WOZA *Shakespeare!*

Titus Andronicus in South Africa

Antony Sher and
Gregory Doran

WOZA *Shakespeare!*

Titus Andronicus in South Africa

with illustrations by Antony Sher

Methuen Drama

This paperback edition published by Methuen 1997

The publisher and authors gratefully acknowledge permission to quote Murray Cox,
Richard Eyre, Michael Kustow and Tom Stoppard. The authors would like to thank
Sue Powell, their research assistant in London, and Bruce Laing, who helped check
some of the details in South Africa.

First published in the United Kingdom in 1996 by Methuen Drama,
Random House, 20 Vauxhall Bridge Road, London SW1V 2SA

Random House Australia (Pty) Limited
20 Alfred Street, Milsons Point, Sydney,
New South Wales 2061, Australia

Random House New Zealand Limited
10 Poland Road, Glenfield
Auckland 10, New Zealand

Random House South Africa (Pty) Limited
Endulini, 5A Jubilee Road, Parktown 2193, South Africa

Random House UK Limited Reg. No. 954009

A CIP catalogue record for this book
is available from the British Library

ISBN 0 413 70270 7 (cased)
ISBN 0 413 70270 4 (paperback)

Typeset in 10 on 13 point Ehrhardt by Dorchester Typesetting Group Limited
Printed and bound in Great Britain by Clays Ltd, St Ives plc

For the *Titus* Company
and the Market Theatre

Contents

Dramatis Personae

The chief characters in the book, listed under their Christian names, in alphabetical order:

Adam Steyn	Stage Manager on *Titus*
Ann Bateson	Arts Officer, British Council, Spain
Barry Ronge	Arts Editor, Jo'burg *Star.*
Barney Simon	Co-founder of the Market Theatre; Artistic Director, 1976–95
Bradley Goss	Assistant Stage Manager on *Titus* (Jo'burg)
Bruce Laing	Actor; playing Publius/Alarbus in *Titus*
Charlton George	Actor; playing Chiron in *Titus*
Christopher Wells	Actor; playing Lucius in *Titus* (London, Leeds, Almagro)
Dale Cutts	Actor; playing Marcus in *Titus*
Dan Robbertse	Actor; playing Quintus/Aemilus in *Titus*
Daphney Hlomuka	Actress; playing the Nurse in *Titus*
Dean Pitman	Production Manager, Market Theatre
Deb (pseudonym)	Member of the Market Theatre staff, communicating with the *Titus* hoaxer, Mr van Schalkwyk
Diane Borger	Deputy Head of Studio, Royal National Theatre
Dorothy Ann Gould	Actress; playing Tamora in *Titus*
Dumi Dhlamini	Composer and Musical Director of *Titus*
Duncan Lawson	Actor; playing Martius in *Titus*
Godfrey Mgcina	Musician; percussion on *Titus*
Grahame Lindop	Chairman of the Board, Market Theatre
Gys de Villiers	Actor; playing Saturninus in *Titus*
Heidi Kelsey	Deputy Stage Manager on *Titus* (Jo'burg)
Helen Chadwick	Voice and Movement, Studio, Royal National Theatre
Howard Sacks	Trustee, Market Theatre
Ian McKellen	Actor
Ivan D. Lucas	Actor; playing Bassianus/Clown in *Titus*
Janet Suzman	Actress, Director
Janice Honeyman	Artistic Director, Jo'burg's Civic Theatre
Jason Barnes	Production Manager, Cottesloe, Royal National Theatre
Jennifer Woodburne	Actress; playing Lavinia in *Titus*
Joan Silver	Partner to Tony's sister, Verne
Joel Sher	Tony's younger brother
John Barton	Associate Director, Royal Shakespeare Company
John Doran	Greg's father
John Kani	Actor; Executive Director, Market Theatre
Leslie Fong	Actor; playing Chief Goth and other parts in *Titus* (Jo'burg)
Lucy Hemmings	Production Manager, Studio, Royal National Theatre
Mannie Manim	Co-founder of the Market Theatre; now an independent producer and lighting designer
Mannie Sher	Tony's father

Margaret Doran	Greg's mother
Margery Sher	Tony's mother
Mark Jonathan	Head of Lighting, Royal Natonal Theatre; Lighting Designer of *Titus* (London, Leeds, Almagro)
Martin Le Maitre	Actor; playing Lucius in *Titus* (Jo'burg)
Michael Maxwell	Manager of the Company, Market Theatre, and Producer on *Titus*
Nadya Cohen	Set Designer on *Titus*
Oscar Petersen	Actor; playing Demetrius in *Titus*
Patsy Rodenburg	Head of Voice, Royal National Theatre
Paulus Kuoape	Actor; playing the Boy in *Titus*; member of Squint Artists, Alexandra Township
Randall Sher	Tony's older brother
Raymond Sergeant	TV Producer; in charge of the SABC recording of *Titus*
Regina Sebright	Administrator, Market Theatre
Richard Barnes	Production Manager, Market Theatre
Richard Eyre	Artistic Director, Royal National Theatre
Ricky Rudolph	Actor; playing Chief Goth and other parts in *Titus* (London, Leeds, Almagro)
Robert Whitehead	Actor, Director; assisting on *Titus*
Roger Chapman	Head of Touring, Royal National Theatre
Sean Mathias	Director
Selina Ntuli	Domestic Worker at Tony and Greg's digs in Jo'burg
Stuart Smith	Master Carpenter, Royal National Theatre
Sello Maake ka Ncube	Actor; playing Aaron in *Titus*
Sue Higginson	Head of Studio, Royal National Theatre
Sue Laurie	Teacher of Alexander Technique
Sue Steele	Costume Designer on *Titus*
Tim Parr	Musician; guitar on *Titus*
Vanessa Cooke	Head of the Lab, Market Theatre
Verne Borchardt	Tony's sister
Wesley France	Lighting Designer on *Titus* (Jo'burg)

Titus Andronicus – Plot Synopsis

Act I. *Scene 1.* Following the death of the emperor, his youngest son, Bassianus, calls for free elections. He regards his brother, Saturninus, as unfit to rule. The Tribune, Marcus Andronicus, announces that the people have chosen Rome's great general, Titus, his brother, as their candidate for emperor. Titus returns to Rome in triumph, after a ten-year war with the Goths, bringing their queen, Tamora, and her three sons, as prisoners. When Titus publicly executes her eldest son, Tamora vows revenge. Offered the candidature for emperor, Titus refuses and bestows the people's vote on Saturninus, who is inaugurated. Saturninus offers his hand in marriage to Titus's daughter, Lavinia, but she is already pledged to Bassianus, who elopes with her. An enraged Saturninus makes Tamora the Empress of Rome.

Act II. *Scene 1.* Aaron the Moor persuades Tamora's remaining sons, Chiron and Demetrius, to rape Lavinia.

Scene 2. Titus arranges a hunt for Saturninus and the court.

Scene 3. During the hunt, Tamora and Aaron make love and plot Bassianus's death. This is carried out by Chiron and Demetrius, who then drag Lavinia away. Aaron causes two of Titus's sons to fall into the pit where Bassianus's body lies. Thus they are implicated in his murder and, despite Titus's pleas, Saturninus sentences them to death.

Scene 4. Chiron and Demetrius mock Lavinia, whom they have not only raped, but mutilated – cutting out her tongue and amputating her hands. Marcus discovers Lavinia.

Act III. *Scene 1.* Titus appeals to the Judges and Senators for his sons' lives, but they ignore him. His distress is magnified when Marcus brings the wounded Lavinia to him. Aaron tricks Titus into cutting off one of his own hands, promising that this will ransom his sons. When their heads are then brought to him, Titus swears to avenge the Andronici's wrongs, and sends his eldest son, Lucius, to raise an army among the Goths.

Scene 2. Marcus kills a fly. When Titus berates him for it and mourns the fly, Marcus realises his brother is losing his wits.

Act IV. *Scene 1.* By scratching on the ground, Lavinia reveals the names of her rapists to Titus and Marcus.

Scene 2. Tamora has given birth to a black baby – Aaron's. She sends it to him to destroy. Chiron and Demetrius are keen to do the job for him. Aaron defends the baby and then flees with it, having killed the Nurse.

Scene 3. Battling his own sanity, Titus instructs a little band of followers to shoot arrows to the gods, appealing for justice.

Scene 4. The news of the Goth army marching on Rome terrifies Saturninus, but Tamora promises to arrange a parley.

Act V. *Scene 1.* In the Goth camp, Lucius confronts Aaron, who has been captured, and the Moor confesses all his crimes.

Scene 2. Disguised as Revenge, Tamora visits Titus, to persuade him to arrange the parley. Titus agrees, on condition that she leave Chiron and Demetrius in his care. Alone with his daughter's rapists, Titus slits their throats.

Scene 3. At the parley feast, Titus produces a large pie. Once Tamora has started eating, Titus kills Lavinia and then reveals that the heads of Chiron and Demetrius are baked in the pie. In an outburst of vengeance, Titus, Tamora and Saturninus are killed. Aaron is sentenced to death, Lucius is proclaimed Emperor of Rome and Marcus advocates the need to heal the wounds of a society devastated by violence.

PART I *Studio Visit*

Johannesburg; September–October 1994

1968   1979
SA No. c11187753   UK No. 010305 E

1990   1994
UK No. 001467418   SA No. L838537612

Passport Portraits

1

Saturday 24 September

I'm about to use my new South African passport for the first time. In the New South Africa.

Sitting on flight BA57 from London to Jo'burg, I'm part of an advance team from the Studio of the Royal National Theatre, visiting South Africa for a fortnight of workshops, classes, skill-sharing. Next to me, Greg is filling in a landing form, along with the rest of the group: all hunched over, like kids in a classroom, copying out details from their British passports. I'm fortunate enough to own one of those as well, and it's a good feeling – belonging to two decent democracies.

As the plane starts to descend, I transfer my South African passport from my briefcase to my jacket. It's sleek, blue, spotless. I'm so bloody proud of this thing. Who would've thought it?

As soon as I was granted British citizenship in 1979, I burnt my old one. And in that small but difficult ritual (the passports of the old South Africa were military green and not easy to torch), I also hoped to incinerate my identity as a White South African. Absolute nonsense, of course. You can't obliterate your past, and anyway, there was no need. My family weren't lawmakers or torturers; they were unpoliticised middle-of-the-road citizens, businessmen and housewives, dutifully voting for the ruling government. But when I arrived in England as the most wide-eyed of nineteen-year-olds, and gained a new view of this thing called apartheid, so normal back at home, so grotesque elsewhere, I went into a state of shock and then, with Jewish instincts akimbo, became possessed with guilt. Leading to the burning of the passport.

Earlier this year, on the day before overseas voting in South Africa's historic elections, a friend phoned me to say that she'd just managed to retrieve her citizenship – at record, red-tape-breaking speed – and was able to vote tomorrow. All thanks to a particular lawyer . . .

Michael Richman turned out to be a kind, quietly spoken South African Jew, a veteran of the struggle, friend and colleague of Albie Sachs and, currently, in charge of the European IEC (Independent

Election Committee). I dashed to his Pall Mall office, and together we rushed to Trafalgar Square and South Africa House. Here, the atmosphere was chaotic, reminding me of movies about the last days of Saigon. With a gesture here, a word there, Michael was able to get us past the long queues in the public halls (were all these people hoping to retrieve burnt citizenships?) and into the heart of the building, the *backstage* area: a warren of corridors and offices where the embassy staff, wearing shirt-sleeves and determined frowns, were boxing or shredding documents and files. They were packing up; they were leaving. The elections hadn't begun, yet they seemed to know the results. They were out; they were finished.

The Chief Immigration Officer was so overworked he'd gone into a kind of daze. 'My last few hours, thank goodness,' he confided cheerfully to Michael as he grabbed my forms, my photos, and my £37, barely checking any of it. Within ten minutes of our arrival, Michael and I were back in Trafalgar Square.

I expressed amazement that any bureaucracy could operate so fast.

'Think of it as a closing-down sale,' said Michael.

The next morning I spent three hours in a joyful queue, inching round South Africa House, through brilliant South African-type sunshine on one side, cool English spring shade on the other; then the final lap – the famous, or notorious, west side of the embassy, where demonstrations were always held ('If this pavement could speak,' someone next to me said) and at last through the entrance and into the rather threatening interior, with its old-regime mixture of the grand (marble pillars, teak furniture) and the provincial (dusty dioramas of South African scenes), and then finally into a booth. It was small and scruffy, with a feel of having been extensively over-occupied, like a toilet on an aeroplane, and the pencil was blunt with use. I was trembling with sweet emotion as I made my cross . . .

Today, five months later at Jo'burg airport, my virginal South African passport takes me through Customs in a flash, while the others wait patiently in the Aliens queue. Led by the Royal National Theatre Studio's boss, Sue Higginson – a lady heroic in thought, deed and build (tall, with a mane of blonde curls and spectacles like search lamps) – the South African visit includes some very classy people. Lady Soames, the Royal National Theatre's Chairman (she insists on the use of *man* not *person*) is coming, so is the Artistic Director Richard Eyre; also the Head of Lighting Mark Jonathan, the Cottesloe Production Manager Jason Barnes, the voice coach Patsy Rodenburg, the designer Alison Chitty, the director Sean Mathias, the writer Winsome Pinnock, the actress Selina Cadell; thirty-two in all. Including Ian McKellen.

He's been good value on the flight. Back at Heathrow our group tried to get ourselves upgraded from Economy by urging him to whip out his knighthood (he was travelling it for use in his one-man show, *A Knight Out*) and impress the check-in lady. He co-operated gamely, slinging the ribboned medal round his neck, but to no avail. The woman didn't seem to have any awareness of him, the National Theatre, or even knight-hoods. But the moment we stepped on the plane it was a different story. Ian – *sans* medal – was instantly the centre of intense admiration: recog-nised not so much for his appearances as Iago, Vanya, etc., but for those at Gay Pride marches and benefits, and a celebrated visit to Downing Street. As we progressed down the aisle, the air stewards (or 'coffee-moffies' as they're known in South Africa) stared at him with expres-sions of almost religious awe. We were given unlimited supplies of champagne, fine chocolates, extra helpings of food and, best of all, a row of seats each, so that for once we could sleep decently on those flying cattle-trucks.

Carlton Hotel. 'Why have you brought along *Titus Andronicus*?' I ask Greg as we unpack our case of books.

'Might use it if we do some Shakespeare classes. It sort of makes sense in Africa . . .' (Greg has been invited to do the play in Lagos with the National Troupe of Nigeria – as a co-production with the RSC – but there's currently a question mark over the project, because of the politi-cal situation in that country.)

I don't know *Titus* all that well. In 1987 I saw Deborah Warner's strik-ing, *white* production (all dust and clay; the characters becoming paler, ghostlier, as they lost more blood) and I've read the text, but that was a while ago. 'Why would it work in an African context?' I ask.

'I suppose because of the violence. It can seem so gratuitous, just a gory melodrama . . . but not here somehow.'

I nod, staring down at the streets of Jo'burg sixteen floors below and thinking of the things that have gone on in this country over the past half-century.

'And', says Greg, 'it's got Shakespeare's *other* great black part.'

I glance at the drawing of Aaron the Moor on the cover of the Arden

edition. Here he's a rather imperious, unsexy, soft-bodied figure standing over Tamora, who looks grumpy and has one tit out. In the background other characters gambol through pretty woods with greyhounds. The whole thing looks about as African as Regent's Park. God, I hate these Brotherhood of Ruralists pictures on the Arden Shakespeares! I ask, 'Is Aaron better than Titus then, d'you reckon – as a part?'

'Not sure,' answers Greg. 'But if the Nigerian production still happens, you can play him.' He laughs. 'I'll have to reverse it all – everyone else black, him white.'

At that moment the phone rings. I'm invited to the British High Commission in Pretoria tonight, for dinner with Prince Edward (here to do a TV interview with Mandela), who, it turns out, was also on our flight last night. Very nice, very flattering, but the trouble is, I'm invited on my own. Which is absurd. If Greg and I were a straight married couple, here together on the Studio visit, they wouldn't dream of inviting one without the other. I try to argue the point, but the High Commission is adamant, claiming it's a small dinner party and they're restricted by numbers. Either I come on my own, or not at all.

'Of course you must go,' says Greg.

'Suppose so.'

We fall into silence. A small humiliation, a small defeat in our lives as an out couple.

On the drive to the dinner I gaze at the streets of Jo'burg. It's a city which I don't really know. I was born and brought up in Cape Town and never came here till last year, just before the elections, when Greg and I did an extensive South African tour, researching my latest novel *Cheap Lives*.

A strange place, Jo'burg. Glassy skyscrapers, fortresses of the old South Africa, hover above a new third-world street life: the pavements crammed with people cooking, sleeping, selling fruit, cutting hair – while crippled beggars limp and crawl their way along. Not a white face to be seen, of course – except in the cars, their windows and doors tightly locked. Then at night everyone disappears. It's like an unofficial curfew. The streets radiate a peculiar, silent danger. Jo'burg, murder capital of the world. We're under strict instructions not to go anywhere by foot, day or night, and not to flaunt cameras, and not to wear jewellery, expensive watches, or even fancy sun-glasses. My spectacles are photochromic (i.e., they go dark in bright sunlight). I imagine them being whipped

off, and me running after the thief, shouting, 'Wait, stop, they're
optical . . . !'

'The thing you've got to understand about Jo'burg is that it wasn't
founded beside a river or bay, like sensible and decent cities are. It was
built on a barren stretch of ground – for one reason only. There was gold
underneath. And because of that gold, the greediest and most dangerous
people gathered . . .'

   This is Barney Simon speaking – co-founder (with Mannie Manim) of
Jo'burg's Market Theatre. These days he runs it with the renowned
black actor, John Kani. The Market is hosting the Studio visit, because
of their long association with the National (*Bopha*, and Fugard plays like
Master Harold and the Boys, The Road to Mecca, etc.).

Barney
Simon

   We're all at the British High Commission, which has a curiously Scan-
dinavian, Habitat look to it, and I've just met Prince Edward for the first
time. He's prettier than in photographs. The meeting was, as meetings
with royalty tend to be, brief and tongue-tied. What to chat about? Last
night's flight? I heard myself saying, 'The turbulence, the *turbulence*! It
made me wish I'd watched the safety video properly, 'cause the only bit I
remembered was about removing your high heels . . .' At which point

the High Commissioner, Sir Anthony Reeve, dislodged me with a well-trained elbow and introduced the next guest.

John Kani (who's been allowed to bring along his wife, *his* partner!) is much easier company. I ask him about the New South Africa and why the blacks have been so forgiving? 'Oh it's all thanks to the Old Man,' he says cheerfully. 'Before he was released, I used to dream of finding the policeman who tortured me in Port Elizabeth. I know he's still there, retired now. For years I dreamed of tracking him down and doing him some serious damage. But now . . . now I just want to bump into him in the street one day and say, "Hey, you know what? – I was right and you were wrong!"'

Sunday 25 September
The Market is one of those perfect theatres. It shouldn't be. There's no natural stage-left entrance and it has some bad sightlines. The acoustics are superb, though. More crucially, the auditorium has life and history. It used to be the Indian fruit and vegetable market of old Johannesburg. Round the auditorium, with its steel arches and dome, they've kept some original signs: 'S. Patel, Vegetables', or 'Spitting is Prohibited/*Moenie Hier Spoeg Nie*'. Like the Almeida in London, which used to be a cock-fighting ring, a Salvation Army Citadel and the site of the 'unrolling' of a mummy from Thebes, or like my favourite theatre, the Swan in Stratford, which used to be a rehearsal room, the Market is one of those spaces – in Brook's words, 'a space which has a special humanity' – where you feel that even the walls have stories to tell.

It opened in June 1976, at one of the most explosive moments in South Africa's history – the schoolkids of Soweto had just rebelled, refusing to continue learning Afrikaans, and the police had just opened fire on them – a moment which some now see as the beginning of the end of the old regime. From then on, with its multi-racial policies, backstage and front-of-house, the Market became a sort of David to apartheid's Goliath. In the old days it was forced to do some performances in secret, or with security policemen lurking at the back of the stalls, waiting for them to put a foot wrong, or with far-right groups issuing death threats to people who worked there. The Market has emerged from all this, battered but victorious – yet still without state subsidy. That's been forgotten in the great, urgent rush to heal the more life-threatening wounds which the Nationalist Government inflicted on this country, and so all public funding still automatically goes to the old state theatres and companies.

Ian as
Iago & Vanya

Nobody has had time to remember what the Market did for The Struggle, both locally and internationally. Its most famous show, *Woza Albert!*, toured the world, educating foreign audiences about South Africa in a humorous, unsanctimonious way. It was directed by Barney Simon, and devised by him and its two actors, Percy Mtwa and Mbongeni Ngema. Playing everything from helicopters and trains to themselves and (donning pink ping-pong noses) their white bosses, they told the story of Christ's return to earth and his bewilderment at apartheid. The Zulu word *woza* means welcome or arise, and the show ended with a call to the dead heroes of South Africa's past, like Robert Sobukwe, Ruth First, Steve Biko and the Nobel Peace Prize winner and ANC President, Albert Luthuli: *'Woza Robert! Woza Ruth! Woza Steve! WOZA ALBERT!'*

Today, in the Market, Ian does *A Knight Out* as a fund-raising performance for them. It's a terrific mixture of Ian as actor-knight performing Shakespeare speeches – the body very still, the great voice going everywhere – and Ian as himself, pottering round the stage, handing his knighthood down to the front row ('Pass that round, but I'll want it back!') and telling anecdotes about his life in gay politics.

There's only one strange aspect to today's show – it isn't full. How can the local theatre going public afford to be blasé about a performance like this – which even London hasn't seen yet?

We've barely time to participate in the standing ovation before we're bustled into a Kombi and hurried to the next event. Richard Eyre, newly arrived, isn't pleased: 'I've travelled half-way across the world, I've never been to South Africa before, I'm only here for forty-eight hours and how am I spending the evening? At an *awards* ceremony!'

These are the Vita Awards (South Africa's equivalent of the Oliviers) at the Civic Theatre, a very different place from the Market – all lifeless, titanic concrete, housing five auditoria. I meet up with its Artistic Director, Janice Honeyman. We've been friends since we were kids. A few years ago she came to London to direct Estelle Kohler and myself in Fugard's *Hello and Goodbye* for the RSC.

'How are you, my boykie?' she says, hugging me.

I also slip into the poor-white accent we used in the Fugard play: 'No OK my sus, just a bit bleddy scared to be back home at last . . . !'

The Studio
WORKSHOPS

Greg teaching
Shakespeare
4/10/94

2

Monday 26 September

Tony is feeling nervous. The Studio workshops begin in earnest today. The groups are very mixed: experienced pros alongside young actors from the townships. Whereas many of our lot are professional teachers, we're not, and Tony's not sure how he'll cope. I've done a lot of teaching so I'll hold his hand and run the sessions with him. But I'm not sure how I'll cope either.

Last night, Barney Simon tried to put our minds at rest. He said the actors were anxious too, and recounted his preliminary discussions with the township groups: 'Think of the workshops', he told them, 'as a big plate of food with *vleis* and *pap*, but also maybe spaghetti and moussaka and shrimps. When you are first offered the plate you may just take the *vleis* and the *pap*, but later you may find you want to try the shrimp.'

Right at the start of our first class, Tony and I make it clear we are not teachers, that we are here to share ideas, experiences, rehearsal techniques, and we begin by playing some preliminary warm-up games; in particular Max Stafford-Clark's game in which you explore status in human relationships by using the numbers 1 to 10, drawing these from a pack of cards.

The ways different actors choose to play status here are complex and unexpected, often dependent on their race. After all, apartheid instituted the Status Game on a national scale.

After a coffee-break, we ask the group what they hope to get out of these sessions. An actor called Jamie Bartlett, brooding cross-legged on the floor, pinches his lower lip and says: 'Ja, I want to find a way of doing Shakespeare in my own voice, using my Africanness.'

Tony becomes impassioned about this. The subject is close to his heart: 'I lost my own South African accent twenty-six years ago when I left here to go overseas to train as an actor. I was embarrassed by it and used to disguise it. And I think I lost my relationship with my own voice.'

He goes on to describe how that relationship had to be nurtured back, by people like Cis Berry and Patsy Rodenburg.

This leads to a long discussion about accent. It's interesting how actors all over the world tend to put on a posh English accent when they do Shakespeare. Why? There's a peculiar assumption that the words are only valid if spoken in this way, or the poetry can only be released in RP (received pronunciation). It's as if indigenous or regional accents are somehow inferior, or lacking in range, or expression, or are just inappropriate. The assumption also presupposes that Shakespeare himself spoke like Prince Charles. He didn't. American English is probably closer to Elizabethan English than our own.

But today's argument is not really about how Shakespeare did or did not speak, it's about our perceptions of language, what Patsy Rodenburg calls 'Vocal imperialism . . . the dominant forms of spoken English that are deemed right and acceptable' and which have been used in the process of colonisation.

The South African actors resist the idea. The only way forward is to explore.

We take the scene from *Antony and Cleopatra* where the Messenger brings Cleopatra news that Antony has married Octavia. The actors try the scene in 'standard' English accents. It's fine, but a bit flat. We encourage them to use their own accents.

First, Basil Apollis, a Coloured actor with a husky voice and a rude twinkle, plays the Messenger in his own Cape Flats accent, while Julie Solomon plays Cleopatra as a *kugel*, the South African version of a Jewish Princess. There are instant laughs of recognition when Cleopatra calls the Messenger 'Boy' or Basil's fast-talking, self-deprecating Coloured calls her 'Madam'.

Next, Patrick Shai, who worked with Tony in a BBC TV film called *Land of Dreams*, plays the Messenger as a Zulu and Dorothy Gould, currently playing Hedda Gabler at the Market, plays the queen.

'Play her like Hester,' says Tony. Dorothy recently scored a hit as Hester in Athol Fugard's *Hello and Goodbye*.

'What, you mean poor white?' says Dorothy. 'Cleopatra, *a poor white . . .*?!' And she does. The accent releases the essential element of gypsy in Cleopatra and Patrick is very funny as the downtrodden Messenger. Why is playing low status so often funny?

'But that's fine for comedy,' somebody says, 'not so good for tragedy.'

So we try the end of the scene, where Cleopatra despairs: 'Let him for ever go; let him not, Charmian!' and Dorothy does it in the same accent. It's a real person suffering real pain, and it strikes chords in all of us.

'This is really fascinating,' says an actor called Dale Cutts, who looks like Rod Steiger's younger brother, 'but a South African audience would never buy it.'

We walk back to the Market at the end of the session through a complex of recycled factory buildings. One is being converted into a new museum of brewing. Another is destined to become a dance studio. A third will house a huge Biennale Art exhibition next year. If all goes well this area could become a real Mecca for the Arts.

Tony is still charged up with excitement about the workshop and suggests that we come back and do a full Shakespeare production here, using South African accents.

'What, you and me?'

'Yeah,' he says.

'Are you serious?'

'I am. I've had such a bloody awful year work-wise back home that maybe it's time to . . . Yeah, I think I'm serious.'

Evening. We are sitting in a funky African restaurant in Yeoville called Iyavaya.

'Greg and I want to come back and do a play here,' Tony says, 'at the Market.'

We've cornered John Kani and are putting our plan to him while we tuck in to the special of the day: crocodile pie.

'Come any time. What do you want to do?' says John.

'We'd like to do a Shakespeare,' I say.

'Great. When are you coming?'

'Well as soon as possible,' says Tony. 'January? Is that too soon? It's just that we both have a gap in the New Year and . . .'

'No ways, my friend, nothing's too soon. That's how we do things at the Market. Somebody comes to us and says they have this idea, they want to do something . . . And *Bang*! suddenly they're doing it. It drives our Board crazy!'

John breaks into a loud laugh which ricochets around the restaurant.

'You must have other things scheduled,' I say.

'We'll change it. You just tell us which play you want to do. Look, Tony, Greg, my brothers, we want you here.'

We haven't decided which Shakespeare we might do. There are several contenders. We've talked about *Macbeth* before, and there's *The Winter's Tale*. *Othello* would have been great, but Janet Suzman's already done a very successful production here, with John himself as the Moor. And there's *Titus* if the Nigeria production falls through.

We've decided, if this goes ahead, that we'll conceive our production together. I think it'll work. Any director consults his leading actor from the very early stages. That collaboration often produces basic concepts and develops crucial production ideas, but it is seldom acknowledged.

In previous centuries, before directors existed, the leading actor would have run the whole show himself: ordering the moves, prescribing the inflections and setting the tempo. They were, in Edward Gordon Craig's phrase, '*metteurs-en-scène,* boss creators of all that goes on on the boards'. It was not until Granville Barker, Reinhardt and Stanislavsky (all of whom had started as actors) that the role of the director really came into existence.

Richard Eyre, Boss Creator of the Royal National Theatre (he also started as an actor) is in the restaurant with us. He came to launch the workshops and present an inaugural lecture, and tomorrow flies out again to open *Racing Demon* in Los Angeles. The lecture this afternoon was excellent; a practical, hard-nosed and funny dissection of the work of a director, delivered with that English passion which burns with a low flame but a white heat. 'My task is to illuminate the meanings of the play; its vocabulary, its syntax and its philosophy,' he said. 'Directing is a matter of understanding the meaning of a scene and staging it in the light of that knowledge . . . and directing Shakespeare is merely directing writ large.'

I wonder what he'll think of our co-conceiving a production? Would he warn me not to lose the whip hand? I think not. He believes, as we do, that Theatre is the most collaborative of the Arts.

Tony sat sketching Richard throughout the lecture, muttering his approbation. One thing Richard said struck us in particular. He talked about the Arts in post-Thatcher Britain being terrorised by 'the three horsemen of the contemporary apocalypse: money, management and marketing'.

Tony has been going crazy this year. Since he finished the West End run of *Travesties* in May, there have been a series of disappointments. The director of a new British film wanted him for a leading role and went into battle over it. But he was defeated by one of the money-men, who reckoned Tony wasn't sexy enough. Then he was offered a big BBC series, but money spoke again. The part was snatched away when a more bums-on-sofas actor (who had already turned it down) changed his mind.

The Richard Eyre lecture

After the lecture we stood outside the Market, breathing the fresh hot afternoon air. 'This country,' he said, 'it's starting to smell cleaner than home. Mind you, where is home now?'

3

Friday 30 September

Educators' Workshop. For people who use drama in education. With Ian (McKellen), Sean (Mathias), Selina (Cadell), Greg and self. Various exercises; each of us takes turns leading, the others joining the group. First big black turn-out in our sessions – at least fifty per cent.

The class is good, but not nearly as good as the tea-break.

Two actors from Squint Artists, an Alexandra Township theatre-in-education group, use tea-time to work out together with mime exercises. They do this in a corner, without meaning it as a performance, but the rest of us become transfixed. The younger of the two, Paulus, who can't be more than eighteen, with slightly battered, angelic looks, is particularly gifted. He transforms himself into an old man with a stick – his smooth face suddenly wrinkled and toothless, his tongue darting like a lizard's – and now a streetwise gangster-boy, playing cards on the ground – you can *see* the cards in his hands as he shuffles them; you can *hear* them slap the ground.

At a company meeting, Mark Douet, the tour's official photographer, announces that he witnessed a murder round the corner from the hotel this morning. A man was gunned down in the 'taxi wars'. Travel to and from the townships is painfully difficult and slow, so black taxis (nothing to with the London variety; these are Kombis which seat about fifteen) are big business.

Mark is shaken, but it's a timely reminder for the rest of us – who've all become careless about security – that this is a dangerous place. Small wonder. It's a city where, until a few years ago, legalised state violence knew no bounds.

John Kani is in our Kombi on the way back to the hotel, playing the tour guide from hell: 'See that blue building with the steel shutters, that's police headquarters, John Vorster Square. See the tenth floor? That's where the torture rooms – known as the "Workshops" – were situated. See the balcony on that floor? That's where prisoners kept throwing themselves from, because, y'know, life had got a bit much . . .' He

John Kani

gives his chuckle, that strangely warm, forgiving sound. 'See this concrete block on the left . . . that's where we used to queue for our pass-
books, for hours and hours and hours. And that was just in order to live
in your own city. God forbid if you needed to *travel*, to travel abroad, like
I did with the shows that went to London and Broadway – my God, you
got chased from one office to the next, like something out of Kafka. And
then you still didn't end up with much. See, here, look at this . . .' He
digs in his briefcase and produces his old passport. In the space for his
nationality, an official has written UNDEFINABLE. 'I remember once arriving at Heathrow – for one of the shows at the National, I think – and this
Customs man looked at my passport and said, "Your nationality is *undefinable*? I can't let you in." And I said, "My friend, please don't give me a
hard time . . ." And I told him my story and luckily he was sympathetic,
against apartheid, in that British way, sorry for us poor little downtrodden blacks, and so he let me in.' John hoots with laughter as he recalls
this, while our smiles freeze – in that British way.

Back in our room, Greg and I become even more fired up by the idea
of doing Shakespeare in this country. The rhythms of Elizabethan and
African society are strangely compatible: the violence and beauty and
humour in both.

'It's *Titus*,' Greg says. 'That's what we should do if we come back
here.'

'But you're doing it in Nigeria.'

'I don't think that's going to happen . . . actually, I'm due to ring the RSC, see if they've heard anything.'

He does. They haven't. The Nigerian *Titus* looks dead. A South African one could be born . . .

Evening. Dinner party at the mansion of Mary Slack, Market Theatre trustee and Oppenheimer heiress, for Lady Soames, National Theatre Chairman and daughter of Winston Churchill. I'm at the Slack–Soames table in the dining-room, while Greg – oh dear – is at a table in the hall-way, the table for *wives*! (Actually, he ends up having a much more relaxed evening than me, who has to be on best behaviour.)

I've never met Lady Soames before and she seems equally intrigued: 'It's so lovely to talk to some *actors* for a change. At the National, I only seem to deal with people connected with ticket prices or lavatories.'

Fascinating to hear her talk of 'my father'. Every time she says these two words, the table goes quiet and people lean forward. You can't help noticing those pale eyes, the curve of her lips – to say nothing of her small cigars, lit by tilting over the candelabra. A debate is currently rag-ing in South Africa about whether to hold Nuremburg-type trials, so I'm interested to hear her say that 'my father' was uneasy about the original ones. '. . . He didn't believe in revenge. Where does it all end, d'you see?'

On the way home, Greg asks what we were discussing at our table.

'Cycles of revenge,' I answer.

'Oh,' he says. 'So you told them about *Titus*.'

Saturday 1 October

What a relief to walk through the streets of Jo'burg at last, and feel *safe*. Mainly because there's about 2,000 of us, participating in the Lesbian and Gay Pride March. Apparently that's double the number of last year's march and a phenomenal improvement on the first one, five years ago, when only a few dozen people marched, some with paper bags over their heads. It's a tremendous boost for the cause to have Ian here and he makes a stirring speech. Then, along the route, he tells me about his visit to New York earlier this year, for the Stonewall Riot twenty-fifth anniversary – commemorating the night in '69 when the cops raided a Greenwich Village gay bar and a group of drag queens *finally* fought back.

'A lot of people', says Ian, 'don't realise that the reason why the queens were so emotional, so defiant that night, is because they'd just buried Judy Garland. Liza Minnelli came to sing at this year's anniversary and said to the audience, "Mama would've been so happy today." At which point Armistead Maupin, who was next to me, whispered, "Happy? We don't want Judy Garland *happy*! That's not why we love her." '

The march takes us through the city centre, where the local residents, ninety-five per cent black, watch from their balconies, some bemused, some mocking – but anyway, all smiling. They must recognise something in us, surely? Jo'burg has known other marches like this . . . people dancing and singing through the streets, demanding their rights.

The only aggro comes from a tiny gang of evangelists (some with American accents – have they flown in specially?) with bibles held alongside their mouths, trying to amplify their heckling against the music, chanting, car hooters of our celebrations. The most disturbing participant is a ten-year-old boy, who keeps screeching 'Repent!'. Some adults, his parents or whoever, have filled him with hatred over an issue he can't possibly comprehend. Dear God, heterosexuality can be so queer.

The march finishes in Joubert Park, where we meet two heroes of South African gay rights, one black, one white, Simon Nkole and Edwin Cameron. Greg and I are forced to leave the festivities soon afterwards. We've come along without hats and are burning. Which is taking pink power too far.

Sunday 2 October
The rest of the RNT Studio group have gone on a tour to Soweto today, without Greg and me. We did a similar tour last year, when our guides were two ANC security men with guns in their belts. As well as showing us the squatter camps, they also took us through the (Winnie) Mandela and Sisulu homes, bedrooms and all, treating the places like shrines.

So we spend today at the swimming pool, on the Carlton roof-top, thirty-one floors in the air, with a dismal view of freeways and gold dumps. I reread *Titus*. I never find Shakespeare easy, but this is tremendous; it reads like a thriller; you can't put it down. And there's so much compassion in it and dark humour.

As a part, Titus becomes terrific from Act III onwards, when he has a great explosion of grief and then descends into Lear-like madness, e.g. the 'death of the fly' scene. But in his first appearance, during the long Scene 1, he's a problem. So irrational. Mourning for his two sons, slain in battle, and yet, at the drop of a hat, murdering another, who tries to

Cox as Titus

block his way during Lavinia's elopement. I finally understand why, in Deborah Warner's uncut version, Brian Cox had to play him bonkers from the word go. Battle-crazed. At the time, although I admired his performance, I wondered why he hadn't given himself more of a journey? But I guess if you're going to kill your own son in the first scene, for a minor misdemeanour, you have to be loony from the kick-off.

Wonder if there's a way round that?

Monday 3 October
Didn't sleep very well last night. Nervous about the Platform Performance Ian and I are doing today on *Richard III*. Had a meeting last week to choose a chairman. '*Chairman?*' Greg said. 'Isn't it a referee you need?'

Anyway, Greg ended up with the job and I don't know if that makes it better or worse . . .

4

Monday 3 October

A packed auditorium at Wits (the University of Witwatersrand) to witness the Clash of the Titans, as Tony and Ian McKellen compare notes
about playing Richard III. It's surprising to see how nervous they both
are, pacing around backstage beforehand.

I kick off by inviting both men to describe their different approaches
to the role.

Tony talks about his research into the precise medical nature of
Richard's disability (a choice between scoliosis or kyphosis) and the
introduction of the crutches, which became the trademark of his interpretation.

Ian says he didn't really do any research into the disability, since he
wanted the handicap to be relatively slight. He invented a mix of a small
hump, mild alopecia (baldness) and paralysis down one side.

Whatever their different approaches, both actors discovered great dexterity in the part: one, able, on his crutches, to swing across the stage and
move faster than anyone else; the other, able to remove his greatcoat or
light a cigarette using only one hand.

In the manner of a breezy talk-show host inviting his guests to sing a
little number, I ask both actors if they'll do the opening speech for us;
knowing perfectly well that they've been rehearsing it in their respective
bathrooms for days. Anyway, the audience demand it, with cheers, and
we toss a coin to see who'll go first.

Ian. He sets the scene briefly. His production, directed by Richard
Eyre, was set in the thirties, paralleling Richard's rise to power with
Hitler or Oswald Mosley. A precise historical context. Now he begins.
He stalks stiffly forward, a cool military man, and in the clipped English
accent of the period, he says: 'Now is the winter . . .'

Tony next. He has concealed a pair of crutches at the back, which he
now produces, blowing any semblance of spontaneity and making everyone laugh. His production, directed by Bill Alexander, was set in a cathedral in the medieval period of the real king. Recreating the opening
moments, Tony broods at the back of the stage. The crutches are held

behind him until the first mention of his deformity. Then he hurls him-self at the audience, scuttling at them like 'a bottled spider'.

The exercise proves a point. There is no one definitive way of doing Shakespeare. Actors are constantly challenged by performances which have gone before them. They dig into the plays, mine the text and re-invent the roles. We are constantly discovering new ways of doing those parts and those plays.

During the session there are further gems. Ian, asked if it is necessary to observe the metre in Shakespeare, says: 'Of course not. But it would be a shame not to, rather like doing *Don Giovanni* without the original music.'

Tony, asked 'why Richard III?', says, 'There are certain parts as an actor that you pick out for yourself. If you are good-looking you play Hamlet and if you're like me you play Richard III.' Big laugh from the audience.

'And if you look like me,' says Ian, 'you play both.'

Round of applause. We finish there.

Emerging into the foyer, both men are thronged by fans. Dave and Rick, the two Americans on the course with us, teaching managerial skills, congratulate me on my role as a 'facilitator' (apparently I give good facilitation); and Lady Soames says, 'Oh I'm so glad I saw that. I'll swank about it at dinner parties for months.'

I heard this morning that the production of *Titus* scheduled for Nigeria has finally been cancelled. The political crisis in that country has deep-ened and things look like getting much worse under General Abacha's ruthless military regime. There have been riots since Moshood Abiola, who unofficially won the annulled presidential election there, was jailed in the summer.

So Tony and I decide to propose *Titus* to the Market.

I love the play. T. S. Eliot thought it 'one of the stupidest and most uninspiring plays ever written'. But I think it's a play about our capacity for cruelty, and our capacity for survival; about the way violence breeds violence; about the search for justice in a brutal universe. It's about a world I recognise around me, particularly here in Africa.

And Titus would be a great part for Tony.

As we get back to the Market from Wits, Barney stops us. John Kani has talked to him about the idea of us coming back in the New Year. 'Oich! Can't you make it September?' he says. 'What do you want to do?'

'*Titus Andronicus.*'

'Ah-ha. Expensive. What do you think, Michael?'

Barney turns to Mike Maxwell, the theatre's valiant administrator. He's a handsome chap, though his face is fretted with the stress of keeping the Market afloat. His hair is beginning to thin a bit at the front, not so much from age as from habitually tearing it out.

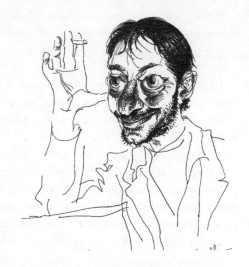

Mike Maxwell

'If we move *Six Characters in Search of an Author* after the revival of *The Island* and the new Fugard, we could do *Titus* once *Hysteria* closes.'

'So when's that?' we ask.

'Start February, four weeks' rehearsal, open March?'

'If we can raise the money,' says Barney. 'And what play do you want to do again? *Titus*? We've got a barman called Titus.' He chuckles. 'He'll think we're doing a play about him.'

My God, could this actually happen? I'm suddenly nervous about doing the play, about directing Tony, about my ability to direct at all. I feel like blurting out, 'Yes, you're right, it's far too expensive. Let's forget the whole thing!' But Tony grins at me. I take a deep breath and grin back.

I had always admired this actor, Antony Sher, and had my first chance to look at how he works when we met in Stratford in 1987, on another Bill Alexander production, *The Merchant of Venice*. I was playing Solanio.

Solanio and Salerio are known as 'the salads' in the business, so I suppose you could say these were my 'salad days' at the RSC. Tony was playing Shylock.

In tackling the part, he explored his own experience of prejudice, as a Jew, as a gay man, as a South African, and lent Shylock the voice of his own anger. And that voice was given added resonance one particular night.

These were the bitter days of the P. W. Botha's State of Emergency in South Africa, immediately prior to the National Party's fortieth anniversary in office.

In Stratford, there was a special gala performance for Shakespeare's birthday. Ambassadors from all the different countries represented at the court of St James were invited. And therefore, despite the acting company's strident objections (even threatening to strike), the South African cultural attaché was also in the audience. Tony had found out where he was sitting.

Line by line hit home. The 'Hath not a Jew eyes?' speech reverberated round the auditorium; and in the court scene, as Shylock pleads with the Duke, Tony grabbed one of the court attendants (played by a black actor), dragged him to the front and, eyes sparking, directed this speech at the hapless attaché:

> 'You have among you many a purchased slave,
> Which like your asses and your dogs and mules
> You use in abject and in slavish part . . .'

The play itself spoke our objections louder than any boycott action could possibly have done.

As Shylock exits at the end of Act III, Scene 3, I had to shout the line: 'It is the most impenetrable cur that ever kept with men.' Only one night it came out as: 'It is the most impenetrable cur that ever *slept* with men.'

And we've been together ever since.

5

Monday 3 October

The only time that Greg and I worked together as director and actor was on an anti-apartheid benefit in London in 1988, a fund-raiser for BDAF (British Defence and Aid Fund, which provided legal or educational fees for South Africans whose bread-winners were victims of apartheid). The show was called *Two Dogs and Freedom* – a quote from a six-year-old Sowetan boy, who said 'When I am old, I would like to have a wife and two children, a boy and a girl, and a big house, and two dogs and freedom.' As well as Greg directing, and self appearing, we were also both part of the organising committee, and helped to assemble a star-studded cast of British and South African performers, alongside Trevor Huddleston, Albie Sachs, the Kinnocks and, courtesy of *Spitting Image*, Margaret Thatcher and P. W. Botha. It played one tremendous Sunday night at Sadler's Wells, was televised by Channel 4, and raised £45,000.

This evening, in Jo'burg, I meet up with one of the key figures of that show – Dali (son of Oliver) Tambo. Back in '88, he was an exile, living in England and working as personal manager for Jonas Gwanga, who did the music for *Two Dogs*. Now he's back in SA, presenting its most popular TV chat show, *Children of the South*, and I'm one of tonight's guests.

The show is two hours late in starting. It's African time gone haywire. It's perfectly p.c. to say that, since all of Dali's assistants appear to be white. As things get worse and worse, I feel less and less angry, relishing what turns into a Fellini-esque experience.

My fellow guests are to include American actor James Earl Jones (here for the remake of *Cry, the Beloved Country*), British tabloid star Samantha Fox, a local drag act called The Weathergirls, Mandela's personal praise-singer (didn't catch his name), and Salif Keita, the albino singer from Mali. By the time things get under way, James Earl Jones's name has vanished from his dressing-room door. Did he get pissed off and leave? (Could mean extra air time for me to plug the RNT Studio visit.) Reaching the studio, I overhear Samantha Fox threatening Dali – unless proceedings start *now* she's leaving. (Could mean even more air time for me to plug the Studio visit.) Samantha's interview is conducted rapidly, and now I'm on. The camera script says, 'Antony joins Samantha on couch' – not something I'd ever imagined doing – but Samantha's already gone, darting away under the studio equipment.

Dali interviews me. In the recording break, he reveals he was busking – they forgot to give him the questions. Summoning a floor manager, he whispers that unless everyone gets their act together, *he's* leaving! (Goodness, I could end up hosting this show.)

When Dali calms down, Salif Keita, the albino singer from Mali, comes on. As I'm being ushered away, I hear Dali ask the first question and Salif reply that he only speaks French. On the monitor, I see the camera sweep across the audience to show a party from the Albino Society of South Africa. One woman is fast asleep.

Tuesday 4 October
Another Samantha, the actress Samantha Bond, has flown in to join the course, as well as Denise Wong's Black Mime Company, who improvise plays about Britain's black issues. Meanwhile, here in our workshops, the number of local black actors are diminishing day by day. (Just when we'd ditched *Antony and Cleopatra* for our Shakespeare workshops, in order to do some practical experiments on *Titus*, and had chosen Aaron's big scene defending his baby.) At first, we covered our disappointment with grim jokes about 'African time' ('Maybe they're just very late for every session'), but it's becoming clear that they really are disappearing. We're assured it's nothing personal.

Barney Simon says to me, 'Look, some were intimidated from the start, some hostile. They've had so many years of white culture. And a lot simply can't *afford* to come along. You're not paying them.'

'Paying them?!' I say. 'We're sharing all our experience, all our skills, free of charge.'

'And that's a luxury they can't afford.'

I frown at Barney. Half guru, half Jewish uncle, with his Yiddish proverbs and Charlie Brown quotes, he isn't always that easy to follow.

He smiles – it's a gentle but tired smile; his small eyes always have a faraway look. 'Listen, every time you hold a workshop, they have to travel in and out from Soweto or Alexandra. That costs money. And while they're here they have to eat. And that costs money. And some have families to support. Which costs money. Now – if you were them, would you go to a workshop, or would you go to work?'

*

Ramalao Makhene & Sam Bond

Tonight, the Squint Artists from Alexandra Township come to the Lab
(the Market's version of the Studio), to show us extracts from their current show, which tours schools, dealing with subjects like sexual harass-
ment in the classroom, and AIDS. Paulus, that remarkable young actor
whom we all noticed during the tea-break in the Educators' Workshop
last week, shines again. Towards the end, a young woman starts to cry as
she sings. Paulus hurries over and mops her tears. They continue like
this, her singing, him wiping her face.

After the show, Greg and I try to compliment Paulus on his work, but it's difficult to communicate. Either he's very shy, or speaks hardly any English – I can't work it out. Michael, his companion from the Educators' Workshop, says to me, 'We thought you were such an old man, till we saw you move on those crutches the other day!'

So they were at the *Richard III* Platform. I'm surprised. If Paulus speaks so little English, what must he have made of that session, with our theatre stories and jokes? Yet something drew them.

Clearly there are some black performers who, despite the economics of attending the course, *aren't* staying away.

Driving back to the Carlton tonight, the streets of Jo'burg are more silent than ever, blocked with empty buses. Another strike, another protest.

6

Wednesday 5 October

We have an afternoon off and escape to the Pilanesberg National Park, a couple of hours' drive north of Johannesburg, in the independent home-land of Bophuthatswana. One of the South African stage managers, the fiery-faced Bruce Koch, is driving. There's Patsy Rodenburg, Ian McKellen, Selina Cadell, Tony and I, and sitting in the back, Sue Laurie and Sean Mathias, who wonder if there'll be any tigers.

The park sits in the massive crater formed by a ring of extinct volca-noes. And here at last, among the thornveld and the sour bushveld, is Africa. Or at least the Africa I dreamed about as a boy.

My *Ladybird Book of Great Explorers* called it the Dark Continent, and back in my native Preston I imagined Africa as one large safari park. I used to have my own game reserve on an old chicken run in the back garden, with a dock leaf swamp fed by a hosepipe waterfall, and a rock-ery volcano smouldering with dead leaves. And dotted about it were my collection of 'Britain's' plastic animals: an elephant, a giraffe, a zebra, two gorillas and a chimpanzee.

Today the Pilanesberg seems less populated than my chicken run, but we see kudu, wildebeest, sacred ibis, a couple of warthog and a black-backed jackal; oh, and a long way off, booming from the other side of a large waterhole, hippopotamus.

The heat hangs on you. It's very dry and parched, and the soil seems leeched out. Bruce tells us that the wildebeest are particularly suscep-tible to droughts; but Selina Cadell thinks he said 'draughts', and the thought of a herd of prissy wildebeest all muffled up in scarves and mit-tens sustains us for several hours.

As we leave, Patsy says: 'Well, I'm sorry we didn't see any lions, but I feel sure they saw us.' And we start singing 'Born Free', which was the first record I ever bought.

Then on to the Lost City, a giant hotel, the latest eight-hundred-million-rand addition to Sol Kerzner's slot machine empire and gambling mecca, Sun City (the Las Vegas of South Africa).

As we drive up in our Kombi, over the artificial lake, the tusk and palm frond turrets of the Lost City are ablaze with flaming torches. This, the brochure says, is the palace built by a long-lost civilisation, destroyed by an earthquake and abandoned 'to the concealing growth of time'; until it was 'restored' in 1992 by big Sol.

We pull up in the courtyard alongside a gilded sculpture of a cheetah pouncing on a herd of startled gazelle. It all looks a bit grand, but Patsy and I (demonstrating a high status 10) march past the palace guards to see what's on the menu.

Meanwhile the others fret about their trainers and jeans, and Knight of the Realm or not, Sir Ian is refused entry (low status 3). He waves and sets off to explore the gambling arena with Sean and Bruce. The attractions of a cold bottle of Chablis inspire Tony, despite his shorts, to follow us to the restaurant.

Inside the atrium, past the sable fountain, through the glittering vestibule with its mosaic marble floor, lashed bamboo pillars and frescoed rotunda ('a homage to art and nature' says the brochure), we emerge at the top of the grand staircase, overlooking the Crystal Court. Several acres of dining-room stretch away below us. In the centre, beneath a luculent rock-crystal chandelier of cascading ostrich feathers, four trumpeting life-size elephants spray water into a hammered bronze bowl.

Tony is stopped as we go in, but after telling the *Maître d'* (who turns out to be from Braintree) that he is writing a piece for the London *Times*, the dress code is instantly changed and we're shown to a corner table overlooking the Valley of Waves.

If I thought the Pilanesberg was real Africa, the Lost City is phoney Africa on an unashamedly epic scale. It's a Rider Haggard jungle fantasy as imagined by Cecil B. De Mille. A stately pleasuredome which redefines kitsch.

'Perhaps the set of *Titus* should be like this?' Tony says, surveying the room with awe. 'An African version of Ancient Rome.' I tuck into my Karoo lamb chops and don't respond.

Bruce doesn't want to set off too late, as the road back to Jo'burg can be dangerous; car-jackings and violent ambushes are common. Bophuthatswana was created by the apartheid regime to serve as a dumping ground for blacks. Unemployment is very high in these homelands and there is terrible poverty.

Just before the '94 elections, we were in the Cape visiting Tony's family. We all sat round the TV in comfortable Sea Point, watching coverage of the rioting in Bop; black looters kicking out plate-glass windows in luxury shopping malls. The Shers shuddered with horror. They were glimpsing their worst nightmares about the New South Africa; soon it would be Durban or Cape Town.

Tonight, back in the Kombi, our driver, Bruce, subverting the new reconciliation-speak, calls looting 'affirmative shopping'.

We stop for a pee-break. I get out and stare at the huge blackness of the sky. So what is this place and what am I doing here? What is the real Africa? The wild one of my childhood imaginings has been tamed in this country and corralled into game parks, like Pilanesberg; the fantasy one, like the Lost City, is a sanitised version of Africa, catering for rich tourists, who just want to escape from it all and don't care to come into contact with the real thing, which is violent and complicated and exhilarating.

But am I not just a tourist, too? How can I direct a play here? Well, South Africa does seem to have been part of my life over the last seven or eight years with Tony, travelling round it, trying to understand it, or working with its exiles and expatriates who were helping to change it. But surely, to be relevant, theatre must have an umbilical connection to the lives of the people watching it. How can I provide that? I suppose the answer is that I won't. Shakespeare will. I'm just a 'facilitator'. Content myself with that thought and clamber back in the Kombi.

Singing a medley of half-remembered Broadway hits, we head home.

7

Thursday 6 October
Oh shit. Arrive for today's Shakespeare workshop, and find there are no black actors *at all*. Have to ask a white actor to read Aaron.

Is this the New South Africa?

Friday 7 October
Last day of the Studio Workshop. Frantic last minute scheduling. I'm torn between participating in Sean's Queer Theatre session and a rehearsed reading of Winsome Pinnock's excellent new play, *The Rebirth of Robert Samuels*. Queer or black theatre? I choose the latter because it seems more relevant. Sean is not pleased. But I don't think we could be accused of underplaying the gay cause during our visit.

Anyway, as it turns out, the audience for Winsome's play-reading is mostly white and, among those blacks who do turn up (do I spot Paulus and Michael there at the back?) several drift out before the end.

Evening. And already it's over. Farewell party in the Market's beautiful upstairs room, with huge domed window – the Art Gallery. Everyone turns up: actors from both weeks' workshops, the Squint Artists from Alexandra, the gay activists we've met, people from the British Council, including its new head, Les Phillips, a tall Welshman with red cheeks and a twinkle in his eye, who has just arrived in South Africa after several years in Pakistan.

Les is cornered by Mike Maxwell, Greg and self. We tell him our proposed *Titus* budget, about a million rand (roughly £166,000) and ask him if he's prepared to underwrite the first stage, so that Greg and I can stay on in SA and return to Jo'burg (after our holiday with my family in Cape Town next week) to start auditions immediately. Les is excited by the project and, there and then, promises an initial sum of money. 'Where's Bob?' he says, surveying the heads in the crowded room. 'He's our Jo'burg chap . . . oh, there he is . . . Bob! . . . *Bob*! . . . come here and give these fellows a few thousand rand . . .'

So. There's still a long way to go – in terms of finding all the money

for our budget – but we've got a green light to *start*. And here at the
Market, that means a go-ahead to do casting, find a designer, a musical
director, etc.

We reel away from the encounter, like kids with armfuls of sweets.
'Can you imagine,' I say to Greg, 'can you *imagine* setting up a project
this easily – and with this amount of support and enthusiasm! – back in
England?'

On my way to the loo I bump into Barney Simon. He takes me aside.
'Listen,' he says, 'about *Titus* . . .'

'Yes. We've got the go-ahead from the British Council!'

'Good. But why don't you do *Macbeth* instead?'

'What?' I say, and again, 'What?' And then, '*What*?!!! But we've been
talking about *Titus* since . . .'

'I know. But nobody knows *Titus* here.'

I stare at him. I've heard he's contrary, but can he really be unpicking
the whole thing now, or trying to change its course?

'Well, they don't really know it in England,' I say. 'But then every few
decades someone does a production, like Brook in the fifties with Olivier
and Vivien Leigh, or Deborah Warner's a few years ago, and everyone
goes apeshit, saying "Hey, this is a great play, why don't we know it?"
Isn't that the kind of Shakespeare the Market should be doing?'

'Maybe. But *Macbeth* is the school set text, and . . . we sometimes have
a bit of a problem with audience numbers these days . . .'

'Barney!' I say, amused and shocked at the same time. 'We're doing
Titus. That's what we want to do, that's what you've said we can do and
that's what we'd like to do.'

'Fine,' he says, dropping his objections as swiftly as he raised them.
'Do *Titus*.' And he smiles in that odd, sad, slightly dead-eyed way.

As I move away I feel, for the first time during these *Titus* discussions, a
slight sense of foreboding. Maybe it's just Barney. He's so unfathomable.

There's no time to dwell on it. The party is taking off and my head is
going along. The celebrations are full-blooded, hilarious and moving,
with people jumping on tables to make speeches, and lots of improvised
dancing and singing. Strange, mesmeric Gregorian chants, which Helen
Chadwick has been teaching her singing groups, or townships songs, and
of course the anthem, 'Nkosi Sikelel'i', which we've all been trying to
learn during the week and still can't get through without our songsheets.
Except Greg. He learned it when we did *Two Dogs and Freedom* and his
fluency surprises the locals.

People loom through the raucous crowd and shout in my ear:

Patsy Rodenburg: 'I had the most marvellous result in a voice class today. This man said, "Thank you – as I did that exercise, for the first time ever, my balls vibrated!" '

Dan Robbertse (actor): 'I've always tried to find something in Shakespeare for me . . . couldn't . . . then you guys said, "use your own idiom" . . . and that was so fucking nice!'

And now an actress, whose name I don't know, says to me, 'Thank you for coming home.'

Her words have more significance than she realises. I go into a corner, hiding my emotion. I feel overjoyed, and sad, and angry, if that makes any sense. Maybe you have to be white South African . . .

8

Saturday 8 October
SA flight 237 to Cape Town.

Knackered. The farewell do lasted most of the night. Tony is next to me, in a light doze. I'm flicking through my copy of *Titus*. I give him a nudge. 'I've just realised something,' I say. 'Do you know what your first lines as a professional actor on a South African stage will be?' I quote them to him:

> 'Hail, Rome, victorious in thy mourning weeds!
> Lo, as the bark that hath discharged her freight
> Returns with precious lading to the bay
> From whence at first she weighed her anchorage,
> Cometh Andronicus, bound with laurel boughs,
> To re-salute his country with his tears,
> Tears of true joy for his return to Rome.'

'That's you,' I say. 'You're coming back to re-salute your country!'

PART II *Auditions*

Cape Town, Johannesburg; October 1994

9

Wednesday 12 October
Suddenly, rushing up from the depths and bursting the surface in a thunderclap of spray, there she is, a Southern Right Whale. And we thought we'd be too late to see them.

They come every spring to mate and breed in the wide waters of Walker Bay, just along the coast from Cape Town. We're spending a few days of whale-spotting with Tony's family, here in the little seaside town of Hermanus, before auditions. We feared, so late in the season, that these great mammals might have upped pods and gone, back to the Antarctic Ocean where they live for the rest of the year.

When we arrived, we spotted a whale down in the old harbour and helter-skeltered down the rocks, leaping chasms, stumbling, grazing flesh, losing flip-flops. But the whale had already dived by the time we got there, leaving only sunlight swimming in forests of gold kelp. Tony was inconsolable, convinced that we had lost our only chance to see them; and was determined to inflate the missed opportunity into a symbol for a spate of bad luck recently.

But now, thar she blows. Like an omen of good fortune for the year ahead. This mighty Leviathan rising just yards in front of us, spouting a jet of spume, its great glossy head bonneted with barnacles, its blow-hole sucking air like a Hoover, before thwacking back down under. Then moments later, breaching her way across the bay like a bouncing bomb. I hear Tony breathe an almost inaudible 'Thank you' from somewhere deep in his soul.

Thursday 13 October
We're driving to our first set of auditions. It's a sparkling, blustery day. We follow the ridge of Table Mountain around the corner and along the coast to a tumble of crags called the Twelve Apostles, standing sentinel over the long white beach of Camps Bay.

Tyrone Guthrie said that directing is ninety per cent good casting. So from my point of view, auditions are probably the most crucial stage in the production process.

Most directors have a team of actors in their heads who spring to mind when casting a play; and browsing through *Spotlight*, the actors' directory, slots the rest into place. Not so here. I know only a handful of South African actors. The community is much, much smaller. PAWE, the actors' union, have less than 1,500 actors on their books (as opposed to British Equity's 45,000 members).

The Market have arranged for us to meet an agent called Sibyl Sands who seems to represent most of the Coloured actors here in Cape Town. We are looking in particular for two who might play Chiron and Demetrius, the younger sons of Tamora.

Sibyl scurries around, bright-eyed and busy, like a Yiddisher Mrs Tiggy-Winkle, fetching us cups of coffee and muffins, and ushering in her clients one by one.

'Coloured means specifically mixed race, doesn't it?' I say to Tony. 'Not Indian, not white, not black, mixed race.'

'Yes,' says Tony. 'Coffee-coloured. Surely you knew that?'

'Of course,' I snap defensively. 'Just checking.'

The play deals with issues of race and therefore we do need to be precise about the colour of actors we choose. Aaron has to be isolated in his blackness. Saturninus and Tamora have to be white, otherwise there would be no scandal when Tamora produces a black child (with Aaron). Nevertheless, since we know Tamora has a penchant for black men, her three other sons don't need to be white as well.

We meet several Coloured actors and a number of contenders emerge. Tony wants to book one immediately.

'Casting is all about chemistry,' I say. 'We need to see the two brothers together.'

This is an unusual situation to be in. After all, we're hiring people on a prayer that the production can go ahead. Equity wouldn't allow it.

Friday 14 October

I love coming down to the Cape. Tony's family make me feel like an honorary Sher, though there's all too little time to relax with them this trip. On our last evening we have drinks at a theatre bar in Sea Point, run by Tony's entrepreneurial niece, Monique.

Tonight there's a one-man stand-up comedy show called *A Klonkie Vol K*k* (which, roughly translated, means 'a Coloured guy who's full of shit'). It's performed by an actor called Ivan D. Lucas.

In a flat cap (covering a shiny pate) and tartan trousers, the unemployed klonkie tells of his hopes and frustrations, queuing to vote for the first time in his life. Beneath the clowning is a politically focused monologue. 'For me,' he chirps, 'a member of the Non-Working Class, change here is like the world turning. It's got nothing to do with revolution but we know it's happening, we believe it's happening, we just can't feel it's happening.'

The show lasts maybe fifty minutes and the audience cheer him at the end. Ivan comes over to meet us. He's an activist, with angry eyes and a hectic laugh. He turns out to be a Shakespeare fanatic to boot and has already played King Lear. Tony wants to offer him a part, any part, immediately.

Meanwhile, Monique serves a lethal stream of novelty cocktails including one which I think was called 'A Woman's Revenge'. You knock it back and it explodes in your mouth. Before we get completely comatose and Tony offers Ivan the part of Titus, we arrange to meet him again, properly, to chat.

The week's been too short. We have to head back to Jo'burg to do some more auditioning and meet our potential set designer.

Ivan D. Lucas

10

Monday 17 October
Strange to be back in Jo'burg, at the Carlton Hotel and at the Market, without the rest of the Studio team.

Here at the theatre, when the workshops were on and the place was thronging with theatre people from all over South Africa and from the National, the place felt as it's perceived internationally – like a major theatre landmark – but now, with the large foyer gloomily lit and sparsely peopled, even at night (despite very good reviews, Barney's production of *Hedda Gabler* is playing to audiences as small as thirty), we're seeing a different reality: the Market Theatre looking a bit lost in the New South Africa.

Anyway, there's still much excitement about *Titus*. Everyone thinks it'll be a sell-out, a big event, just what the doctor ordered. The enthusiasm is palpable, both within the building and from the actors who stream in today to meet us.

Auditions.

God, I hate them. Nowadays I'm lucky I don't have to audition for theatre jobs any more, but I do for films and the humiliation stays the same. American film-makers, who tend to be oblivious of British theatre careers, have a particular way of making me feel that the last twenty years never happened and I've just left drama school. Actually, the bigshots themselves seldom attend the audition. You play the scene to a casting director and a video camera, and the tape is then sent back to the States to be flicked through on fast-forward. To anyone who believes, as I do, that acting is about preparation, transformation and, above all, inter-action with your fellow players, the kind of instant performance required in these situations is so nonsensical that I seldom agree to go along, and consequently seldom appear in films . . . !

Anyway, here I am today, on the other side of the table, and it's making me hate auditions even more.

I hate seeing actors as vulnerable as this. So hungry for the job, and so nervous. Dry-mouthed, they spend the first part of the audition – the *chat* – trying to separate their lips from their teeth, and then they spend the second part – the *speech* – trying to remember their lines. It's surprising how most of our visitors forget their lines.

Equally surprising is how Greg is able to prompt them, from memory, no matter what Shakespeare speech they're doing.

He treats our visitors well. He bounds across the room to meet them, rather than expose them, as some directors do, to that long, lonely walk over to the table where we're sitting. He makes sure there's a jug of water on the table, for those dry mouths. And he gives everyone equal space and time, even when the person is clearly wrong for the part, or not on our wavelength

Although we stress that we want to find a South African way of playing Shakespeare, practically every actor does his or her speech in an assumed English accent. The workshop syndrome again.

I'm on the edge of my seat, fascinated and tense – because, of course, that's *me* on the stage. I've spent a lifetime burying my South Africanness, in the belief that good acting, proper acting and certainly Shakespearian acting, has to be English.

As soon as Greg encourages the actors to try again, using their own accent, their own energy, their own *centre*, they transform. Suddenly they become the actors who amazed audiences around the world on those Fugard tours, those Market tours – amazed audiences with their rawness, their passion.

And now I sit there thinking, this could be me, this could be *me*.

What's it going to be like, playing Shakespeare in an accent like this? – an accent that isn't all smooth and rounded, but full of muscle and edges. An earth accent, a root accent, instead of one that floats and flitters around in the air.

I've been longing to find something like this. It would've been so useful for some of the classical parts I've played – most of all, Tamburlaine, the peasant warrior, stinking like a butcher, dreaming like a poet.

But clearly my appetite for this aspect of our production isn't immediately shared by the local actors. We meet quite a lot of resistance during the day. Don't know why I should be surprised. In Britain it's taken decades to fight off the Victorian legacy of performing Shakespeare in wrinkly tights and starched vowels. Barry Rutter's Northern Broadsides Company, which exclusively uses Northern accents to play Shakespeare, is still fighting the battle, still coming up against the purists. So South Africa might have a long way to catch up.

11

Tuesday 18 October

Nadya Cohen's shoulders seem permanently shrugged and she generally wears an expression so laden it suggests that if doom is not actually imminent it is nevertheless inevitable. And I like her from the moment we meet.

Nadya is one of South Africa's top designers and has a long association with the Market. We stand in the main auditorium at the theatre, on the set of their current production of *Hedda Gabler*, and imagine endless possibilities.

The Market is a truly Shakespearian space. Standing on the stage you feel that, if the auditorium were full, you could shake hands with everyone without having to stretch. I'm keen to open up the stage as much as possible, to allow the action of the play to flow swiftly. I want the space to allow any location. Not 'Nowhere-in-general', but 'Everywhere-in-particular'.

Nadya has read *Titus* and responded to it just as we have: not intellectually, but emotionally. She can smell it, she's detected its force field. 'I've got something I want to show you,' she says.

It's a black-and-white photograph of Gloria Swanson posing in the ruins of an old cinema. The only thing left standing among the rubble is an ornate pillar. She wears a long black velvet evening gown and her arms, theatrically draped with a white feather boa, are flung wide.

Completely irrelevant to *Titus* you'd think. But the photo strikes a chord. Don't know why. It's a starting point, a reference. It catches the play's mood, and our early sense of the production.

My brain's antennae get so tuned in to a play at this stage, before rehearsals start, that every conversation, every newspaper article, *everything* seems to be on the right wavelength. For instance, we are driving through Jo'burg's business district to the Market. Suddenly, among all the high-rise corporate granite and mirrored glass skyscrapers, there's an open space where a building has recently been demolished. Buckled metal and rusty iron rods writhe in the rubble. Behind stands the neoclassical portico of a municipal library. Then further along Jeppe Street the construction workers are hosing down the tarmac which had become caked in the deep-red earth on which Johannesburg is built. The street seems to stream with blood.

These are the colours and textures of *Titus*. We decide to bring Nadya back to have a look.

Mike Maxwell has recommended a musician called Dumisani Dhlamini to be our composer and Musical Director. Michael's advice is invaluable, as he's a talented musician himself.

We meet Dumi in the yard of the Yard of Ale, the pub in the Market precinct. The waiter, Shadrach (I want to ask where Meshach and Abednego are) takes our order of Castle beers.

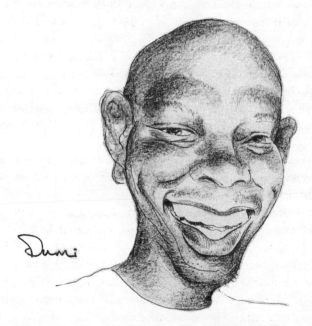

Dumi is tall and slightly stooped, and has the cheery, ascetic look of the Dalai Lama.

We talk in very general terms about the music. I think we may need a military band sound for the triumphal return of the Andronici, and a musical theme for the Goths which is more elementary, more primitive, more percussive.

Dumi begins to firecracker off different ideas. Shadrach brings another round of beers and we toast Dumi: 'Welcome, you're hired.'

*

We're thinking of playing the Andronici as Afrikaners. Titus's family are of old Roman stock, with a self-righteous belief in their own importance. Like the Afrikaner nation, they are God-fearing and pure-bred.

Shakespeare even gives Titus the surname 'Pius'. Roman piety meant unswerving loyalty to Family, Church and State. Such piety is quintessential to the old Afrikaner mentality. And it's eloquently expressed in the Voortrekker Monument. In order for me to get a fuller picture of Afrikanerdom, we snatch some time to pay a visit to this most sacred temple of the Volkdom, and head north on the N2 towards Pretoria.

The Monument suddenly rises before us, like some huge granite tabernacle, near a place called Valhalla. It commemorates those Afrikaners who lost their lives in the Battle of Blood River, in 1838, when the Boers, rejecting British Rule, trekked north from the Cape, and encountered 12,000 Zulu impis. The Boers were less than 500 in number, but they defeated their assailants – a sure proof both of divine intervention and their status as a chosen people.

This stone blancmange, as someone once called the Monument, was built in 1938, the centenary of the famous battle. With its stripped-down classicism and grandiose scale, it could have been designed by Albert Speer, Hitler's architect.

As we make our way into the precincts of the Monument I keep thinking someone is going to stop us and ask for ID, or a blood sample. There's a stone wall carved with 'Jawbone' ox wagons circled into a defensive laager, and the building is buttressed by graven images of famous Boer heroes like Andries Pretorius and Piet Retief, looking like supermen.

A party of black workmen are busy repairing the flagstones as we clamber up the steps. We go in. My hand automatically reaches for the holy water – it feels like entering a cathedral. And in a way that's what it is. Inside the cool, hushed Hall of Heroes, the walls are lined with an epic bas-relief which details the Afrikaner version of the Trek, and the subsequent battle, with almost bibilical reverence.

We wander round, gazing suspiciously at the marble friezes, with their one-sided view of history. Tony's dimly remembered school lessons do little to fill in the gaps. And I wasn't taught about the Boers at school. Certainly not about the Anglo–Boer War in which 26,000 Boer women and children died in British concentration camps. Yes, concentration camps – we invented them.

In the centre of the basilica you can gaze down into an inner sanctum.

There is an altar inscribed with the words '*Ons vir jou, Suid Afrika*'.

'It means "We for you, South Africa",' Tony translates. 'It's from the old National Anthem.'

On 16 December each year, the day of the Boers' astonishing victory at Blood River, a shaft of light streaks through a hole in the dome and, with Druidic precision, hits the altar, illuminating the oath. According to the guide book, this symbolises the light of civilisation which the Afrikaner Volk have created in Darkest Africa.

There is some debate as to whether the Voortrekker Monument should be allowed to remain in the New South Africa. Apparently the compromise suggested, in this period of compromises, is that another monument should be built, on one of the neighbouring hills, to commemorate all those who gave their lives in the struggle to rid the country of apartheid.

As we leave, I wonder if the black workmen replacing the flagstones ever pop in to look at the friezes and see how their ancestors are depicted.

On the steps, we take snapshots for the family album. Tony does an impersonation of Eugene Terre'Blanche, the charismatic leader of the neo-Nazi Afrikaner Resistance Movement, the AWB. And I recall that the first time I heard of the Monument was in 1989, when Terre'Blanche drunkenly stormed the gates one night in his jeep. Apparently, he wanted to exhibit his white supremacy to his girlfriend, the gossip columnist Jani Allen.

Over the main portal, the carved head of a buffalo, the most dangerous and unpredictable of African animals, glares down at us.

Back at the hotel, I spot a porn magazine on the news-stand. A sleezy tide of pornography is flooding the New South Africa, while it decides what its stance should be on censorship. The magazine's cover shows something that many people in this country would consider sacrilegious and perhaps it was prompted by Terre'Blanche's escapades. It pictures a topless nurse romping about in the hallowed environs of the Voortrekker Monument.

12

Wednesday 19 October
We auditioned fifteen Lavinias today . . .

Lavinia is one of Shakespeare's most untypical creations. For a writer whose characters use language incessantly – 'words, words, words' – and who are so articulate, it is remarkable that, in Lavinia, he develops a role, a leading role, which is mostly mute.

(Lavinia is Titus's daughter, who is raped and mutilated by Tamora's sons; both her hands are chopped off and her tongue cut out.)

In today's auditions, Greg asks each actress to pull socks over her fists and, without using speech, to communicate the story of some traumatic event in her life – a real one – to me. Unintentionally, a lot of the actresses turn this into a game of charades, with me going, 'You were travelling in a car . . . no it wasn't a car . . . a motor cycle? . . . a bike, right . . . uh-huh . . . and you were hit by a car . . . nope . . . a truck? . . .'

But then an actress called Jennifer Woodburne comes in. Mid-twenties, open personality, angular beauty, hennaed hair. She's very convincing as Lavinia, both with speech (playing her as a kind of Afrikaner princess) and without. Her sock-fisted, dumb-tongued story – about an intruder breaking into her flat one night – is very upsetting, without a hint of charades to it.

After she goes, I say to Greg, 'I think we've found Lavinia.'

More experienced at auditions, his reaction is calmer: 'Could be, but we've got more girls to see tomorrow.'

I'm very convinced by Greg's ideas about how Tamora should be played. So often she's simply the wicked queen from *Snow White*, but, as Greg points out, she begins as a victim: defeated in the long war with Rome, captured and dragged in chains through the streets, and then forced to beg Titus for the life of her son who is selected for sacrifice. When she fails, and he's slaughtered in the street, she starts to wreak havoc, which continues throughout the rest of the story. This case history – of the persecut*or* beginning as the persecut*ed* – has been the starting point for some of my own performances, like Shylock and Singer.

The actress we've always wanted for Tamora is Dorothy Ann Gould, currently playing Hedda. It's a real heavyweight part, and she's a real heavyweight actress – with sexy, slightly Oriental, slightly simian looks.

Trouble is, her partner is Mike Maxwell, our show's producer at the Market. He's been very good about not mentioning her during casting discussions. Too good. Anyway, we now ask him to ask her . . .

Thursday 20 October
Saturninus, the emperor of Rome, is a terribly difficult part, both to cast and to play. I've had some experience of it before, because my former partner, and now closest friend, Jim (Hooper), played it in Deborah's RSC production and we talked a lot about the character's violent mood swings.

Is he mad? Is he drunk? Is he on some drug?

Here in Jo'burg, we've seen some fine actors for the part (it's very flattering that the city's leading actors are all prepared to come and meet us), but then this afternoon someone arrives who shoots straight to the top of the list.

Gys de Villiers. Mid-thirties, Afrikaner, tight, muscular build, a wolfish quality. Bald, with a moustache and goatee which emphasise a flashing smile. Big powerful eyes. He seems to have no problem with the psychology of the character. When he reads the speeches, you don't ask yourself, Why is this man so irrational? – you just think, This is how this man *is*. And he brings a sense of fun to it, as though Saturninus's life is just one long, wild rave-up.

After he goes, Greg says, 'Well, we dreamed of finding a South African John Malkovich for the part. I think we just did.'

It's my turn to be cautious. 'I wonder if he's trouble . . . ?'

We check with Mike Maxwell, who says, 'Not at all. Not if he respects the work. Then he's incredibly committed.'

A wild boy who works hard? You don't normally find both things in the same person.

Friday 21 October
Last day. We're flying home tonight.

It's terrific – in one week we seem to have assembled a first-rate cast. Dorothy has agreed to play Tamora; Gys has said yes to Saturninus; Dale Cutts (the Rod Steiger look-alike from the workshops) will do Marcus; Jennifer Woodburne is playing Lavinia; Martin le Maitre, a huge baby-faced rugby-forward of a bloke, who's just played Hamlet in Durban, is going to be Lucius; Ivan D. Lucas has agreed to a double of Bassianus (a chance for him to play straight) and the Clown (a chance for him to do his klonkie stand-up stuff); two stalwarts of the Market's Lab Theatre, Dan Robbertse (who gate-crashed our auditions!) and Bruce Laing, both very decent guys and excellent actors, will be invaluable in an assortment of parts; and we've found a way of changing the Boy in Act IV, so that he doesn't have to be Lucius's son, and can be played by Paulus Kuoape, that outstanding young actor from Squint Artists, who inadvertently auditioned for us during a tea-break in the workshops.

A few parts are still uncast, including Chiron and Demetrius. The Coloured actors we wanted from our Cape Town auditions are unavailable. But Mike Maxwell has promised to continue auditioning, on video, and to send us the tapes. (Oh God, we're going to be like those American film-makers I was moaning about.)

Apart from Chiron and Demetrius, only one other major part to cast . . . Aaron.

We've seen several fine black actors, but Aaron has some of the longest, most complicated and most beautiful speeches in the play – which is very difficult if English isn't your first language. Also he has to be dangerous (he causes the downfall of almost everyone), yet sympathetic (his black-is-beautiful speeches will have special resonance in this country) and, finally, he must be extremely dishy (despite the fact that she's now married to the emperor, Tamora still can't keep her hands off him).

It's a tall order. But there's one actor who has been recommended by everyone. Barney Simon mentioned him to me, even before we thought of doing *Titus*. 'You must see this actor – he's very beautiful,' said Barney, emphasising the last word in a way that wasn't referring to his looks. 'He's just been in my production of *The Suit*, and when Janet Suzman saw it, she said, "That actor is going to be the next great Othello."'

'What's his name?' I asked.

'Sello Maake ka Ncube.'

'Pardon?'

'Sello. Just remember – *Sello*.'

At lunch-time today, there's another awards ceremony, the Critics' Award, and our man, Sello Maake ka Ncube, has been nominated as Best Actor for his performance in *The Suit*. At about 2.30, Sello arrives, beaming from ear to ear, having, yes, won.

Sello

Sello is a charismatic mixture of maturity and openness. Walking with a rolling gait that never becomes a swagger, his body is powerful, yet his face is gentle. Barney was right. He is beautiful. And not just physically. Something shines within him: a grace, a humility. You sense it the moment you meet him. So it comes as no surprise to learn that, before becoming an actor, he was a lay preacher. He's now a big TV star, from a soap called *Generations*. He was brought up speaking Sotho, yet reads Shakespeare effortlessly. Last year he played Mark Antony in *Julius Caesar*.

Greg and I are both about to offer him Aaron then and there, when he says, 'There is a problem . . .'

We both say, 'Uh-huh?'

'I've been offered Othello – for CAPAB – over the same period, and I've half committed myself . . .'

I go 'gulp', while Greg barely pauses for breath: 'Yes, you must play Othello . . . you're born to it . . . I know Janet Suzman said that very same thing . . . but I think you should play Aaron first. He's the rough sketch. For Othello *and* Iago actually. How old are you?'

'Thirty-five.'

'Thirty-five. Yes, well, y'see, Othello describes himself as "declined into the vale of years".'

Sello goes, 'Uhm . . .'

Greg says: 'Look, you must play Othello, you *will* play Othello, there will be many opportunities. But not so many to play Aaron.'

Sello says he needs to think about it and talk to his agent, and that he'll let us know as soon as possible. As he's leaving, he suddenly says to me, 'You know – I was expecting you to be taller. Forgive me, but I didn't realise you were so small.'

I answer, 'Sello – ever since you walked through that door, after winning that award, you've been floating six inches off the ground. How can you possibly judge what size anyone else is?'

He laughs and I feel we're going to be OK here. The lay preacher has a sense of humour.

A few hours later, just before we're about to leave for the airport, his agent rings back to say, yes, Sello would like to play Aaron. It's the best farewell present anyone can give us. The dark heart of the play – Aaron and Tamora – that dark, blood-red heart is going to be as strong as an ox.

In the circumstances, we don't really need a plane to fly us home, but we get on to one anyway and climb into the sky of a South African spring night, and turn towards the northern hemisphere and its autumn. Which Greg loves ('There's so *much* weather in England – in South Africa there's hardly any!') and which I hate.

But on this particular Friday night I'm full of hope.

I can't wait to get back to my novel, *Cheap Lives*, and do the final draft, armed with rich new material from this trip, like the whales at Hermanus, and Ivan D. Lucas's revisions to the Cape Coloured vernacular.

What with *Cheap Lives* and *Titus*, my world is beginning to orbit round South Africa again. 'What would you say', I suddenly ask Greg on the flight, 'to the idea of us going back to South Africa on a more . . . permanent basis . . . as many people have done since the elections . . . what would you say?'

He takes a long time to consider it, then answers, 'I'd say . . . why don't we use *Titus* to find out?'

PART III *The Workshop*

London; January–February 1995

13

Thursday 19 January

'You haven't forgotten we're popping into the Studio after lunch?' says Greg, when I reach home from the optician.

'Oh, I had,' I say, giving a series of exaggerated nods, as I tilt my head around, trying to find a way of looking through these, my first, bifocals. They're the new, expensive kind, where you can't see the join. 'Why do they want us?'

'Final arrangements for the South Africans. Who's going to the airport, at what time, whether we serve them breakfast when we get them back to the Studio, what to serve, that sort of thing.'

'Well, you don't need me for that, do you?' I ask, holding up a page of the *Guardian* and watching it slide in and out of focus.

'*Yes!*' growls Greg. (Sub-text: You're not just doing the fun bits of this venture.)

'But I promised to look at the new proofs of *Cheap Lives* before . . .'

'You're coming along!'

'Mind you,' I say, giving in, 'don't seem to be able to look at anything with these things.'

'And John Kani rang.'

'What did he want?'

'I didn't speak to him. He left a message on the machine, said he'd ring back.'

'Mh-hh,' I murmur, finding that the only way to read the *Guardian* is to hold my head back stiffly, as though surprised.

'He sounded a bit odd.'

'Odd?'

'Muted.'

'Muted . . .' I repeat absently. I turn to Greg with my stiff-necked pose. 'How am I going to rehearse like this? Titus can't be permanently surprised.'

'Well . . .' says Greg, starting to laugh. 'His homecoming doesn't turn out quite as he expects.'

*

Driving to the Studio, we reflect on the circumstances which are leading to the arrival of our principal actors in London this Saturday, plus the Musical Director, and then both our designers next week, to start work on *Titus* here, instead of us getting on a plane and going to them.

Back in November, just when we'd finally finished casting (via video auditions), Mike Maxwell rang, his voice heavy, to say that the Market was finding it difficult, *very* difficult, to raise the money for *Titus* – sponsors were worried that they didn't know the play, that it wasn't a school text, that it was too violent – and so, at this point in time, there was still not a single cent in place. The Market were seriously considering whether to scrap the whole idea.

We told Sue Higginson at the Studio and, always game for a challenge, she wondered if they could help? Make it a co-production with the RNT Studio? Share some of the costs, like the two-week development period. The Studio's involvement would be a logical progression from the South African visit. Might it be possible to develop the production in London, at the Studio, then rehearse and play it in Jo'burg, and then bring it back for a short run at the National?

Sue's idea was that by becoming *more* ambitious for the production, by giving it a higher profile, it might be easier to raise sponsorship, both in South Africa and the UK.

From then on Sue threw herself, heart and soul, into making *Titus* happen. First of all she enlisted Richard Eyre's support. He promised to try to find a slot for it at the Cottlesloe. 'It's a project made in heaven,' he said to me. Now the Studio was able to allocate its own money for a development period that would happen *here*. Then Sue chatted up the British Council. They were inspired by the idea of a British arts presence in South Africa during the Queen's first visit there in March. So they weighed in with £15,000 to fly over the principals.

So far, so good. But, as yet, we didn't have the main body of money – for the production itself. The Market still had to find this themselves.

And then, early in December, there was a phone call from Barney to report that sponsorship, big sponsorship, had finally been found.

National Panasonic, SA, were giving us R600,000 – about £100,000!

National Panasonic normally only sponsor sports events, so nobody had bothered to approach them during the initial search for money, but this time round, a junior member of the Market staff decided to have a go, and to everyone's surprise and delight they said yes.

The worst remaining problem, as we drive to the Studio this Thursday afternoon, is whether to serve croissants or buns when the South Africans arrive on Saturday.

'Have you guys talked with John Kani this morning?' asks Diane Borger the instant we arrive at the Studio. Sue is away on her Christmas holiday, so Diane, the deputy head, is in charge. A short, auburn-haired American, Diane is normally bubbling with wisecracks (I keep telling her she's Jewish and she keeps telling me she's not), so it's a surprise to see her looking solemn today.

Greg tells her about John's message on our machine. Diane says they had one too. 'He said there was a problem, said he couldn't give any details and that we were to stand by for a fax this afternoon.'

'A problem?' I repeat. 'What can it be?' The three of us stare at one another blankly. I ring the Market. Can't get through to John. Or Mike Maxwell. And Barney is away, in mourning – for his friend, Joe Slovo, the leader of SA's Communist Party, who died a fortnight ago. Eventually, I'm put through to Regina Sebright, the administration manager. Her voice is measured. 'Yes, there is a problem. I can't talk about it at the moment. Please wait for the fax. That will make everything clear.'

What the fuck is going on?

So we sit around for an hour or so, trying to go through our agenda of last-minute details for Saturday morning, while jumping out of our seats every time the phone rings.

Eventually it starts – the fax machine goes into its humming, grunting, tummy-rumbling mode – and begins to spew out the goods. Greg dashes over, twists upside down and starts reading: ' "Market Theatre . . . Extremely Urgent . . .".' He frowns. 'It seems to be addressed to Panasonic . . .'

'To Panasonic?' Diane and I cry in unison.

'To the Chairman,' gasps Greg, now almost standing on his head in an effort to read it. ' ". . . Panasonic was approached . . . with regard to sponsorship of our production of *Titus Andronicus* by William Shakespeare, starring the world's leading Shakespearian actor, Antony Sher . . . " '

I laugh grimly. 'I've been promoted.'

' ". . . Subsequently, it would seem that we have been the victim of what appears to have been an enormous hoax, which could have catastrophic consequences for the Market Theatre . . ." '

'A hoax!' gasps Greg, coming up from his handstand. He carefully rips the first page from the rest.

He and Diane almost bang heads as they rush to read it upright. I try to join in, but can't find the right focus with my new bifocals – that precise, stiff-necked position – it's all just a soft, faxy blur to me.

Meanwhile Greg and Diane are already on to page two, going 'Jesus!' and 'Wow!'

'What, what, what?' I ask, dancing round them like a kid being excluded from a grown-up crisis.

'Shush!' goes Greg.

It's agonising. Page after page comes off the machine, but try as I may, my head jerking back and forth like a stork's, I cannot read a word.

At last all the pages are out, all five of them, and Greg and Diane sit back, pale, wide-eyed and breathless.

I say, 'Will someone *please* tell me . . .'

Greg says, 'There's no money for the production. None at all.' He reads the letter aloud. It's from John Kani to the Chairman of Panasonic.

It describes how, after a junior member of the Market staff (whom I'll call Deb) had approached Panasonic for sponsorship, a Mr van Schalkwyk phoned her to say the proposal had been accepted. He gave Deb a telephone number which he claimed was his direct line and from then on, all her calls to Panasonic were made on this number.

Then follows a bizarre account of why the sponsorship cheque never reached the Market. On one occasion, Mr van Schalkwyk was due to deliver it personally but, because of a storm that afternoon, he never arrived. On another, he invited Deb to collect it and, to save time, offered to meet her in the Panasonic car-park. When she reached the car-park he apologised, saying the cheque wasn't ready. Later he rang to say the cheque was being posted by registered post. When it didn't turn up, he blamed the Christmas post.

Finally, two days ago, Mike Maxwell rang Panasonic personally, only to discover that they knew nothing of this. The proposal to sponsor *Titus* had been rejected, not accepted. And no one of the name of van Schalkwyk worked for them.

Reaching the end of John's letter, Greg reads: ' "We may have to cancel the production. This would place the Market Theatre in great jeopardy, severely affect its local and international reputation. The totality of this may affect the future of the Market Theatre." '

'Then', Greg says, 'John asks the Chairman whether he can throw any light on this mess . . . and to reconsider backing the production.' He lowers the pile of fax pages.

Now I'm as white-faced as the rest.

We sit in silence for a while.

Then: 'We've been asking to see confirmation in writing ever since we heard about the sponsorship,' Greg tells Diane. 'Why was no one at the Market doing the same? Why were they leaving it to a junior member of the staff?'

'That's right,' I say. 'Why wasn't John or Barney ringing the Chairman of Panasonic, and saying, Can I take you out to lunch, can I kiss your feet?'

'Five weeks,' says Greg, checking the fax again. 'Five weeks of everyone leaving it to this junior member of staff . . . !'

'While cheques were about to be picked up in a car-park,' says Diane. 'A *car-park*? What is this – "Deep-throat" and Watergate all over again? Handing over big corporation cheques in *car-parks* . . . ?'

I bury my head. The poor Market, after its heroic struggle against apartheid, unfunded by the government, fighting for every penny for every production . . . now here's the Market in the New South Africa, without enough business sense to insist on confirmation of Panasonic's sponsorship *in writing*.

Diane says, 'Let's just go step by step here' – and picks up the phone. She dials Roger Chapman, the RNT head of touring, and within minutes he's dashed over and is manning the desk and phones.

A big, forty- or fifty-something Yorkshireman, Roger is an impressive mixture of charm and practicality. He's listened to our story and read the fax, while uttering no more than a quiet 'My goodness!' and now says, 'Well, the British Council are paying for the workshop, so we might still be able to get this thing started.'

'But what's the point,' I ask, 'of starting, if you can't carry on?'

'Ah-hah!' he says. 'The point is once you've started, you find a way of carrying on!' – and gives a wide explosion of a laugh.

Roger belongs to a rare and valuable species: he's a theatre enthusiast.

He rings the British Council, drags the head man out of some important meeting, explains the situation, says we're hopeful of finding a solution and asks for permission to proceed as planned – to fly out the South Africans on British Council money.

The answer is – go ahead.

Roger plops down the phone, asks us if he may come along and say hello to the South Africans on Saturday morning and then, excusing himself politely, hurries back to work.

We sit amazed – as amazed as we were by the first news.

'Wasn't that great?' says Diane eventually. 'Wasn't that like Daddy coming in to make it all better?'

Back at home, without the tension, the craziness of the last few hours, Greg and I go into a slump. The shock hits us again and again – this bizarre hoax, it's like a bad B-movie.

And then there's the reality of what's ahead. As Roger said, 'It's going to be most tough for you chaps, to run this workshop, not knowing if it might just be an end in itself, or whether it might still become a production.'

Jesus, what's going to happen to *Titus*?

And to the Market?

I imagine, in the future, someone asking, 'Did you ever work at the Market?' – and me replying, 'No but I helped to close it down.'

Friday 20 January
Finally get to speak to John Kani.

He says that the Chairman of Panasonic responded promptly to yesterday's fax, and they're washing their hands of the whole business. Quite rightly. They were approached for sponsorship, as they constantly are, and said no, as they mostly do. The rest had nothing to do with them.

John says he's thinking of calling in the police.

I express amazement that he hasn't already.

'Ja, my friend . . .' says John, 'it's just that the Market's had such a bad relationship with the police over the years . . . it's hard to explain . . . even now, we don't think of them as people you turn to for help.'

I ask whether Deb has any ideas about who Mr van Schalkwyk is? No. The Market's solicitor interviewed her yesterday for several hours and she told him everything she knew.

John says they are determined to find the money – he and Barney are personally going to ring the Market's friends, in South Africa and round the world.

I mumble something like 'Good luck', suddenly feeling tired and upset. 'Now about the actors . . . have they been told?'

'No.'

'We'd like them to be told.'

'Well . . .' says John. 'We're not so sure that's a good idea. It'll go right round town in a . . .'

I interrupt, telling John that if they don't tell them, we will. The moment they arrive. It's their right to know. We think they should be told before they get on the plane. I mean, they could be out of work in two weeks. They might want to start looking for a job.

'My friend, you're right,' he says immediately. I give a little smile and I sense he does too. After all, we're talking about actors – we're talking about *us*.

In the evening, Mike Maxwell rings to report that John did what we asked. When the actors all gathered at the Market *en route* for Jan Smuts Airport, John made a stirring speech, as only he can. He explained that the production had been the victim of an extraordinary hoax and that it was now in jeopardy, as was the future of the Market itself. He said everyone was determined to find a solution – but if any of the cast wanted to hand in their plane ticket and go home, they could.

'They all sat in silence for a moment,' says Mike. 'And then they stood up and surrounded John and hugged him. And then they all got on the bus and went to the airport. I've just got back from there. They're on their way to you . . .'

When I relay this to Greg, we both start crying, for the first time since the news broke, and then laughing.

'He's a wily old bugger, is John Kani,' says Greg.

'That's right,' I say. 'He waits till they're all packed and excited and ready to go, and then he tells them there's a bit of a problem, so they must choose between a two-week holiday in London, or going home and being out of work. And guess which they choose?'

Saturday 21 January
Heathrow, 5.30 a.m. Tears and smiles again. How many times have I stood here, in the Arrivals hall, scanning the passengers flocking through that blank, vaguely sinister partition which separates us and them, scanning them for some South Africans? In the past, until Dad's death just over a year ago, they've numbered two and been of a parental persuasion. Today there are ten and they seem more like kids; beaming, excited, some on their first visit to London, and one never having been in an aeroplane before! This is Oscar Peterson, one of the two young Coloured actors, whom we've cast, via video, as Chiron and Demetrius, but never seen till now. In his early twenties, dark-skinned, bespectacled, unshaven (we've asked all the men to grow beards), Oscar seems totally and utterly

Oscar

Charlton

fazed: by his first ever flight, by being in London, by meeting us. The other one, Charlton George, is slightly older and skinnier, much lighter skinned, and with remarkably blue eyes. In the bad old days, he could've found himself in one of those nightmare cases of race classification – Coloured or white?

Diane Borger and Lucy Hemmings (production manager at the Studio) are also at the airport to meet our brood and now transport them back to Waterloo.

Roger Chapman, hero – and father-figure – of Thursday's crisis, arrives to greet the group, to tell them of the National's commitment to the project, and that he's spoken to the Market and agreed that if the money isn't found by Friday next week, the production will be cancelled. The group would then have another week's workshop, which they could just treat as training, and that would be it.

(Exit Titus Andronicus.)

Greg leans forward and says, 'Good, right, OK, and that's the last time we're going to talk about it. From now till next Friday we're proceeding as though this workshop is the beginning of our rehearsal period. We can't go through the next week prefacing every remark with, "*If* we do the production . . ." ' The group agrees to ban the subject for the next six days. Then Greg turns to me, 'Tony, do you have anything to say?'

I do – I want to tell them how much this means to me, to see all these South African actors here, in London, where I came as a frightened nineteen-year-old, to see them – to see *us all* – here at the Royal National Theatre for God's sake . . . ! But I'm too emotional and just mutter, 'No, I think we've covered everything.'

Greg turns to the group. 'Anyone . . . any questions?'

'Yes,' says Ivan D. Lucas, the sharp stand-up comic we saw in Cape Town. Bald, bespectacled, gleaming, Ivan hasn't been sitting in his chair, but limbering up behind it. 'Why *Titus Andronicus*?'

'How d'you mean?' says Greg.

'Why are we doing that play – that particular play?'

Greg thinks, then says, 'I'm not going to answer that question. I hope the next fortnight will answer it for us.'

14

Sunday 22 January

'Why do I always do this?' Tony snaps at himself, as he stomps about trying to get himself ready. Sometimes, getting Tony out of the house is like trying to winkle a barnacle off its rock.

Today we're giving the South Africans a tour of London. It's the last thing I feel like. This whole project may collapse at any moment. We're treading water. But I'm not meant to talk about that.

I'm standing in the hall waiting patiently. On the wall is a panorama of London as it looked in Shakespeare's day. It was engraved by Visscher in 1616, the year of Shakespeare's death. I bought it from the Museum of London and Tony had it mounted for me one birthday. There's always something different to find: a coach waiting to cross the bridge, windmills on the hills in distant rural Hampstead, or the man peeing against a wall in Borough High Street.

While Tony continues to search frantically for whatever it is he's searching for, I'm back in Tudor London on a winter morning in 1594, imagining Will Shakespeare, not yet thirty, leaving his lodgings in Silver Street on the corner of Cripplegate (somewhere underneath the present Barbican Centre) and hurrying down to St Paul's Churchyard. There, at the little north door under the sign of the gun, a bookstall owned by Ed White and Tom Millington, I picture Shakespeare clutching a copy of the first of his plays ever to be printed, *The Most Lamentable Roman Tragedy of Titus Andronicus*, hot off the press. I can see him stroking it, and sniffing it, and feeling like a real writer.

The play is already a huge hit. It has been rushed into print because the Plague has broken out once again and the theatres have been closed. So if people can't see it, at least they can read it. And it would run to two further editions, one in 1600 and one in 1611. Long after Shakespeare had retired to Stratford some twenty years later, his rival Ben Jonson would complain that people still considered *Titus* one of the best plays around.

It's been a bad couple of years for the theatre. Plague has swept away 20,000 people, nearly ten per cent of the city's population, and the churches stink of rotting corpses. But just after Christmas it has abated sufficiently for Philip Henslowe to reopen his new theatre, the Rose, in the Liberty of the Clink.

My Lord the Earl of Sussex's Men mounts a season of plays, including Will's new play, *Titus*, his first tragedy, on 23 January. (When our workshop starts tomorrow it will be exactly 401 years later, to the day.) It packs the house. Henslowe records receipts of £3 8s, the best takings of the season, and puts it on for another two performances.

I imagine Shakespeare crossing London Bridge on his way to work, gazing downstream past Billingsgate at some great merchant galley corralled below in the Pool of London. At the end of the bridge, a row of traitors' heads are spiked up on the gate. I wonder if Shakespeare was inspired by this grizzly phalanx when writing *Titus*, or if the Rose's stage manager was tempted to borrow a couple as props for the show.

Or perhaps Will would avoid the busy traffic of the densely populated bridge. Perhaps he would go down to the stairs by Fishmongers' Hall, and hail one of the Thames watermen to ferry him across to Southwark. The tilt-boats, shallops and wherries make a brisk traffic criss-crossing the river, avoiding the swans, hay boats and gilded royal barges.

The south side of the river is the 'West End' of Shakespeare's day. The Rose Theatre stands among the stews, brothels, prisons and taverns on Bankside, next to the Bear Gardens, where bulls and bears are baited by ferocious mastiffs and terriers. The bears can be stars in their own right, like Harry Hunks, a great favourite during James's reign. Or the polar bear, which the Spanish ambassador was delighted to see loosed in the Thames so the dogs could fight it as it swam. No animal rights protesters then.

I first came to London with my family when I was five. Like Christopher Robin, I was impressed by the Changing of the Guard at Buckingham Palace; and I was frightened by the wolves in the Zoo. But my most vivid memory is one of absolute awe. I can still feel the lump in my throat and a dizzy rushing in my ears. Wandering around the galleries of the Natural History Museum we came face to face with the sixty-foot bulk of a Blue Whale, plunging in airy space.

Seeing the real thing at Hermanus a few months ago, I felt just like that five-year-old again.

'All right, I'm ready,' says Tony. 'We can go.'

Finally we meet the company and our tour begins. I'm meant to be the tour guide. I've planned a route setting off from the Studio in Waterloo, taking in the major sites and ending up for lunch below Tower Bridge.

Everybody clambers on to the coach. I feel quite nervous. I've never been a tour guide before. Unfortunately, since I can't tell my right from my left, important monuments fly by on one side, while the company are looking out of the other.

As we drive through the City, I do manage to point out the golden statue of Justice standing atop the Old Bailey, in her sturdy blindfold. She appears a lot in the play.

'The first South Africans to visit London were brought here during Shakespeare's lifetime,' I bark into the mike. 'A group of Khokhoi herdsmen from the Cape were shown off at court.'

It was a fashionable novelty to display exotic natives in England:

Have we some strange Indian with the great tool come to court, the women so besiege us?' (*Henry VIII* Act V, Scene 4)

My knowledge of London tends to be rather eclectic and anecdotal. I can tell you why Lambeth Bridge is surmounted by pineapples, or the names of the pelicans in St James's Park, but I'd be completely stumped if someone asked me about house prices, or the public sector borrowing requirement.

'You know the difference between streets in London and streets in Jo'burg?' says Ivan. 'The detail. There's so much detail in the streets here. So much architecture, so much history, so much . . . detail.'

He's right. London is a palimpsest on which many different ages have engraved their marks. Sometimes those marks have almost been erased, but their faint outlines still remain, even if only in the odd street name: Seacole Lane, Apothecary Street, Bear Alley. History is palpable in London.

Today, our tour bus crosses Southwark Bridge and turns right. As we round the corner of Rose Alley, I shiver. It's a real Blue Whale of a shiver. My eyes moisten and I struggle to keep my voice from breaking. A thatched roof has come into view. And rough-cast plaster walls. 'And here, folks, is Shakespeare's own theatre. The Globe.'

For twenty years the project to reconstruct the Globe was the brainchild of the American actor, Sam Wanamaker. Sadly, he died last year, before seeing the completion of the project. But now here it is, nearly finished, Shakespeare's most famous theatre just yards from its original site.

We are met by Patrick Spottiswoode, education director of the Globe, who takes us into the theatre.

We stand huddled in the wind and the rain. The Wooden O is minus its tiring house and stage, and the floor is asphalt instead of a 'clunch' of hazelnuts. We watch as the specially turned green-oak balustrades are pegged into place on the galleries, and the roof is thatched with reeds from the Norfolk Broads.

The spirit of Shakespeare affrights the air!

Now that we are about to tackle one of Shakespeare's plays (fingers crossed), I feel we are part of a continuum. Part of a process, a thread which stretches back in an unbroken line to the company who first performed Shakespeare's plays. On this site, or as near as dammit, in the original Globe, Richard Burbage played Hamlet and passed it on to his understudy, John Taylor; Sir William Davenant saw Taylor's Hamlet, and taught Betterton, whose company passed it on to Garrick and so on through Kean and Irving, Gielgud and Olivier to the present generation.

'Are you cold, Oscar?' I ask.

'Agh, man,' says Oscar, from deep inside his anorak. 'It's not cold I'm shaking with . . .'

In the Globe's shop you can buy Shakespeare heritage fridge magnets, Bard coasters and key-rings, Shakespeare bubble bath probably, and the company roam around picking up souvenirs.

Dumi is looking at a tiny edition of the sonnets. 'Oh, I think I'll have this for Lulu. My wife likes to read sonnets to me when I'm in the bath.'

For two pounds, Ivan, the Bard fanatic, has bought a brick. It's his contribution to the Globe. He waves his certificate: 'You see,' he cries delightedly. 'I may just be a klonkie from Cape Town, but now there will always be part of Shakespeare's theatre that's mine!'

15

Harry has finally taken me to his heart. Which is very important if you're working at the Studio. Get in Harry's good books and you gain access to some vital necessities, like a space in the car-park and fresh milk for your coffee. As the caretaker, Harry Henderson rules the place with a rod of steel. His room is, in fact, filled with rods of steel: old-fashioned dumb-bells and gym equipment. A Londoner, in his seventies, Harry is a body builder, with biceps erupting out of shirt-sleeves rolled up so tight they look like tourniquets. Before he worked here, he was a stage hand at the Old Vic and used to weight-train Olivier – 'the Guv'nor' – and before that he served in the army, as is evident from that rigid back, those massive teeth, built to bite not smile, and that tendency to address me – now that he's decided I'm all right – as sir, or rather *sah*!

'How are you this morning, Harry?'

'Bearin' up, *sah*, bearin' up.'

When I worked here before, on *Uncle Vanya* (which the Studio developed), he was less sure of me, often not recognising me from one day to the next. But this morning he's full of warmth when Greg and I arrive, and laughs when I say, 'You've got all these South Africans here for the next fortnight, Harry – don't frighten them too much.'

A cavernous, ugly, great aircraft hangar of a room, the main rehearsal area at the Studio is nevertheless, like the Market, another of those really good spaces. Today it's freezing, and noisy with big fan heaters. The South Africans arrive, wrapped in coats, scarves, woolly caps, looking more like the cast of a Chekhov play than one by Shakespeare, which is set, unbeknown to the author, in hottest Africa.

We start work. This isn't focused on the *Titus* text. That's for rehearsals, when the whole cast is assembled. Instead, our daily schedule involves an assortment of voice and movement classes, acting exercises, and sessions on our two main topics:

Shakespeare. And How to Speak Him . . .

Violence. And How to Avoid the Clichés . . .

For both of these, we'll have visiting experts working with the group, but Greg is basically in charge of the Shakespeare side and I'm in charge of Violence.

'Why that way round?' I asked, when we were planning the schedule. Greg laughed in my face. Then reminded me of the other day, when we were sorting out our collection of video tapes. Coming to my stack, Greg said, 'Right, well, we just need three shelves here, labelled . . . Apartheid, the Holocaust and Mass-Murderers.'

Tuesday 24 January
As part of our work on violence, we've asked each member of the group to recount a personal experience of it. Today, someone volunteers to begin . . .

A member of his family was raped and murdered. He recounts all the details of this in a calm, quiet voice, both far away from, and very near to, the edge of tremendous emotion.

When the worst of it was over – the discovery of the crime, the breaking of the news, the investigation, the trial – another member of the family revealed a startling thing. He had been given, and had kept, the police photographs of the event. Graphic close-ups of the body. Then the empty bed, with two deep patches of blood, where her head and loins had been.

The victim was white, the two murderers black. Only one had been caught and he was sentenced to death; then pardoned – as part of the death row amnesty after Mandela's release.

The whole story is shocking, but I'm most disturbed by the photos – and I ask how anyone could bear to keep them?

The answer is: 'They were part of *us* . . . my family . . . part of our history.'

I half understand . . . but I'm trying to imagine, just imagine, seeing photos of Mom or Verne (my sister) like that . . .

The whole group is sitting in silence, maybe thinking similar things.

I'm chairing today's session and it's my job now to draw comparisons, to fit this personal story into the scheme of our work – but it's difficult to speak.

After another long pause Greg says, 'I think we'd better take an early lunch . . .'

Later, another shocking story . . . of a different kind.

I'm on the phone to the Market, talking to Mike Maxwell. They haven't found any money yet, but are following some hopeful leads. I say, 'And what about the hoax . . . what's the news there . . . did you people get the police in?'

'Uhm no,' he says, sounding uneasy.

I feel myself losing patience. I want to say, You're in the *New* South Africa! – John Kani is a personal friend of the President! – how can you still be frightened of the police? But this would be impertinent. So I say, 'Well, how on earth are you . . . are *we* going to find out who Mr van-fucking-Schalkwyk is? How can we do that if you won't . . .'

Mike interrupts, sighing deeply: 'We're beginning to wonder if he ever existed.'

'What do you mean?'

'We've checked the phone number he's supposed to have given us, and it's nowhere near Panasonic. It's in Hillbrow. It's the building where the lady lives . . . the lady who was dealing with Panasonic . . . the lady on our staff.'

A prickle goes up my spine.

Oh I see . . . of course . . . it's so obvious.

The hoaxer was Deb herself.

No one else was ever involved. There was no Mr van Schalkwyk, no phone calls, no trips to car-parks. Nothing, other than her fantasies. Which she then relayed to Mike Maxwell, or John, or anyone else who asked how the Panasonic deal was going – 'Yes, the cheque is in the post', or 'I'm just going to collect it' – and, amazingly, she got away with it for *five* weeks!

Mike tells me that, since last Thursday, Deb hasn't been back to work.

After the phone call, Greg and I try and unravel what was going on in her mind. Was the hoax done out of vengeance, settling some grudge against her employers? Or was it done out of love? The Market desperately wanted to do this show, but couldn't raise the money. So she raised it for them – in her head.

Out of love, and *for* love. I'm recalling the phone call from Barney on the day they heard about the sponsorship – telling me how Deb ran into his office whooping, 'They're giving us six hundred thousand rand!' – and how everyone congratulated her, and how the Chairman of the Market, Grahame Lindop, phoned personally to thank her, to praise her . . . she was the heroine of the day, the heroine of the next five weeks. That's an awful lot of love.

And now I vaguely remember Deb from the Studio visit last September . . . a huge, very jolly lady – overpoweringly jolly – who buttonholed me one day in the Administration building, and told me how *thrilled* she was that the National was there, and how *thrilled* she was that I was there, and how *thrilled* she was about our plans to do *Titus*.

Wednesday 25 January
Very productive day, with lots of material that can go straight into the production. In the morning we look at violence from the victim's point of view, in the afternoon from that of the perpetrator.

First, Lindy Wooten from the Support Centre for the Victims of Violence. She deals with a lot of rape victims, so she's particularly useful for Jennifer Woodburne (Lavinia). With regard to Titus himself, I'm struck by two things she says. 1: How people will fight to make sense of senseless violence. 2: How violence robs you of power. The latter point drives Titus to distraction. He is a father who has been unable to protect his daughter from rape and mutilation; he is an army general who is unable to save the lives of his two sons. So when that bizarre moment comes Aaron claiming the sons will be spared if someone cuts off his hand – Titus volunteers because, perversely, it's a way of regaining power. It's a way of him doing *something*. Cutting off his hand becomes a positive action.

After lunch, Dr Murray Cox, consultant psychotherapist at Broadmoor, the secure psychiatric hospital. Murray is a donnish character, with a quick, dancing mind (it's hard to keep him on one subject), a most original sense of humour (which you'd need in his job) and a great theatre fan. He uses Shakespeare extensively in his work and has published several books on the subject, most recently, with Alice Theilgaard, *Shakespeare as Prompter*, which has a drawing of mine on the cover: Shakespeare's face melting into Freud's, within a womb-like, spermy swirl of quotes from the plays. I was first introduced to Murray by Patsy Rodenburg, when she and I were doing preparatory vocal training for *Tamburlaine*. I was getting hung up on the problem of how this violent barbarian comes to express himself through the beauty of Marlowe's mighty lines. Murray unlocked the problem by describing the language sometimes used by patients, which can be full of dark and peculiar poetry. The *Tamburlaine* problem is pertinent to several characters in *Titus*, particularly Aaron. So today, with Murray present, we pass his books round the circle and read quotes from therapy sessions:

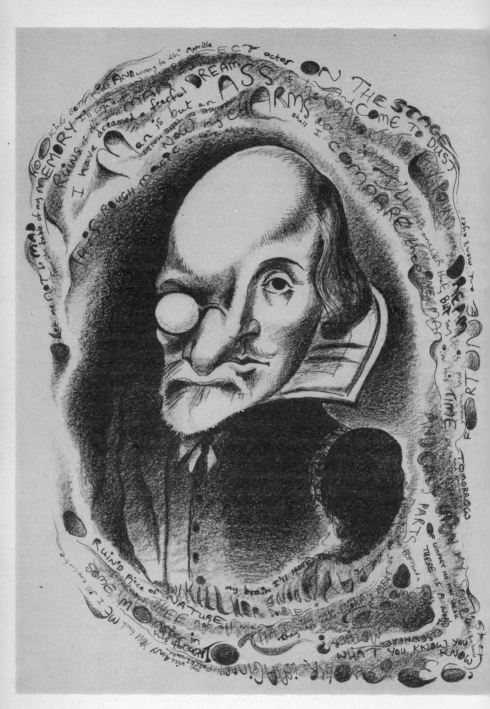

"Shakespeare as Prompter"

'I'm blind because I see too much; so I study by a dark lamp.'

'I just went on killing him. It never occurred to me that he'd die.'

'I heal her with colours and images to counteract the strong smell of blood.'

'I have met people who have walked off the edge of language – and then they *do things*.'

When we finish reading these strange, beautiful, chilling fragments, Murray is pensive, like a playwright who has just heard his work interpreted by actors for the first time. 'Thank you, that was fascinating, it really makes one think.'

More dramatic developments in Jo'burg . . .

The good news is that Barney has found the money. An American friend of the Market, Michael Kaiser, is giving it.

The bad news is that some of the Market trustees no longer want to use the money for *Titus*.

It now appears that the Market is in much bigger trouble financially than we realised. A section of the Board, a group of businessmen, have become increasingly dismayed by how the theatre is run, and last week's development – the hoax – was the final straw. They want to use Kaiser's money to close the theatre temporarily, refurbish it and replace some of the staff, maybe even Barney himself . . .

They're calling an emergency Board meeting either Friday or Saturday, to decide which way to go.

The first few days of the workshop have been stimulating but exhausting, and Greg and I have avoided discussing the crisis, even privately. Now we're forced to face it again. What to do? Celebrate or grieve? This is a cruel development. Talk about *violence* . . . this is a torturer's touch, stroking and scratching at the same time.

Thursday 26 January

A new addition to our daily routine is a session of army drill – for the Romans. The Goths are off in another room, with Dumi, our musical director, trying to devise a war-dance; Greg's nicknamed it the *hakka*, like the New Zealand rugby ritual . . . that ape-like display, designed to terrify the other team, with stamping squats and booming, panting chants. Our hope is that the two sides, the Romans and Goths, will each develop their own style of movement. The Romans upright, rigid, conventionally militaristic, the Goths lower, more sinewy, earth-bound –

a ferocious guerilla force pitted against a giant war machine. Like the
Vietcong in relation to the US forces, or the Kurds to the Iraqi army, or
SWAPO to the SADF (South African Defence Force).

Gys de Villiers, the Afrikaans actor who's playing Saturninus, trained
as an officer in the SADF, so he's taking the drill sessions.

Apart from moments when he breaks up laughing, I find these sessions
unpleasantly reminiscent of my nine months of National Service before
leaving South Africa. As a pampered little Yiddisher whitey from the
beachfront suburbs of Cape Town, the army was another world to me,
like Mars or hell. For starters, I had to *wash my own clothes*, I had to *make
my own bed*. We new recruits were used by the older ones to alleviate
boredom, with torture-games and as slaves. In British terms, it was like
the fag system at public schools; in South African terms, it was like
becoming a 'kaffir'.

And then finally there were the authorised bullies, the sergeants and
officers, screaming Afrikaans into your face.

Gys does a very good impersonation of those SADF professionals and
all I can say is, it's a good thing he keeps giggling . . .

16

The Studio has provided a great team of people to help hone our skills. Each morning, Helen Chadwick leads an easy limbering-up session. Its effect is just like that old advert for Ready Brek where the kids march off to school radiating a warm glow.

Sue Laurie gives a class in Alexander Technique, getting us all to relax, lying on the floor with a book under our heads. The books, from our research table in the corner, all have titles like: *The History of Torture* and *Nam*, but the technique still seems to work.

Patsy Rodenburg teaches exercises and techniques to help the company connect to the language and discover the physicality of the words.

And, because we know South Africa is short of fight choreographers, Terry King comes in to give us some professional advice.

We look at the plethora of deaths at the end of the play. The text just has a lot of stabbing: Titus stabs Tamora and gets stabbed by Saturninus, who is then stabbed by Lucius.

Swiftly we build up a scenario which we can develop later. Dorothy is pursuing the image of Tamora as warrior queen. Once she has vomited out the meat of the pie, Tamora falls on Titus, ripping at his eyes. And in the ensuing scuffle, Titus drowns her in the pie. Yes, well there's no actual stage direction to this effect, but it's an idea Tony has.

Gys is investigating the possibility that Saturninus is hooked on something. Perhaps he has a ventilator-inhaler (like Dennis Hopper in *Blue Velvet*) which he snorts at odd moments. What's in it? Coke, morphine, opium? Anyway, as Saturninus sees his wife choking in the gravy, he seizes the knife (used to cut the pie) and stabs Titus.

Reeling away, Saturninus then seizes the ventilator for a quick fix of his drug. Lucius grabs him, clamps the inhaler over the emperor's mouth and administers a lethal overdose.

Tony, who has been enthusiastically helping Terry and me to conceive these deaths, now looks at us expectantly, as if to say, 'What about me?' He is the only one still left with a common-or-garden stabbing. I point out that no one has ever seen Titus stabbed with a pie slice before.

Dumi Dhlamini has been busy plundering sound archives and collecting musical instruments and inspiration from the NT's Sound Department.

After work one day he plays through a few ideas for me in the sound booth. I notice he has odd socks on. In fact he's been wearing odd socks all week. 'I can't believe it,' he says. 'She's always doing this. I don't have a single pair of socks with me that actually match. I think she must be colour-blind.'

'Your wife?'

'No, no,' he corrects me. 'My maid.'

I don't know why I'm so surprised.

The other major area of work we want to tackle in the workshop is the actual business of speaking Shakespeare.

As a young actor arriving at Stratford, I remember a terrible sense of inadequacy and (despite having already done quite a lot of Shakespeare) a lurking unease that, if challenged, I couldn't actually tell my caesura from my iambic pentameter.

This sense of inadequacy afflicts many actors. They feel there's some kind of divine panel sitting in judgement upon any actor foolish enough to take on Shakespeare; ready to pounce on any delinquent stress or defend any violated rhythm.

But I needn't have feared. If great teachers are great artists, then Cis Berry, the RSC's head of voice, is one of the greatest. The first and most important lesson she teaches is that there are no rules about how to do Shakespeare, just clues. Everything is negotiable. Of course that sounds too simple, but it is immensely liberating.

Once you know how to identify the clues, you can read the map and walk through the maze.

Another great RSC teacher is John Barton. John has been with the company since 1960. He's its resident guru. John has agreed to visit us in Waterloo to do some intensive work with the South African actors. He's coming at the end of next week.

17

Friday 27 January

Jennifer has revealed that she is the daughter of South Africa's equivalent to the First Lord of the Admiralty, Admiral Woodburne, known as Woody to his men. So she knows all about having a war-like father, a hero of the state, and all about him going off on dangerous missions, and then the homecomings.

Jennifer's mother works as a medical technologist at Groote Schuur Hospital, and this has enabled Jen to research Lavinia's hand and tongue amputations.

She fed questions to her mother, who would quiz her colleagues. One doctor became confused. 'This girl, with these injuries, is she in hospital . . . ?'

They gave her access to medical books and she's brought along photocopies. They show severed hands, looking like water-filled gloves, lost gloves, and there's one of a young boy's mouth after a gun went off in it, turning his lower face into a flattened, bubbling wound.

I'm a great believer in research myself, but find it difficult to confront these photographs.

Jennifer had the same problem initially. 'But now', she says, 'I just feel possessive about them . . . terrified someone will take one of them off the wall . . .'

She glances over to the notice-board near the door, where we've pinned up relevant images. Like the colour photo, which has recently been on the front page of every newspaper, of a girl in Grozny, after a shell exploded near her – she stands doll-like, frozen with shock, coated completely in white dust, except where there are splashes of blood ('I could use that for Lavinia's make-up,' whispers Jennifer. 'The way her lips are outlined in red, her eyes too'). There's also the article from last week's *Independent* telling how, in Saddam Hussein's Iraq, the traditional Muslim punishment of hand-chopping is now no longer done with a sword in the town square, but surgically, in operating theatres, by doctors. It is still public though – they show it on TV.

Another newspaper clipping which Jennifer brought is from a Durban paper. The headline says HAND SEWN BACK, and the photo shows a Zulu man, with an oxygen mask over his face and one arm in bandages, giving the thumbs-up sign with his other hand. His name is Ambrose Sibiya. He interrupted thieves, who struck him with a panga (machete).

Jenny (with dyed hair)

Jennifer went to visit him and interviewed him through a translator. She reads from her notes, quoting him: 'They wanted to cut off my head, but I put up my hand . . . so they cut that off instead . . . when I saw the blood, I knew that if I didn't stop it, I would die. It felt like my heart was going like a hammer and there were a thousand voices in my head, a thousand clear thoughts.'

Jennifer asked him what the pain was like?

He answered, 'No pain. My head went mad, my heart went like a hammer.'

Jennifer asked if he wept?

The nurse, who was translating, replied for him, indignantly; 'Of course not. He's a Zulu. He's a *man*.'

Ambrose Sibiya continued, 'I couldn't leave the hand lying there . . . not because I knew it could be sewn back, but because it was *mine*.' So he picked it up and went into a nearby shop. They put it into a bucket of ice and rang the emergency services.

It was only after Ambrose Sibiya had finished his story that he asked Jennifer *why* she wanted to hear it.

'It was difficult to explain through the translator,' says Jennifer. 'At first he thought it was something on TV . . . but eventually he understood – it was for a stage play – and then he began to laugh. He asked, "But how will they cut off your hand each night, and put it back in time for the next one?" He became quite hysterical with laughter . . .'

(Soon after Titus loses his own hand, he begins to laugh. When the shocked Marcus demands an explanation, Titus replies, 'Why, I have not another tear to shed.')

Now Jennifer says, 'And then I went to meet a man who'd lost his tongue . . .'

I interrupt, 'Thanks, but I'll hear that story another time.'

Well, our deadline is upon us – end of work, Friday – when it's to be decided whether the production is happening, or not.

Roger Chapman, *Titus*'s new foster-father, comes to talk to the group. Tells us that he's agreed with the Market to extend the deadline by twenty-four hours, to allow time for their emergency board meeting tomorrow morning, when the trustees will choose whether to use Michael Kaiser's American money for *Titus*, or to refurbish the Market.

Roger makes a heartfelt speech, about how the Market *mustn't* close . . . how it's among the five most famous theatres in the world.

Afterwards, Greg and I ask him why he was talking about the Market *closing* – not just going dark for a few months to refurbish, but *closing*? He says he's very worried by conversations with the Market over the last few days, and now he's finding the word 'refurbishment' increasingly sinister. He believes, as we do, that there's a considerable number of trustees who are so dismayed by how the Market is run, that they either want to change it out of all recognition, or close it down.

A surprise piece of news is that they're voting tomorrow. The trustees are going to use a vote to decide whether to use Kaiser's money for *Titus* or not. So our fate depends on how many supporters we have among them.

I say to Roger, 'By the way, they think they know who the hoaxer is. One of their own staff. The lady who approached Panasonic.'

'Ah,' says Roger. 'What's happening to her – d'you know?'

'She's left, or they've asked her to go. They're being quite cagey about it. She's a single mother . . . they're all worried about what she might do.

I guess, after what the Market has been through over the last few decades, they look after their own.'

Roger bobs his eyebrows – as though saying, Who are we to judge? – then goes. Greg and I take a deep breath and make one last effort to save this production.

First of all, we waylay Janet Suzman at the Old Vic stage door (across the road from the Studio) as she arrives for a performance of *The Sisters Rosensweig*, and ask for her help. She goes through her address book, finding phone numbers of the various trustees, saying, 'Oh *him* . . . he'll be a friend . . . I'll ring him . . . oh *her*, she's an enemy, not worth wasting our time . . . oh *him* . . . well, you've met him, so you can ring him yourselves . . .'

Then she dashes off to her performance and we start phoning. We track down various trustees in different parts of South Africa: Howard Sacks in Durban (he's specially flying back to Jo'burg for tomorrow's meeting) and Janice Honeyman in Cape Town, who's going to phone in her vote.

Much, much later, back at home, we make contact with a vital trustee, Mannie Manim, co-founder of the Market, and now an independent producer and lighting designer (in fact, due to light *Titus*). He's been a big supporter of the production, yet there's negativity in his voice tonight . . . and it isn't just because we've dragged him from his bed (it's now past 2 a.m. there). Yes, he says, he has been canvassed by the other side. I talk to him for about an hour, trying to win him round again.

I think I succeed, but I still fear for tomorrow.

Finally, at about 4 a.m., we fax the Market chairman, Grahame Lindop, urging him to support us, offering to cut our fees drastically (and pointing out that the Market have contracted the *Titus* cast, so if they cancel it, they'll still have to reimburse everyone) and then, finally, *finally* we collapse into bed.

The sense remains of being caught in a terrible B-movie. Tomorrow – or no, *today* – is going to be another succession of hair-raising deadlines. We're taking the *Titus* group up to Stratford-on-Avon, to visit Shakespeare's birthplace. Once there, we're going to phone Howard Sacks or Mannie Manim, to get the results of the board meeting, and then, if it's negative, we'll have to reach our two designers, Nadya Cohen (set) and Sue Steele (costumes), who are due to fly out tomorrow night, so that we can stop them getting on the plane . . . !

18

Saturday 28 January
Set off for Stratford.

We take the M40 to Oxford, then the A34, the old slow route to Stratford before the motorway was extended. We keep checking our watches. It's nearly eleven here, so it must be about one in South Africa. Will the trustees have decided our fate by now?

It's a bright, damp winter day. My first summer as an actor in Stratford was so wet that Brian Johnstone, the cricket commentator, dubbed it a '*Madam Butterfly* summer', in other words '*One* fine day'.

On that one fine summer Sunday, Tony and I had driven off in search of somewhere to picnic. We found a cornfield tucked away in a secluded valley. The only sign of civilisation was an elegant seventeenth-century windmill (designed by Inigo Jones), on a hill in the distance. We spent a long afternoon, lazing in the blond corn, with a feast of figs and Boursin cheese and a bottle of chilled wine.

The following year we sought out our special place again, only to find a churned-up battlefield of mud and bulldozers. The route of the new M40 was being torn right through the centre of *our* cornfield.

Today we avoid that stretch of motorway and go via Woodstock, which for some reason raises a laugh among the company. Woodstock, Tony explains, is also the name of a suburb of Cape Town. When he was growing up it was a notoriously rough, poor–white area.

We pull up for what Gys calls a wet stop.

Tony and I whisper to each other: '11.30: half past one in Jo'burg. Shall we phone now?'

'No, let's wait till we get to Stratford.'

We go into the Bear Inn. It's a real piece of Merry England, an ancient country hostelry which, as they say, was 'old when the Palace was new'. Blenheim Palace, the Duke of Marlborough's pad, with its grounds and landscaping by Capability Brown, stretches out expansively to the south-west of the town.

'I love this. It is so beautiful. You know?' sighs Martin le Maitre over a jar of nut brown bitter. 'God, even the fireplace is twelfth century!'

We arrive in Stratford. We've arranged to take the company backstage before the matinée. I point out a tiny African statuette in the Green Room. It commemorates Edric Connor, who played a Calypso-singing Gower in Tony Richardson's production of *Pericles* in 1958. 'He was the first black actor to appear at Stratford,' I say.

'But not the last,' says Sello, with an ambitious glint in his eye.

In the main house, as we walk out from the wings, I suddenly remember we are on the very stage where Olivier himself had played Titus in Peter Brook's production in 1955. A sort of hush falls over the company.

It was here that Anthony Quayle had blacked up to play Aaron, and shone exotically in pearl and gold. Maxine Audley gave her glittering Tamora, and from that very wing Vivien Leigh had emerged so memorably, everybody says, as the ravaged Lavinia, streaming with red chiffon. Once again we feel part of a process. Or we might be, if the word from Johannesburg is good.

We point the company in the direction of the Dirty Duck (the RSC's favourite watering hole), while Tony and I go off to find a phone to ring South Africa.

Luckily lots of old friends from our time here are around to help. Eileen Relph is on duty front-of-house and she lets us use her office phone, and Betty Southwood on stage door gets us the number in South Africa. We hold our breath.

'Hi, Mannie? It's Tony, how did it go? . . . Aha?'

I try to follow the conversation by a mixture of sign language and deciphering the scribbles Tony makes on his pad. 'A leap of faith . . . Like the old days . . .'

Tony nods frantically at me. We're on, we're safe. Thank God.

In a five-hour meeting, expertly chaired by an independent arbitrator, Ian Steadman, the trustees have agreed that the Kaiser money should be used for *Titus*.

Apparently, Mannie says, it was like the old days with the trustees bonding together to keep the Market afloat. We stumble out of the theatre dizzy with relief.

We've arranged to meet everyone for a photo call outside the theatre at 3 p.m. We arrive with long faces. I ask the photographer to give us a few minutes alone.

'As you know, the Board of Trustees of the Market met this morning to consider whether *Titus* can go ahead. I think it's only fair to tell you . . .'

The company huddle closer and Jennifer's lip is trembling.

' . . . I think it's only fair to tell you . . . that they've said "Yes". We're
on.'

Disbelief explodes into hysterical cheers, threatening to disrupt the
matinée of *Measure for Measure*. The photographer thinks we're nuts. We
move down to the river bank among the wet willows. The Avon has over-
flowed and is washing the terrace. Tony cracks open a couple of bottles
of brandy and splashes out 'dops' for everyone.

The rest of the day goes by in a flurry. We take a lot of touristy shots of
the company draped around the statue of Shakespeare in the Bancroft
Gardens. Sello poses with Hamlet, and Ivan, muffled to the eyebrows
like some mad Cossack, clambers half-way up the pedestal to be immor-
talised worshipping at his hero's feet.

We have a fascinating session with Professor Stanley Wells, the director of the Shakespeare Institute, in the Buzz Goodbody Studio at the
Other Place. I haven't been in here since directing Derek Walcott's
adaptation of *The Odyssey*.

'Tony's playing Titus presumably?' Stanley asks. 'Of course, he'd have
made a superb Aaron, in days gone by.' (He's referring to the policy,
adopted by both the RSC and the National, not to do *Othello*, for example,
unless a black actor plays the title role.)

We laugh. Imagine Tony making his professional début in his post-
apartheid homeland, blacked-up!

Much later, the company emerge from the evening show, *A Midsummer
Night's Dream*. They look exhilarated.

'I'm jealous,' says Gys. 'The buzz in the auditorium, man! It's like
being at a rugby match.'

On the coach home, while the company sing endless choruses of
'We're marching to Pretoria', 'Sarie Marais' and 'Nkosi Sikelel'i'!, I say
to Tony: 'I suppose we should be thankful to Deb, you know, "The
Hoaxer".'

'What?' he yelps.

'Well, if it weren't for her this whole production would have been
cancelled back in November. At least the hoax kept it going, until it had
built up such a momentum nobody could stop it. I suppose we should be
thankful to her for that.'

So we toast Deb in flat beer, and I fall fast asleep.

Sunday 29 January

We've brought our designers, Sue Steele and Nadya Cohen, to lunch at Marsden's in Upper Street. We come here almost every Sunday. The head waiter, Luciano ('Call me Lucifer for short') Molina, welcomes you with such cheeky delight it's impossible to disappoint him. So it's the only restaurant we phone if we're *not* coming.

The girls are both exhausted, having just crawled off the plane. Nadya says she's left her stomach at Jan Smuts.

Until today, we haven't actually met Sue, our costume designer. But she comes highly recommended. She recently won a VITA award for her designs for *Scenes from an Execution* at the Market.

Sue is a Pre-Raphaelite with zest. Her hair might not cluster in auburn cascades, but it has a sort of fiery éclat. She is wearing one of her own creations, a great black mochado velvet gown, with Renaissance gold frogging, chunky paste jewellery and wellies.

I have an increasingly clear idea about how the production could look. And I need to bring her up to date.

Titus Andronicus is the only one of Shakespeare's plays for which we have a contemporary illustration. It is called the Peacham drawing and it belongs to the Marquess of Bath at Longleat. It shows Tamora pleading to Titus. Standing behind him are two soldiers, Elizabethan men-at-arms, presumably representing his two sons.

Titus wears a sort of token toga and a laurel wreath. Everyone else is in Elizabethan costume – in other words, modern dress. This reinforces my sense that Shakespeare intends to address modern issues through an ancient setting, and his audience would have recognised that.

I suggest to Sue that we should be looking for a contemporary costuming for our production; but we should push back our reference a few decades, in order to avoid confusing parallels with modern figures. A world, not elsewhere, but else*when*.

Sue says her major thought about the costumes is that each of them should be a fashion statement. I'm worried. Perhaps the way we want to do *Titus* won't suit her.

Sunday evening. I realise that *Titus Andronicus* bookended my first experience of the Complete Works of William Shakespeare. Browsing through my bookshelves I come across a postcard of a costume design for *Titus* which I've had since school-days. It shows Saturninus, in a beautiful design by Ann Curtis. He is wearing a trailing toga of Tyrian purple,

encrusted with gold embroidery and tassled fringe. His earlobes are dis-
tended with heavy gold jewellery and his jet-black hair is wreathed with
tiny golden leaves.

I bought the postcard at a touring exhibition which came to the Harris
Art Gallery and Library in the centre of Preston in about 1973 or '74. It
was called 'Staging the Romans', and it celebrated the season of Roman
plays (including *Titus Andronicus*) which the RSC had mounted in Stratford in 1972, directed by Trevor Nunn. John Wood played the Emperor
Saturninus.

This was my first exposure to Shakespeare in production. From then
on, I couldn't get enough. Apart from the annual Shakespeare school
play, I began mounting my own Shakespeare plays, at the age of sixteen,
with a group of schoolmates. We called ourselves the Poor Players, and
barnstormed the North-West, playing in the courtyards of stately piles,
from Astley Hall in Chorley, to Houghton Tower just outside Preston.

In the seventies the reps could still afford to do productions of Shakespeare, in which young actors could hone their craft. In a host of school
trips I saw Shakespeare at the newly opened Royal Exchange in Man
chester; the Duke's Playhouse in Lancaster; and a whole season of
Shakespeares at Wilfred Harrison's Bolton Octagon. The New Shakespeare Company came to the Royal Court Theatre in Liverpool and
Theatre North toured to Southport.

There were school trips to Stratford-on-Avon, but not enough for me.
So Richard Sharples and I used to hitch-hike from Preston and camp
overnight on the race course. We queued for hours to see Alan Howard
as Prince Hal and Henry VI, Nicol Williamson and Helen Mirren as the
Macbeths, Judi Dench and Donald Sinden in the Raj *Much Ado*.

At university, I completed my Bard score card with *Titus Andronicus*
(oddly enough) at the Bristol Old Vic, when Adrian Noble directed the
play in a sort of sandy bear-baiting pit with Simon Callow as Titus,
Sheila Ballantine as Tamora, and Pete Postlethwaite, blacked-up as
Aaron.

I had seen every Shakespeare play by the time I came of age. That
same year, 1979, Margaret Thatcher came to power and her opposition
to the subsidy principle radically changed the Arts in Britain. These
days, it would be impossible for the most fanatical 'bardolator' to see live
productions of the whole canon while still in their teens.

Monday 30 January
The company gather in the NT Studio for the second week, and I
remind them of the premise of the workshop. Sometimes our research
will seem haphazard, sometimes irrelevant, sometimes symbolic rather
than practical; but we'll continue to lob it into the melting pot and watch
the ripples.

Then we all describe our current images for the play to Sue and
Nadya, and the cast show a photo or picture which best expresses their
character. It's an interesting selection. Jennifer produces photos from an
appalling fashion magazine called *Dazed and Confused* in which all the
models seem to be bruised and crying.

Up till now Sue has been looking sceptical. This is the first time she
responds positively. She wants a Rome-in-Africa look. Togas made of
adire cloth and batik fabrics perhaps. It's a way of doing the play, but it's
not our way. But I think she'll come round. That's what the workshop is
for.

19

Wednesday 1 February
Cold, dark February weather. Struggling through the traffic to the Studio this morning, I feel overjoyed that we'll be climbing on a plane in a few days' time and escaping all this. In winter, London resembles one big underground car-park, its routes choked with vehicles, its sky like a stained grey ceiling just above your head.

Our exploration of violence has been hard going, but worthwhile. When we come to reproduce it, we will be compelled, as Greg puts it, 'to honour the real thing'. Today's work especially convinces us that we're on the right lines with this production. The South Africans have a very intense, *personal* attitude to violence.

We show the group a TV documentary about the My-Lai massacre in Vietnam – a useful model for the Roman–Goth war. The film has testaments from people on both sides. Gaunt Vietnamese women, who saw their daughters and sisters raped, and who are unable to forgive. A negro Vietnam vet who, back in 1968, gorged himself during the rampage, and today is haunted by the incident, with a scrapbook of press clippings on his lap, and bottles of tranquillisers at his side. It's not easy to watch him: bloated, quivering, pouring with sweat; a man frying in his own fat, roasting in hell.

Greg and I believe he's a good example of how real life confounds the clichés about violence. Here's a man who would be described, in tabloid-talk, as a monster, or, in Shakespeare's day, as a villain (like Aaron, or Chiron and Demetrius) and yet who, in reality, is sick and in pain.

But the South Africans are curiously unmoved by him and the film. Having grown up with violence, they view it in a more cynical, less sentimental way than Greg and I. The neurotic negro got what he deserved, some say . . . others find his uncontrollable jitter-bugging funny. (They often find aspects of violence *funny*.)

Maybe the Vietnam war is just too far away from their own experience. Their reactions are very different when we show them images of themselves.

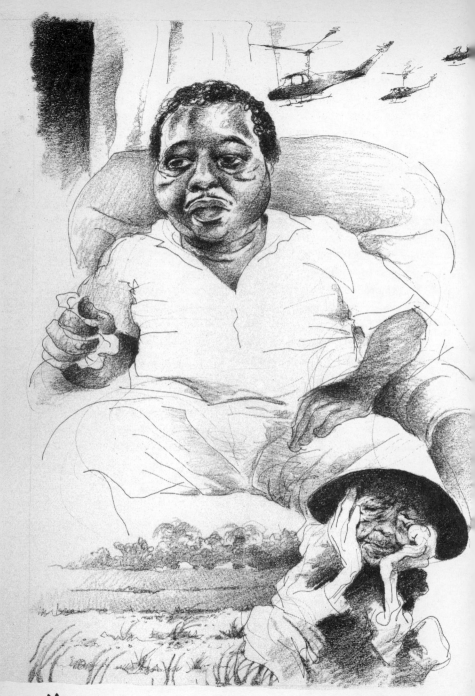

My-Lai

This is in Michael Buerk's harrowing 1987 report on his time as the BBC correspondent in South Africa, which includes graphic footage of a young man being surrounded by a mob and knifed to death. There are several stabbing scenes in *Titus*, but without this kind of research, actors wouldn't think of playing them as happens here. The man's panic, his adrenalin level, is so high, that he doesn't seem to notice as blades go into him – he just keeps arguing with the mob, trying to *reason* with them. There's a particular look on his face . . . a particular kind of bewilderment. Gys de Villiers says, 'It's as if his spirit is saying yes this is happening to me, but his body is saying no it isn't.' Jennifer says, 'And then there's a moment . . . you can see it in his eyes . . . when his spirit gives up, when it leaves his body . . . and it's *before* he's actually killed.' The last shot shows his corpse jerking and bouncing, as people run in, with a strange terror of their own, still to stab at him, to make their mark on the sacrifice.

Nobody in our group finds this material irrelevant, or reckons that anyone is getting what they deserve. They watch it in shocked silence – some weeping – these are images from their own nightmare. Like photos of a loved one raped and murdered, this *belongs* to them.

As we're winding up for the day, Ivan addresses the group: 'If anyone thinks they've had as much horror as they can take, may I just remind you that tomorrow we will each be doing a Shakespeare speech in front of John Barton . . . !'

20

Thursday 2 February
John Barton's workshop. John asked each actor to learn a speech by the time he came to join us in Waterloo. So inevitably the session begins with the whiff of abject terror in the air. John occasionally falling out of his Hush Puppies or getting tangled in his cardigan, urges and prompts and encourages.

The Market is snatching the opportunity to record these workshops. The Stage Manager, Bruce Koch, on secondment from the Market as a result of the Studio's visit last September, is standing at the back videoing the proceedings.

John begins by describing the difference between the modern acting tradition and acting in Shakespeare's day. There were no drama schools then, no directors, and actors might have to learn parts in forty plays in one season. They weren't issued with the latest Penguin edition, they would only be given the text of their particular parts with the cues. The advantage of this, John points out, is that it made you listen carefully. And that's key. 'Shakespeare put masses of acting tips in the writing,' he says, and goes on to show us what he means as each speech is done.

Oscar is first in the hot seat. He does the fourth-act Chorus from *Henry V*, describing the English camp the night before the battle of Agincourt.

'Well done, very good, very good . . .' says John. 'But you're making statements and that's a bit boring. Rather tell us the story more, be like a camera moving through the camp.'

Oscar shakes himself out in a jerky paroxysm of nerves and does it again.

'Very good,' says John, squatting down by Oscar's chair. 'Now a great phrase that's used about Shakespeare is that he sets the word against the word. Look at that bit "the foul womb of night . . .", those vowels put together, setting the word "foul" against that word "womb", neither word by itself quite does it. "Stilly sounds", there's another example, not a statement, not a description, it's dynamic, it's moving. Go on, try it again, choose those words, make them your own, fresh-mint each image.'

John Barton

'Let me check that out,' says Oscar, stabbing the air with his finger, and he does the speech perhaps two or three times, each time discovering more, enjoying more, taking his time to explore.

'Perhaps this would be a good time to talk about the whole question of accent,' John says. 'It's something I've encountered a lot. It might be useful if I did a few lines of the Chorus that Oscar has just done, as the Elizabethans may have pronounced it.' (Ripple of excited applause.) '. . . because ironically enough, there are one or two Elizabethan sounds which have been kept pure in South African terms and we've lost over here. I don't do it well, but it goes something like this . . .' And he gives us his party piece, delivering Oscar's speech in Tudor! An extraordinary sound collage of Celtic brogue, West Country and a bit of American, with God knows what else thrown in.

He's not suggesting that we should try and copy or recreate how Shakespeare was originally spoken, he's simply pointing out that there's no empirical reason why modern English RP should be adopted either. Tony and I wink at each other. It's great to hear our own preoccupation about doing *Titus* in local accents validated by the experts' expert.

John goes on to talk about the rhythms of blank verse – 'Anyone using the words "iambic pentameter" will be flogged mercilessly,' he japes. 'All we're talking about is a ten-beat-to-the-line rhythm which goes di-dum, di-dum, di-dum, di-dum, di-dum.'

He describes how the writers of the time like Shakespeare and Marlowe got excited by this new verse form, got hooked on it, when Thomas Kyd invented it, writing *The Spanish Tragedy*.

He talks a lot about how once you've understood how the verse operates, you have instinctively to surrender to the rhythm of the verse.

'Like going with the wave,' someone says. 'You have to surf the verse!'

'That's a very South African way of putting it,' I whisper to Tony.

To demonstrate how powerful that wave, that current, that rhythm can be, John gets Tony to throw us a length of Marlowe's mighty line and do a speech of *Tamburlaine the Great*. Tony played the megalomaniac Scythian Shepherd in Terry Hands' RSC production in 1992.

Tony drives the verse through with relish, firing on all cylinders.

> 'I will with engines never exercised,
> Conquer sack and utterly consume
> Your cities and your golden palaces . . .'

John points out that Marlowe uses the verse form in a very regular way; indeed, the beat is so regular in Marlowe, it's easy to become monotonous. He gets rather carried away with the music, whereas Shakespeare energises the form by making it irregular, going against the stress, adding an extra note and so on, like a jazz musician improvising around the beat.

John also makes the point that people use blank verse in everyday life. It's a simple way of phrasing and ironically, rather than heightening the language, often it can help the actor to become more naturalistic.

Sello's next. He moves towards the chair. 'It's so hot, this seat, it's burning!' he jokes nervously. He does Sonnet 130, 'My Mistress' eyes are nothing like the sun'.

'Now,' says John, 'this brings up perhaps the single most important acting note, in my opinion, when approaching Shakespeare. It's something Shakespeare uses all the time, it's often the basis of the whole dramatic structure of a speech . . . It's antithesis.'

'Say what?' Sello asks, jerking his head forward and tugging his woolly hat.

'Antithesis: setting one thing against another, balancing two phrases or ideas. My mistress' eyes, and the sun. If snow is white, her tits are the colour of shit,' he paraphrases, 'an antithesis of some richness! If you unlock the antithesis, then you'll get it. Try it again, share it with your audience, provoke them.'

Sello does, he begins to contact us, to make us laugh, and the laughter liberates him.

'Nobly done, nobly done,' John says. 'Now use those rhymes . . . use those pay-off words at the ends of the line,' he cajoles. 'It's much easier to play rhymes, if the character consciously makes it up, because he needs it.'

Gys next. I've given him a piece of Richard III, a part he's born to play. It's the speech at the end of the Lady Anne scene, and it contains a terrific example of John's antithesis:

> Was ever woman in this humour *woo'd*?
> Was ever woman in this humour *won*?
> I'll *have her*, but I will not *keep her* long.

Gys has a good stab at the speech, finishes and spins round on one leg.

'Right,' says John. 'Now, after those first three lines, where's the next full stop? How many lines down?'

Gys squats and begins to count. 'One, two, three . . . four, five . . . Okay-eh . . . six, seven, eight. Fuck me! It's all one sentence. Jees!'

'That's right, you gave it a lot of welly . . . you sort of went full out on each line and hoped for the best, but the speech doesn't achieve its meaning until you reach the end of the sentence. You need to organise it a bit more, make us follow the argument, head for the full stop. Go for the argument, not the emotion, otherwise all we get is generalised delight in the situation. You merely present a mood. Do you see?'

And Gys does, and we all do. All round the room people are making frantic notes. As if the manna dropping from heaven has to be collected with the dew still on it.

Gys tries again.

'I know this sounds obvious, old thing,' said John, 'but you've got to ask the question, "Was ever woman in this humour woo'd?" It launches the storyline. It's written as a series of questions. Play it as questions and as soon as you do you'll find your interpretation.'

I've given Dorothy a speech by Constance from *King John*. Constance believes that her child is lost, and probably dead, and tears her hair with grief. The speech contains one of my favourite lines in the whole canon: 'Grief fills the room up of my absent child.' It could be one of those phrases collected by Murray Cox from his patients in Broadmoor.

The speech is relevant to *Titus* for two reasons: (a) because Dotty has to play a mother distracted with grief at the loss of her son, Alarbus; and (b) because it deals with a recurrent problem in *Titus*: the articulacy and great intellectual skill with which people express their deepest emotions. They cling to language and somehow translate their pain, sorrow, hatred, ecstasy, into words in order to cope with it, in order to understand it. When Marcus discovers his mutilated niece in the forest he says:

> Shall I speak for thee? Shall I say 'tis so?
> O, that I knew thy heart and knew the beast
> That I might rail at him to ease my mind.

– as if the very practice of putting his disgust into words will cure him.

Dotty makes the speech very contained, determinedly keeping control, observing all the gear changes in the speech.

'It's a balancing act isn't it?' says John, tucking his chewing gum round his molars. 'One rehearsal I might say to you, "OK tear your hair out a bit more, go for it" . . . another day I may say "Stop emoting", and we'll eventually find the balance which suits both of us. As long as you surrender to the text and let the words work for you.'

Dotty looks super-charged with nervous energy. She wants to get it right and is kneeling at John's feet biting her knuckles. Like all of the company, her appetite for this work is enormous.

'I tell you another thing,' says John, fiercely scratching his salt and pepper thatch of hair. 'Respect the monosyllables. Almost all the great lines in Shakespeare are monosyllabic, have you noticed? "I am the sea" – Titus's great line. Simple human speech. Constance's "I am not mad", Hamlet's "To be or not to be" – see what I mean?'

This man's brain is a modem connected to the Shakespeare Internet. He's an access provider and the company are busy downloading. Everybody does their speech. Everybody forgets their words and winces. Everybody grows.

We decide to end by summarising what we've learnt over the two sessions and then distilling that down into ten major points, and prioritising them. The list will be particular to this group; a subjective choice, not necessarily definitive or exhaustive.

John suggests a headline for our list: TO MAKE AN AUDIENCE LISTEN.

I go round the group for contributions.

'Tell the story,' says Jennifer.

'Aim for the full stop,' says Tony.

'Own the words,' says Ivan.

'Go for the antithesis,' says Dan.

'Play the argument,' says Sello.

'Surf the verse,' says Martin.

'Fresh-mint the images,' says Oscar.

'Ask the question,' says Gys.

'Decide who you are talking to,' says Charlton.

'Respect the monosyllables,' says Dotty.

And Bruce Koch, who has been standing quietly at the back, adds: 'Learn your lines!'

It's the last afternoon, and Sue and Diane come in to distribute the T-shirts they have had made for everybody, with a few extra to take back to South Africa. TITUS is written in bold red letters across the front. We all put them on. Jennifer discovers that by folding the fabric you can make your T-shirt read 'TITS'; and like a bunch of schoolkids everybody follows suit.

We're finishing off the two-week workshop with a reading of the whole play. Sue and Diane are our audience. They haven't actually seen any of the work we've been doing, so this is partly to thank them for their hospitality.

The South Africans take a collective deep breath. Most of them are not used to reading Shakespeare. Tony also takes a deep breath. He's very used to reading Shakespeare, but not in a South African accent.

Dumi adds some drumming as we chart through the play, and at the end everybody picks up something: a tambourine or a rattle or a tin and shakes out all their tension in a furious drumming session. It's an exhilarating catharsis. Suddenly I understand why Elizabethan actors performed a jig at the end of every play, whether comedy or tragedy. And it gives me an idea for our own curtain call.

We say farewell to the Studio staff.

Sue is coming over for the first night. 'Well,' she says. 'See you in Jo'burg. All the luck in the world.'

PART IV *Rehearsals*

Johannesburg; February–March 1995

21

Sunday 5 February

What is it about packing and unpacking? I have only to stand in a room, which can be familiar or strange, and look down into a suitcase, which can be hollow or brimming, and hold an armful of my belongings, or be empty-handed, and I experience vague, distant sensations – of fear and sadness – which I can't explain.

When we're joking about it, Greg says, 'Oh, it's just the Wandering Jew in you.'

When we're not joking, he says, 'Oh, it's just your way of getting *me* to do all the packing!'

There's probably an element of truth in both, as well as a memory of that big, real, alarming journey I made when I was nineteen and travelled from South Africa to the place we called *overseas*, and started life all over again.

Yesterday, when I was faced with that journey in reverse, going back to South Africa, not just to visit, but to live and work there for the first time, the packing syndrome was at its worst. I was very tense, Greg was doing all the work and both of us were caught in a kind of chaos, badly unprepared and racing against time, because of the last fortnight, the pressure of the workshop, the suspense surrounding the hoax and all that.

Anyway, we're here now. In South Africa, in Jo'burg, in a car with Dorothy and Mike Maxwell, driving towards the house which will be home for the next four months.

There's a story to these digs . . .

We specified that we wanted a place with a garden, so I could wander around and learn lines; that the property should be totally secure, so we wouldn't have to worry about Jo'burg's reputation as the 'murder capital of the world'; and that it should be completely private, so that we could relax when we weren't working.

When the Market mentioned this particular house it sounded ideal. Apparently it was in a safe area, a suburb called Greenside, and it was spacious, with a garden and swimming pool (I've always wanted to live alongside a pool), and it would be serviced, which is the p.c. way of saying that there would be a maid popping in – a *domestic* as South Africans tend to say these days.

It was owned by the father of one of the Market's stage managers, but he was prepared to move out while we were there.

Perfect.

Then the snag . . .

There was a lodger. Would we mind if he didn't move out? He was hardly ever to be seen, very quiet, very solitary, busy at work during the week, often away at weekends, bird-watching; we'd never know he was there. So would we mind?

While we were deliberating – could we bear to bump into a stranger over coffee in the morning? – the Market phoned again, with more information about the lodger, meant to entice us. He was a Shakespeare enthusiast and very excited about meeting me.

That decided it.

It wouldn't just be a case of bumping into a stranger over coffee – him with nose buried in a book on the Shaft-tailed Whydah or the Pygmy Goose – it would be, 'Excuse me, Mr Sher, what do you think Shakespeare intended by removing the Fool half-way through *King Lear*?'

We rang back with our answer, but before we could say a word, Mike Maxwell told us gleefully, 'It's all right, no problem, the lodger's gone, he moved out this afternoon. The moment he was told it wouldn't just be Tony on his own, but Tony with his boyfriend, he packed his bags and left.'

As Greg and I said to one another, 'Prejudice has its virtues.'

The house in Greenside is terrific, very reminiscent of houses from my childhood. Built round about the turn of the century, single-storeyed with a grey-green corrugated-iron roof, cool passageways inside, one very mannish room that serves as a den-bar (my family had a room like this), everything a bit worn, well-lived-in, a real *home*. The garden is large and rambling, with one secretive part – holding someone's childhood memories, I'm sure – and the pool is long enough to exercise in.

So those are all the pluses. The first minus is the noise. You stand in the garden, longing for its sounds to be African, birds and insects, or at least suburban, sprinklers and lawn-mowers, but instead it's traffic, traffic, traffic – the house is situated on a corner. The other minus is the security. There isn't any. Just two dogs, a collie called Laddie, and his son, a labrador cross, Grunter. Both gangly, friendly, eager to be loved. 'They'll lick burglars to death.' Dorothy laughs as they fall upon her. I'm less amused. All the neighbouring houses have high walls topped with razor- or electric-wire, a sign on the gate from one of the Armed Response Units, *and* dogs. Massive, black hell-hounds, which hurl themselves at their garden gate as you go by, chewing on the bars, trying to dig under them, *determined* to reach you. Admittedly, Laddie and Grunter do a version of this; bounding along the inside of our hedge and barking at passers-by in a rather cheerful way. In fact, their sport has led to a further security problem. The neighbours complained about the barking at night, so now the dogs have to be locked in the backyard when darkness falls, leaving the grounds completely unprotected!

'We don't get trouble round here,' says Hugh, the house's owner. 'Not yet. Touch wood.'

I smile politely, while imagining the headlines: VISITING THEATRICALS IN MANSON-TYPE SLAUGHTER.

Hugh shows us around and then leaves, as do Mike and Dorothy, who have kindly brought supplies for the fridge.

(Greg said the other day, 'Do you realise we've become the *friends of Dorothy?*')

So now here we are . . . in our home, our South African home. I feel so strange; it's hard to describe . . . a peculiar nostalgia, which somehow takes me forward as well as back, and what I see in both directions fills me with confusing, bitter-sweet sensations . . .

The afternoon is sweltering. The sunlight grows steadily weirder and the clouds gradually gather into a single bank, swelling and bubbling, a thundery bleakness in the centre, a beautiful gold lining on the edges. The Transvaal storm arrives with tremendous violence, driving us indoors. Hailstones, big as ice-cubes, bounce off the lawn. Tired and bewildered, we stand in the doorway watching this hot, dark African spectacle.

Monday 6 February
Slept badly.

The bedroom is, well, unconventional . . . with a circular bed, upholstered in ruched bright-blue velvet, and a mirror above the headboard. Floor-length velvet curtains, this time in imperial purple, cover the windows. The ceiling is typical of these houses, made of thin white metal, pressed into rococo patterns. You feel like you're sleeping in a biscuit tin. And then there is the electric fan. One of those ceiling fans which you see in tropical movies, it hangs from the biscuit lid above our circular bed.

As we retired for the night we realised we had two choices. Either to leave the fan off and be dive-bombed by a peculiar breed of kamikaze mosquitoes. Or leave the fan on, which created an insect-free area below, but added another unrestful noise. *Doef, doef, doef.* Just a little too fast for your heartbeat. We settled for the fan and Greg immediately fell into a deep sleep (as he is wont to do). I lay there worrying about intruders, listening to this noise, *doef, doef, doef,* feeling I was in a thriller . . .

I haven't mentioned Selina.

Soon after our arrival yesterday, Hugh said, 'You must meet Selina, she's about to leave for church.' He summoned a middle-aged black lady, who was dressed in a crisply ironed, red-and-white Methodist suit. As we greeted her, it was clear she spoke little English. When she was gone, Hugh explained that he would continue to pay her wages, but we should give her a weekly allowance of R20 (about £4) for food. She would clean the house, make our bed, wash and iron our laundry, but not cook – which suits us fine. Then came a surprise. As he was showing us round the house, he revealed that her room was next to ours.

When I was growing up in South Africa, it would've been an anathema for Selina to sleep *inside* the main house. The 'maid's room' was at the end of the yard . . . and then later, after the Group Areas Act, when blacks were discouraged from tainting the white cities, the servant population lived in the townships and commuted to and from work.

Of course it's good that Selina should have a room within the house. But why did we go through all those deliberations about the lodger, if there was already someone permanently installed in the house? Or didn't it occur to the Market people – even liberals like them – that Selina *counted*?

And how does she feel about it? These two strangers in the house (her home), these two men in the big round bed?

Yesterday, while she was at church, I looked into her room. Converted from what must have been the *stoep* (porch), it has virtually no furniture. Shelves are improvised out of planks, there's a Baby Belling next to the door and her bed is propped on stacks of bricks, lifting it high off the floor.

Apparently this is so that the *tokoloshe* can't reach her. An evil spirit from African mythology, usually represented as a hairy, dwarfish man, who is sexually insatiable, it is most likely to attack at night – so you're most vulnerable in bed.

(*Oich*, now it isn't only intruders I've got to worry about, but dwarfish spooks with rape on their minds . . .)

Tuesday 7 February
We've been given these few days to acclimatise ourselves, before rehearsals start tomorrow. I want to start *now*. At least we've got publicity and production meetings today.

Waiting for the taxi, I absently watch the telly, while Selina cleans round it. The news is on, and the neo-Nazi AWB leader, Eugene Terre 'Blanche (they call him E.T. here) suddenly makes an appearance under her duster. First some old stuff – with him as a wild animal, snarling and slavering – and then more contemporary footage, with him as a white-haired old dinosaur, saying, 'If the war is over, let's send the soldiers home,' referring to the AWB men still in prison. His array of actor's equipment – his eyes, his voice, his passion – is impressive, but he has always mesmerised me in a more personal way, the same way that Hitler does (*I haven't done anything to this man, but he wants to get rid of me*), and I expect him to have the same impact on Selina. But no, she just carries on dusting. As though he's just another baddie from one of the dreadful American soaps which swamp SA telly.

Our meetings are at the Market – our first time back. Bump into John Kani, who is as warm as ever, hugging us, saying, 'You're here, you're here, I'm so happy you're here'; and Barney Simon, who gives a cursory handshake and says, 'People are very worried about you doing Shakespeare in South African accents.' What an extraordinary greeting after all we've been through. I'm flabbergasted. It draws a gloomy cloud over the day.

Wednesday 8 February
In just over an hour we start our first rehearsal of *Titus Andronicus*.

I've had my daily swim, with Laddie and Grunter yelping round the poolside, we've breakfasted in the garden and now set off in the white Fiesta which the Market has hired for us; Greg driving, me trying to navigate from Mike Maxwell's sketch map.

I've banished Barney's strange, cold greeting from my thoughts. I'm just terribly excited . . .

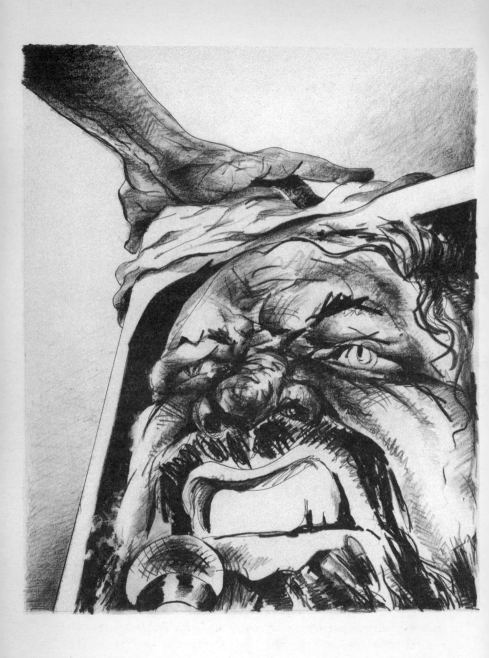

Cleaning the telly

22

Wednesday 8 February
The first day of rehearsals.

As Tony and I walk into the theatre, a group of the Market handymen are sitting in the sun.

An imposing man, with a proud bald head, strides up to us. He's wearing oily blue overalls open to the waist. 'Do you know who I am, eh?' he asks. Before I can reply, he continues. 'I am Haccius. I am the stage crew. And I'm very, very glad you are all here. I love Shakespeare. We've been waiting for you.' He introduces the little team around him. There's Oupa, a beefy chuckle of a man with wide Zulu features; and a short wiry chap called Matthews who wears the cap and badge of the Christian Zionist Church. The cap seems a couple of sizes too big.

'Oh and these are Mabel and Agnes,' he says, pointing out two elderly ladies moving slowly across the way with their brooms, like storks wading across a pond in search of frogs. 'They have cleaned the Market since it started,' says Haccius.

They all greet us. I'm touched by their welcome. And it gives us a lift for the first session.

Our rehearsal room at the Market is in a deplorable state. It used to be a scenery store, but an arson attack on the theatre a few years ago reduced their new store to charcoal and everything had to be moved back in here. Now the room is overflowing with stacks of old theatre seats, flats, timber, treads and junk. It's a high, gloomy space with a corrugated-iron roof, which amplifies every raindrop. It is situated across the precinct from the Market, tucked away behind the Yard of Ale pub. Electric fans from the kitchens pump a sort of school-mealy smell into the room and the stage crew and handymen have a changing room in the corner.

Adam Steyn, our stage manager, and his team have cleared the decks so we can begin. Adam is a long, languid Afrikaner with hooded eyes and cropped blond hair. In contrast Heidi Kelsey, the deputy stage manager, is short, bright-eyed and feisty; a terrier to Adam's Afghan hound.

*

'*Titus Andronicus* was written yesterday.' I scribble this on the wall of the rehearsal room. Not just to stop a lot of classical posturing, but to get the actors to approach the text as if the ink was still wet on the page, as if the author was writing about their lives here and now. Holding the mirror up to show them their own reflection.

It's not really like a normal first day of rehearsal because we've done our first read-through in London. The most important task is to incorporate the new members into the company and to convey some of the things we've discovered, so that everyone is talking the same language.

Apart from Dale Cutts, now joining us for the first time as Marcus, and friends from the Studio visit, the beetle-browed Bruce Laing (Publius), and Squint Artist Paulus Kuoape (the boy Lucius); there are also some newcomers.

We had to audition a couple of the actors by videotape, Fed-Ex'd to London. One actor, Duncan Lawson, in a supreme piece of hard sell, sent over a tape with himself doing soliloquies from *Hamlet*, filmed in some courtyard. His initiative (and talent!) won him the part of Martius, Titus's youngest son. Daphney Hlomuka, a Zulu actress with a singing voice to melt stone, has agreed to play the Nurse. And the last member of the cast is Lesley Fong. Lesley would have been officially classified as Coloured in the old South Africa, although the predominant characteristic in his racial make-up is Chinese; another ingredient in the great melting pot (or boiling pot) that is South Africa. Lesley is playing the Chief Goth.

So finally, after a couple of ice-breaking, group-warming games, we begin to rehearse. The first few days will be rigorously devoted to taking the text apart so that everybody understands each word. This involves long sessions of sitting round a table reading the whole text, line by line, and paraphrasing.

It is the words which will stimulate the audience, the words that must excite them; the words that must release their imaginations; and the words, then, that must be our priority.

'You are going to cut it, aren't you?' Mike Maxwell had asked a little nervously, back in October, hinting that audiences in Jo'burg are not used to lengthy plays. 'Two hours is about the limit.' *Titus* is quite a long play (though it's shorter than the first three acts of *Hamlet*). Shakespeare tends to go at about a thousand lines an hour, which means cutting

around 500 lines from the text if we are to comply with the Market's
dictum.

Back in 1955, Peter Brook cut 650 lines, including glories like 'both
baked in this pie' [see page 178]. When John Barton did it in Stratford as
a double bill with *Two Gentlemen of Verona*, he cut 850 lines. Deborah
Warner didn't cut a syllable, and though good, her production lapped the
famous 'two hours' traffic of our stage', going on for nearly four.

Anxious to alert the actors to any major cutting as early as possible, we
decided to prepare our own text long before the workshop, with the cuts
removed. Otherwise the censored lines lurk on the page, tantalising the
actors. We also removed the footnotes. I don't like footnotes in a working
copy; as someone once said, reading them is like having to run down-
stairs to answer the door on the first night of your honeymoon.

We reached a crucial decision. We'll be cutting the death of Mutius.
Within minutes of his first entrance, Titus kills one of his sons for dis-
obeying him. It's a tricky one. How do you find any journey for Titus to
go, if he's barking mad to start with? From a close study of the text, it
seems that the death of Mutius might have been an afterthought, a late
rewrite. It interrupts a conversation, and Marcus is given the clumsiest
segue imaginable in an attempt to get back to the plot: 'My lord, to step
out of these dreary dumps . . .' Mutius is for the chop.

Thursday 9 February
The first act of *Titus Andronicus* is so action-packed it's like watching one
of those frenetic trailers for a Schwarzenegger move. There's an election
rally, a human sacrifice, a double funeral, an imperial inauguration, an
elopement and a royal wedding. And that's all in the first half-hour. The
story-telling has to be crystal clear.

Today we get to Titus's first entrance and when Tony finally has to
utter those first few words about re-saluting his country with his tears,
neither he nor I have any difficulty producing the goods.

Friday 10 February
I have an idea for an opening image. I want the arches and the columns
of the Market to be illuminated by the flickering light of an eternal
flame. It's both ancient and contemporary, and I hope will convey a sense
of a mausoleum for the honoured dead, and later the Andronici
monument.

I ask Adam if they will allow live flame on the stage and he assures me

it'll be fine. The theatre here doesn't seem to be as restricted by fire regulations as at home, where the whim of the local fire officer can close a
show. Apparently, Adrian Noble's production of *The Cherry Orchard* in
the Swan Theatre is having to tackle the cigar smoking without lighted
cigars!

Monday 13 February
We've decided to begin the play with the late emperor's funeral, in order
to establish that the city is in mourning. We pool ideas and come up with
the image of Ayatollah Khomeni, whose shrouded body was pulled from
its coffin and born aloft by the crowd, hysterical with grief.

The whole company try carrying Charlton (who is the lightest) above
their heads, in an extension of a trust exercise. They get so good at it that
Charlton falls asleep. Dumi finds a deep drum beat, and Daphney
Hlomuka sings a Zulu dirge as the cortège stumbles around the room.
Her voice soars, aching with grief.

Tuesday 14 February
The first moments of the play concern the struggle over the crown, as
the emperor's sons fight for the succession. Bassianus parades himself as
the democratic choice. He ends his opening manifesto with an appeal for
his followers to 'fight for freedom in your choice'.

It is fascinating to be doing a play in which a fiercely contested election threatens to topple the state into chaos, here in South Africa. The
first anniversary of the country's historic elections will take place during
the run.

It's vital that the audience don't miss the plot while their ears are still
tuning in.

The costume can help. Sue Steele (now enthusiastically in step with
the production) comes in to chat to Gys and Ivan. Ivan wants to play the
rebel Bassianus as a Left-Bank radical in a black leather jacket, while
Gys, as his playboy brother Saturninus, could wear Italian designer suits.
Sue will see what she can find.

She is also gathering together a collection of cut-down jeans and T-
shirts, for the Goths. And for the Roman Army she's brought back a pile
of sandy camouflage fatigues from a shop in London's Mile End Road.

Thursday 16 February
Our first production meeting.

'Now what about this jeep for Titus?' I begin.

We've decided that the chariot on which Titus makes his first entrance should be a burnt-out jeep, laden with the dead bodies of his sons for burial.

'You really want a jeep, hey? On the Market stage?' Our hard-pressed pony-tailed production managers, Dean Pitman and Richard Barnes, take the task on board. Because the Market has no wing space to speak of, there is only just room to conceal a jeep stage right. But Dean has some ideas and Heidi's dad knows someone who has an old jeep they might let us use.

There is a lot of work to do and we're already stretching the budget.

Friday 17 February
God, this first scene is huge!

Tony's finding it difficult to chart his way through it. Titus seems one step behind everything, oblivious to Saturninus's psychotic mood swings and willing to accept the most absurd developments, like the marriage to Tamora.

Once we finish the scene, I make the mistake of suggesting we slowly mark through the whole thing to end the week. It's too soon. Tony isn't ready and we have a (I hope rare) spate of bad behaviour as he sulks his way through it, barely audible.

Determined to end the week well, however, I decide it's time to try staging the end of the scene.

By this point in the play things have turned upside down in Rome. The old order has been swept away, the new emperor is clearly unstable and Tamora, who began the play as a prisoner, is now empress of Rome. In the opinion of the Andronici, the Barbarians have entered the gates. We title the end of the act 'The Rise to Power'.

'What happens in Rome is just what all the whities feared would happen after the Elections here,' someone says.

'Like the looting in Bop, that gave everyone the jitters. A real fright. Terrible!'

'That's what Chiron and Demetrius would do, given the chance, they'd go on a spree.'

'And Tamora wants some new clothes.'

It's Nadya's photograph of Gloria Swanson in the rubble.

I begin with a brainstorming session and fire a lot of questions. (Who said 'Directing is not about knowing all the right answers, it's about asking the right questions'?)

'What are they looting?'

'New suits . . . shoes, televisions, anything . . .'

'How? What do you see? What do you hear?'

'Bricks through plate-glass windows . . . You remember that footage of boys kicking in that metal door . . . And those two women taking away a fridge in a shopping trolley. People wearing balaclavas, in case there are cameras about. Everybody's running, ducking, on the look-out. Chaos. Alarm bells going, all different alarm bells. Flashing lights.'

I set up an improvisation, pooling all the ideas, editing and selecting. Tamora spots a designer dress in a department store window. Saturninus himself picks up a rock and smashes the window. Alarms. The boys kick in the door and run into the store. The mannequin is lowered down to Tamora, who rips off the dress and pulls it on. The boys charge in with stolen suits. They strip off their old rags and clamber into their new clothes. People run past with shop racks glittering with trinkets, shopping trolleys filled with boxes.

'And what's Saturninus doing?' I ask.

'Fiddling while Rome burns,' someone says.

'I don't fiddle,' says Gys, 'but I can play the sax.'

Dumi invents a jaunty tune with echoes of Cape 'Coon Carnival' music. Ivan jumps up, grabs his guitar and strums, and somebody else attacks the drums. It's very rough, but in about thirty seconds of stage time we see the Goths take over Rome.

Saturninus (Gys)
...while Rome burns

Saturday 18 February

Back home in Greenside, we discuss the stagger-through and Tony's resistance to it. He talks about the need to move on. Often, the path ahead and the view it affords of the overall journey will explain why there was so much mud behind you and help you get through it next time around.

A solution emerges for Tony. It's very basic and simple. Titus is old. He *is* one step behind. As a loyal servant of the State he will support anything the State does. At first. Titus's journey is painful because he learns that the State isn't always right, or good, or just, and that he can challenge it.

23

Sunday 19 February

I'm more and more intrigued by Selina, the lady with whom we share our home in Greenside. She has a heavy, measured walk round the house, as though she's outdoors, in hot countryside . . . a slight frown on her face, as though squinting into sunlight, which gives her an expression that's both tired and sorrowful.

Her lack of English, and mine of Sotho, make conversation difficult, but I managed one the other morning, before we went to rehearsals. She's from the Transkei, where all her family still live, and when she gets leave, she makes the long trek back to them. Her husband died long ago and she's the mother of five children, though three of them are dead as well. 'How did they die?' I asked. She replied slowly, 'I don't know.' Amazed, I persisted. 'Was it during . . . ?' (I wasn't sure what word to use – apartheid, the Struggle?) ' . . . was it during the troubles?'

'The troubles, maybe,' she said, sounding very unsure.

(I'm remembering a speech Mandela made to a group of supporters, myself among them, in London in 1993, when he said something which led to the title of my new novel: 'In South Africa, at this time, life is very cheap indeed . . . we must work to change that.')

Selina's gone to church and we spend today swimming, sunbathing, leafing through the SA *Sunday Times*, writing our diaries, reviewing the first fortnight of rehearsals.

Greg read somewhere that a version of *Titus* exists with a happy ending! God knows what this entails – they sew back the hands? Tamora is vegetarian? – but anyway it was written by the Restoration playwright Edward Ravenscroft, who said of the original Shakespeare play: 'More a piece of rubbish than a structure.'

I don't understand why *Titus* sometimes gets that kind of reaction. I simply can't comprehend it. But then I'm an outsider, belonging to three minority groups (Jewish, gay, white South African), so my view of things is always askew; I'll never see them as Mr Normal does. Over the past two weeks, the more we've explored *Titus*, the more it excites me. It's a roller-coaster ride through a world full of violence and compassion. Mr Normal's world, in fact.

I'm getting very excited by the role too. Now that we've cut his hysteria in Scene 1, killing his own son, I think I can map out an interesting journey for him – from rock-solid pillar of the community to bewildered outcast to wounded animal to psychotic avenger.

The *character* of Titus feels like it's coming together. Ever since that discussion with Greg about Titus's curious behaviour in the first scene – why is he one step behind everything? – and our solution – because he's old – I sense Dad coming into the picture. In the last few years of his life, he was a very *old* old man, and I can easily imagine him behaving as Titus does in the first scene, somehow not noticing Saturninus's wild mood swings.

Dad was what's called a *Boerejood*: born Jewish, but bred as an Afrikaner, on the baking plains of the Karoo, in a tiny one-horse *dorp*, Middlepost (which I used as the setting for my first novel). He grew up speaking Afrikaans as his first language and had a strong Afrikaans accent. That's become the basis for the one I'm using for Titus.

The accent feels like a gift. It's allowing me to do things with my voice which more typically, as an actor, I do with my body. It gives me new muscles. It lets me flip through the air. Or rest on the earth. Or sink into it. It instantly creates Titus's dogged patriotism ('I hold me *highly honoured* of your majesty') and his fury ('Rome is but a wilderness of TIGERS!'), and his disgust ('My bowels cannot hide her woes, but like a drunkard must I vomit them!').

Its *R* sound is fantastic. It allows you to claw through certain words, possessing them, or the opposite. Rome becomes *Rrrrrome*. Bitter becomes *bitterrrrr*.

My voice, my vocal range, feels liberated by this full-blooded Boer accent, and yet it's not that much closer to my original childhood accent – mildly Jewish, English-speaking South African – than the RP British accent I later learned at the Webber-Douglas Academy of Dramatic Art in London.

So it hasn't really solved a question which has always nagged at me: What is my *identity* as an actor?

I'm thinking of an article which Richard Eyre wrote for the *Evening Standard* after the Studio visit to SA: 'We can dress up in the clothes of other people, we can borrow the rituals of other societies, we can pillage the plays of other languages, but we must always do it in our own voices, not mimicking either the people we would like to be, or the people we feel we ought to be.'

It just keeps coming back to the same thing . . . I'm a *character actor*. Like our play, that phrase has an unfair and unfortunate reputation. It's traditionally used to describe supporting actors who play eccentric people. Margaret Rutherford, for example, would have been known as a character actress. But she wasn't remotely. She played every part exactly the same way – and very delightful it was too – she was a *personality actress*. It's whether you travel towards a role, or bring it towards you. Neither kind of acting is better or worse than the other, but I happen to lean towards character work. I hope in the best sense. Approaching a role from the outside and inside simultaneously. In other words, a combination of assuming the superficial behaviour of other people, their mannerisms, their accents, with things that really matter, things from your own heart. The latter is crucial. Two of the leading character actors this century have been Laurence Olivier and Peter Sellers, but the difference between them is that Olivier never put his heart into the people he played. Although Sellers's characters are comic, they all have a living, beating heart – Sellers's own. Among the pieces of character acting that I most admire are Sellers in *Dr Strangelove*, Meryl Streep in *Sophie's Choice* and Brando in *The Godfather*.

Sellers in "Strangelove"

Brando in "Godfather"

I'm borrowing Titus's military bearing from another favourite film performance, George C. Scott in *Patton*; a soldier down to the soles of his boots and, even deeper, to the souls of great warriors, long buried ... a soldier by *destiny*. That movie is also inspiring some of Dumi's music – stirringly militaristic at first, echoed later with thin, eccentric versions of the same marches.

So, at the moment, there are two sides to Titus. Privately, he moves and talks a bit like Dad and, publicly, he behaves a bit like George C. Scott's Patton. It's the prospect of the mixture which excites me. Moments when, even in his madness, Titus can use his military training to pull himself together. Even though he'll stoop more and more as the play progresses, every now and then he should be able to snap back to attenSHUN!

We want the facial look of all the Andronici to be very old-style Afrikaner, like the Voortrekkers, or those people in the Anglo–Boer War book, *To The Bitter End*, which I showed Sue Steele during the design session in the London workshop. So I've grown my beard and the plan is to wear it big and square, and to cut my hair almost to the skull, in a military crew cut. This arrangement, with the main weight of the face being round the jaws, should also help the ageing. As for the colour of my hair and beard, I want it to be white, and the appropriately named Robert Whitehead has demonstrated how to achieve this.

A warm, rudely twinkling character, Robert is helping on *Titus*. Since he's one of this country's leading actors, and a distinguished director, we were flattered when he offered his services. Greg says it's like having Simon Callow as an assistant director.

When Robert walked into the rehearsal room on our first day, I did a double-take. Currently playing Freud in the Market's production of Terry Johnson's *Hysteria*, Robert had his black hair and beard bleached snow-white. He said the great advantage is that you don't have to spend hours doing make-up before each performance. The only minus is that you can't take it off at the end of the show. I'd have to live with the Titus-look for three months, and maybe longer – if the National brings the show to London.

I broke the news gently to Greg; 'I hope you fancy old men ...'

George C. Scott in "Patton"

24

Monday 20 February
Solo with Sello.

Aaron has been silent for the whole of the first act. We've worked in a moment when he prowls through the looting scene, watching everyone else clambering up the social ladder but him. Now he enters the action.

Most actors corral their characters within the bounds of their own personality. Others, like Tony, investigate how different they are from the character, and that necessarily involves transformation. They are *Comediens*, the French would say, as opposed to *Acteurs*. Sello has another distinction.

'Acting', he says to me, 'is wearing a character inside yourself.'

Tuesday 21 February
Another brainstorming session today before embarking on the hunting scene. The text says 'The morn is bright and grey', which sounds like a contradiction in terms. The company conjure up the early morning scene:

'The hadedahs are calling . . .' says Dan.

'The what?'

'The hadedahs, they're ibis, they're called hadedahs because that's what they cry.' And someone does an impression . . .

'Oh, yes, they fly over our house in Greenside in the morning,' I say.

'And the hunting party have probably got a flask of hot coffee which steams in the headlights of the bakkie . . .' someone else chips in.

'The bakkie?' says I, the *dof rooinek* ('stupid redneck').

'The bakkie,' everyone choruses at me, 'the jeep. All South Africans go hunting in a bakkie.'

'With dogs . . .'

'And Marcus is bound to have brought along his hip flask of brandy to warm up the coffee,' says Dale.

'Oh so has Titus,' says Tony. 'These Andronici hunts are heavy drinking affairs, everybody gets drunk.'

Then we start joking about how people probably dread these hearty

Andronici hunts, and the only way of getting through it is to get completely plastered.

'That can explain why Martius falls down the pit,' says Duncan. 'He's pissed.'

'No, he's probably high,' says Dan. 'They've all been smoking *dagga*.'

So, we've got it. The scene will start with Lucius and his brothers having staked out the hunt, smoking a joint . . . ('No. Lucius wouldn't. He's alert,' says Martin. 'He'll just have a fag . . .') They're broody and disconsolate. The sound of a bakkie, dogs barking. Titus arrives. They rouse the emperor and his party, sleeping in the hunting lodge, by hooting, clanging pieces of metal (which they use to beat game from cover) and parping the car horn.

'Greg, I've been called for this scene,' says Sello, 'but I don't know, is Aaron in this scene?'

Well, no, he's not. But it's a good idea. As the guests arrive, Aaron, still the servant, still the 'boy', can hold the tray of coffee while Titus and Marcus slosh Oude Meester Brandy into their steaming cups.

I congratulate my perspicacious stage management for making a wrong call.

We try running the scene, but when Tony delivers the line 'I promised your grace a hunter's peal' in his gruff Afrikaner accent, the company crack up laughing. Apparently the Afrikaans word *piel* is slang for penis!

Evening call.

Dorothy keeps herself constantly fit. It allows her to explore the physicality of Tamora. The way she's beginning to play the Goth queen's sexual appetite makes you taste it. It's salty and, like sweat, it oozes from every pore. From her toes to her fingertips, she itches for the Moor's body.

We're rehearsing the scene where Tamora slips away from the hunt to meet her lover Aaron in the forest. Tamora is using Aaron for her own pleasure. He worships her.

Dotty tucks her rehearsal skirt into her waistband so she can really move. She'll do this with the ball dress she loots in the 'Rise to Power' section; turning it into a sort of jump suit, so she can run and squat on her haunches. Her Tamora is always attached to the earth.

The scene is very sexy, a power struggle between two powerful people.

*

In the scene where Bassianus and Lavinia walk into the trap, we run into problems.

There is a danger that as the actors make more and more discoveries about their characters the text can become colonised by a host of irrelevant emphases, quirky stresses or empty pauses. Everybody does it.

Ivan is an offender today. He's so passionate about the text that he wrings every drop of meaning out of it. Here Bassianus reveals his innate racism, when upbraiding Tamora about her relationship with the Moor. The speech goes:

> Believe me, queen, your swart Cimmerian
> Doth make your honour of his body's hue,
> Spotted, detested, and abominable.

But the way Ivan's doing it, the speech seems to go: 'Believe me (not anybody else, *me*) queen (if you deserve the name) your (what shall I call him?) swart (let me show off to my girlfriend by using long words) Cimmerian, Doth make your (huh!) honour, of his (I can hardly bear to say the word) body's hue, Spotted (and not only that), detested (and just wait while I vomit), abominable.'

I'm not against any of Ivan's nuances of meaning, or his attempts to make the speech sound spontaneous by carefully choosing each word, but it detracts from the impact of the whole speech. He must head for the full stop.

Ivan is one of those actors who never takes a note until he's fully justified his position. But he's beginning to get it. Still, today I'm quite relieved when we reach his stabbing.

During the workshop someone brought in a picture of a line of squatting prisoners in Vietnam, each with an identity tag round his neck. We used this in Act I. All the Goths are given tags. After the execution, Lucius carelessly chucks Alarbus's identity tag at his weeping mother's feet.

Dotty's decided that Tamora keeps her dead son's tag with her, wearing it round her neck, to give her strength to pursue her sworn vengeance on the Andronici. It comes in very useful in Act II, Scene 3.

Lavinia is begging for mercy. She makes the fatal miscalculation of appealing to Tamora to spare her, for her father's sake.

Dotty grabs Alarbus's tag and kisses it, reminding her sons that Titus showed their brother no mercy. The raw, guttural, poor-white accent she's using turns the words into weapons:

'Hadst thou in person ne'er offended me,
Even for his sake am I pitiless . . .
Therefore away with her and use her as you will,
The worse to her, the better loved of me.'

Lavinia is lost. 'That's when she gives up her spirit,' says Jen. 'It's like that moment on the video we saw . . . when the man was being chopped by knives and finally he knows it's finished and the spirit seems to leave him; he gives it up. Do you know what I'm saying?'

I do. At the point when Chiron drags her away, Lavinia gives up her spirit and he finds a rag doll in his hands. Suddenly Oscar tries something. He begins to dance with this rag doll and waltzes her off stage. His brother drags Bassianus's body with them to use as a 'pillow to our lust'.

Wednesday 22 February

Hillbrow is apparently the most densely populated square mile in Africa, consisting almost totally of high-rise apartments. It used to be a place of retirement for white senior citizens, but now it is flooded with people from the townships and beyond, including illegal immigrants from Zaïre and Zimbabwe, Malawi and Mozambique. It teems with all sorts of street life.

Tony has sent four of the actors to Hillbrow on a research trip for the 'dump people'. I've put him in charge of this area of work because it's right up his street. He has a painterly eye for the humanity within the grotesque, and vice versa.

At the start of our second half, Rome has practically disintegrated. Nadya has designed the set so that, all being well, the central area of flagstones can break in half, revealing a gash of red Johannesburg sand underneath. It's as if the very stones of Rome have eroded away; the forum has crumbled and been overwhelmed by a tide of detritus. There are flies everywhere.

Picking their way through the encroaching dump will be an underclass of drop-outs, runaways and homeless tramps. They'll be useful later on in the play as a little tin-pot army which Titus gathers around him, replacing the rather anonymous family group Shakespeare has written. Tony has asked each of the actors to observe a fragment of behaviour by real characters on the street, and then reproduce it. Today we see the result of their investigation.

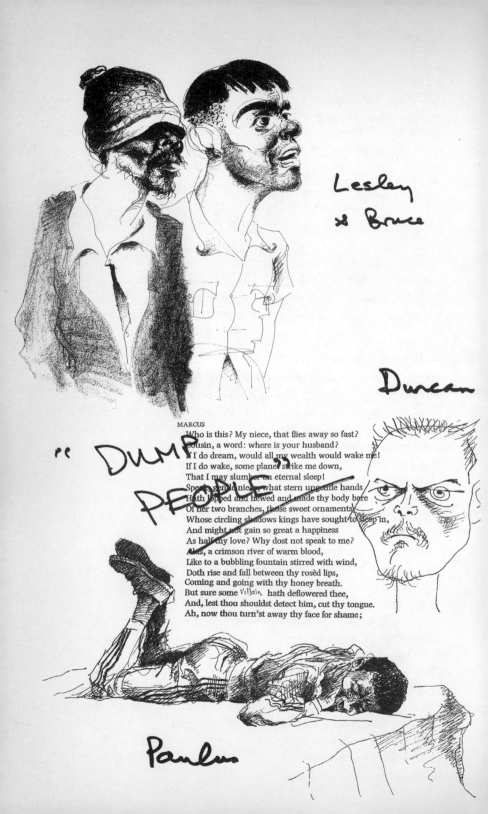

Lesley & Bruce

Duncan

" DUMP PEOPLE "

MARCUS
Who is this? My niece, that flies away so fast?
Cousin, a word: where is your husband?
If I do dream, would all my wealth would wake me!
If I do wake, some planet strike me down,
That I may slumber an eternal sleep!
Speak, gentle niece, what stern ungentle hands
Hath lopped and hewed and made thy body bare
Of her two branches, those sweet ornaments,
Whose circling shadows kings have sought to sleep in,
And might not gain so great a happiness
As half thy love? Why dost not speak to me?
Alas, a crimson river of warm blood,
Like to a bubbling fountain stirred with wind,
Doth rise and fall between thy rosèd lips,
Coming and going with thy honey breath.
But sure some *villain* hath deflowered thee,
And, lest thou shouldst detect him, cut thy tongue.
Ah, now thou turn'st away thy face for shame;

Paulus

Swiftly a real world emerges, populated by street-kids and substance abusers. Duncan invents a hunched, hostile figure with an unblinking reptilian stare, like Jack Nicholson without the twinkle, hoarding things in a black plastic bag. Lesley, unrecognisable beneath a dirty orange woolly hat, plays a drunk, so sodden his body's turned to jelly; while Bruce, in a scout uniform three sizes too small for him, sits watching the world, pining for something lost, and picking his scabs. And Paulus comes into his own. His character lies asleep among the rubble, endlessly pestered by flies. It's an accurate piece of observation and therefore very effective. It reminds me of the first time we met him, improvising with his fellow Squint Artist in the National Studio workshop all those months ago.

Thursday 23 February

Last night we were fast asleep in Greenside, when I suddenly found myself out of bed, flat on the floor and crawling for cover. Someone was firing a gun outside. Tony snored throughout.

Today, we try to recreate that sense of night fear in staging the arrival of Revenge and her ministers in Act V. They mustn't just be Hallowe'en trick-or-treat freaks; they must genuinely terrify Titus and the audience. If, in the middle of the night, Titus were to hear a car revving madly in the dark outside his house, and a violent knock at his door, that might create the tone of anxiety we need.

We decided to use Titus's jeep (which has been dumped by this point in the play) as Revenge's chariot. It'll mean rigging up lights in the jeep and finding a smoke machine. I want to start in darkness, until a glare of headlights reveals the figure of Revenge, in a cloud of exhaust fumes. I talk it through with Dean and Richard. As usual, they nod, take the idea on board and quietly go about seeing if it can be achieved.

We're rehearsing Act II, Scene 4. It is one of the most violent scenes in all literature. Chiron and Demetrius taunt Lavinia, whom they have just raped and mutilated.

We've tried it hundreds of ways. Finally we take the cue from Jennifer's sense that Lavinia has 'given up her spirit', that somehow she has retreated into her own mind to shut out the horror of her attack. The extremity of her pain has numbed her and made her incapable of understanding what has happened to her.

Oscar's improvised waltz off with her in Act II, Scene 3 gives us the

idea that Lavinia waltzes back in, all muddied and mutilated, dancing to
a tune in her head.

'A bit like a ballet dancer in a musical box,' says Dumi. 'You want a
sort of tinkly waltz tune.'

While she dances, the two boys can taunt her by raping the mannequin that has been abandoned at the end of the looting scene.

We try it. The rape of the mannequin is appalling. The boys lick and
fondle the dummy's breasts, and simulate violent penetration, using a
knife; all while Lavinia distractedly dances around them. Demetrius
pulls off the dummy's hands and waves them at her obscenely. Then they
run away laughing, leaving their victim in the forest.

'That's the moment when she comes to,' says Jen. 'It's then the full
impact of the pain hits and she panics, tries to run, but can't because of
the bruising between her legs . . . and that's how Marcus finds her, running away, trying to hide. She doesn't want anybody to see her.'

Marcus's discovery of his niece is very difficult to achieve. He has an
inordinately long speech, during which he seems to make no effort to
help or comfort her.

'You know if you've ever been in a car accident,' Dale says, 'suddenly
everything seems to go in slow motion? I think that's what happens to
Marcus. A hundred thoughts go through his mind in a second. That's
what this speech represents.'

'That's exactly what Ambrose Sibiya said when his hand was chopped
off,' says Jennifer, grabbing her notes. 'Here it is: "My heart was going
like a hammer, and there were a thousand voices in my head, a thousand
clear thoughts." It's exactly what's happening here.'

Still, how do you make the audience understand that, and not wonder
why Marcus isn't calling for an ambulance?

Tim Parr, our guitarist says, 'You know the moment in *Jaws* when Roy
Scheider realises that his son is in the water and the shark has got into
the lagoon? Spielberg does that amazing shot where he zooms in to
Scheider's face and tracks back at the same time. That's what you need
here.'

Tim tries an idea. We do the scene, and at the moment Marcus actually
sees his niece's injuries, Tim gives us a chord on the guitar, with masses
of reverb, to echo in the head. It helps the moment. It stops the record.
Freezes time. But we may be overloading this badly and should just let
the words do it. We leave it open.

Tim Parr

We've managed to get through the whole play now and at least identified all the major problems.

Sello's offered us a lift to the airport. We're taking a long weekend to fly down to Cape Town to see the family. It's the only chance we'll get before the show opens. And after last night's gunshots, it's good to get out of Jo'burg.

I breathe a sigh of relief as we get into the car. Sello apologises that it's not the BMW. I wonder if he's joking. But he's not. He bought a BMW with the money he made from his soap opera, *Generations*. It was his pride and joy. It was stolen last week.

25

Thursday 23 February

Sitting next to us on the plane is Oscar, who's missing his girlfriend so much, he's splashed out on the air fare. This is still only his third flight ever and he sits in the window seat, looking slightly grey with nervous excitement (he went this same colour when he had to do a Shakespeare speech for John Barton), grinning and shaking his head, or leaning his forehead on the glass. During the flight, we've talked about our very different experiences of growing up in Cape Town – me in a rich, white, beachfront suburb, he in a poor Coloured area. Now, as the plane starts to descend, offering a dreamy, tilting, bird's-eye view of Table Bay and its great mountain, and Oscar's jigging excitement turns into something stiller and quieter – complete bloody wonderment – I'm hoping he can't hear my puffing noises as I stifle my emotions.

It isn't only Oscar's joy that touches me. As the character of Titus slowly grows, there's more and more of Dad in him – I'm moving like Dad, sounding like him, *being* him – and there's a profound connection between Dad and the airport, D. F. Malan, which we're about to reach . . .

In November 1993, he and Mom were staying with us in Islington.

Earlier in the year he'd been ill and it seemed like, for the first time ever, they might not be able to make their annual trip. Along with the wear and tear of old age (eighty-one), he'd become increasingly agoraphobic, following a savage mugging a few years earlier. South Africa had given him a fright. He'd always been master here, *die ou baas* (the old boss), patronising but genial, held in affection by his staff, both at home and at the business (a skin and hide export firm), but now it was as though the land itself, and not just two poor black youths, had pulled him down and stolen his money and smashed open his head. He never reported it to the police – 'What's the point?' he said – and just became steadily more frightened by the changes around him, good and bad, the reforms, the violence, Mandela's release. Refusing to leave the house, except by car, he'd spend day after day sitting on their little patio, or pacing round it, hemmed in by its walls and security system, like an old zoo animal longing to return to the Africa it once knew.

But then he suddenly rallied, they arrived in London and the stimulation of new surroundings did wonders for his health. Their trip culminated in a visit to Buckingham Palace. As President of the RSC, Prince Charles had organised a fund-raising gala. I was part of the evening's entertainment and managed, in exchange for a few limbs and part of my soul, to get Mom and Dad invited. They were as thrilled by the evening as Oscar is by flying. Maybe quite similar experiences. 'I just never imagined doing that,' Dad kept saying afterwards. 'Me – from Middlepost – me going to Buckingham Palace. Hell's Bells!'

This was just before their return to South Africa, which Dad was dreading. We planned to spend the final few days up in the Lake District, where Greg's folks live.

Then, three mornings after the Palace visit, a phone call from Israel, where Mom's sister, Rona, emigrated with her family some years ago. Her son, Mark, had died of a heart attack. He was only a year or two older than me. His brother Neal was summoned after he collapsed, but by the time he arrived, Mark's face was already covered with a towel. Neal lifted it and kissed him goodbye. They were identical twins.

Mom

My mother is a very strong woman, unafraid of death (spiritualism is her faith), but I've never seen her as shaken as she was that morning. Dad was just very quiet.

They flew to Israel the following night, a Wednesday. They'd spend a few days there, come back to London for a couple more and then return to SA the following week.

Mom rang from their hotel in Herzlia on Thursday afternoon. They'd just got back from Ra'anana, where Rona, Neal and the rest of the Hesselberg family live. It was terrible, she said, the grief was terrible. They'd come back to the hotel for a rest (Dad was napping) and in the evening would go back to Ra'anana.

Greg and I held our own little wake for Mark and were quite drunk when the phone rang at about 9 p.m. Greg answered it, then quickly handed it to me. I heard Mom's voice, low and dry, say my name, and then, 'Dad has died.'

He'd carried on napping – very restlessly – through the afternoon and then – more peacefully – in the early evening. Not wanting to disturb him, Mom watched a Woody Allen film on the movie channel. Noticed he was quite still. Went for a bath. Returning, she noticed his lips were bluish. Tried to wake him, couldn't. Called down to reception. They sent a security man, who pulled Dad on to the floor and tried to revive him. A doctor arrived, tried various things . . .

(I'm haunted by these images . . . these strangers with Dad, holding him, kissing him . . . he and I never touched, except to shake hands . . . we had shaken hands on the Wednesday evening at Heathrow when they left for Israel, and I'd watched them walk away, him looking very small, wearing his blue sailor cap and his step slightly unsteady, slightly baby-ish, searching for the ground each time.)

Now Mom and I both had dreadful tasks. She had to phone the Hesselbergs and add to their grief and ask for their help. I had to phone South Africa and tell my sister, Verne, and my two brothers, Randall and Joel, what had happened.

I never thought it would be this way round, me phoning them . . . ever since leaving South Africa, I've dreaded the moment when the phone would ring and I'd pick it up and one of them would deliver this news.

Greg and I flew to Israel first thing Friday morning, pausing only to ring my agent from the airport, to warn the RSC that I'd probably be missing the performances of *Tamburlaine* on Monday and Tuesday.

Now I embarked on a most peculiar journey, both within myself (until recent years, Dad and I never got on that well, chalk and cheese really, the businessman and the artist) and in physical terms, travelling half-way round the world in six days . . .

The weekend in Israel . . . with Greg having to fly back early Sunday morning for work, and being stopped, and grilled, and strip-searched by the zealously security-conscious Israeli Customs people; they couldn't believe anyone would fly in for just one and a half days, and for some reason he couldn't say the words, 'My lover's father has just died, so I came here with him.'

And then, on Sunday evening, Mom got on a plane to South Africa and I found myself boarding with her. We made every effort to take along Dad (or 'the body' as everyone suddenly started calling him), but were in a bureaucratic nightmare – the Israeli sabbath is on Saturday and the South African one is on Sunday – meaning nobody could do the paper-work. So we had to leave him behind, which distressed me.

(When his transportation was eventually arranged, the cost was obscene. About £4,000. As my younger brother Joel, the grim joker in our family pack, said, 'People spend fortunes to be buried in Israel – trust Dad to do it the other way round!')

Anyway, of all the events during those few days, it was the arrival of Mom and me back in Cape Town, at D. F. Malan Airport, that still upsets me most to remember . . .

As Mom and I turned into the Arrivals area, Randall, Joel and Verne were immediately apparent among the crowd – the smiling crowd, all there to meet holidaying family or friends. Joel didn't wait for us to reach the barrier, but rushed forward and hugged Mom. I heard her sob for the first time since this thing happened. Now Verne was at my side and we hugged. And now Randall also, and we were all standing there, hugging and crying, exchanging partners like in some strange, slow dance. Mean-while other passengers from the flight were battling to squeeze past us and the spectacle was being watched by the people behind the barrier, as by an audience. We presented a long tragi-comic scene, played in silence, except for our weeping.

This afternoon, as Greg and I – and Oscar Peterson – reach D. F. Malan Airport and walk into the Arrivals hall, there's the family waiting behind the barrier again, but this time smiling like the rest of the crowd and we hug without sobbing. Mom's there, and Verne and her partner Joan (after twenty-five years of marriage and three kids, Verne came out – joy-fully – as gay), and my older brother Randall, wearing an apron from his new take-away shop.

Mom is glowing with good spirits these days. As Dad grew sicker and angrier in his last few years, raging against the dying of the light, she found his company increasingly exhausting and nerve-racking. Now she's been given, as they say, a new lease of life.

The drive from D. F. Malan (will the new government change these airport names – all ex-prime ministers?) begins with a display from the past, from the old South Africa we all knew and hated. First the road is flanked by billboards advertising expensive cars, jewellery and perfumes, and then, immediately, stretching for mile upon mile, it's flanked by the townships and squatter camps.

From then on, it becomes, for me, the loveliest journey I know. The road climbs up the flank of Table Mountain, showing its trees and colossal slopes and sky beyond, and then seems suddenly to dip, almost tumble – like a fairground ride – offering a huge, open view of the city and the docks and the bay. On these drives, these re-entries to my birthplace, these returns home, the weather always seems perfect, as it is this afternoon. Cape Town air is surely brighter and fresher, and the sky more blue, than anywhere else in the world!

Along the way, Mom is eager for news about the rehearsals, and then, as we enter Sea Point, our suburb, she suddenly says, 'Did you ever do that painting of Dad?'

'No,' I say evasively.

After his cremation, I brought some of the ashes back to London, intending to mix them into an oil painting of him. It seemed like a good idea at the time (borrowed, I think, from Derek Jarman, who did that with a painting of a friend), but though I sometimes look at the last sketches I did of him, in '89 and '91, and feel pleased with them, I never feel inclined to turn them into that painting.

So his ashes are still there, in a little plastic container, among the paints and brushes in my artwork cupboard. On the adjoining shelf is a framed photograph of Dad . . . a special photo. Taken after that evening at Buckingham Palace, which thrilled him so much. When we reached home, Greg took a few rather formal shots of Mom, Dad and me in our finery, proudly holding the official programme and the red sticker which allowed my dusty old Jetta to drive through the palace gates. Dad then went to change out of his Moss Bros DJ, while Mom sat at the dining-room table, still fully bejewelled and frocked, relaying the highlights of the evening to Greg. A few moments later, Dad reappeared, now wearing dressing-gown, vest and slippers, but with the bow-tie still round his neck . . . he couldn't unfasten it. Either Greg or I grabbed the camera

Dad at Delcombe Rd 4/10/89.

Dad

and caught the moment when Mom turns and sees him. She explodes with laughter. He stands there, clown-like, in bow-tie and underwear, grinning at us. As though he's saying, 'Ja, I may be that *plaasjapie* from Middlepost, but I damn well made it to Buckingham Palace!' And that's the last photo ever taken of him.

Friday 24 February
This whole *Titus* experience seems to be one long catalogue of nail-biting deadlines.

We spend this morning sitting nervously on the *stoep* of Verne and Joan's house (we're staying with them), waiting for Roger Chapman to ring from the National.

Today's the day we hear whether we'll be doing what Roger calls 'Stage Three' of the *Titus* journey. The return to the National. There have been enormous problems finding the money, just for a change.

Roger has promised to ring at one o'clock. At about five to one I go into the lounge and pace around, watching the goldfish do something similar in its bowl.

The phone rings.

Roger is his good old warm no-nonsense self: 'The answer is *yes* – so long as you chaps are prepared to make some compromises. At our end it's been one hell of a battle to make the sums work, but we've found a way, and I just hope it's acceptable to you . . .'

The main compromise is that we don't get a two-week run at the Cottesloe, as originally hoped, but only one, the second being in Leeds, at the West Yorkshire Playhouse, who will share some of the costs. This doesn't strike me as a hardship at all. Jude Kelly has turned that place into one of the most exciting theatres in the country. In addition, Roger tells me that by chance the Playhouse is also hosting the Market Theatre production of *Jozi Jozi* the same week that we'll be there. 'So we can really do a big number on the Market Theatre,' enthuses Roger. 'Get a load of publicity . . . really show that the Market is alive and well!'

Roger is pleased by my positive response, but warns me that the deal is non-negotiable. He asks me to discuss it in detail with Greg, to check with the company, and with the Market of course, and to let him have an answer by Tuesday afternoon – when the National's new brochure goes to print.

Greg, Verne and Joan have all been watching tensely while I've talked with Roger. Now, as I put down the phone, they all say in unison, 'Well?'

'Well . . . I think our production of *Titus Andronicus* is going – briefly
– to the Royal National Theatre of Great Britain!'

Even the goldfish seems to grin.

To celebrate, a champagne and bagel lunch at Montagu House, where I
was brought up, and where Mom still lives. The bagels have been baked
by Katie, Mom's *domestic*. They're her speciality and I don't know of any
Jewish bagel better than the ones made by this Coloured lady. And as
usual she's done two dozen extra for Greg and me to take back with us.

Katie Roberts has worked for my mother for almost half a century
now; and during that time she's been at the heart of family life. Literally.
Often expressing the emotion that the rest of us hold back.

When Mom and I reached Montagu House on our return from Israel,
after Dad's death, it was Katie who wailed. We had wept – she wailed.
And back in 1968, when I left home for London, while the rest of us all
just bit our lips and frowned, it was the farewell to Katie that almost
broke my nerve – as she stood in the doorway of the 'maid's room', sobbing uncontrollably.

Today she's all smiles. '*Haai*, Mister Antony, Mister Greg, how are
you? . . . And Mister Jim, how's he?' She always asks after my ex-
partner. As a pious church-goer, she has, I think, a different interpretation of these relationships of mine. I once overheard her talking to
Dad, during a visit with Jim: '*Hulle is net soos broers*' ('They're just like
brothers').

Saturday 25 February
Bright, sunny afternoon. I stroll down to the beachfront on my own. I'm
feeling very tense about *Titus*. It's difficult working at the Market. I
mean, it's not their fault – they get no government funding – but everything is less efficient than we're used to.

I think, I hope, this weekend in Sea Point will be what the doctor
ordered.

I walk all the way to Rocklands Beach and then back. Approaching
Graf's Pool (a men-only nude sunbathing enclosure), I'm walking along
that section of the promenade where there's a great curve of sea wall . . .
and suddenly become aware that, held in that curve, like in a bowl,
there's a powerful mixture of sensations. From one side, a smell of the
sea, like bright mist, and from the other, a smell of mown grass, that
watermelon smell. A group of young men are playing football on the

lawns, blacks and whites together, as though this is, and had always been, the most natural thing in the world. Many of them are semi-naked. I stand there, breathing deeply, smelling the smells and admiring the players. And then, in this Proustian stupor, I half-remember some fragments from childhood; seeing boys like this, thinking how beautiful they were, how plain I was, and how never the twain could meet.

This afternoon's experience only lasts a few seconds, but it's good, there in that curve, that long rounded corner, man and boy meeting, swopping a few notes.

Sunday 26 February

I should never have agreed to it. Giving up a morning on this precious weekend for a *press interview*.

But the Market said it was important, to be used in both South Africa's *Cosmopolitan* magazine and *Sunday Times*, and recommended the interviewer, Dr Something-or-other (can't remember his name, because everyone just keeps stressing the *Dr*), who is a Professor of English at one of the universities.

He turns out to be a short, aggressive man. His opening question is: 'So why are you back here? Because it's *chic* to work in South Africa now?'

I blink at him, amazed.

I hadn't seen South Africa's progress in terms of *fashion*.

Is that why apartheid fell? Because it was a bit *passé*?

I don't, of course, say this. Instead, I relax and become very courteous, answering his questions as best I can, while trying to figure out why he's so negative about everything.

When, finally, he goes, and I'm left sitting there, appalled at the waste of my Sunday morning, it dawns on me that I've met his type before in this country. Always white, often journalists. The press was particularly angry with me after the burning of my passport (widely reported when I won the Olivier and *Standard* Awards in '85) and it might still be run by the same people, still confused as to why anyone was ashamed of the old South Africa.

So far, my homecoming has been marked by two general responses. Blacks tend to say, 'Welcome home, thanks for your efforts abroad.' Whites, like Dr Whatsisname today, tend to say, 'Oh *you're* back . . .'

*

To salvage the day, Verne and Joan drive us to a couple of favourite spots, which we four have made our regular haunts. The Brass Bell in Kalk Bay, where we lunch on the linefish and drink fine South African wine, and then the beach at Fish Hoek, where the small warm waves of the Indian Ocean gently knock us about.

Let's hope the next three weeks are as kind.

26

Monday 27 February

'*Goeie mõre dames en here, ek het baie goeie nuus*' ('Good morning, ladies and gentlemen, I have very good news'), I announce to the company, in my best Afrikaans, which I have been practising since yesterday. '*Ons se produksie van* Titus Andronicus *gaan London toe.*' We're going to London. The company whoop and cheer.

The deal is explained and everybody has to let us know by the end of the day whether they can come or not.

Daphney comes up to me in a break. 'Oh, Greg,' she says, 'I'm so excited to be going back to London. It's great news.'

'Going back, Daphney,' I say. 'Have you been before?' I had forgotten that Daphney famously played Lady Macbeth in *Umabatha*, the Zulu *Macbeth*, which took London by storm in the early seventies, arriving at the Aldwych as part of the World Theatre Season.

Over the weekend in Cape Town, I came into Verne's kitchen to find her youngest son, Dean, showing off his skills with a new knife he'd bought. She isn't too pleased with the new acquisition.

Oscar & 'Okapi' knife

'It's called a butterfly blade,' he explained, and I can see why. The double-flick action is like watching some deadly species of steel butterfly fluttering in your fist.

'That's it!' I said to Tony. 'Chiron and Demetrius must have butterfly knives. Where can we get them?'

Today, Oscar and Charlton take to the knives at once, as if Tamora's sons have just looted them along with natty zoot suits, flowery shirts and clashing ties, in the 'Rise to Power' sequence. We decide that Chiron, the older brother, will have a butterfly and Demetrius will have an 'Okapi' (a more conventional folding knife), which his brother scornfully can refer to as a 'dancing rapier' and a 'lath' (a toy sword), which his mother has given him. Throughout the play both boys can be seen constantly practising their skills, opening and closing the knives.

Today their first scene with Aaron springs to life as the two develop a whole blade culture, a series of lunges and threatening tactics which are dangerous and thrilling, and yet funny at the same time.

We also take a look at the boys' last scene in the play. Titus finally comes face to face with his daughter's attackers. He shows them the result of their crime, the damaged Lavinia:

> Here stands the spring, whom you have stained with mud,
> This goodly summer with your winter mixed.

They are dead meat. He is going to cut their throats, drain their blood and bake them in a pie.

Charlton & butterfly blade

My image for their execution is inspired by *The Long Good Friday*. There's a scene in a cold store, where Bob Hoskins deals with his gangster enemies by hanging them upside down from large meat-hooks. Titus can do the same thing, once the boys are in his power.

I ask Oscar and Charlton how they feel about hanging upside down. They agree to try, although Charlie looks a little green around the gills. It is another stunt which will take a lot of rehearsal. Adam informs Dean that we need a wire to fly in (and support) two bodies, and two pairs of ankle straps. And we need them now.

Oscar has had a hangdog look about him all day. I'm anxious to find out whether something in rehearsal has troubled him. Perhaps the stunt idea? I finally catch up with him at the tea-break. He tells me his fiancée finished with him, back in Cape Town at the weekend. He's devastated. The news that we are going to London hasn't cheered him up. 'What's the good if you don't have anybody special to share your excitement with,' he says.

Inevitably, everyone responds very quickly to the London deadline. Martin le Maitre's wife is due to have their first baby in June, so he won't be able to come; and Lesley Fong has been offered Mephistopheles in a world tour of William Kentridge's *Faustus in Africa* for Handspring Puppets.

Now only Paulus hasn't said anything. Tony and I seek him out. He's sitting in the sun against the yellow wall of the Flower Market, rifling through the 'Chocolate Log' sports bag he always has with him.

'Chocolate Log!' says Tony in a little gooey voice. Chocolate Log bars were his favourite sweets as a kid. Whenever we come over here, he rushes to the nearest confectionery counter to sate his appetite. Funny the things you miss.

'What about it Paulus, are you coming with us to London?'

'Uhh . . . you see, ummm, it's just . . .' Paulus looks embarrassed and struggles to explain. 'I don't have anywhere to stay . . . in London.'

'Paulus!' we chorus in disbelief. 'Oh, Paulus, Paulus!' And we go on to explain that the arrangements will be made for him and detail the money that he will be getting in per diems and salaries. His eyes start popping.

'Is there someone you need to check this with Paulus?' Tony says. 'Any family? Before you decide if you will be coming with . . .'

'No, no,' he interrupts. 'I'm coming with, I'm coming with!'

27

Tuesday 28 February

There are two ways you can represent the amputees' stumps in *Titus*. Either realistically, as in Deborah Warner's production, where Lavinia and Titus wore costumes with long sleeves, or stylistically, as in Brook's production, where Vivien Leigh held red ribbons in her hands, to symbolise the blood.

We're going for the second option. No long sleeves, no concealment. In fact, probably the opposite. Greg wants the audience to *see* whatever device we use, so that they don't waste time wondering how it's done. He's thinking of having someone wrap Jennifer's fists in bandages – onstage – during the first part of Act II, Scene 4, while Chiron and Demetrius describe how they've mutilated Lavinia.

This morning, before we drove to work, I popped into the chemist in Greenside and bought a sprained-wrist support. Stiffened by a strip of plastic inside, and with velcro fastenings, it locks the lower arm and hand. That's what strikes you when you see a real amputee's stump – how the limb ends in a rigid shape, rather than the dexterity of a hand or foot. I intended the wrist support as no more than a rehearsal aid, but Greg and Jennifer both think we could use it in the production, wrapping Elastoplast over the top.

Later, Jenny tells me that when the hoax happened, and the show was almost cancelled, she was most worried about the people who'd helped her research Lavinia's injuries. 'I felt such responsibility to them. If we didn't do the play, I would've sort of cheated them.'

Now she relates, finally – I've been resisting hearing this – the story of the man with no tongue; an elderly Coloured man, a cancer victim. Jennifer's contact at the hospital, the speech therapist there, asked the man to let Jennifer look in his mouth.

'He was so sort of *proud* to do it . . . obviously lots of medical students came to look . . . there was just saliva inside, no teeth, nothing, just saliva. Even when his mouth was closed, it kept running out. He had a little folded handkerchief, very soiled . . . and he kept dabbing his mouth.

This seemed to embarrass him the most . . . that he couldn't stop the saliva pouring out. You can't swallow properly, y'see, if you have no tongue. He kept talking to me as if I could understand him . . . his focus was amazing . . . I couldn't understand a word . . . but his *focus*. You see, he was illiterate, so he couldn't communicate by writing either.

'Later I kept remembering his embarrassment about his saliva. I thought, what would it be like for Lavinia, who had been this, like, *princess* in Rome . . . what would it be like for her to have saliva running out of her mouth all the time, and no hands to wipe it away?'

In rehearsals, this has helped us develop our rapport in the second half, as father and child, nurse and patient: Jennifer's saliva keeps spilling out of her mouth and I keep wiping it away with my handkerchief.

Some other excellent things have come from her research.

A doctor explained about the difficulty of eating and this has led to a moment where Titus has to try and cajole her into eating, like with a baby – 'Come, let's fall to, and, gentle girl, eat this' – and she refuses, scrambling off his lap.

Another doctor spoke to her about the shock effects of the mutilations and rape – 'Lots of weeping, regression to childhood, either needing constantly to be hugged, or not wanting to be touched at all' – and this has led to a messy, scrabbling tussle when Titus first sees her in Act III, Scene 1 and tries to comfort her, saying, 'Gentle Lavinia, let me kiss thy lips, or make some sign how I may do thee ease . . . *What shall we do?*'

I'm making Jennifer sound very intense. She's not. She laughs a lot, and at herself. For example, her research finally went OTT, when yet another doctor pointed out that she might be pregnant after the double rape. She asked Greg whether she could get steadily more pregnant through the second half. He said no, and I added: 'You're heavy enough on my lap as it is.' The subject wasn't discussed again until one day last week, when we were rehearsing the Arrows scene.

Greg: 'Jennifer, why are you squirming like that while they're speaking?'

Jennifer: 'Well, you remember I asked if I could be pregnant?'

Greg (guarded): 'Yeees . . . ?'

Jennifer: 'And you said no.'

Greg: 'Yeees . . . ?'

Jennifer: 'Well, I went back to the doctor, and said, "My director won't let me be pregnant, so now what do I do?" And he said, "Well, if there was any chance of your rapists having a sexually transmitted disease . . . ?" And I interrupted and said, "There's *every* chance!" And he said, "Well, then she might miscarry . . . " '

Greg: 'Yeees . . . ?'

Jennifer: 'Well, that's what I'm doing with the squirming. I'm miscarrying.'

Me (spluttering): 'What . . . ? What . . . ? While I'm busy acting my bollocks off . . . doing all my poignant Don Quixote acting . . . she's over on the other side of the stage having a *miscarriage*?!'

Greg and I look at one another, then Greg says, 'Which one of us should remind her that, as written, Lavinia isn't even in this scene, and that if she doesn't keep very, *very* still, she could find herself taken out of it again . . . ?'

My own research into Titus's disability was done, unintentionally, several years ago, when my friend Richard Wilson (now best known as V. Meldrew) and I workshopped and then made a film called *Changing Step* — me writing it, him directing for BBC Scotland. Set during the First World War, it told the stories of injured soldiers returning from the Front, and how they were nursed by the daughters of the aristocracy in a VAD hospital. Several of the wounded were amputees, and Richard and I were determined that they shouldn't be played by actors with arms or legs tied behind them. So we found real amputees, many of whom hadn't acted before, and then spent many months living and working with them, months which were full of enlightenment for me. The group used to describe Richard and me as 'People with more than the average number of limbs'.

"Changing Step"

28

Tuesday 28 February

Rhetoric should be a compulsory subject at all drama schools. It's the art of persuading people.

Shakespeare would have been taught rhetoric as a formal discipline in the curriculum at Stratford Grammar, alongside Latin, and logic, and some mathematics.

Gys is working hard to maximise the effectiveness of the long speech in Act IV, Scene 2. We explore the conscious and deliberate construction of the argument, the placing of key words, the bombardment of rhetorical questions, the gradual lengthening of phrases until the last six lines drive through to Saturninus's rallying cry for vengeance:

> But if I live, his feigned ecstacies
> Shall be no shelter to these outrages;
> But he and his shall know that Justice lives
> In Saturninus, whom if Justice sleep,
> He'll so awake as she in fury shall
> Cut off the proud'st conspirator that lives.

It's a claptrap. The speech builds so effectively to its climax that his audience should be left with no option but to burst out in rapturous and sustained applause. But it seems at odds with Saturninus's character. It's almost as if he's just rehearsing it. In fact, Tamora tells him to calm down – a neat piece of deflation.

Wednesday 1 March (Ash Wednesday)

Half-way through rehearsals. Lent begins.

We've gone back to the Pit scene. I'm irritated because we still can't rehearse this properly.

Aaron lures Titus's sons to the edge of the pit; Martius topples in and discovers the dead body of Bassianus. Quintus, trying to rescue his brother, also falls in. At the start of rehearsals we decided that the fall would be achieved by a stunt fall from the gallery of the Market, down camouflage netting, a drop of some eighteen feet.

Tony has a great deal of experience himself with these very physical moments of theatre, particularly during his training for *Tamburlaine the Great* (or 'Trampoline the Great', as it was known by the company at the time) and I placed him in charge. He insisted the boys practise on a daily basis. Now we're half-way through rehearsals and the damn net still hasn't arrived. So Duncan and Dan can't rehearse it.

Tony is also uneasy about the rest of the scene. The decision to make the pit on stage level means that he has to play Titus's discovery – that his sons have been sentenced to death – way up on the gallery. The trouble is compounded by the fact that Shakespeare seems to have forgotten to write Titus into the scene, or indeed for most of Act II, a curious omission.

But if we do change everything round and play the pit more conventionally, using a trap, the scene will literally disappear into the floor. So I hold my ground.

Thursday 2 March
The war-dance is beginning to look very impressive. The role of choreographer has devolved on to Oscar. Every able-bodied member of the company has been drafted into the Goth army for this, including Dale and Gys.

In Act V, Scene 1 we want to achieve a real sense that the Goths have assembled into a mighty fighting force. They have rallied behind Titus's banished son Lucius. The Chief Goth swears allegiance:

> Be bold in us. We'll follow where thou leadst
> Like stinging bees in hottest summer's days

It reminds me of a trip Tony and I made while researching *Cheap Lives*, to Isandlwana, the sight of the disastrous British defeat in the Zulu wars. One January morning in 1879, thousands of King Cetshwayo's warrior impis descended on the British infantry 'humming like a swarm of bees'.

We recreate the buzzing war cry – 'Ohgee! Ohgee!' – underneath the Chief Goth's speech. Then as Lucius commands his troops to march on Rome, the Goths, hooting and ululating, break into a war-dance.

Oscar's using the early work we've done creating a Goth *hakka* in the chilly studio in Waterloo. His starting point is a *ratieb*. A *ratieb* is a type of ritual dance, performed in the Malay communities in Cape Town.

The *ratieb* dancer, in a frenzied trance, slashes his forearms and body to prove he is impervious to pain and to testify to the power of mind over matter. In this state of ecstasy, swords might be drawn across tongues and stomachs, and skewers pierce cheeks, but no blood flows. It is performed to the frantic beating of drums and tambourines, and must be thrilling to watch.

Friday 3 March
I completely ballsed up the beginning of Act III, Scene 1 last week. I tried to invent a sequence where Lucius takes the law into his own hands and attempts to spring his brothers out of jail. Not distinguishing between fortifying the story-telling and over-elaborating it.

However, good things come out of it today. We have the boys harried through the streets, chained to the same yoke the Goth sons use to drag in Titus's jeep in Act I. The crowd jeer and yell at them.

In order to avoid any naff stage blows from the crowd, we create a rule: they can't actually hit the boys. But they can wield sticks and knobkerries; they can rattle cans and whistle at them, but perhaps the most ugly thing they can do (and which is possible to achieve effectively) is to spit at them. The boys should drip with gobs of rheum. Having double-checked that there are showers backstage, Duncan and Dan agree to the spitting. Although it is restricted to run-throughs!

Saturday 4 March
We've instituted weekend rehearsals.

Tony and Dotty have been to the fleamarket this morning, and bumped into Sue Steele, the costume designer. They arrive back glowing with pride, having discovered a fearsome-looking African mask with salamanders clambering over its brows.

'Wouldn't this be great for Revenge?' Tony says. It looks good, but is so heavy, Dorothy will need a neck brace to sustain its weight.

The first problem in Act V, Scene 2 is how to present Revenge, Rape and Murder. Of course you can begin by saying it doesn't really matter what Tamora and her sons wear, because they believe Titus is two slices short of a toaster, that he'll accept whatever they tell him. But apart from anything else, that's not nearly as dramatic. Taking the cue for how Chiron and Demetrius might be dressed from Titus's reference to them as 'a pair of hell hounds', we're making them hyenas.

*

We're still working through Act III, Scene 1.

We've got to the section where Titus appeals in desperation to the tribunes and judges for his sons' lives, but is left weeping to the stones. It is Lucius who has to bring his grieving father to his senses. We're trying an idea that Titus, in his grief, actually rips up one of the loose paving stones.

Further torment is to follow, as Marcus appears with the mutilated body of Lavinia.

And just as things seem incapable of getting worse, Aaron comes running on, claiming that Titus's sons will be released if Marcus, Lucius or Titus will chop off one of their hands. There follows a ludicrous squabble between the men.

> *Marcus*: My hand shall go.
> *Lucius*: By heaven it shall not go!

Tony is very nervous about this sequence. He thinks we should cut it. 'The audience will laugh if we're not careful.'

'Yes,' I say. 'I think they may, and we'll monitor that, but I think if we get it right, they *should* laugh. It's daring writing, teetering on the brink of absurdity. Shakespeare makes you laugh, then he undercuts it . . . pulls the carpet away from under your feet.'

'Ummm,' Tony grunts. 'It's a good theory.'

Now we get to the hand-chopping. The stage management have brought in a cow's thigh bone. We're still clinging on to an idea which we first tried in the London workshops; a complicated effect of displacing the audience's focus at the crucial moment by showing a bone being hacked through at the side of the stage, at the same moment that Titus's hand is chopped.

Essentially it's a film convention, where you can intercut rapidly from one image to the other. The technique doesn't work on stage. It interrupts the flow of the action. Today, after trying unsuccessfully to chop through this revolting thigh bone, we abandon it completely.

Instead, Aaron grabs a piece of black plastic from the rubbish heap around the stage and lays it out to perform the amputation. After three terrible chops of the panga, Titus pulls his mutilated arm away from a pre-wrapped hand, which Aaron has already palmed (excuse the pun), and wraps his stump in the plastic.

Black plastic bags have become a big feature of the production. When the messenger brings Titus the severed heads of his two sons, they are delivered in one of these bags. I hope this moment is somehow made worse by the black plastic, both concealing the obscenity and allowing our imagination to provide the awful reality.

Shakespeare piles horror upon horror. Titus has to deal with the sentencing of his sons, the mutilation of his daughter, the pointless loss of his hand and then the spectacle of his sons' heads being presented to him. It is as if Shakespeare challenges himself by pushing his characters to the limits of human endurance to explore how the human psyche deals with trauma.

Whereas the scene can be absurd and revolting elsewhere, doing the play here in South Africa, a society which has suffered decades of atrocious violence, a strange reversal occurs. The acts of brutality, instead of being gratuitous or extreme, seem only too familiar, and the focus turns instead on to how the characters deal with that violence and the impact of grief.

I watch Tony turning into Titus. Sometimes it's like watching his father, Mannie, shuffling round the stage, stooped and tired, with his hands

The trees, though summer, yet forlorn and lean;
Here never shines the sun, here nothing breeds,
Unless the nightly owl or fatal raven;
And when they showed me this abhorrèd pit,
They told me here at dead time of the night
A thousand fiends, a thousand hissing snakes,
Ten thousand swelling toads, as many urchins,
Would make such fearful and confusèd cries
As any mortal body hearing it
Should straight fall mad, or else die suddenly.
No sooner had they told this hellish tale
But straight they told me they would bind me here
And leave me to this miserable death.
And then they called me foul adulteress,
Lascivious Goth, and all the bitterest terms
That ever ear did hear to such effect.
And had you not by wondrous fortune come,
This vengeance on me had they executed.
Revenge it, as you love your mother's life,
Or be ye not henceforth called my children.
DEMETRIUS
    This is a witness that I am thy son.
        He stabs Bassianus
CHIRON
    And this for me, struck home to show my strength.

Titus...

slapped behind his back. Tony soaks up direction like a sponge, always ready to try something new. The key, I discover, is not to explain an idea too much, but just to suggest it, pour it in and leave it to percolate.

At these moments of deepest grief, I see Tony trawling through recent events in his life for a sense memory to draw upon. It's a painful process, painful in its honesty. Where do you look to find a recollection which can qualify?

It was not until months after Mannie's death that I saw Tony cry for his father, crumpling at the waist, reaching out to clutch me, gulping with sobs. That's what Titus does now. I recognise it. But never let on. He has filed away the physical memory of that experience and calls it up now.

We keep the rehearsal very free, setting nothing in stone until the actors have had time to chart the impact of what happens to them, and understand the emotional journeys they have to travel.

We finish the session by running the scene. It's the first time the whole company have seen it. There is absolute silence. At the end we break, and shuffle out into the light. In the courtyard people are standing around, quietly sipping cups of coffee.

Dan comes up to me. 'Look at the state of this,' he says, pulling at his T-shirt. It's wet. Wet with tears.

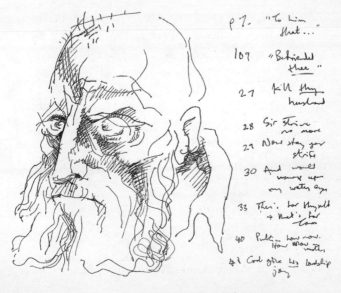

... script sketches

29

Sunday 5 March

5 a.m. I've just had a dream scripted by Shakespeare. Greg and I were on a kind of rocky shore, looking out to sea. The sky and water were lit by a bleak light, not stormy, something weirder. There were small choppy waves everywhere, but no wind on us. Suddenly I said, 'Look!' and we turned round – to find that the same seascape stretched away behind us, and on either side. We weren't on a shore, but on a tiny island. We gazed at the view. It was both frightening and beautiful.

Waking, I remember those lines in Act III, Scene 1, when Titus, who has just seen Lavinia's injuries for the first time, says:

> For now I stand as one upon a rock,
> Environed with a wilderness of sea,
> Who marks the waxing tide grow wave by wave,
> Expecting ever when some envious surge
> Will in his brinish bowels swallow him.

After yesterday's (terrific) run of Act III, Scene 1, Greg and I identified this speech as the moment when Titus starts to go mad. I asked, 'What does he mean by a *wilderness of sea*? What would that look like?'

I've just seen it.

Never mind Titus's madness, there are times when I feel I might go thither myself. The pressure is enormous. Not just the familiar pressure of grappling with one of Shakespeare's big roles, but the pressure of sharing, as co-conceiver of the production, a *wilderness* of problems surrounding us. It's not the Market's fault – why doesn't the government give them some *funding* for fuck's sake? – but every single department is understaffed, so none of them can deliver the goods. Everyone is working their socks off, yet nothing, in a way, *works*.

The Poster. We still haven't got one. And here, unlike at the RNT or RSC, posters aren't souvenirs, they're crucial advertisements. But despite us forsaking a whole afternoon's rehearsal in our first week for the necessary photographs, and despite the fact that we open in just over

Wilderness of sea

a fortnight, no poster has appeared. Plenty of excuses, but no poster.

Publicity. There isn't any. I've done a few interviews for glossy magazines, like the one in Cape Town with Dr Death, but they won't come out till after we open, and so focus more on *Cheap Lives* than *Titus.* Yet it's vital to prepare people for this show. Now. As Janet Suzman said, when she popped into the Market last week, 'The critics here are not like the London bunch. You're going to have to help them. Give them a *handle* on what you're doing.' The head of publicity here is a kind, hardworking chap, but he's new to the job. Previously he ran a take-away food shop. When we complained to Mike Maxwell about the lack of publicity, he said, 'The problem seems to be that Tony's work isn't known here.' Greg said, 'But what about his *reputation* – that's known, surely?' Maybe, but it's what I've said before. Having been excluded from the outside world for so long, South Africans are not that interested in it.

Marketing. There isn't any. No marketing at the Market. Well, to be fair, everyone in Marketing is beavering away, but nobody knows how to sell this show – normally the only Shakespeares done in South Africa are school set texts. Maybe the department is also still in shock. Our hoaxer, Deb, worked there.

Bookings. There aren't any. This is truly worrying. We could suffer the same fate as other Market shows. Greg and I saw their production of *Hysteria* recently. It's had rave reviews, and they're well-deserved. Robert Whitehead was excellent as Freud, and Dawid Minaar very funny as Dali. No audience, though. Maybe sixty, seventy people there, in a theatre which seats 450. The show is coming off a week early.

Production Team. Yes, there is one – an exceptionally committed and industrious one, yet defeated, like everyone, by the lack of resources. Props keep not arriving, or are wrong. Sometimes for bizarre reasons. They brought me an officer's baton, a real one, which had belonged to a South African Field-Marshal in the last war. I began rehearsing with it. Then one day Heidi, the ASM, said to me, 'Please, would you mind not throwing it on the floor when you go mad – it's an *antique.*' Apparently valued at several thousand rand, it had only been loaned by the military museum because someone got Jenny to phone them. ('Hello, yes, this is the daughter of Admiral Woodburne – I need your best baton please!') I said to Heidi, 'But Titus is in a terrible state, his sons are about to be executed, his daughter has just been raped and mutilated . . . he is seriously losing the plot . . . I can't just neatly lay the thing on the floor.' So then they went away and crafted one from scratch and showed it to me.

It was a stick painted brown (to represent the leather), and with some kitchen foil scrunched round the top (to represent the silver insignia). I immediately asked for the antique back and am now investigating the possibility that grief-stricken madmen don't always throw things.

Whatever problems we may have on the technical or marketing side of the show, there are absolutely none among the company. I'd say that South African actors are more energetic and enthusiastic than their British counterparts. There's huge appetite for the work. They remind me more of a dance company – there's that degree of dedication. No one's phoning it in, nobody's signalling, 'Been there, done that.' Wherever you turn, inside the rehearsal room or outside in the Market precinct, people are *busy*. Oscar and Charlton spend hours practising with their Okapi and butterfly flick-knives; Martin, Dan and Duncan endlessly revise the march steps for the triumphal entry; Gys blows and tickles away at his saxophone – twiddling as Rome burns.

And then there's me, wandering around, just trying to learn my lines . . .

The other evening, I was ordering a round of drinks in the Yard of Ale, when the barman said to me, 'Are you OK?'

I said, 'Yes. Why?'

He said, 'I keep seeing you on the pavement out there, talking to yourself.'

This production of *Titus* is going to have no villains or heroes, and it's very much to Greg's credit – it reflects his view of the world (a remnant of his Christian upbringing perhaps). Dorothy as Tamora is a million miles away from the wicked queen of stage tradition . . . the new Arden edition shows a photo of Maxine Audley in the Brook production, all bejewelled, shimmering, glacial evil, her arm out- stretched, condemning somebody with one deadly digit.

Dorothy rehearsing

Dorothy, on the other hand, is a fighter, a hunter, simply obeying the laws of nature, where mating and murder are just part of the same cycle. *Evil* doesn't come into it.

The same is true of Sello as Aaron. Another photo from the 1955 Brook production shows a blacked-up Anthony Quayle cloaked in more finery and haughtiness than Maxine Audley. This Aaron has realised his ambition: 'I will be bright, and shine in pearl and gold.' Sello, on the other hand, will never change out of his ragged clothes. No 'Rise to Power' for him. Just life at the bottom of the heap, as everyone's servant, everyone's 'boy', whether kitchen boy (he serves us coffee on the hunt) or toy-boy (for Tamora). Sello's Aaron moves with a muscular, rolling prowl, half threatening, half submissive, someone who keeps to the walls, to the sidelines, someone whom everybody else forgets to watch. (Except the audience, that is. Sello's charisma is phenomenal. I'm glad I don't have to share any scenes with him.) Like Tamora in this production, Aaron wrecks lives around him without leering or winking at the audience. It's just par for the course, the law of the jungle. A harsh urban jungle, like Jo'burg.

Every day as we drive to work, carefully following security instructions as we reach the city streets, rolling up our windows and locking our doors, the place seems full of Aarons – people whose capacity for violence stems sometimes from the need to survive, sometimes because they've forgotten any other way.

I believe we are achieving what Greg urged . . . we're 'honouring' the personal stories we heard, those films we watched, Jennifer's research.

Two weeks to go . . .

30

If you ask actors to squeeze their lemons, or pull down their bolero, and they understand what you're talking about, then you know they trained at the Bristol Old Vic Theatre School.

These are just two of the dictums of a formidable teacher and prophet of non-specialisation. His name is Rudi Shelly. I find myself recalling Rudi constantly during rehearsals.

I did a postgraduate acting course at the school, after Bristol University. And fell in love with Rudi, like generations of students before and after me. He is a perfect Puck, with a nice line in batik cravats, a boundless curiosity and a sense of humour as rude as his nose, a most erotic appendage.

Rudi is an Austrian Jew by birth, schooled in East Prussia, where he trained as a dancer. He escaped from Nazi Germany and fled first to Palestine, then to England, where he took up teaching at the BOVTS when it opened in 1946. Fifty years later he's still there, at the ripe old age of eighty-six. For at least twenty years he has described himself as the superannuated doormat of the school.

Everybody can do impersonations of Rudi. 'My Go-ord,' you drawl, shrugging the vowel up and down in time with your shoulders, and wagging your finger as if it is one of those nodding dogs you see in the backs of Ford Sierras. 'But what are you doing? This is *show* business, you must *show* me!' Countless times during my professional life I hear Rudi clucking at me: 'Greg, you are wanking in your mind, don't want to be clever!' or, 'Don't hug yourself, hug the audience.'

I spent many hours perched on a sofa, in his 'junk-shop' living-room while he played me old 78s of Hindemith, Ligeti and Javanese gamelans. The lime-green walls hung with masks and naïve paintings of summery landscapes. On his mantelpiece a colourful array of wooden penis sheaths from Polynesia, a vulgar monk with a big surprise under his cassock and clay figurines from Portugal and Latin America, handmade of course. Everything handmade. 'I am a one-man revolt against mass-production,' he always says. He loves folk art, perhaps because it reflects the elusive qualities of simplicity he tries to teach and describe.

Rudi looks for three things in an actor: a love of craftsmanship, a desire to communicate and the courage to make a fool of oneself. He taught me that theatre is not apart from life, it is a distillation of it. And he taught me about red noses.

Rudi's red-nose class went like this. He would produce a clown's red nose and offer it around the students, bidding each of us to put it on and try to make everybody laugh. Inevitably, one after the other, we would don the nose and lark about, raising hardly a titter from our peers. Then Rudi would put it on and simply carry on talking, completely oblivious of the nose. And it was hysterical. It was hysterical precisely because he ignored it. He didn't acknowledge it, as we all had done. He didn't play the nose.

'Don't play the red nose' is a note we are particularly applying to the second half of *Titus Andronicus*.

Monday 6 March

We're rehearsing the fly scene, a little scene with the soul of Samuel Beckett in a previous incarnation. Shakespeare probably wrote it much later (possibly around the time he wrote *King Lear*). It does not appear in any of the three quarto versions of the play (the paperbacks), but had to wait until the omnibus edition of the collected works, gathered together after his death.

Titus berates his brother for killing a fly. It is the last straw. Amidst all the carnage, on the very threshold of despair, Titus can endure no more violence. It's a turning point in the play. Here's how it goes:

Marcus: Alas, my lord, I have but killed a fly.
Titus: 'But'?
How if that fly had a father, brother?
How would he hang his slender gilded wings,
And buzz lamenting doings in the air!
Poor harmless fly,
That with his pretty buzzing melody,
Came here to make us merry! And thou hast killed him!

I love the image of the fly mourning his dead dad, and buzzing his lamenting 'doings' in the air. It's as if Titus is unable to think of quite the right word and suddenly invents 'doings' to fill in.

It's brilliant comic writing, with the options for laughs built in by Shakespeare. Particularly the opening short line 'But?', which is mistakenly added to the following line in some texts, losing the laugh; and the way he builds in a comic climax by pushing through from the second short line, 'Poor harmless fly', right through to the outraged exclamation in the last twelve-beat line, 'And thou hast killed him!'

Tony instinctively drives it through and nails the laughs home.

Tuesday 7 March
During the London workshop, Tony and I bumped into Guy Woolfenden at the Green Room bar one night. He was waiting to note a preview of *The Merry Wives of Windsor*, for which he had composed the music. (Guy has composed scores for the full canon of Shakespeare's plays.) He told us the following story:

Apparently, when the Oliviers were doing *Titus* in Stratford, Noël Coward came to see the show.

When they got to the scene where Lavinia writes in the sand, Vivien Leigh was so nervous that she dropped the stick. It had to be rescued and replaced, for her to continue.

After the show there was a knock on her dressing-room door and Coward appeared. He wagged his finger and said brightly, 'Butter-stumps!'

Vivien Leigh's nerves provide us with an idea. As our Lavinia struggles to master the technique, she should drop the stick. Her uncle then gently guides it back into place, prompting his angry outcry, 'Cursed be the heart that forced us to this shift.'

Titus swears to engrave the rapists' names so they will never be erased. What if Titus does this literally and grabs a rock from the ground to scratch 'Chiron' and 'Demetrius' on any available surface he can find?

Wednesday 8 March
'You can guess what they're going to call this production, already,' says Robert Whitehead. 'The Shopping Trolley *Titus*.'

He's referring to the shopping trolley which we had in the looting scene, and which we're using to bring on Titus in Act IV, Scene 3, to parody his triumphal entry.

We call this scene the Don Quixote scene. Titus gets his men to shoot arrows to heaven to appeal for justice. We're going to achieve the arrows with a selection of old crossbows fired over the heads of the audience. There won't be any bolts, just a lot of twanging.

At this point the clown enters.

Ah, Shakespearian clowns! The trouble with all Shakespeare's clowns is that like an '84 Burgundy, they don't age well. But Ivan makes this one a little Coloured pigeon fancier from the Cape Flats, a klonkie who can't say his Rs.

The danger with this scene is that we begin to play the absurdity (Don't play the red nose!), enjoy the gags and forget the story. 'What is the scene about?' we keep on reminding ourselves. Titus is looking for Justice. That objective has to be kept constantly in mind, otherwise the scene seems a silly distraction which holds up the action.

Thursday 9 March
Gales of laughter in the ladies' loo today.

We're rehearsing Act IV, Scene 4 again: Saturninus and Tamora. Can't quite remember where the idea came from that Saturninus should be rehearsing his speech while sitting on the loo; but it certainly has its pay-offs. When the clown is ushered in and starts to address Tamora (supposing her to be the emperor), she tells him: 'Empress I am, but yonder sits the emperor.' On his throne, you might say.

Saturninus is paranoid with jealousy. He knows the citizens would rally to Lucius should he return. To see him quivering with fear and anger, having retreated to the bog, bravely but ineffectually rehearsing his attack on Titus, seems to us to capture precisely the absurdity into which the play descends in this act.

The basic situation leads to a whole host of possible gags, all of which we resist. No flushing the loo, no getting tangled in a toilet roll, definitely no toilet brush, no arrows in the backside or stuck in the toilet door. Instead we'll play the situation absolutely and totally for real.

Once we play it in front of an audience, any hint that the actors are pleased with themselves (smugly winking at the audience as if to say 'look at us, aren't we funny') will kill the scene dead. Don't play the red nose.

Daphney and Ivan are arguing. In Act IV, Scene 2, Chiron and Demetrius are waiting for news of their mother, who is in labour. Our production will fortify this with a story-telling beat by glimpsing Tamora at an upper window in the throes of childbirth, attended by the Nurse. However, Daphney, like any good midwife, adds the instruction 'Push'. Ivan, our resident purist, objects that it is not in Shakespeare.

Our percussionist, Godfrey Mgcina, has persuaded his sister to lend her baby daughter, Nana, for today's rehearsal, in order for the actors to recall the mewling-puking reality of holding a child.

We'll be using a doll in performance, concealed in a black bin bag – after all the Nurse is bringing the baby to Aaron to dispose of it.

In one and the same moment, he beholds his child for the first time *and* contemplates its execution. 'Zounds, ye whore!' he cries. 'Is black so base a hue?'

I encourage Sello to honour that thought. It's not just a throw-away. It's a moment when perhaps for the first time Aaron dares publicly to claim his rights as a human being, and a black man. It releases something. And suddenly we're blasted with his anger. A lifetime of the humiliations of apartheid, decades of his people's struggle, centuries of his race's oppression, howl up through Sello now as he delivers the line.

Shakespeare slams on the pressure now, shortening the lines from ten beats down to seven or eight, then down to four:

> *Chiron*: It shall not live.
> *Aaron*: It shall not die.

The two sons sniff around the child like a pair of hungry hyenas unaware that they are about to encounter a mountain lion. Listen to the contrast (just in the consonants and vowels) between the nipping petulance of Demetrius's line, as opposed to Aaron's powerful open roar:

> *Demetrius*: I'll broach the tadpole on my rapier's point.
> *Aaron*: Sooner this sword shall plough thy bowels up.

To make the actors really experience that contrast in their throats and mouths, I try a favourite Cis Berry exercise and make them say each line just voicing the vowels, the emotional heart of the words, and only then adding consonants.

I asked Tony in to this rehearsal last week to see what he thought of the slaughter of the Nurse. We've done it as a friendly hug which turns into a stab, as Aaron rips his scimitar-shaped panga up her spine.

Tony winced. He said it reminded him of those off-cuts from the South African news footage which we saw in the London workshops. So I knew we were OK.

Left alone, Aaron experiences new sensations of tenderness. He tells his baby that he will bring him up in the wilderness to fight, as his father has had to fight. He resolves to flee Rome and escape back to the Goths.

I was skimming through this scene in the text which appeared in the programme of the 1987 RSC production of *Titus*. (Methuen used to publish the text of all Swan shows in the programmes.) In Aaron's speech to the baby, he's meant to say:

> I'll make you feed on berries and on roots,
> And feed on curds and whey, and suck the goat.

There's a typo in this edition. It reads:

> I'll make you feed on berries and on roots,
> And feed on curds and whey, and suck the goat off.

Friday 10 March
Run the play.

We're reminded how much stamina it takes to play Shakespeare. The play runs out of steam in Act IV, as actors get tired. It's almost useless to say to an actor 'you're slow, be faster' because pace is clarity of thought.

If the thinking is wrong, or slips between the lines rather than keeping on the line, then the result from out front is bound to be a gradual loss of power. And certainly with an early play like *Titus*, Shakespeare keeps the momentum going, not just from scene to scene, but from line to line, from word to word. It has the heartbeat of a young man pounding through it, and that vigorous pulse is exhilarating.

This afternoon, we work through notes from the run, concentrating on one scene in particular. Tony's not in it, so he can go home early.

We go back over the discovery of Lavinia in Act II. Dale is having difficulty remembering the words of the big speech. He's very tired, playing Dr Yahuda in *Hysteria* every night after rehearsals. He keeps scrubbing his face with his hand to wake himself up. But I'm sure that's not it. He doesn't usually have any difficulty with lines. Sometimes this crops up if an actor is unhappy with a scene. We keep working on it.

We're in the middle of the speech. We're making progress. I tell Dale only to move on to the next line when he has to, when he has fully realised the impact of the last one, until his mind can comprehend the atrocity before him. I want him to explore the sensations of outrage, anger, incomprehension, pity, physical revulsion, the extremity of grief. It is quiet, breathless, intense, painstaking, difficult, emotional . . . and then somebody walks through the room whistling.

> And what he is that now is leapt into it.
> Say, who art thou that lately didst descend
> Into this gaping hollow of the earth?
> MARTIUS
> The unhappy sons of old Andronicus,
> Brought hither in a most unlucky hour,
> To find thy brother Bassianus dead.
> SATURNINUS
> My brother dead! I know thou dost but jest;
> He and his lady both at the lodge
> Upon the north side of this pleasant chase;
> 'tis not an hour since I left them there.
> MARTIUS
> We know not where you left them all alive,
> But, out alas! here have we found him dead.
> _Enter_ Tamora, with attendants, _Titus Andronicus_
> _and Lucius_
> TAMORA Where is my lord the King?
> SATURNINUS
> Here, Tamora, though grieved with killing grief.
> TAMORA
> Where is thy brother Bassianus?
> SATURNINUS
> Now to the bottom dost thou search my wound.

It's one of the Market's casual workers. Nobody's told him to go round the other way. Perhaps he's forgotten. For weeks I've been asking for some sort of partition to be erected in the rehearsal room. I blow, and the poor guy jumps out of his skin. I'm beginning to behave like some colonial bwana!

31

Friday 10 March, Afternoon

Greg doesn't need me for the rest of rehearsals. I feel edgy. Both tense and bored. We're too close to the opening – the only thing my body knows how to do at the moment is *work*. So what am I going to do with the next few hours, suddenly free?

I wander through the Market. Mabel and Agnes are cleaning, as always. An abiding image is of them, with buckets and brooms, touring round the building's empty, dusty corridors and cleaning, cleaning, cleaning, like people trying to sweep sand out of a desert.

I catch a taxi back to the house in Greenside.

This morning's run was OK, but – damn! – we've lost our way with Act III, Scene 1, the big grief scene. We cracked it a couple of Saturdays ago, just by taking a wild, unprepared tumble at it. With all its talk of death – and Dad's still fresh in the air – and with Jenny's performance – her research has produced shockingly real stuff – I had no problem unlocking the real emotions needed. You can't bluff it. Well, you can, but the scene becomes boring, an exercise in self-indulgence. So it's essential to really go for it. Which we did that Saturday. And the scene worked.

But how to keep reproducing the emotion?

It's why acting is so much easier in movies than the theatre. You only have to do it *once*. Or maybe go to a few takes.

When I started out as an actor, my heroes were, as I've said, the great character actors: Olivier and Sellers, or Alec Guinness in the Ealing films. But now I've become as interested in another side of acting, what the Americans call Method Acting . . . actually, I've never quite understood what that is . . . but what I mean is a kind of acting where you invest – personally, passionately – in the part and the play, and use emotional recall to make the moments of sorrow, joy, fear, etc., completely real. Instead of Method Acting, it could just be called good acting.

Perhaps because of a degree of reserve in the British character, actors in the UK don't always do this kind of acting and audiences are forced to sit through endless scenes where the emotion is presented at arm's length, rather than experienced.

Fiona Shaw in "Electra"

I think Market Theatre actors have more immediate access to their feelings. The shows born of apartheid (which I've heard some whites sneeringly dismiss as *protest theatre*), shows like *Woza Albert!* and *Sizwe Banzi*, were always too close to the bone to hold at arm's length.

There are, of course, exceptions in the UK, and they mostly tend to be female. Judi Dench, Vanessa Redgrave and one or two others – above all, Fiona Shaw. In the space of one year, 1992, I sat in two different theatres, watching *Electra* at Riverside, then *Hedda Gabler* at the Playhouse, and both times was stunned by what I saw. Two human beings in unspeakable trouble. As we've all seen in news bulletins: whether reports from Bosnia, Northern Ireland, South Africa, or press conferences where a mother appeals for the return of her abducted child. Fiona Shaw inhabited Electra and Hedda totally. No cheating. In a way, no *acting*. The real thing.

How did she do it night after night?

Anyway, that's what's needed for Act III, Scene 1 and I had it briefly, and maybe it'll come back, but what the fuck do I do in the meantime?

Blame Greg, maybe.

The other day he fixed the moves a bit too much for my liking. The mad scrabble round the stage as Titus tries to comfort Lavinia. He said it was becoming one big mess. Well, perhaps, but at least it kept surprising me and Jennifer. In real life, big emotions always *surprise* us.

We'll get it back, I must keep believing that . . . the untidiness, the emotion, everything . . . we'll get it back.

32

Friday 10 March, Evening
Things are going from bad to worse.

I realise that this is not the RSC or the National Theatre, but I'm unprepared for the level of inefficiency which dogs us at every step in this place. It is exhausting.

This afternoon's fracas about the partition has lead to promises that one will be erected for the last week. I'll believe it when I see it. An upper level has been sorted out above the ladies' toilet, for Titus's study, but it's choking with dust. A family of cicadas have taken up residence in the rafters somewhere, and because the room is so gloomy they chirrup away all day as if it is midnight. A large mouse (which might actually be a small rat) keeps popping out from the stack of theatre seats behind me and making my spine judder, and we had to stop the run for twenty-five minutes this morning because it rained so hard it sounded like a herd of elephants gumboot dancing on the roof.

Heidi has found a pair of highly strung pigeons for us to rehearse the clown scene (they won't be used on stage); but they haven't yet solved more vital props like Lucius's pistol. What props they have found get distributed untidily all around the room, so in advance of the run, and as tactfully as I could, I demonstrated how a prop table should be laid out, with a taped section labelled for each prop.

The body bags in Act I keep ripping, and we keep running out of Elastoplast to bind up Titus's and Lavinia's hands. I'm told that every chemist in Johannesburg is out of stock, and it's too expensive anyway. So our Titus is getting grumpy, understandably grumpy, but grumpy nevertheless. And now my stage management team have stopped talking to each other.

Jennifer has been to the hairdresser three times to have her hair dyed, and they still can't remove the henna. She's meant to look like Grace Kelly, not a satsuma. The eternal flame still looks like an old wok (perhaps because it *is* an old wok). The dead emperor's body looks like a wrapped shop dummy (ditto). And despite long hours of gallant welding and soldering in the workshop, the triumphal jeep still looks like Chitty-

Chitty-Bang-Bang; and we have to continue wheeling Titus around in an old sound amp dolly.

The net for the fall into the pit has not arrived so the boys have never rehearsed their stunt; the meat-hook hasn't been hung, nor the ankle straps found, so Oscar and Charlie can't try out hanging upside down by their feet for the slaughter; and the rope ladder hasn't been rigged, so Titus can't practise coming down it with one hand. All this means that when we come to a run, like this morning, I keep having to interrupt it and say, 'And this is where that is meant to happen . . .'

I don't know what to do about Dumi's synthesiser. Either it or Dumi seems to have a defective memory. Every time we get to a music cue I hear something I've never heard before.

The pigeons sit on their perch looking miserable and are beginning to smell.

The publicity is frankly a joke and Barney wants me to take time out in the middle of my technical rehearsal to explain to a few key critics what the show is all about, and perhaps 'run a scene or two'. And now, *now*, I've just been told we've lost our lighting designer. Nobody can tell me why and he's not answering his phone. There don't seem to be any other lighting designers available in the whole of southern Africa.

I get back to leafy Greenside this evening to be told by our landlord that yesterday, three doors away, two black youths walked up to a man as he was parking in his driveway, held a gun to his head, told him to get out of his BMW and drove off in it. Although no self-respecting mugger would be seen dead in our grubby Ford Fiesta, I nevertheless double-lock the gates behind me. Laddie and Grunter lollop up to say hello but I shove them out of the way grouchily. They bear no resemblance to the slavering, rabid hound on the 'Keep Out' sign on the gate. We might as well be protected by Pluto and Goofy.

Tony has been sitting by the pool all afternoon going over his lines. Titus has a third of the play off and I have to rehearse the rest some time. But he gets tetchy when he's not rehearsing and is feeling isolated because the phone in the house has been cut off again for no discernible reason and the mobile we've been given requires a password which nobody seems able to recall. Tony has a long list of concerns to chat through from the run. I just need a few moments' silence to sit by the pool, with a gin and tonic, and watch the ibis hadedah their way home to roost on the roofs across the way.

There's no food in the house. The only time Tony ever tried cooking he let a pan of potatoes boil dry until they disintegrated and claimed they had 'self-mashed'. But surely he could have got something ready. Opened a can, something! He may be a white Jewish South African brought up with people to do all that sort of thing for him, but that's no excuse. In all honesty, as I had the car, I had agreed to pick up a take-away, but with other things on my mind I'd forgotten. However, I am damned if I'm going to admit it. We order a home-delivered pizza. They're about as tasty as old jiffy bags, but I can't be bothered to go out again.

The weather has turned from the blistering hot days we enjoyed when we arrived. It's a shame, because I could do with a swim to clear my head. It's all the fault of the Queen, who starts her official visit in a week's time. She's sent her English weather on ahead.

In fact, the British High Commissioner has invited us both to attend a reception to greet their majesties. But it's on the day scheduled for the dress rehearsal so we can't go. Now Tony has also been commanded to attend a private reception on the royal yacht *Britannia*. It's a great honour, since there are only forty guests. 'It would mean flying down to Durban and staying overnight,' he muses.

I can't believe it, he's actually wondering whether he can squeeze it in. Trying not to sound as if it's just sour grapes because I haven't been invited, I tactfully remind him that as it coincides with our first preview, he may be needed.

There's nothing on TV, apart from tired American soaps with double-barrelled titles like *The Bold and the Beautiful, The Young and Restless* (what next? – *The Old and Incontinent*). They're all power-dressing and pectorals, and they make *Acorn Antiques* look slick. The home-grown South African soaps seem to ape them, although there's one decent one called *Egoli*, which is set here in Johannesburg, the City of Gold. We did join the local video store in Greenside, but when we tried to fit the tape into the machine above the telly, we realised it was actually the receiver for the M-Net channel. This means we can get CNN, but America is still obsessing about the O. J. Simpson trial and the rest of the world may as well have stopped turning.

Flop down in front of a vintage episode of *Birds of a Feather*, of which South African TV seems to be doing a serious retrospective. But Tony wants to talk. The food arrives. Can hardly distinguish the pizza from its cardboard box, but we go back out to the terrace to eat it anyway.

He starts running over his concerns. When are we going to integrate the 'dump life' properly? What about the hand–chopping? Are the pigeon shadow puppets going to work? And what about that bit in Act III, Scene 1 when . . .

At the end of a day like this, you need somebody you can let off steam with, somebody who'll be supportive and sympathetic, someone to bitch *with* you, not *at* you.

I can't quite remember what happened next, but I do recall wondering whether the dinner plate was part of a set, whether the glass went into the pool, and being amazed at quite how many pieces a cut-crystal salt cellar can explode into.

I don't know how Michael and Dulcie, or Timothy and Prunella do it, but as I storm my way to bed, slamming several doors behind me, I make a mental oath that if we should ever work together again, which at this point seems very unlikely, that we'll never, *never* bring work home with us.

33

Sunday 12 March
We spent yesterday afternoon combing the lawn, flower beds and pool, with me saying things like, 'Crockery in a swimming pool – do you know how dangerous that is?' or 'A fork in the grass – the dogs could've stepped on this!' I got so much mileage out of it that I'm tempted to hide some more things round the garden, so that I can keep discovering them – whenever the need arises, in our own status game.

Anyway, this morning, with the pool cleaned and Selina away at church, and Laddie and Grunter locked in the backyard (an audience wasn't welcome), we had a great swim, making up.

Evening. The Market has won some award and there's a ceremony-celebration at the theatre. It's the last place we feel like going tonight, the last thing we feel like doing, but I guess it would be impolite to stay away.

The place is buzzing. The invitation said, 'Formal – black tie or traditional', so Lesley Fong is looking magnificent in a green kaftan, and Paulus, grinning away, is unrecognisable in a DJ.

Mike Maxwell explains to us that the award, called the Jujamcyn, from America is very prestigious (and worth a lot of cash). Previously given to the American Repertory Theatre and the New York Shakespeare Festival, this is the first time it's going to a theatre outside the States. All the Market stalwarts are here, Mannie Manim, Janice Honeyman, even Athol Fugard.

'How's *Titus*, chaps?' Athol asks us.

Greg says, 'Well, we've got one or two technical hitches . . .'

Athol gives a small, grim smile of recognition.

'. . . but a wonderful cast,' Greg adds. 'They could grace any stage in the world.'

'I'm very proud to hear you say that. I can't wait to see it.'

I can't wait for him to see it either. Athol has never seen my work and I'd like him to. His performance as Johnnie in the original production of *Hello and Goodbye* in 1965 (directed by Barney) was one of the only examples of fine theatre acting I saw before leaving SA. It inspired me to go into the profession.

Inside the Market auditorium, the Soweto String Quartet, dressed in zebra tuxedos, are playing their hit, 'Zebra Crossing'. As they finish, John Kani bounds onstage and makes another of those speeches of his, full of wit and insight (they seem off-the-cuff, and are done without notes) and then invites the chairman of Jujamcyn to join him. Mr Binger is a tall, elderly gentleman, who looks and sounds a bit like Jimmy Stewart. Jujamcyn is presenting the award he says, 'to recognise the Market Theatre's demonstration that art can change society'.

Now Barney goes up to accept the award. Unlike John, he's not adept at public speaking. He produces a few scruffy sheets of paper and, with a little shiver in his voice, apologises that he's going to read his speech.

I sink in my seat. I'm still angry with Barney over his strange, cold greeting when we arrived, and I'm angry with the Market over a hundred different things, so I'm not really in the mood to hear its history read out by someone with the stage presence of a gnat.

But within seconds, I realise I'm experiencing something unique. Both the speech and the spirit of its author:

'. . . I believe we live in a place of miracles. I haven't seen a burning bush, except in a veld fire or two. I've never followed a travelling star or even fantasised a flying saucer. But that's not a complaint. The miracles that interest me are not wonderful or delightful, or much to do with the divine. The ones that I like best are those that give evidence of the grace that is in all things. They're the hardest to come by in a world as tormented as ours. There might be miracles in heaven, but I suspect that they're not nearly as rewarding as miracles in hell. Every adult South African sitting in this auditorium was born into an insane world. Insane because it denied and confused mankind's greatest gift, the equality of our humanity. We were forced to behave as if cultural differences between human beings were stigmas, separations, that curiosity and passion could be crimes, and we were denied the dignity of even comprehending the lives being lived beside us.'

By now I'm bolt upright in my seat.

'. . . And here's a miracle. Despite our beginnings, there's our people. Multiple, vivid, absurd, treacherous, generous, adventurous, divinely pragmatic, and always capable of our sound of survival – laughter. We who began the Market, did it out of love for this.'

His voice still trembling slightly, like the paper in his hands, he turns to Mr Binger:

'You honour us for what we have been. I hope it is also for what we are. We undertook a task in the terrible year of 1976 that many called, according to their prejudices, absurd, criminal or super-human, which is my preference. It's not a vanity. Camus said that tasks are called superhuman when men take a long time to complete them. We're very far from completion. Our journey is as various and difficult and extraordinary as any that strive for dignity and clarity in this country at this time. Thank you for helping us to continue.'

As the audience applauds, I look at Greg and find him shaking his head. 'What?' I whisper.

'To think', he answers, 'how we've been moaning for the last couple of weeks. About the Market. We're so lucky to be here. Privileged!'

Afterwards, we congratulate Barney and ask if we could have a copy of the speech. He looks surprised, but says he'll arrange it.

Nearby, two of his closest friends are beaming with pride. Vanessa Cooke, who runs the Lab, and Bruce Laing, our Alarbus/Publius.

Bruce is a lodger in Barney's house, and tells me that Barney spent hours last night writing the speech. At about 3 a.m., when Bruce got home, after his usual Saturday night *jawl* (rave-up) at Bob's Bar, Barney was just finishing and asked if he could read it to Bruce. 'So then,' Bruce says, 'he read it out. A bit nervously, like back in there. At the end I had, y'know, my jaw hanging open. He said, "D'you think that's OK?" And I said, "Ja, Barney, I think that's probably OK." '

34

Monday 13 March
'One week to go!' Robert Whitehead smiles darkly. Robert is meant to be my honorary assistant director, but since he's just been playing Freud in *Hysteria* it's been more like having a friendly psychiatrist sitting behind me. *Hysteria* finished on Saturday and he's shaved off his bleached hair and beard. Now he looks like Picasso.

Hysteria's early finish should be a huge advantage for us. It means that we can get the set in to the theatre a week ahead of schedule and possibly even have some extra rehearsal time on the stage at the end of the week.

Today we're hanging Sello.

We've finally managed to get a rope and Ivan expertly slings it over one of the rafters in the rehearsal room, dislodging a cloud of black dust.

In Act V, Scene 1, Lucius comes face to face with the man responsible for maiming his father. Should he seek revenge? Should he take the law into his own hands?

'Instead of hanging him, why don't we put a tyre round Aaron,' someone suggests, 'and douse him with petrol?' There's a little argument. Some people think it's gimmicky. Others think we should try. I suggest we continue with the hanging.

Somebody works out how to tie a non-slip noose and puts it over Sello's head. Suddenly the central image of the scene comes into focus. It's shocking.

'It's just like those old photos of blacks being hanged in the Deep South,' says Martin. He's right. Necklacing is a system of execution used by blacks on blacks, but this is a lynch mob. And it gets more like the Ku-Klux-Klan, when Lucius instructs the Goths to hang Aaron's baby in front of its father's face.

Martin allows no flicker of sentimentality to invade Lucius. He is playing him as a hard-line man of war, reactionary, racist, his father's son. Does Lucius actually mean to sacrifice a child? It oddly shifts our sympathies towards Aaron. Now we see him as a parent fighting for the life of his child. The audience are thrown into a moral turmoil, forced to use their own judgements, to view the dilemma from 360 degrees. That's part of Shakespeare's genius.

Now the text goes into rhyme and I urge Martin to enjoy them. Lucius is taunting his captive with the rhymes, pushing Aaron to see if he will crack:

> *Lucius*: A halter, soldiers! hang him on this *tree*
> And by his side his fruit of *bastardy*.
> *Aaron*: Touch not the boy, he is of royal *blood*.
> *Lucius*: Too like the sire for ever being *good*.
> First hang the child, that he may see it *sprawl*
> A sight to vex the father's soul *withal*.
> Get me a ladder.
> *Aaron*: Lucius, save the child.

The rhymes stop. Aaron cracks. He begins to brag of his deeds. Sello and I have great difficulty with the tone of these speeches. Aaron seems to be hammering nails into his own coffin. Has he gone mad?

It then strikes us that he is lying. Why? Because he is performing the role that white society expects him to play – the devil. Since medieval days the devil has always been pictured as black. To Sello, this psychological profile seems accurate and familiar.

Dan is certainly making the most of his cameo role as Aemilius.

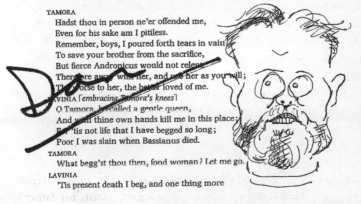

TAMORA
Hadst thou in person ne'er offended me,
Even for his sake am I pitiless.
Remember, boys, I poured forth tears in vain
To save your brother from the sacrifice,
But fierce Andronicus would not relent
Therefore away with her, and use her as you will;
The worse to her, the better loved of me.
LAVINIA [*embracing Tamora's knees*]
O Tamora, be called a gentle queen,
And with thine own hands kill me in this place;
For 'tis not life that I have begged so long;
Poor I was slain when Bassianus died.
TAMORA
What begg'st thou then, fond woman? Let me go.
LAVINIA
'Tis present death I beg, and one thing more

Aemilius arrives in the Goth camp to invite Lucius to the parley. Dan is exploring the comic potential of the Roman envoy's discomforture, edging his way among the hunkering warriors in the Goth hill camp.

Once he's dressed in a sober suit and homburg hat, gripping his attaché case in one hand and hanky in the other, mopping his forehead and thick red beard, it will look for all the world as if someone has sent Lytton Strachey as UN envoy to Bosnia.

Tuesday 14 March
There's a gift from Barney in the office this morning. It's a photocopy of his acceptance speech at the Jujamcyn do – signed (as if it were a limited edition) with his love. I'm delighted that he remembered. Like Titus, someone should 'go get a leaf of brass, and with a gad of steel' engrave his words and put them up somewhere to remind the Market of its mission.

We make a breakthrough with the Revenge scene today. It's seemed a bit of a slog up to now: Tamora pretending to be one of the Furies and Titus going along with it, while indicating to the audience that he knows who she really is all along.

'It seems to contain a tension factor of nil,' Tony complained. 'Which is a pity at this point in the play, just before the climax.'

Today's discovery is that Titus *wants* to believe she is Revenge. He slips in and out of sanity. He recognises her as Tamora one minute, the next as Revenge. Titus must be so hungry for revenge that he goes on a giddy trip of 'Is she? Ain't she?' and he can take the audience on the same ride, judging his sanity: 'Is he? Ain't he?'

Tony has extended the idea of Titus scrawling the names of his daughter's rapists all over the set to carving messages into his own flesh, attacking his disabled arm with a knife. 'Witness this wretched stump, witness these crimson lines.'

The idea comes from one of the most harrowing violence stories told us in the workshop. One of the group spoke about a friend who began mutilating herself regularly, filling a washbasin with her own blood.

Titus's mania for revenge prevents him from understanding the needs of his daughter. Jennifer discovers and mines a rich vein here. Having researched rape, she decides that Lavinia would be traumatised by having to face her attackers and is not only reluctant to assist her father in their slaughter, but repulsed by it. She is so revolted that she rejects her father. It is a rejection he cannot comprehend.

Wednesday 15 March
The birdies have arrived.

Terry Hands (who always lights his own shows) taught me how useful these powerful little spotlights could be to pinpoint or highlight a particular moment. When we discovered that they don't have birdies over here, Tony came to the rescue and offered to buy a set and donate them to the Market. Today they arrived from London.

The pie scene.

Titus serves up Tamora's sons baked in the pie. We imagine that he has instructed his private army of strays to set up the banquet on the dump where they live. So the banqueting table is an old door supported on crates, the chairs are car seats and boxes and they put up a string of festive light bulbs for the occasion.

Lavinia has been curled up in a corner of the dump, pining like a sick dog (Giulietta Masina in Fellini's *La Strada*). Her relationship with her father has ruptured badly. She is horrified that he has turned into the same kind of torturer as her attackers. He is weary of her crippled whimpering presence. She now emerges to watch Dad.

Titus serves out the pie (tricky with only one hand) to the emperor, and his empress. Tamora, having learned very little Roman etiquette, tucks straight in.

'Surely Marcus would expect a bit of pie,' says Dale. 'Marcus doesn't know what's in it!'

Very good observation. We mustn't anticipate the story there. So we build in a moment of suspense as Marcus hands out his plate to be served. If Titus does not serve him he will give the game away. To prevent her uncle being served, Jennifer, as Lavinia (who *does* know about the pie), hurls herself forward and flings the pie to the floor.

Titus throws himself into action and embraces his daughter, attempting to calm her down. As he rocks her backwards and forwards, he slowly waltzes her round. I get Dumi to reprise the tinkling waltz tune we heard when Lavinia 'gave up her spirit'. A tune we now refer to as the rape waltz. Titus suffocates her in his embrace and she slips quietly to the floor. It is all over almost before anyone has noticed.

Some of the company worry *why* Titus kills his own daughter. Tony's solution is simple. 'She's a sick dog,' he says. 'She needs to be put down.'

Tony has been concerned that Shakespeare has given Titus no death speech. But it seems to me that he does have a final speech. It comes now. Titus has killed his daughter, he has nothing left to live for. The rest of it, the revelation of the pie filling, the retribution which must follow, is merely something that has to be done.

Tony takes up the note and illuminates the moment. As Titus lays out his daughter's twisted limbs, Tony howls out his grief like an animal:

> 'I am as woeful as Virginius was
> And have a th-*ouwwwww*-sand times more cause than he
> To do this outrage . . .'

then he collapses with the words '. . . and it now is done'.

The emotion seems so real. He's trawling his memory again. Perhaps it's the thought of his father, lying dead on the carpet of that Israeli hotel, those strangers leaning over his body trying to revive it. Perhaps.

As the tragedy dawns on the guests, they back away appalled, except for Saturninus. He demands to know the reason for her execution. Shakespeare uses rhyme again, a whole cataract of rhymes, to create tension and drive the text on to its inevitable revelation:

> *Saturninus*: What! was she ravished? Tell who did the *deed*.
> *Titus*: Will't please you eat: Will't please your highness *feed*?
> *Tamora*: Why hast thou slain thine only daughter *thus*?
> *Titus*: Not I, 'twas Chiron and Deme*trius*.
> They ravished her and cut away her *tongue*,
> And they, 'twas they that did her all this *wrong*.
> *Saturninus*: Go fetch them hither to us presently.
> *Titus*: Why here they are both, baked in this pie.

You can feel the sense of disappointment in that last couplet. It's a sensational revelation, but somehow it misfires because there's no rhyme. In Shakespeare's day, 'presently' obviously did rhyme with 'pie'. It would be arch and silly to try and force the rhyme, and pronounce the word 'present*lie*'.

In order to preserve Shakespeare's intention, we change Saturninus's line to 'Go fetch them hither to us, bring them *nigh*'. A little clumsy, perhaps, but it maintains the breathless ding-dong rally at this point in the play and I doubt anyone will notice the substitution.

Thursday 16 March
Our hopes that we might be able to rehearse on the stage in the theatre

by this time seem to be evaporating. Things have got behind.

The end of the play is still a problem. After the multiple deaths, the winding up seems either too long or too abrupt.

In the later tragedies, Shakespeare wraps the play up in twenty or thirty lines. In *Titus* he excels himself with five times that length.

Lucius commands his soldiers to stay behind and bury Aaron up to his chest, and leave him to starve. We'll retain this as the last image of the play; aware that this might be politically sensitive, and there might be those who would read Aaron's fate not as a harsh sentence imposed on a man brutalised by oppression, but as a generic punishment to be meted out to his race.

We decide to temper the image by moving Marcus's plea for healing to this point. After such appalling tragedy on both sides, this healing must be the prevailing priority.

> Oh let me teach you how to knit again
> This scattered corn into one mutual sheaf,
> These broken limbs again into one body.

These words hold such resonance in South Africa, where the new political orthodoxy is reconciliation. But in order for this unifying idea to be meaningful, justice must be done, and be seen to be done.

We want Marcus's words to resonate with the audience, for them to hear the echo. I'm anxious that we go no further. Otherwise we would be twisting the play too far, creating specious parallels and appear to be trying too hard to apply a relevance which the play does not admit; destroying the text's application to the universal by limiting its relevance to the specific.

We have chosen to do the play in this way in order to liberate it, to make it accessible and relevant not in specific, but in general terms. We are certainly not presenting allegory. We are localising the play by highlighting its themes of racial tension and cycles of violence.

Friday 17 March
Final Run.

I'm expecting all the staff to be present: my designers and production managers etc. But they are all too busy getting ready for the Technical on Monday. However, Wesley France, whom we have persuaded at the last minute to step in as our lighting designer, is going to watch the run. He's trying to get to grips with the play. And Nadya, the set designer, is watching too.

The run is OK. There's still a lot to do. But Nadya comes up afterwards to tell me how much she liked it, and how moved she is. When I tell the company, they are startled.

'Nadya liked it!' someone says. 'Wow, Nadya never likes *anything*!' So I regard that as high praise indeed.

We clear out of the rehearsal room. Funny, over the last six weeks I've become rather fond of it.

35

Tuesday 21 March
I stare into the mirror, frowning.

I mean, you wake up in the morning . . . you're just *you* . . . you get up, you go to the loo . . . still just *you* . . . you go into the bathroom, you pass the mirror and then you freeze . . . it's no longer *you*.

The man staring back at me has short white hair and a massive white beard. In the beard, under the mouth and on the cheeks there are streaks of yellow and brown, tobacco colours, like you see in the facial hair of old men . . . and even some strands of the dark brown hair that this chap must've had as a younger man.

Hang on, *I* had dark-brown hair yesterday.

(But was it yesterday? How long have I slept?)

Heidi warned me this would happen. This shock.

Heidi Fleish works for Goldwell, the hair cosmetics people. It was she who transformed Robert Whitehead into Freud, and it was she who transformed me yesterday from a youngish-looking forty-five-year-old to this weathered old man in the mirror.

The job took four hours and wasn't pleasant. Heidi explained that the ammonia bleach is only designed for the hair, not the face, and that my skin might not like it. In fact, apart from a slight prickling sensation, my skin was fine. It was my nostrils and eyes that didn't like it – the ammonia fumes encasing my head. 'Won't do you any harm,' said Heidi, who is a glamorous, self-satirising *kugel*; '– it's not a train crash.' So I sat fanning myself with a Goldwell brochure, while Heidi applied more and more of a foamy mauve gunge, and then left it to, as she said, 'cook'. This literally seemed to happen. The heat from my head caused the mauve gunge to swell and flop like dough. It looked like I was melting. Like I was one of those coloured candles after a long party.

But I was thrilled by the end result. Perfect for Titus. Makes me look so old, so Afrikaner, so Christian.

Now all I have to do is learn to live with it for the next few months.

After this morning's shower, I go into the kitchen, where Selina is washing dishes. She was in bed by the time we got back last night, so she hasn't seen my transformation yet. Now she glances round, looks at me, then turns back to her work without a word. I'm puzzled. Why wasn't she more surprised? And why didn't she say 'Morning Tony' like she usually does?

Then it dawns on me. She hasn't recognised me.

'Hi, Selina, how are you today?' I say.

Hearing a familiar voice, she turns again. Her customary expression (as though frowning into sunlight) breaks into one of disbelief, horror even – before she starts to laugh, giving her whoop.

'It's Tony . . . ! Hooo . . . ! Greg, come quick! . . . look at Tony! What thing has happened to him? Hooo . . . !'

Afterwards, Greg says to me, 'But if she didn't know it was you, who did she think it was – walking into the kitchen, just wearing a dressing-gown, at seven-thirty in the morning?'

I shrug. 'Some elderly party you'd picked up for a night of wild abandon?'

The Tech starts . . .

The Market only has two dressing-rooms, one for guys and one for gals, and for some reason they've put me in with the gals. Greg says it's for reason of numbers, but I'm not convinced. Anyway, for the next two months I'm an honorary gal. An improvised curtain hangs down the middle of our dressing-room, for modesty. My side has also to serve as the stage managers' room, so they're busy improvising another curtain. I ask them please not to. With all this hanging material I feel I'm in a tent; a speciality act in some kind of circus.

(Maybe not a million miles from the truth.)

Today, adding my new facial look – the old Boer – to the military costume, pleases me hugely.

In the tea-break I change back into my civvies and stroll outside for some fresh air. A woman comes up to me and asks for a job at the Market. I take a moment to work out what's going on. It's the white beard. She thinks I'm Barney Simon.

Titus (before)

Titus (after)

Wednesday 22 March
The Tech continues . . .

Greg had to go in first thing. I arrive at the theatre mid-morning. The auditorium is in darkness, as Wesley plots the shadowy forest lighting. I'm fumbling my way down the stairs when Greg notices me. He smiles. This is unusual to see these days. The Tech is in a terrible mess. Despite the lead start we got when the last week of *Hysteria* was cancelled, we're now hopelessly behind. Usual story. Underfunding, understaffing. The two production managers, Dean and Richard, are working round the clock. Literally. They stay here till the early hours, maybe grab three or four hours' sleep and then start again – but there's only so much that a production team of two can do for a show as big as this. At the National, say, there would be dozens of people involved; whole departments of builders, carpenters, electricians.

Anyway, there's Greg smiling at me this morning . . .

He holds up a parcel. A Fed-Ex parcel. Intrigued, I make my way along the row to him. The parcel clearly contains a book. I glance at the name of the sender. Little, Brown. My London publishers.

My God, this is my book.

This is *Cheap Lives*.

I've been so absorbed in *Titus* that I forgot it was due.

Greg whispers to Wesley, 'Excuse me a moment' and follows me out into the foyer.

The next sensation is one of the best I know. Seeing your new book for the first time. Holding it. Smelling it. Even though I've designed the jacket and seen the text in proof form, there's something quite unique about this object. The sheen of it, the precision of its shape. Its absolute newness. It seems to represent the whole journey. The journey behind, of writing, when the relationship was just between me and the words, and the journey ahead, when it becomes a book in a shop. My pleasure makes everything a blur. The book melts in my hands.

Late afternoon. We're ploughing on, but it's uphill all the way. It's hard to hang on to the feeling we got at the Jujamcyn Award Ceremony last Sunday: that it's a privilege to work at this place.

I'm sitting in the stalls, waiting to do Act III, Scene 1. Jennifer has just entered for the previous scene, where Marcus discovers her after the rape. She's still wearing her first, beautiful, white, Grace Kelly-type frock of the pre-rape scenes, instead of the second, broken-down version.

Greg says 'Hold it' and strides down to the front of the stage. 'Jen, is that your second costume?'

'Well, no,' she answers. 'I'm wearing this because the other one isn't ready yet.'

Greg runs his hands through his mane of hair. 'But how are we going to do 3.1, where you're crawling around all over the place . . . ?' He turns to the Dress Circle, from where our stage manager runs the show. 'Adam, could you please ask Sue Steele to come into the auditorium.'

'Sorry,' comes the reply. 'She's gone home.'

'She's gone *home*? We're in the middle of a Tech and the costume designer has gone *home*?!'

Greg knows as well as we all do that Sue hasn't gone home to put her feet up in front of the telly, but to work. Her cutting rooms, her dyeing rooms, her storerooms, they're all there. But at this moment he needs her here and that's all there is to it. He looks round, stumped by the problem. 'But how are we going to . . . ? We can't do any of the next few scenes if Jen isn't . . .' I start to head down towards him, planning to suggest that Jen change into her jeans so that we can carry on, but I'm blown back, as from a bomb. 'FOR CHRIST'S SAKE, *NOTHING* IS READY! THE SET'S NOT READY! THE COSTUMES AREN'T . . . !'

He dashes up the aisle to the fire doors and smashes them open, suddenly presenting us with a framed picture of daylight and the outside world, the ordinary outside world where people get to do their jobs with all the necessary equipment. These same people have finished those jobs for the day and are presently strolling along the Market precinct, or having a drink at the Yard of Ale. Alongside, on the paving stones, our camouflage netting is spread out, being spray-painted. Supervised by Nadya, in conversation with Mike Maxwell.

'Nothing is ready!' Greg yells at Mike. '*Nothing*! I've just teched two acts of this play, and I'm going to have to tech most of it all over again! This is a complete fucking waste of time!'

Mike and Nadya look startled. Justifiably. A wall has just burst open and unleashed one of the Furies.

Before either can reply, Greg charges back into the theatre, forcing them to follow. Someone discreetly closes the fire doors, excluding the Yard of Ale clientele from what happens next.

Greg marches up and down the rows of seats, with Mike behind him, as though they're playing a kind of party game: catch-me-if-you-can.

'. . . The sound isn't ready, the props aren't ready . . . We can't steer the fucking jeep, we're behind with the lighting, which isn't Wes's fault, but . . . nothing is ready, *nothing*!'

(I'm starting to wonder: is Greg's explosion genuine or tactical?)

'. . . Scene after scene – we fucking crawl through them! . . . Not one scene, *not one scene*, is ready! . . . The smoke gun isn't here yet!'

Dean and Richard, our production managers, have crept into the auditorium, while our ASMs, Bradley and Heidi, peek out from the wings. Everyone is grey with exhaustion.

'Where's the eternal flame for Scene 1?' Greg is demanding. 'Not here! *Nothing* is here! We may as well . . .'

He suddenly stops, then says quietly: 'Right, I'm going for a walk round the car-park for ten minutes, then we'll discuss what we're going to do.'

When he comes back, he's very calm.

(I think it was a tactical explosion.)

'All right everyone,' he says. 'We've obviously got some problems to sort out, so I'm breaking the company for the rest of the day. Apologies if I offended anyone.' His apology surprises people more than his outburst.

Market Theatre veteran, Dale Cutts, says: 'Oh *every* director who works here blows up. We just couldn't understand why you took so long.'

And Wes says to us privately: 'When they couldn't get it together for us to work on Sunday, I rang Mike and said, "We're not going to make it, y'know, there's going to be an explosion – roundabout mid-week." '

A group comprised of Greg, self, Mike, Wes, Nadya, the production and stage management teams, hold a powwow in the theatre, bleakly lit by its working lights. Greg decides to give the evening over to the production team, so they can catch up.

'Much appreciated,' say Dean and Richard in unison, sitting on the steps of the auditorium.

Now follows a most exceptional evening.

One of the problems which has been driving Greg mad is that half the set is missing – the so-called 'dump', on either side of the stage: rubbish heaps of objects mummy-wrapped in black plastic – which has become the motif of the production. This aspect of the set isn't crucial, in terms of the action (which is why Nadya is leaving it till last) but *is* in terms of its look. Without the dump, the set appears rather featureless.

So tonight, a group of us resolve to build the dump. Some of the group are from the production – self, Mike, Nadya, Robert Whitehead –

and some are from other Market departments, like Karen Cutts, the
operations manager (Dale's wife), and the Lab's director, Vanessa Cooke.
People have heard we're in trouble and are coming to help.

We cross the precinct to the Market's administration block and climb
the stairs to the furniture and props storerooms above. These turn out to
be dusty, dim attics filled with what some might describe as junk and
others as treasures. 'This was in *The Blood Knot* I designed . . .' says
Nadya, pointing to some broken piece of furniture. 'And this was in
Sophiatown,' says Mike pointing to another.

Then we process back to the auditorium, each carrying a hat stand or
Hoover or traffic cone or bed-head and, along the way, pass Greg, who is
now sitting on one of the concrete blocks in the precinct, *sewing*. Sewing
fiercely. He's making a plausible, jointed, properly weighted doll for
Aaron's baby . . . another prop which has been driving him mad. He
smiles as we pass.

(It *was* a tactical explosion.)

Back in the theatre, we find that some of the actors have stayed behind
to help and we all set about wrapping our chosen pieces of junk in black
plastic and then giving Nadya a hand to build the junk-sculptures on
either side of the set. I fetch some beer from the Yard of Ale and some
fine wine from Gramadoelas Restaurant, Greg joins us and we work on
through the evening. It's one of the best – of this whole experience so far
– and one which gives me another insight into this place.

'It's like the old days,' Vanessa Cooke says. 'When we were in trouble,
we'd all work together. Whatever our actual jobs, we did anything to get
the shows on.'

Even the weather, which had become autumnal and chilly recently,
seemed warmer this evening, and the sunset was golden, like nostalgia . . .

Thursday 23 March
The magic of last night has vanished and things are very tense again.

We're finally able to practise the deaths of Chiron and Demetrius,
when their throats are slit as they hang upside down from a meat-hook.
The equipment is here at last. The hoisting system, the hook, and the
ankle supports for the actors.

I was expecting moon boots, as used in London gyms. Solid, well-
padded anklets, they fasten with a reassuring metallic snap and have a
curved spur on the heel to latch over the bar (or, in this case, meat-hook)
from which you hang.

Instead, due to lack of funds, Dean has had to improvise his own ver-sion. An elastic thong which goes round the ankle (apparently they use this in bungi-jumping), with a dog-clip to attach it to the meat-hook.

I don't like it. I don't like the fact that you *can* slip your foot out of the thong. In the heat of performance, say . . . in the heat of a death scene. I've experienced too many stage injuries myself (an Achilles tendon rup-turing in *Lear*, the time I fell off the rope in *Tamburlaine*) to let anyone take this risk. 'I'm sorry,' I say. 'I don't think we've cracked this and now it's too late to keep trying. I suggest we cut our losses and scrap it.' Everyone agrees, reluctantly.

As people drift off the stage, Greg says to me, 'I'm not blaming you . . . you did the right thing . . . but it makes me angry . . . it could've been a good moment . . . it was one of the moments that were important to me . . . to the production . . . it makes me *very* angry.'

'I know,' I say. 'But we've rehearsed without it, we've done all our run-through without it. Maybe it's like the hand-chopping – it's too late to impose something new. The scene has found its own rhythm now. Maybe it's Shakespeare's rhythm and we should leave him to it.'

'Yeah, maybe,' he echoes gloomily.

Re-teching Scene 1.

The main problem is that there isn't enough space in the wings to pre-pare for the triumphal entry: me in the jeep, all the Goth prisoners and my three soldier sons, who lead the procession with a slow march, which has been meticulously timed and rehearsed.

Today, Greg tries a new solution. The three soldiers will wait on either side of the wings, then scurry together as the music starts, straight into march formation. Needless to say, their drill falls apart.

'Greg,' I say from the jeep. 'I don't think we should change anything to do with the marching . . .'

'It's fine,' he says from the stalls. 'They just have to practise it a few times.'

'No. They've been doing it like this for weeks. We mustn't change it.'

'It's fine. Let's carry on with the scene.'

'You don't understand! One can't start a march formation from split-up positions!' I say, aware I'm losing my cool, then add, 'I've been in the army . . . !' – aware how silly this sounds.

'Carry on with the . . .'

'Greg!'

'*Carry on with the scene – please!*'

So . . . for the second time I sulk through Scene 1, barely audible. Half-way through, I realise that there's a small group of spectators at the back of the stalls. Among them Barney Simon and, just arrived from London, Sue Higginson.

God, I hate it when this happens. When Greg and I come to blows in front of the company. I hate it.

Later, in the car-park, when I complain to him about it, he says, 'You're crazy . . . go and ask the company . . . go ask them if their impression is of us fighting . . . they'll say no – their impression is of us in harmony . . . in perfect harmony . . . go and ask them!'

We drive home in silence.

Friday 24 March
Well, the day has dawned. The day of my professional début in my homeland.

An exhausting day.

In the morning we finish the Tech.

In the afternoon we do a dress rehearsal.

In the evening, the first preview.

Beforehand, making up in the dressing-room, I feel very emotional, imagining the moment of the jeep turning on to the stage, and of me saying the lines about re-saluting my country.

A sinister sign just before we start. Peering through a hole in the set, I'm amazed how small the audience looks. The Market auditorium has the same ghost-town feel that it's had every time we've sat in it recently, watching *Hedda Gabler* or *Hysteria*.

Anyway, the show starts . . . in darkness, with Daphney's soaring lament for the dead emperor . . . and the Roman crowd shuffles on, carrying his wrapped body . . . and the spot finds Gys following it, slowly flicking his fly whisk . . . and, in the wings, I'm climbing into the jeep, with Bradley and Heidi holding it steady . . . and onstage, Gys takes the crown, and is about to put it on, when the crowd starts baying at him and he shouts the first line, 'Noble patricians, patrons of my right!' . . . and now the cast are hurrying backstage, gathering round the jeep, shedding their *crowd* coats and scarves and hats, and preparing for their main characters . . . Dorothy and her sons are struggling into their yoke and chains and my soldier sons are pulling on their webbing and rucksacks, and bracing themselves into ramrod military stances . . . and my spine is stiffening too, along with the fingers of my left hand, holding the baton in just the way I've been taught (by Gys) . . . and Sello is leaning into the jeep, gripping the steering wheel, and Paulus is behind, holding the T-bar which also steers the vehicle . . . and now Dumi's music starts, the triumphal march music, and Lesley, as the priest, is stretching his arms wide and proclaiming, 'Romans, make way!' . . . and now we reach the cue and the soldiers scurry together and march off, and Dorothy and the yoked prisoners follow, giving the jeep a little jerk . . . and I raise my chin (thinking of Dad more than George C. Scott) . . . and Sello starts to swing the steering wheel . . . and we're heading into the light . . . and I'm aware something is wrong . . . our *angle* is wrong . . . and in the next moment we hit the back wall and scrape along it . . . and Sello and Paulus are fighting to free us . . . and downstage, the soldiers are coming to the end of their march . . . and the music is finishing . . . and I'm due to say my first line, 'Hail Rome!' any moment . . . and we can't prise ourselves off the back wall . . . and we're stuck, we're well and truly stuck.

My mind is racing.

What do I do? Speak the speech from here, or climb out?

In this split second, another thought occurs, very clearly:

I've waited twenty-seven years to step on to a South African stage, and what happens? I crash.

36

In the audience my heart stops.

A shudder ripples down my spine and my shoulder-blades crack together. I want to yell out, 'It's my fault. How did this happen?' I want to rush down and hug him, but without a pico-second's pause, Tony has abandoned the wrecked jeep, marched down to the front of the stage and, as if nothing has happened, launched into that first speech.

Immediately I begin to rehearse what to say to Tony afterwards. Be brisk: 'Good job this happened in the preview. Means we can sort it out . . . so it will never happen again.'

The rest of the preview goes by in a blur. In fact the accident has kick-started the show with a jolt of energy and the company career through it at breakneck speed.

As I poke my way backstage at the end, Sello and Paulus, who control the jeep, are ashen with apology. Though it's not remotely their fault. Despite an absolute embargo on anything being changed between dress rehearsal and first preview, they'd been given new broken-down shoes to wear. The soles gave them no purchase on the slippery stage floor, so they couldn't steer the vehicle. All they could do was watch, dismayed, as it crashed.

It's an object lesson. The reason you have a technical rehearsal is so that you can try everything out beforehand. Otherwise it's impossible to foresee potential disasters. Who would have thought changing a pair of shoes would wreak such havoc!

In the pre-show pep talk to the company I had insisted that previews were rehearsals and that things were bound to go wrong. And among the usual rallying talk about the audience being the last piece of our jigsaw, and dotting the eye of the dragon, I had also begged them not to dwell on things that might go wrong: lines they fluffed, cues they didn't get, laughs or reactions they didn't expect. I impressed upon them that they must not carry this baggage around with them, or by the end of the show they would be on their knees. Considering the magnitude of what has gone wrong, I'm proud of them for heeding that counsel so well.

I go straight to Tony's cubicle. 'I'm sorry,' I say.

'Not your fault. The rest went well,' he says. I know he's avoiding the subject. It'll bubble up some other time. Later. Unexpectedly. I feel lonely.

'Yep. We'll sort it out,' I bluster.

'Of course. Get me a gin eh?'

'Yep.'

As I trail back up the aisle, Sue Higginson gives me a thumbs up. I know she's waiting for the right moment to respond and look forward to that.

At the top of the steps Barney Simon greets me. I'm longing to know what he thought.

'Greg,' he says, 'you look like a cow, trailing its afterbirth.'

'How do you mean exactly, Barney?'

'I once saw a cow in the country, trailing its afterbirth. They had to put a stone on it. You look as if someone needs to put a stone on your afterbirth.'

'Thanks, Barney,' I say, with a baffled grin.

Saturday 25 March

Before the second preview, I take a turn around the fleamarket on the car-park outside the theatre, looking for something as a first-night present for Tony. It's good to be outside and away from everyone, and thinking of other things.

Zulu women sit on the pavement, sewing. They are wrapped in blankets, despite the hot sunshine, laboriously threading tiny coloured beads to make necklaces or bangles, traditional dolls and brightly patterned wall hangings. One lady, with a towel on her head, is making little colour-coded bead badges, known as love letters, with secret messages sewn into the pattern. Now they are even turning out bead badges of AIDS ribbons and the New South African flag.

One man sells fabrics from all over the continent. He's spread them out on the tarmac: Kuba cloth from Zaïre, pounded from the bark of trees and dyed with gardenia juice and carbon; roughly woven cottons and raffia canvas, appliquéd and embroidered in rusty terracottas, earthy madders and charcoal black; rich African colours.

There's township art on sale, an object lesson in recycling: a tin crocodile which snaps as you push it along; a flapping bird with a wonky beak; a briefcase of Coca-Cola cans; and saxophones, motor bikes and windmills made of bent wire. The vivid patterns and colours of the imbengi baskets are ingeniously twisted out of stripped telephone cables.

There are wooden fertility fetishes, coptic icons, animist bronzes, decorated calabashes, grass baskets, malachite animals and grizly iron weaponry.

I find two tiny carved masks from the Cameroons, which the man says are called passport masks. They are like the miniature cabinets and chairs which itinerant carpenters used to take around with them in England, to prove their skills in craftsmanship. One of them has a chalky face and a prim smile, the other has a long, thin, miserable expression and looks like Stan Laurel. They could be Comedy and Tragedy. I buy them for Tony. I can't know what significance they originally had, what spirits they manifest, what dreams inspired them, what social function they served. They are invested with the vitality of their makers, their beliefs, their hopes, their fears. Most likely, these small masks were made as powerful charms, fostering well-being, destined for personal protection or enhancement. I adopt them, invest them with my own significance, my own hopes and fears, for Tony, for the show, for our lives together, and carry them back to the theatre in a black plastic bag.

Sunday 26 March
It's not a great day. The interview which Tony gave on his free Sunday back in Cape Town, with 'Dr Death' has appeared in today's *Sunday Times*. It goes on about how arrogant Tony is.

Dorothy phones mid-morning. She's incensed. 'I'm going to write to the paper,' she says, 'the picture this guy paints of Tony . . . I just don't recognise it, none of the company would. This isn't the man we've been working with for the past three months.'

But that's how bad reputations are built up, I suppose. Through sour little character assassinations like this one.

Then Barney phones to give me his notes. 'It's a stunning production, Greg, really. I'm not just saying that. And Antony is superb, really. I've got one or two notes. Do you want to hear them?'

Do I want to hear them? I've been dying to hear them. Barney continues, rambling around the play in quite a disjointed way. But I have been warned about this. Robert Whitehead says that Barney once told him his performance was like green smoke.

There's wheat and there's chaff, but in between the parables there are genuine insights to be gleaned.

37

Wednesday 29 March

The day of our opening night. It's a bit of a blur. Here are some impressions from the first half of it:

An overcast day, threatening storms. When HM was in the country last week, the weather was so bad they dubbed her the Rain Queen.

Mom, Verne and Joan fly up. They're staying with us.

In the afternoon, we – the *Titus* company – sit in a circle in the rehearsal room, in that dark, dirty, noisy, stuffy room (but Janet Suzman was right – you do grow to love it), and do a speak-through of the play. Incredible to think these are the same actors who stumbled through their speeches in the John Barton workshops. Today they make Shakespeare's language sound like it's second nature to them. You can understand everything – *everything*. It's wonderful: the journey they've travelled, and their appetite for it, and their joy. Sello is particularly good this afternoon, playing the part with such *passion* – sitting on the edge of his seat, tilting the chair precariously, his trouser legs so rucked up it looks like he's wearing shorts. As always, with speak-throughs, when the whole cast is gathered, I find it valuable to remind myself who my character is talking about . . . like being able to see the faces of Dan and Duncan, when the heads of Quintus and Martius are brought to me.

Daphney is late for this afternoon's call and everyone becomes worried about her. She doesn't arrive till towards the end. Turns out she's been in a car accident. Someone crashed into her from behind. She's very shaken. not so much by the accident as what happened afterwards. As she tells me, 'The other driver was a white man. The whole thing was his fault, but he jumped out of his car and shouted, "You bloody kaffir bitch!" He said it again and again. "Kaffir bitch, kaffir bitch." It shouldn't still be like that. Not in the New South Africa.'

When we finish and drift into the theatre, the foyer is crammed with trestle tables. Tonight is a big night for the Market . . .

38

Wednesday 29 March, 5.30 p.m.
After the speak-through, I pop out for some air and finish my first-night cards. I've written notes to the company. There's only Tony's to go. I try several times, but keep tearing it up. I can't seem to say exactly how I feel: how proud I am of what we've done, and how excited, how nervous, how grateful I am. So I just scribble a thank you and leave the masks to do the rest.

6.30 p.m.
We all gather together again for a vocal and physical warm-up. Everybody runs to a different part of the auditorium, from the gallery right to the back of the stalls, to get used to the size of the house. In turn, each person has to come up on stage and say one of their lines. The rest repeat it back to them. Even the musicians join in. The last one on the stage is the percussionist, Godfrey. One line has become his special favourite, and he delivers it in ringing tones: 'Zounds, ye whore!'

Godfrey

Finally we draw together and talk about the subject that's on every-body's mind. First Night means Press Night means Critics. I urge the company to face them as a company. Once we place our work before an audience, we step into a Hall of Mirrors. Some distort, some flatter and some reflect accurately what we have done. But we have, as a company, to step into that bewildering, beguiling room together, know what we think, accept praise collectively and together protect each other from unattrac-tive or painful reactions to our work. That said, we wish each other well and break.

I hate first nights. Once the half-hour has been called the director is irrelevant. If you pad about backstage you get in the way, the actors are far too busy getting ready. If you hover about front-of-house, it looks as if you are courting sympathy and the wrong people always come and give it to you.

I pace about, trying to look as if I'm going somewhere.

Out front, preparations are in full swing for the bash afterwards. Dezi Rorich, the freelance press agent employed by the Market to publicise the show, is flitting about. 'Howzit?' she says, a little flustered.

'Fine!' I lie. 'Nothing I can do about it now anyway. What are you serving for the reception? Meat pies and Bloody Marys?'

'No.' She laughs. 'Just a finger buffet.' Well I suppose that's sort of appropriate too.

It's great to have Sue Higginson around for moral support. And Jason Barnes, the production manager from the Cottesloe is here too. They buy me a drink. Which I promptly forget. Then I discover there's a VIP guest bar upstairs, slide in for another to steady my nerves and finally get to meet the real Titus. He's serving behind the bar. I take this to be a good omen.

I hob-nob politely for a moment or two. It's good to see Helen Suz-man, with her daughter; and Albie Sachs, and Judge Edwin Cameron. But I'm terrible company and I'm beginning to sweat. I wander out into the precinct and think about running away.

Some directors don't even watch the show on a first night, but I feel you have to, just as a sort of solidarity with the actors. Although the sense of impotence you experience sitting in the audience is awful. Needing to keep my escape route free, I always sit at the back.

My first 'real' first night was a production of *Romeo and Juliet* I had directed for a tour which began at the Mayfair Theatre in London. I was twenty. My sister Jo sat next to me. Every time anything went wrong (and everything did) I mangled her hand so hard, it was bruised by the interval.

The family arrive. There's Tony's mum, Marge, and Verne with Joan and her mum, Sadie. (Sadie runs the best Jewish deli in Jo'burg.) Joan and Verne present me with a severed hand made of glass beads and twisted wire, township art style; there's champagne from Tony's mum and some wine from Mic, his literary agent, and flowers. My pockets are already stuffed with a clutch of unopened cards and telegrams.

Nadya appears and presents me with a first-night medal, which consists of a ribbon bar from which hang a variety of severed limbs. Pinning it on, I nip backstage to deliver the presents to Tony. This play has brought out a ghoulish sense of humour all round. Bruce Laing is giving everyone amputated limbs ripped off Barbie dolls, and Jen's doling out rubbery lips and tongues you can eat. There are loud guffaws coming from a group of people gathered around the notice-board. A cartoon poster on the wall announces 'The *Titus Andronicus* Shameless Marketing strategy', with Shakespeare wearing a T-shirt saying 'Tarantino fan club', and advertising 'Lavinia Hand Cream'. It's from Bradley and Heidi, the ASM and DSM.

Among the other good-luck cards and messages pinned up on the wall, there's a fax from Richard Eyre and Genista McIntosh, and another from Roger Chapman.

I squeeze into the little curtained-off cubicle in the girls' dressing-room. Tony has a paint brush and some Crimson Lake. He is busy deepening his wrinkles, though tonight they probably don't need it.

39

Opening Night, 6.45 p.m.

Greg's changed into his blue suit, decorated with the brass chameleon brooch I bought for him at the craft shop in Ruthin, Wales (where Mark, his brother, lives), as well as a bizarre piece of amputee jewellery, and he's sweating. He offloads an armful of gifts and cards on to the table next to me. I won't have time to look through them all – except his – till later; I'm already behind with my make-up. Now he wishes me well, kisses the top of my head and goes. How strange to be separate tonight.

Word comes from front-of-house that we'll probably go up late. The guest of honour, Dr Ben Ngubani (Minister for Arts) hasn't arrived yet.

When I'm made-up and costumed, I do a tour of the dressing-rooms (Sello, Bruce and Paulus have created a third one, upstairs in the laundry room) to wish everyone luck. Whenever I do this, I remember being featured in the *Guardian*'s Questionnaire column. Q: On what occasions do you lie? A: On first nights, saying 'It's going to be all right.' Duncan remarks he's surprised how calm I seem. When I reach Jennifer I find that, instead of good-luck cards, she's covered her mirror with a mass of her research material. Photos of the Grozny girl, Ambrose Sibiya with his sewn-back arm, etc. 'I can hardly see myself.' She giggles. Then, without the smile, she adds, 'How am I going to do justice to all these people?'

From front-of-house, the news that Ngubani is here, but one or two other VIPs aren't. We wait. African time . . .

Back in my dressing-room I search through the cards for Greg's handwriting. His gift to me is beautiful: two miniature African masks. I've saved reading his card till now, the last moment, expecting it to trigger the emotion with which I must play Titus tonight, but it's curiously restrained. *Dearest Tones . . .* 'Cometh Andronicus bound in laurel boughs to re-salute his country with his tears.' Welcome home. And thanks. Greg. I wonder if he's disappointed with my performance? Mustn't dwell on that just at the moment . . .

The show is so late starting that my fire goes out slightly. I wasn't expecting to have trouble summoning up real emotion tonight – not with

Mom in the audience and Dad in my mind, as well as a memory of
Daphney saying, 'That shouldn't still happen, not in the New South
Africa' – but I do. And then the interval goes on for ever as well. I guess
the audience is more interested in itself than us. Anyway, I'm better in
the second half, the easy half, the mad half. And real emotion certainly
flows at the end, at Lavinia's death. When it's over, John Kani comes
onstage, and introduces Dr Ngubani, who says, 'I wish all South Africa
could see this great show.' Then he pays me a wonderful compliment.
He calls me *mdodana yesizwe*; 'son of the land'. And then he announces
that the government is giving the Market a subsidy.

At last!

A massive cheer goes up from the audience. And from us onstage. I'm
laughing and crying, and trying to clap – except that one of my hands is a
stump.

Afterwards, Greg comes backstage. He's now wearing – round his
neck – a severed hand, made of wire. We hug. I say, 'Sorry I wasn't on
top form tonight.' He laughs with surprise. 'But you were!' he says.
'What, even in the first half?' I ask. '*Specially* in the first half.' Since he
doesn't bullshit me, and since he's hardly been forthcoming with compli-
ments during rehearsals, it's perhaps another example of the fact that
actors aren't the best judges of their performances.

Now to front-of-house, which is crammed with people. Lovely to see
Helen Suzman again. As witty as ever. She's complimentary about the
production, but not the play – its violence has horrified her – so when I
mention that we're hoping to do a Sunday performance in Soweto, she
says, 'Oh don't – it'll give them ideas!' Albie Sachs hasn't stayed, and
someone says he left at the interval. Was it because of the play? John
Kani assures me that Albie, who is one of the ten judges appointed to
supervise the new Constitution, had to leave for a late-night meeting.

All this history surrounding us . . .

Barney's guest for the night is Joe Slovo's widow. (Of course, that's
why he was away from the Market when the hoax was discovered – Slovo
had just died and Barney was in mourning.)

Sue Higginson and Jason Barnes seem genuinely moved by the show.
As does another Britisher who's flown in specially – to write a piece for
the *Sunday Times* – Michael Kustow. He tells me an extraordinary piece
of British theatre news: Stephen Fry has fled from Simon Gray's new
West End play, *Cell Mates*. Without warning or explanation. This fills
me with mixed emotions: sadness for what Stephen must be feeling and

a sort of admiration. He's done what we all think about doing. (The show *doesn't* always have to go on.) What I've certainly thought about doing in the last fortnight.

Meet Jenny's mother. Says she was very disturbed by the atrocities committed on her daughter in the first half and was almost sick in the toilet during the interval, but then comforted by how my character took care of Lavinia in the second half. 'Thank you for doing that,' she says, as though it had happened in real life. I'm touched by this.

Finally get to hug Mom, Verne and Joan. They seem to have liked the show, although Mom says she wasn't at all happy with my Afrikaans accent.

Poor Mom – tonight she so wanted to show off her son, the British actor, the Shakespearian actor.

It's like the woman who came up to me at the bar after one of the previews. She was a teacher and had brought a school party, and they were all raving about the show, calling it the best Shakespeare they'd seen. 'Only one query,' she said to me. 'Why didn't you speak Shakespeare like you'd been trained?'

Hours too late, I finally composed a reply: 'Because I was trained – not at drama school, but at the RSC, by people like John Barton and Cis Berry, to believe that Shakespeare isn't an élitist artist, but a popular one. That his poetry isn't airy-fairy, but full of blood and guts. If I'd spoken Titus as you and your pupils expect him to sound – as *you're* trained – none of you would have enjoyed it half so much!'

40

3 a.m. or thereabouts

Back at Greenside, everybody's gone to bed: Tony, Marge, Verne and Joan. I've flopped on to the deep leather sofa with a single malt. Behind me, the illuminated fish tank farts a quiet stream of bubbles.

There's just me and the guppy, in a bluey-green glow. I finally read through my cards.

There's one from Ma and Pa, and a telegram from my twin sister, Ruth, not with good wishes, but with the news that I am to be an uncle again. They all seem worlds away.

I find an address for Sadie's shop in my pocket, the best Jewish deli in Jo'burg. Despite being a goy (and a gay goy at that), I swore to Sadie that with Pesach coming up, I would buy all my chopped liver and gefilte fish from her.

On the table, there's a scribbled message from Selina to say that my best and oldest friend Richard phoned this morning from London to wish me luck. He never forgets.

Then I reread Tony's card.

He always gives me a cartoon on a first night. I have a whole book of these silly little sketches, which I treasure. This time he's been too busy. I do understand. Of course. There's a note: 'Dearest Greg, such huge emotions swimming around in me today . . .'

In the public occasion of the first night our private moments have been trampled. There have been too many other people to think about or take care of and we got out of synch.

I feel oddly depressed. The play is no longer mine. And though I'll still work on it, giving notes throughout the run, I feel as if I've lost something. Perhaps Barney's right after all. I need someone to put a stone on my afterbirth.

The guppy blows me kisses and I go to bed.

PART V *The Run*

Johannesburg; March–May 1995

41

Friday 31 March
We bump into Dan outside the Market. His face is grim. 'Have you read Digby Ricci?' he asks.

'Who or what is Digby Ricci?' I ask.

'The critic for the *Weekly Mail & Guardian.*'

'Ah,' says Greg.

'It's not good, I'm afraid,' says Dan. 'Not good at all.'

We're not unduly worried. We've already had terrific reviews in the Jo'burg *Star* ('Stunning and highly theatrical evening's entertainment') and the main Afrikaans paper *Die Beeld* ('A masterpiece that can be shown to the world with pride') and, in turn, we weren't unduly excited by those. It's hard to be, when we don't know any of these critics. I mean, are they any *good* at their jobs? What are their prejudices, their tastes? In the UK there are critics I respect and those I don't, but I don't know this crowd, so they haven't the power to make my blood race or boil.

(During my career I've gone through various phases of addiction to, or abstinence from, reading reviews. For the last few years I've been in a sort of middling stage. Which basically means that Greg reads them all and only hands over the good ones. This isn't conceit – it's self-preservation. Recreating a performance night after night in the theatre is difficult enough without a load of abuse banging around in your head. But for *Titus*, as co-conceiver of the production, I've resolved to read them all.)

Dan is clearly upset by the *Weekly Mail* review. He's fiercely loyal to the production, and to the *Weekly Mail*. That paper is a sort of journalistic version of the Market. During the bad old days, it bravely criticised the insanity of South African society and became a symbol of decency and honesty. But, like the Market, its role is no longer clear in the New South Africa and, like the Market, it is now no longer safely perched on the moral high ground, beyond criticism itself. Many readers are increasingly irritated by its intellectual posturing.

Take Digby Ricci on *Titus*. In the space of one normal-sized review, he manages to make references to Aeschylus, Ovid, Christopher Marlowe, Dr Johnson, Samuel Beckett, Athol Fugard, Kenneth Tynan, Peter

Brook, T. S. Eliot, Bertrand Russell and several others . . . all before
starting on us.

Oh, I see. It's not so much a review – it's an *essay*.

Titled TITUS TOPPLES INTO THE 'RELEVANT' PIT, he hates the South
African flavour of our production:

> The accents. Why, there's the rub. Nobody is demanding the crys-
> talline voices of a Vanessa Redgrave or a John Gielgud from a local
> cast, but it does seem wilfully perverse of a director to rob most
> lines of beauty, grandeur or even meaning by an insistence on relent-
> lessly rolling Rs and pancake-flat vowels.

And so on. All in the same pompous, olde-worlde style – for which he
can't be blamed. To echo his own sentiments: Nobody is demanding the
crystalline opinions of a Kenneth Tynan or a Harold Hobson from a local
critic.

As for my performance, it is praised only when it achieves 'an appropriate Olivier-like ring' (appropriate to what? – some secret blueprint of
how the play ought to be done?), or pleases with a 'rendition of one of
my favourite passages', but is finally summed up as 'a ridiculous, misconceived waste'.

Greg calls the company onstage before the performance and makes a
light-hearted speech about how we mustn't let the reviews, good or bad,
affect future performances. While he talks, he nonchalantly tears the
Digby Wigby review into tiny pieces and throws it into the air like con-
fetti. The company laugh and clap.

Afterwards, we're talking about how a certain type of white South
African is fearsomely snobbish about the Afrikaner accent. I understand
this keenly, having been one of those South Africans myself.

Martin tells us a story:

Back in the old South Africa, an actor dared to play the Duke in
Measure for Measure in an Afrikaner accent. One of the critics wrote that
he didn't want to hear Shakespeare spoken as if by his plumber! The
actor wrote back, saying, 'I wasn't speaking it like your plumber. I was
speaking it like your State President.'

Saturday 1 April
Our first experience of a matinée day. Pretty tough. The early show finishes at the *half* of the second show; i.e. there's just thirty-five minutes

between them, during which stage management have to rebuild the set and we have to get costumed and made-up for the beginning again, while trying to muster the energy and grab some fuel. Thank goodness for Dorothy, a Market veteran, who's brought in some snacks from Woolworths (their equivalent of Marks & Spencers), which she shares out generously. Slugging through this bruising show twice, back-to-back, is made all the harder by the size of the audiences – the houses for both shows are very poor. Mike Maxwell says, 'The weekends are always our low point.' This odd, upside-down syndrome (in the UK, all shows pick up at the weekend) is apparently caused by security fears; Jo'burg, the murder capital, turns into a ghost town on Saturday and Sunday nights.

Appropriate to today – April Fool – everyone else knew this would happen, except us.

Sunday 2 April
The SA *Sunday Times* review is a rave. The opening line goes, 'This *Titus Andronicus* is stunningly sensuous theatre . . .' Very nice, but again we can't get over-excited. White South Africans are very free with their superlatives. They say stunning instead of good, gross instead of bad, and call every second bottle of wine a Grand Cru.

Tuesday 4 April
I may have misjudged the *Weekly Mail & Guardian*. They've been in touch with the Market, saying that *they're* unhappy with Digby Wigby's review and want to do a second opinion this Friday. The journalist is to be Mark Gevisser. He's asked to talk to us personally for Friday's piece and Greg elects to take the call. This lasts about an hour, during which Greg makes several thumbs-up signs. Afterwards, he says, 'We're going to be all right.'

Friday 7 April
Sello and I do an early-morning radio interview. The theme of the programme is the *new voice* of radio in the New South Africa. Instead of using plummy, pseudo-BBC tones, the announcers now use their own South African accents – Zulu, Xhosa, Afrikaans, etc. There have been numerous complaints and a controversy is building up. (Sounds familiar . . .)

After the interview, I buy the *Weekly Mail* and read Mark Gevisser's piece. It's as bad as Digby Wigby's effort, maybe worse. If this is a *second opinion*, I'm glad the guy isn't a doctor. Later, someone in the company mentions that Gevisser has a nickname among the profession: 'Ge-vicious'. (We walked into it again . . .)

Why are there no black voices in any of this? Why hasn't the *Sowetan*, say, bothered to review us?

Sunday 9 April

At last, a grown-up view of what we've done. The British *Sunday Times* devotes a two-page spread to our production, with photos, and an article by Michael Kustow. It isn't the fault of Digby Wigby or Mark Ge-vicious that their practical experience of Shakespeare is limited (though they could be blamed for shouting their ignorance from the roof-tops), but Kustow has spent a lifetime Shakespeare-watching, both in the UK and abroad, culminating in his much-praised season of International Shakespeare for the RSC at the Barbican last year.

In today's *Sunday Times* piece, he writes of us: 'What we see is not just theatre production. It is a significant act of cultural cross-fertilisation, cooked up in South Africa, not imported from abroad.' And later: 'Shakespeare wrote templates for times to come, and this play has found its time and place.'

Kustow is helpful in analysing why we've encountered such hostility:

By performing the play in indigenous speech, rather than getting their cast to ape Olivier or Gielgud, Sher and Doran have confront-ed deep cultural preconceptions in their white audiences. A rich-looking white man behind me, hearing me speak English-English, butts in and angrily asks why Sher is playing Titus with a broad Afrikaans accent. I say we don't know what Elizabethan English sounded like, that it was not like 'refined' English now, but that it was close to its own audience's speech. My neighbour is unim-pressed. 'I think they're trying to make fools of us,' he growls . . . There is a great knot of post-colonial cultural reflexes in all this. After years of cultural isolation, it is not surprising that South African whites should want to make up for what they have been deprived of: well-spoken English versions of the Bard, presented as if he were grand opera. But Sher and his colleagues have tried for something more dangerous, more urgent, as befits the Elizabethan roughness and vitality of the Market Theatre itself, which would have been a good neighbour to the Globe on Bankside. Quite simply, they have sidestepped all the 19th-century wrappings in which an older idea of Britishness embalmed Shakespeare.

And he's great on Sello:

> But it is through the reinterpretation of Aaron the Moor, casually vilified for his black skin and soul by everybody in the play, that this production strikes its shrewdest notes. Played by Sello Maake . . . this Aaron is no longer the malevolent villain of tradition, but a despised and taunted outsider, good enough for dirty tricks, learning fast from the villainy of his masters. But when he has a child with the empress Tamora, he refuses to let her thugs kill it. 'I am of age to keep my own,' he cries, clutching his baby son to his chest. Next to me, a young black man in a business suit yells approval of Aaron's affirmation. No cultural obstacles for this spectator.

42

Now the show is up and running, I'm meant to be flying to Thailand to complete an AIDS film I've been working on with the Worldwide Fund for Nature and the UN.

By the end of the century there could be thirty to forty million people infected with the HIV virus (so says the World Health Organisation), or a hundred and twenty million, depending on how it's handled in Asia. Thailand has been described as a virtual AIDS greenhouse; but most of Asia is still either asleep or in the early stages of denial, or worse, blatantly lying about HIV infections, and Japan's the worst.

Last November, I flew to Bangkok, in the middle of preparations for *Titus*, to research the film. I remember being momentarily surprised to find in my hotel tourist guide a section entitled 'Phuket at a glance'.

But this morning there's bad news from London. The Swedish company funding the film has backed out, for a variety of reasons, none of them very convincing.

It's a project I felt was really worthwhile. Anyway it looks as if the film can't go ahead at the moment. And I won't be flying to Bangkok.

Tony tries to seem disappointed and manages a rather winsome look of sympathy. He has not been looking forward to my going. 'Does that mean you'll be staying in Jo'burg then? . . . For the run?'

It looks like it. It means I'll be able to keep my eye on the production; prepare the filming of *Titus* which the SABC (South African Broadcasting Corporation) have proposed. And spend time with my parents when they fly out here towards the end of the run. It also means that I have more opportunity to see what other theatre is going on in town.

At the Market itself there are excellent productions of Steven Berkoff's *East*, in the Laager Theatre, directed by Barney (he first directed it in 1979 in a private performance, because the play was banned in SA); and Zakes Mda's *The Hill* directed by Philiswa Biko, in the Upstairs Theatre.

The Hill tells the story of two migrant workers trying to get work at a local mine and the hardships they endure. There are two startling performances from Mokete Moeketsi and Job Kubatsi. There's another of Zakes Mda's plays in the Pieterroos Theatre at the Civic.

Two American plays, Wendy Wasserstein's *The Sisters Rosensweig* at the Alhambra, and Jonathan Tolins's *Twilight of the Golds* in the Tesson Theatre at the Civic, seem to have been scheduled particularly to appeal to Johannesburg's Jewish audiences.

Twilight of the Golds deals with the ethics of genetic research. A study by the US Cancer Institute claims to have found an unidentifiable and unnamed gene, located in the X chromosome, that is believed to 'cause' homosexuality. The play imagines that advances in screening procedures allow this gene to be identified in the foetus. An expectant Jewish mother discovers that her child will be born gay and ultimately decides to terminate the pregnancy.

The play is flawed, but I am grateful for the programme notes, in which I finally discover that what sets me apart from my heterosexual kin is the interstitial nucleus of my anterior hypothalamus, and I don't want to brag, but my Corpus Callosum is probably thirteen per cent larger than theirs. I always had my suspicions. *Twilight* is the only play I watch in a full auditorium.

In a one-man show in Pretoria, called *Get Hard*, the gay theme raises its head once more, as a very earnest if rather pudgy young man tries to demonstrate the beauty of the higher faith by removing all his clothes. I think it's intended as a political act. He then proceeds with truly barefaced cheek, to walk between the rows of audience displaying his credentials. I've never liked politics shoved in my face.

The least successful performance I see is a production of *Macbeth* by the Performing Arts Council of the Transvaal (PACT). Part of the problem of staging this play is creating a society which believes in witchcraft. In South Africa many people do. Local sangomas or traditional healers sell their roots and herbs and charms on street corners. Over two hundred people died in witchcraft-related killings in this country within the last year. Over a hundred accused of witchcraft were necklaced with tyres, doused in petrol and burned alive. But none of this reality informs PACT's production. I get the sense that *Macbeth* has been scheduled from a set-text mentality rather than from any burning desire to do that play. And it's clear, by the time I see it, that any faith the company had in the production has been whittled away by too many rowdy schools matinées. This is witnessed by the fact that at a performance on Red Nose Day, when Macduff holds Macbeth's head aloft at the end of the play, it's wearing a red nose. Depressingly, when the schools break up for the Easter hols, PACT are forced to cancel a week of performances. Who goes to Shakespeare, unless teacher says?

Tuesday 11 April
I go in to note *Titus* at least once a week. Usually, there are masses of tiny things to check. Tonight I have another duty to perform. Roger Chapman phoned me from the National this morning to tell me that *Titus Andronicus* has been invited to an international Classical Theatre Festival in Spain, at a place called Almagro. Cheek by Jowl went there last year with their production of *Measure for Measure*.

The company are thrilled. They've all remained immune to the problems we have encountered (the production hassles, the *Weekly Mail* reviews, the poor houses). That's probably because they've had regular injections of good news. First there was the National tour, then the filming for SABC, now a Spanish trip. Only Paulus seems to be hesitating again.

'What is it this time, Paulus?' I ask.

'It's the date,' he says. 'Squint Artists, we have our monthly meeting. I'll have to ask them if I can miss.'

Wednesday 12 April
The Anglican Church Society of Soweto has bought out this evening's performance, our first totally black audience. I'm not sure what a church party are going to make of *Titus Andronicus*.

They come with no preconceptions about Shakespeare, or about how it 'should be done'. They remain quite quiet for the first few minutes, until they have tuned in to the language, then their involvement in the story becomes total. We say afterwards how 'Elizabethan' they were, but how can we know? What is true is that they vocalise their involvement, chatter and comment on the action and occasionally shout out at the characters on stage.

And of course they love Sello. We've changed one phrase in his first scene with Tamora's sons. In the text he shouts out 'Clubs! Clubs!' as they fight around him. 'Clubs!' was the cry raised in Tudor London to call the watch in the event of a public brawl. In Soweto they shout 'Baba Phoyisa!'. It's a perfectly justifiable substitution in this context, so Sello slips it in and the audience erupt. In fact they identify with the way Sello plays Aaron to such an extent that they cheer him right the way through the plot to rape Lavinia. It is not until he hacks off Titus's hand that they suddenly turn against him. When Aaron turns to the audience and says defiantly:

> 'Let fools do good, and fair men call for grace
> Aaron will have his soul black like his face.'

– the Anglican Church Society jeer and boo him.

Then, in the second half when the Nurse brings Aaron's black child to be killed, the audience rally to his side once again. Aaron defies the order to murder his child just because of his colour:

> 'Tell the empress from me, I am of age
> To keep mine own, excuse it how she can.'

The reaction Michael Kustow witnessed at this point is now amplified throughout the whole house: 'Yebo!' the audience shriek out, 'Yebo!' yelling their approval and their solidarity. A memorable show.

Afterwards standing in the bar, one of them comes up to us. 'I didn't understand it all here,' he says, pointing to his head. Then he bangs his chest. 'But I understood it here.'

Thursday 13 April

We're at Horatio's in Melville, an excellent fish restaurant, crammed with maritime tackle and Nelson memorabilia (the Lord Admiral, not the State President). We're having lunch with Ian Steadman, a valiant supporter of *Titus*, the arbitrator of the trustees meeting back in January and Dean of the University of the Witwatersrand.

Wits has been experiencing a great deal of trouble over the last few months. There have been student strikes and boycotts, rioting, campus trashing and intimidation, all over the problem of increasing entry for black students and quota systems. This transitional period is proving a strain on the country's education system. Some people fear that here in microcosm they are witnessing the eventual fate of the country.

Ian looks drawn, but happy to be in other company, discussing other issues. He tells us how he managed to identify some small funding from the University to assist the production, in return for a promise from Tony and me to give a class or two to his drama students. We are very happy to oblige. I enjoy teaching and it will give me something else to do until filming starts.

The waitress arrives and rattles off the specials with the speed of a patter song. 'The fish is excellent: the linefish we have today are Cape Salmon, Rock Salmon, Kingklip, Red Roman, Stumpnose, and Yellowtail . . .' We plump for the prawns in lime and ginger.

'Queens?' she enquires.

I'm taken aback. Do we get a discount? 'I'm sorry?'

'Queen prawns or king prawns?' she asks again.

Friday 14 April

We have no performance on Good Friday, so we decide to host a party in the garden and announce the '*Braai* of the Century'.

The *braai* is a national institution in South Africa, a cultural phenomenon akin to a clambake in New England. It's what they call a 'barbie' in Australia; a barbecue.

Dale brings extra chairs, Dotty and Michael bring a spare *braai* and Dumi another. Dan takes charge of lighting up and Gys quickly prepares a starter of hot spicy mushrooms and gets his kingklip on the go. Everybody brings something: bread, meat or fish, salads, fruit, and booze, plenty of booze. And Jennifer brings Easter eggs to hide in the garden for an egg hunt later.

In a matter of moments a whole band of instruments have appeared: guitars, bongos, shakers and tambourines. Even a didgeridoo. The swimming pool glitters like tinfoil in the afternoon sun; the garden hums with a harmony of cooking smells and music, and the neighbours' children scale the wall to dance in the pepper tree.

The day jigs away and people have just reached that falling-into-the-pool-fully-clothed stage, when Selina arrives.

Selina seems to have spent most of Holy Week at church. She disappeared for two whole nights, returning only to snatch an hour's sleep, before buttoning herself back into her smart red jacket with its immaculately starched puritan collar, and rushing out again for another service. She looks exhausted.

'What do you Methodists get up to all night Selina?' I ask.

'Oh we sing, yes, we dance, oooooh, we have a *great* time!' She blinks at me blearily.

Another round of meat has been placed on the *braai*, so I tell her to help herself. And she does. Selina takes me at my word, gets a large plate and piles it high: boerewurst, steak, chops, sausages, burgers, the lot; there's nothing left. And she pads quietly back to her room.

43

Saturday 15 April
The '*Braai* of the Century' has left everyone with the hangovers of the millennium. Luckily we only have to do one show today. As with *Hysteria*, our audience numbers haven't warranted the double show on Saturdays and the second one has been cancelled for the rest of the run.

Tuesday 18 April
For the next few nights the great jazz musician, Hugh Masekela, is playing next door to the Market, at Kippie's Bar. When I arrive for tonight's performance of *Titus*, the precinct is already thronging with people, many of them black.

(When we fret about the size and colour of our audience – we're playing to houses of about twenty-five per cent, and these are about ninety per cent white – we're told that blacks can't get back to the townships afterwards; an argument which seems not to apply now, when it's music, not theatre, on offer.)

As I make my way through the crowds and into the Market, I wish I were a musician too, and could steal some of Masekela's audience, leading them, Pied Piper-like, after me.

Instead, I go alone into the foyer, which is gloomy and chilly on these autumnal nights. On my right is the box-office. I no longer stop to ask how many are in tonight. I go backstage, into my cramped, curtained-off section of the female dressing-room, change into Titus's shirt, trousers and boots, and then start the make-up. No one else has to age up in the show, so it's a delicate job – just deepening the existing lines.

I love this half-hour . . . a painter's half-hour.

Over the tannoy, I hear members of the company doing their various warm-ups onstage.

As I work, I think of the photos of Olivier as Titus. His ageing was extremely ornate. As well as sticking on a putty Roman nose (strong and straight) and a wig (sculptured silver curls) and huge false eyebrows (like a parrot's plumage), the grease-paint design on his face was as much an exercise in cartography as make-up. Forehead, cheeks and jaws were

"...anything, so long as we can see those lion eyes
search for solace, that great jaw sag." Kenneth Tynan

Olivier as Titus

criss-crossed with a network of lines and wrinkles, as though this general's every route march was etched into his face. All varnished in a dark, weathered, leathery finish, it's a brilliant piece of portraiture, and of transformation. (Did he devise and execute these make-ups himself? If so, he must've been a painter too.)

But how did he *work* in this amount of make-up? In this mask of putty, glue, hairpins and grease-paint. Everything could be dislodged or smeared. My own minimalist make-up has vanished entirely by the time I see myself in the dressing-room mirror again at interval-time, after Act III, Scene 1, washed away by the sweat and tears (flowing freely these days), or smudged in the hugs and grapplings. So did Olivier never touch his own face? Never embrace anyone else? Did he never sweat?

Like Digby Wigby, I'm fascinated by the Brook–Olivier–Leigh *Titus*. Unlike him, I don't believe it need stop the clocks.

The other day I read – for the first time – Ken Tynan's review of that production, in Greg's battered old Pelican paperback, *Tynan on Theatre*. At the end of his piece, Tynan imagines other 'grand unplayable' roles which Olivier might now play, ' . . . Ibsen's Brand, Goethe's Faust – anything, so long as we can see those lion eyes search for solace, that great jaw sag.'

Before leaving London, I met John Standing at a party and he told me stories from that production, in which he was a spear-carrier.

It was during the period when Vivien Leigh was in a bad way. One matinée, she was so far gone that she kept muttering through her scenes, long after the loss of her tongue.

John demonstrated how Olivier did the famous line, 'I am the sea. Hark how her sighs doth blow.' He drew out the *H* of 'hark' into a rasping, hissing sound, gargled at the back of the palette – 'HHHHHHHark' – so that the audience *heard* the water and air.

'No, I don't remember that, but I do remember him howling as Titus . . . but then he was famous for his howls, wasn't he? He howled in everything.' (This was Janet Suzman talking at the Market Theatre bar last week, after she had seen the show. She was in town to help out with the local production of *The Sisters Rosensweig*.)

'When in the play did he howl?' I asked. 'When exactly?'

'Oh I don't remember . . . I was only a kid when I saw it,' she said, giving her husky laugh. 'No, what I remember most clearly was Vivien Leigh as Lavinia . . .' (Janet was a notable Lavinia herself, in Trevor

Nunn's 1972 Roman Season.) '. . . her entrance after the rape. That's what I can picture clearly.'

'Mh–hh, the famous image,' I prompted. 'Arms outstretched, red ribbons dripping from her stumps instead of blood . . .'

'The whole audience gasped,' Janet said.

'Because it was so shocking?'

'No, because she was so beautiful!'

I'd been apprehensive about Janet seeing *Titus*. Her own fine Shakespeare production at this theatre was everything that we're not: traditional (with English accents, sumptuous sets and costumes) and sold-out. But she seemed genuinely excited by what we've done with *Titus*. 'It's going to take the roof off in London,' she said. So why hasn't it done the same here? Janet blamed the cultural boycott. 'People have lost their sense of curiosity,' she said. 'They were deprived of outside culture for so long that they've got to the point where they say, "What we can't have, we won't want." '

What a frightening idea – people losing their sense of curiosity. That's a terrible amputation.

So – is it all because of the boycott?

The Cultural Boycott: a brief history.

1945   American Actors' Equity pass a resolution dissuading its members from performing in South Africa.

1954   Writing in the British *Observer*, Father (later Archbishop) Trevor Huddleston calls for a cultural boycott: 'I am asking those who believe racialism to be sinful or wrong . . . to refuse to encourage it by accepting any engagement to act, to perform as a musical artist or ballet dancer . . .'

1956–7   The British Actors' Union, Equity, and the British Musicians Union forbid members to work in South Africa.

1963   Forty leading British playwrights withdraw the rights for their plays to be performed in South Africa.

1969   The United Nations General Assembly pass a resolution urging member states to suspend 'cultural, educational, sports and other exchanges with the racist regime'.

1975   Just before TV is introduced to South Africa, British Equity interdict the BBC and ITV from supplying South Africa with programmes that feature its members.

1976   New York anti-apartheid groups successfully picket the South

African musical, *Ipi Tombi*, and close it. The show, featuring throngs of joyous migrant workers and bare-bosomed brides, is accused of promoting the notion of black *joie de vivre* under apartheid.

1985   Paul Simon records his album *Graceland* in South Africa with the black group, Ladysmith Black Mambazo. *Graceland*'s release and subsequent tour begins to blur the issues. Is this another *Ipi Tombi*, or is it, in the words of Hugh Masekela (participating in the tour and a stalwart of the anti-apartheid struggle), a 'development project for South African artists'?

1983–8   The UN Special Committee Against Apartheid issues a series of lists of entertainers who have breached the ban on performing in South Africa, including those who have appeared at Sun City, the playground used by the apartheid regime in the 'independent homeland', Bophuthatswana. The UK list includes Max Bygraves, Rod Stewart, Oliver Reed, Robert Stephens, Jeffrey Archer, Barbara Woodhouse and the Male Voice Choir of Wales. The ensuing adverse publicity persuades many artists to support the ban in exchange for the deletion of their names from the list. Even Frank Sinatra, having initially insisted on his right to play anywhere, eventually submits to the pressure.

1987   Conference of South African artists in Amsterdam. They decide that the boycott will henceforth be applied selectively.

1991   Among many reforms and changes following Mandela's release in the previous year, the cultural boycott is lifted.

As an Equity member, I naturally supported the boycott, but always cautiously, with a kind of agnostic spirit – it was hard to decide whether this was a good thing or not. I felt relieved when the boycott was applied selectively, allowing, for example, Janet to direct *Othello* in SA, with the full blessing of the ANC, and me to publish my books there.

Peering out at tonight's audience, I get a fright. Scattered in little clumps around the centre block, and making the half-lit auditorium look vast and cold, it's the smallest turn-out yet. (Later we're told they numbered forty-nine.)

As the show starts, I stare at myself in the dressing-room mirror. Not sure I've got the energy for Titus's journey tonight . . .

Through the back wall of the theatre, I can hear Hugh Masekela playing his trumpet in Kippie's Bar, to roars of pleasure from the packed audience.

I'm thinking of Stephen Fry walking out of that play in London . . . I wonder if he did it mid-performance, or now, just before his first entrance . . . ? It would be nice to change back into my own clothes, go out the back door and slip into Kippie's . . . (They'd never think of looking for me next door.)

No. I don't have the courage or stupidity or whatever it takes – the *wildness* – to do that. I'll go for a different option. I'll stroll through tonight's performance, I'll phone it in. If people can't be bothered to come and see me, fine, I needn't bother doing the real thing.

Then I hear Gys and Ivan over the tannoy, as the emperor's warring sons, lashing into one another, and I hear the rest of the cast, as 'the crowd', supporting them with passionate cheers and heckles. And I think, Everyone's really going for it tonight. Why? Why are they working so hard? For such a small audience.

The answer is like a splash of cold water. This isn't unusual for them – tonight's house – this is normal; this is what it's like being an actor in this country. They've had years of this. And along the way, they've made a decision – a decision to serve up the goods, whatever the circumstances. It's why they come in early each evening to do long warm-ups, it's why they were so nervous in the John Barton sessions and learned his lessons so keenly, it's why they reacted so emotionally to the workshops on violence, laughing or crying, it's why Jenny went to meet a man who's had his hand chopped off and another who'd lost his tongue. It's why, at the end of every performance, Gys – wild-boy Gys – comes into my dressing-room, and says 'Thank you', and then seeks out the stage managers and says it again, in Afrikaans, '*Dankie.*'

Tonight we end up doing one of our best shows ever and the tiny audience give us our first standing ovation. Among them is the actor Ramalao Makhene (he was in *Master Harold* at the National), who is choked-up when he comes backstage. 'Boy, what you guys have done . . . getting Shakespeare to speak to me like that!'

Very high afterwards, we pop into Kippie's Bar. Masekela is between sets, so we don't hear him play – although I do get to meet him for the first time. Dumi introduces us.

'Wow, you're shorter than I thought!' he says to me.

'Yeah, yeah.' I laugh. 'Everyone says that.'

'You're almost as short as me. Still, it's only a problem when we're vertical, hey? Nobody complains in bed.'

We swop notes about our mutual friend, Monty Berman, my

ex-therapist and Masekela's godfather, who, after thirty-four years' exile in England, finally moved back to the New South Africa a few months ago.

Thursday 20 April
Bump into John Kani in the Market foyer.

Me: 'John, our houses . . . ! They're getting worse and worse. What are we going to do?'

John: 'I don't know, my friend. It's a problem we've been having for a long time.'

(Thanks a bunch – why did nobody warn us?)

Me: 'But what is it? The latest excuse I've heard is that the Market is associated with protest theatre and people have had enough of it.'

John: '*Protest theatre*? Is that what we were doing all those years? Man, we didn't even know how to spell "protest". We were just telling the stories of our lives!'

(That statement is wonderfully, typically, John Kani. Satirising a certain white attitude to his race, and throwing it back in their faces.)

Me: 'So what are we going to do about these terrible houses?'

John: 'I'm not sure, but you must speak out about this while you're here. Hold a public debate, go on radio, go on TV. When we say anything, they just shoot us down. But maybe they'll listen to you.'

44

Friday 21 April

The papers are full of stories about the Deputy Minister of Arts, Culture, Science and Technology, Mrs Winnie Mandela. She's been snatching the limelight with court-room dramas and sudden well-timed appearances at funerals, then, just before she was about to be axed from her post, she resigns and swoons into a luxury private hospital.

Her life is truly Shakespearian with its revolutions around the Wheel of Fortune. And South Africa sits back and watches each episode as if it were the latest American soap.

However, as Barry Ronge (the country's ubiquitous arbiter of cultural taste) points out in his regular column as Arts Editor of the Johannesburg *Star*: 'a larger tragedy directly connected to the ex-minister's escapades is busy playing itself out: South African Theatre is on the verge of extinction.'

He spells it out with typical South African hyperbole: 'We have Antony Sher in town. He is one of the top five classical actors in the English-language theatre. He is certainly one of the top three classical actors in the world . . . Are people standing in line to see this remarkable event? Is there a black market in tickets? Of course not. The show is playing to half-full houses. The same is true of the Civic Theatre where the Royal Shakespeare Company are presenting *Les Liaisons Dangereuses*.'

Ronge berates the apathy which, he says, has turned Johannesburg audiences 'into a generation of sugar-seeking weevils who only go out at Christmas to see *Me and My Girl*'. He threatens that, if things go on as they are, the city's three major theatres will close. The Civic will be turned into a supermarket, the Market into a gym and the Alhambra into a massage parlour, before the good Johannes-burghers know what has hit them.

Tony decides that he should take up the cue delivered so passionately by Ronge and write an article in reply. He'll 'come out' about the poor houses we've been getting. It is normally regarded as a taboo subject in the theatrical community to admit to poor houses. Even I find myself spin–doctoring, when Tony describes our houses as 'half-empty'. Somehow 'half-full' sounds more optimistic. But to be honest, for whatever reasons, our audiences have now fallen to more like quarter-full.

Sunday 23 April
Shakespeare's birthday. We had been invited to the Johannesburg Shakespeare Society's celebration of the day, but it coincides with the launch of *Cheap Lives* at Exclusive Books in Sandton.

Apparently the birthday bash turned into an explosive event. Two of our company, Martin le Maitre and Dorothy Gould, were just about to start their readings when one of the audience shouted out, 'I hope you won't be performing in *those* accents.'

Martin

The can was opened and out wriggled the worms. One of them, Digby Ricci, perpetrator of the *Weekly Mail*'s scathing review and a devotee of the Society, suddenly found himself confronted by Martin le Maitre.

'You've been enjoying yourself insulting us in public,' Martin declared. 'Now it's our turn.'

Ricci, backed into a corner by Martin, finally made the mistake of attacking Sello's performance. At which point Dorothy joined the fray: 'Do you mean to say you would prefer to see a white actor black-up to play the part?'

'Yes,' said Ricci emphatically, to howls of derision from the room.

Past midnight, and Tony is finishing his article for the *Star*:

> Serious Theatre is in serious, serious trouble in this city. [He lists the reasons or excuses which have been trotted out for our poor houses, including Janet Suzman's suggestion that the cultural boycott is partly to blame.]
>
> I was very moved by what she said, that because of the boycott, people's range of artistic experience got smaller and smaller, and their range of vision got smaller too – literally – until they were just holed up in their homes watching a video of last year's hit movie.
>
> People's sense of curiosity has been whittled away, and curiosity is at the heart of all artistic activity, both for those who make art, and those who watch it.

In conclusion, he poses a simple question: 'South African Theatre is an incredibly rich and original product. The rest of the world already knows that. When will Jo'burg audiences catch up?'

Tuesday 25 April

The article is printed, not in the arts section of the *Star*, but on the editorial page. It lights a blue touch-paper.

During the week the debate moves even further centre stage. The editorial itself leads with its reaction: 'The cultural boycott is a plausible culprit, as are street crime, and the cost of tickets.' It goes on to propose a cure, a promising rescue plan: a system of properly funded regional theatres, promoting healthy competition at the commercial end of the market and at the subsidised end to allow more controversial or experimental projects freedom from the tyranny of the box-office.

But the editorial is accompanied by an angry open letter to 'the

Government of National Unity, the South African Broadcasting Corporation and to Antony Sher' from one Israel Motlhabane, the first black
voice in the debate. After showing his colours by proclaiming provoca-
tively that 'to the theatre lover in the townships, Shakespeare is sawdust',
he outlines his grievances with the State of the Art.

He attacks the TV companies for not addressing black audiences, nor
employing black directors or writers; and accuses those in positions of
power of frustrating the aspirations of black artists: 'We did not vote for
a government that appoints black men with white mentality to push our
culture and aspirations down the drain the way apartheid did.'

At the heart of this impassioned diatribe is a radical proposal. He challenges the establishment to build top-class theatres in the townships.
There is an audience, still deprived of facilities, eager to see good theatre.

Two days later the *Star*'s letters page is given over to the continuing
debate. One melancholy correspondent talks about the guilt white audiences have been made to feel, in recent years, by plays which he
describes as 'paeans of political correctness'. In his assessment, the result
is that once the alternative escapism of farces and musical comedies has
palled, people retreat to sport and TV soaps.

Another writer blames 'a post coital depression following the union of
all South African people last year'.

But the argument about the cultural boycott raises the most vociferous
response. While hailing *Titus* as 'superb quality theatre', one woman
blames Tony for supporting the cultural boycott, which 'has now come
back to bite him'.

Another goes further, accusing Tony of creating a 'cultural desert' by
actively advocating and promoting the boycott over a quarter of a century
and declares that he deserves 'neither our sympathy nor our support'.

But perhaps the most extreme reaction comes from one reader who
protests that far from being criticised, audiences should be congratulated
for staying away from *Titus*! 'By not going, South African audiences have
made their presence felt more than they could have done by their atten-
dance.'

Others cite the accents as their reasons for staying away. Here's one
response from Sandton: 'He has foisted a poor Shakespearian play on
South Africa. He is using pronunciation unacceptable to a discerning
Shakespeare audience. These are my reasons for not even considering
attending his play.'

In a letter sent privately to Tony at the Market, one woman actually apologises for not coming to see the play, but she 'could not abide the excruciating experience of the ugly accents of southern Africa abusing some of the most beautiful language ever written'.

Everybody is talking about it.

We go to the Civic Theatre one Sunday night to see South Africa's most popular satirist, Pieter Dirk Uys doing a single performance of his new show, *You ANC Nothing Yet*. He comes on and says, 'I believe Antony Sher is angry with Jo'burg for not coming to the theatre . . . I hope someone tells him how full we are tonight!' to which the (ninety-nine per cent white) audience cheer and clap, applauding themselves for braving it from their fortress-like houses to the fortress-like Civic.

On the way home we stop off for a Steers take-away, only to hear a radio DJ saying that *Titus* is continuing at the Market Theatre, 'if Antony Sher doesn't get too angry to finish the run.'

But Tony isn't angry and neither am I. The debate is stimulating, often surprising and even occasionally supportive. The novelist Jenny Hobbs (author of *Thoughts in a Makeshift Mortuary*) urges the *Weekly Mail* readers to ignore the 'tendentious and mean-spirited review' in that paper and to 'take your kids to *Titus Andronicus* to revel in what Shakespeare's really about. 'Strue's bob, it'll be a night to remember.'

The thing that pleases us most is the informed debate about what should actually be done about the crisis. Solutions are offered in two major articles within the same week in the *Star*.

The first, by theatre critic Garalt MacLiam, advocates 'a full scale revolution in the selling of tickets', including more aggressive marketing and subscription schemes, and extensive research into audience needs, including starting times and travel to and from the theatres.

Joyce Ozynski (at one time on the Board of the Market Theatre) argues incisively that with greater resources, theatre in South Africa will eventually prevail; that the current malaise is the effect of undergoing a transitional phase in the country's history. She points out that the Market is 'the place where over the years discoveries have been made and democracies affirmed'. She analyses the demographic changes that had occurred in Johannesburg. 'With the weakening of apartheid, the city centre areas, ghettoised as white by the Group Areas Act, changed. As the blacks moved back, many of the whites moved out to the suburbs. "Town" vanished. And now, in its place is an African city, densely inhab-ited and seething with taxis, pedestrians and hawkers.' This dynamic, she argues, had landed a potential audience of thousands on the doorsteps of those city centre theatres. But it is an audience which needs cultivating. Theatre must reach out in direct and innovative ways, conventional methods of audience development may not apply.

She proposes lowering ticket prices to around R5 (under £1), otherwise a system of economic apartheid would prevail – the *Titus* tickets were R26–30 (£5–6) – along with other practical measures such as Sunday afternoon performances, early evening shows and theatre buses. She ends her excellent article with a clarion call for optimism: 'We are entering a period when, if things are managed well, the arts will be supported by far greater numbers than was ever possible when a fraction of an élite had to be relied on. For the first time, some of the conditions necessary for the flowering of the arts are in place.'

A final rallying cry of celebration comes from Pieter Dirk Uys, who describes himself as one of the T-cells of this ailing body theatrical for the past few decades. 'Theatre is not dead,' he cries. 'It's just being upstaged by modern life!' He ends with a plea for folk to get up and go to the theatre. 'It's your democratic duty. It will also be a great pleasure.'

Ironically, the debate seems to me to be a measure of the production's success. A mission statement, drafted by the Market in its early days, declares: 'We invite risk rather than comfortable certainty. We have learnt to measure our accomplishments through an account of challenged minds rather than economic gain . . .'

Sunday 30 April

We are surprised to discover just how little of the debate has trickled through to Cape Town, when we fly down here to launch *Cheap Lives*.

The launch takes place in Exclusive Books in Claremont, and is like a big Sher family party. The book has just hit the South African best-seller lists and the publishers have invited Albie Sachs to introduce the event.

Albie is a hero of the freedom struggle. I first met him when I asked him to participate in *Two Dogs and Freedom*. He was in England recovering from the assassination attempt, which had blown up his car, damaged his sight and hearing and ripped off his right arm.

Like Mandela, Albie Sachs is remarkable for his forgiveness, his deep humanity, his large vision of life, which allows his suffering to have meaning. 'It was for something,' he has written. 'For democracy, for dignity, for a decent country to live in.' He calls it his 'soft vengeance', the personal triumph of being above the people who tried to kill you. 'I don't want everyone in South Africa to walk around with short arms, just because I have one,' he says.

Back in 1988 he had quizzed me about the nature of the *Two Dogs* benefit we were organising. 'South Africa is full of life and colour and laughter. If your show reflects that, I'll do it. If it's all doom and gloom, I don't want to know.'

The performance marked his first public appearance since the bomb. I remember him coming onstage, his balance unsteady, and lifting his stump to the audience as a kind of salute.

Before the elections last year we met Albie again at a party at the house of Kader Asmal (then on the ANC's Executive Committee). Much heady excitement as someone appeared with the design for the new South African flag drawn on a paper napkin. Then Albie arrived with a draft of the interim constitution which he had been working on, hot off the press. He proudly showed us the clause prohibiting discrimination in the New South Africa, on the grounds of race, creed, colour, gender, disability *or* sexual orientation; the first time any such clause had been included in any constitution in the world.

Today, speaking at the launch in Claremont, Albie describes his hopes for the country a year after the elections. Some people talk about the honeymoon being over, but Albie detests any desire to wallow in pessimism, determined and eager to embrace the will to overcome the country's enormous problems. 'It took three hundred years to mess it up, it won't get cleared up in three hundred days.'

He talks about those deep African qualities of vitality and musicality witnessed in the wit, the laughter, the very body language of its people – qualities which will ensure the health and vigour of its culture in the coming years.

Tony has been anxious to know what he thought of *Cheap Lives*, as Albie famously wrote a jail diary, about his own experiences in prison (later turned into a play by David Edgar). Albie publicly praises Tony's novel, calling it an entrancing book on a gloomy subject. 'It anticipates the mood of the democratic South Africa,' he says, 'while dealing with the rigor mortis of the old.'

He urges Tony to come back here, to do more theatre, something a little lighter maybe, less intense, to celebrate the future, not castigate the past.

I had been wondering what he had thought of *Titus*.

'Well,' he said. 'It's not a play for amputees!'

45

Thursday 27 April

Freedom Day. The first anniversary of SA's first democratic elections. A public holiday, so no performance tonight.

This morning is bright and warm, but we stay indoors, with the curtains half closed, watching the celebrations on TV. They're being held nearby, in Pretoria, in front of the grand old Union Buildings. So strange to see the podium full of war-horses from the old police force and army (a squad of Tituses), hefty, white-moustached Afrikaner generals. A few years ago these men were running the prisons that housed that *kaffir terrorist* Mandela, or mowing down his people in the townships. This morning they're acting as his guard of honour, his security system, his military might. It's very odd. Because they really are the same people. There's been no purge yet, no Nuremburg-type trials, just vague talk of a Truth Commission some time in the future. The crimes of the apartheid era have gone unpunished and a proportion of culprits must be among the people on show today . . . maybe that granite-jawed officer in sun-glasses at the back of shot during Mandela's speech.

Nothing is straightforward here. You applaud the spirit of forgiveness embodied by people like Mandela and Albie Sachs, while at the same time thinking that this will be a healthier place when children don't have to look at their elders and think, What did you do during apartheid, Daddy?

Meanwhile, I watch today's celebrations in delight, pointing at the screen and yelling, 'There's John Kani! Look – that's him coming on to the podium! He's shaking Mandela's hand! Look – it's John!'

Selina is doing her morning work as we sit in front of the telly. We keep inviting her to watch with us, to join us on the sofa, and she keeps being tempted, not sitting down, but hovering in the doorway. However, the conditioning of the old South Africa weighs heavily on her, and her duties call: the slow journey round the house every day, sweeping and cleaning.

It's only when they sing 'Nkosi Sikelel'i' that she finally abandons her duster and stands in the middle of the room, grinning at the telly and singing along, her right fist raised. 'Is that the man?' she asks, as an elderly white man joins Mandela on the podium. 'Joe . . . is that the man's name?'

'Do you mean Joe Slovo?' I ask.

'That's him!'

'No. He died.'

'Oh shame. That was a good man.'

Friday 28 April

Today's the day of our workshop with the drama department at Wits University – part of the deal which enabled Wits to give *Titus* some funding. I'm not experienced at teaching – or particularly comfortable with it – but Greg is, so I've left all the arrangements to him. He imposed two conditions on anyone wishing to attend the workshop. One, that they should be able to perform a Shakespeare speech, so that we can work on our feet, and two, that they should have seen *Titus*, so that we can refer to it. Neither condition seemed stringent. But this is Jo'burg – where the attitude to theatre is weird, even in its only drama school. We were told that many of the students didn't have a Shakespeare piece and weren't prepared to learn one in time for the workshop; and many hadn't seen *Titus*, and couldn't now, because they were in rehearsal for a musical version of *A Raisin in the Sun*, and its director – who happened to be the head of the drama department – wouldn't let them have a single evening off rehearsals.

'I'm terribly sorry,' says David, the tutor who's organising today's event, when we arrive at Wits. 'What with the students who aren't here because they can't meet your conditions and those who've gone home for the long weekend . . . there's not much of a turn-out, I'm afraid.'

'That's OK,' I say chirpily. 'We're used to small audiences.'

So we do the workshop with only about ten (one black) students, then drive back to the Market, more bewildered than ever. I think Janet Suzman was right. South Africans have lost interest in the outside world. I mean, modesty aside, surely Greg and my joint experience of British theatre, and particularly of Shakespeare, should have been of more interest to Wits's drama department . . . ?

Tuesday 2 May

This morning, Barney rang to say he won't be around for our last night (only ten days away!), because he's going overseas this coming weekend

and that he'd like to see us; to talk and to show us some student films
he's involved with. So would we come round for supper one evening?
'But Barney,' said Greg, who was taking the call, 'Tony is performing in
the evenings, at your theatre.'

Barney said, 'Oh, that's right.'

It's a pity we can't meet up. I'm sorry we haven't got to know him
better – specially after his Jujamcyn speech – but then I wonder if anyone does?

At lunch today, at Gramadoelas, with some of the company, we get into
gossipy, giggling mode, and I ask them about Barney. No one knows of
any intimate relationships in his life (perhaps because of his psoriasis
skin condition, someone suggests), or even whether he's straight or gay.

Well, if he isn't gay, why is he always surrounded by attractive young
men? His assistants, his actors, or, sitting opposite me, his lodger, Bruce?

Kind-hearted, hard-working (as well as playing various parts in *Titus*,
he also helps Vanessa run the Lab), Bruce has dark, intense, Afrikaner
looks, which glow from underneath heavy eyebrows, joining at the middle.
Barney has a nickname for him, O.E.O. (One Eyebrow Only), and they
clearly have an affectionate relationship.

'But it's nothing to do with sex,' laughs Bruce, seeing which way my
mind is going. 'He's a sort of father, a wise uncle, a teacher. The most
incredible teacher!'

'Yes, OK,' I say. 'We all know about Barney the guru, but what does he
do for . . . ?'

Suddenly Gys wheels on me. 'Do you also want to know if I've got a
foreskin or not?'

I blink at him. He's stopped laughing.

'Barney's private life is *private*. Can we leave it like that please?'

We change the subject.

Wednesday 3 May
This coming Sunday is scheduled for our performance in Soweto, just in
a hall, without sets or costumes, on the principle that if the people can't
come to the show (because of ticket prices or transport problems) we'll
take the show to the people. It's Sello's brainchild, his dream project.
But there have been problems. John Kani was supposed to be organising
it. Except he thought Sello was. Another essential participant is the editor of the *Sowetan* – to let residents know it's happening – but he's disappeared today, on a holiday or something, and his staff claim they can't

reach him. So, finally, we're forced to cancel Sunday's show. Sello is heartbroken.

His nine-year-old daughter, Lerato (the word means 'love'), who's profoundly deaf, came to the show last week. She sat in the front row. I've never heard Sello do Aaron's speeches to the baby better. Such tenderness. At the curtain call, Lerato applauded by raising both arms and slowly waving them from side to side, while she and her dad grinned at one another. Afterwards, in the bar, she told us that actually she liked Paulus best – as the street-kid in the second half – she liked the way he sticks his bum out as he walks.

Talking of parents and children, there has been much excitement at Greenfield Road over the past few days, as preparations are made for tomorrow's arrival of Greg's parents from the UK . . .

46

Thursday 4 May

Pick up Ma and Pa from Jan Smuts Airport.

They look tired. It's a long journey from the Lake District to Africa, in more ways than one. My mother, Margaret, is a Yorkshire lass from Huddersfield. My father, John, is a Scot and has spent most of his working life in the Nuclear Power Industry, until he retired as General Manager of Sellafield a few years ago. He's travelled all over the world on business and Ma often went along. But this is their first view of the southern hemisphere. We drive past the great tawny mine dumps which skirt this City of Gold.

Greg's Pa, John

'Greg's developed Jo'burg elbow since he's been here, Margaret,' says Tony.

'Oh,' says my mother anxiously. 'Is it contagious?'

'It's an automatic reaction that happens whenever you drive up to a traffic light – you jerk your elbow back to lock your door. They call it Jo'burg elbow.'

And, as if to prove the point, we approach a junction and immediately hear the rapid chunk-chunk of doors locking all around us. Standing on the corner there's a beggar, with a sign round his neck which reads: 'Retrenched since November. Family to feed. Please help.' He's white. It's a new sight for Jo'burg.

I start trying to point out the landmarks, but the only places I recognise are the Carlton Hotel (where we stayed on our first visit) and the blue diamond De Beers building. We've always avoided the city centre because of its reputation for hold-ups and car hijackings.

In most places flyovers are designed to protect a city from the traffic. In Jo'burg, they protect the traffic from the city. We whisk around the elevated ring road and head for the leafy northern suburbs.

Back in Greenside, Selina, who has been excited about my parents' arrival for weeks, rushes out from the backyard waving her arms. She grabs my mother's hands and kisses them. 'Hoooh, Selina is so happy to meet you,' she coos, in that way she has of referring to herself in the third person. 'Hoooh, welcome, welcome!'

We're going to take it easy for the first few days. I think Ma and Pa are secretly quite relieved that the Soweto show has been cancelled and they can spend their first Sunday with us just pottering about.

Of course, I could take them on one of the organised tours of Soweto which are gaining popularity now. One company's brochure promises 'A real cultural soul experience' and entices you to 'Drive through dusty roads and collapsed services. Taste African meals in five-star shebeens. See people who drink *imbamba* [home-brewed beer pepped up with battery acid]. Visit Nelson and Winnie Mandela's house. Experience the *ubunthu* [humanity] of Soweto. Full security.' But I think I'll take them to Gold Reef City or the Diamond Mine instead.

Friday 5 May
I realise my first introduction to *Titus Andronicus* was that old Hammer Horror film *Theatre of Blood*; a cautionary tale for critics. Vincent Price, as an old classical actor so ham you can taste the mustard, gets his own back on those who have 'spewed vitriol on the creativity of others' and ruined his career. He murders them all, one by one, in the manner of the most gruesome deaths in Shakespeare. Thus Arthur Lowe's wife wakes up to discover her husband's head has been surgically removed (*Cymbeline*), Coral Browne is burnt like Joan La Pucelle (*Henry VI, Part I*), by being fried alive under her hair drier; and one old soak is drowned in a butt of malmsey wine (*Richard III*).

'So what happens in *Titus Andronicus*?' asks the bewildered police inspector.

'Oh some poor queen is made to eat her children baked in a pie,' comes the reply. Moments later, Robert Morley (outrageously camp in pink seersucker) is forced to eat his pet poodles for lunch, served up in a pastie.

The Rabelaisian pies we have in our show are made by Gramadoelas, the restaurant at the Market Theatre, run by Eduan Naude (the only man I know with a palindrome for a name) and Brian Shalkoff. We need the recipe for the tour to pass on to the caterers at the National. Apparently Brian has been quite cagey about it so far. Today we drop in to see him and take Ma and Pa along for their first real taste of Africa.

'Gramadoelas' means the back of beyond, or the middle of nowhere, and Eduan and Brian have created a splendid haven, with faux marble pillars, and apricot walls hung with a huge variety of African masks and colonial prints. It is one of our favourite haunts. Gramadoelas specialises in pan-African cuisine. Tony, being ethnically timid, tends to stick to the tomato bredie, and I venture around, trying everything from the sosatie to the swatsuur; the kudu to the ostrich steaks.

'Now what haven't you tried since you've been here?' says Brian with a hint of challenge in his voice.

The only thing left untested is the mopani worms.

'You ate worms as a child,' says Ma.

'Yes,' says I, 'but that was a one-off experiment.' Nevertheless, a little nervously, I go for it.

The worms arrive. They look like large black caterpillars in ketchup, but there's no going back now. As I dig my fork in one, red stuff shoots out of either end. I rush it to my mouth, chew quickly, swallow and honourably acquitted, ask Brian to take the plate away. There is no goodness in the worm.

Brian reappears with the *Titus* pie recipe. Perhaps as a reward for my bravery. It requires 7 kilos of flour. The National won't believe it!

As we leave, we scan the visitors' book. It has been rapidly filling up over the last year. There's Prince Edward, Hillary Clinton and Norma Major, François Mitterand and Catherine Deneuve, David Bowie and Iman. Since South Africa made her dazzling quick change from pariah to paramour of the international community, the world's literati and glitterati have swarmed here, and most of them seem to have pitched up at Gramadoelas.

47

Our final week here . . .

Saturday 6 May
I'm useless at public speaking (which people never believe of an actor), but there's no way I'm going to get out of this one. I rise to my feet. 'Thank you, Grahame, for those kind words, and for this splendid lunch . . .'

We're at a long table on the terrace of Market Theatre Chairman Grahame Lindop's fabulous Sandton home. Several other board members are here, with partners; also the former (and first) chairman, the charming Ian Haggie, very ex-pat, very enthusiastic; also the Editor-in-Chief of the *Star*, Arthur Maimane, whom I met when he was an exile in London; also Greg's parents, who seem to be enjoying it all.

'. . . As you probably know, we've had a bit of trouble getting people to come and see our show at the Market,' I say, to polite laughter. 'Anyway, the SABC are filming our last three performances and the idea is to make it clear that the show is live, in a theatre, not in a studio, so . . . the Market mustn't be empty for those performances. This film will be shown nation-wide. So can I ask you to please get out your address books and phone everyone you know, and ask them to come to the theatre on Thursday, Friday and Saturday night . . .'

'Oh!' exclaims a woman next to me. '*You* shouldn't have to do this!'

'Yes, well, I'm sorry . . . I'm sorry if this is a bit vulgar, but I do have to. We must make those last performances full. For the cameras. So please help. Thank you again, Grahame and Barbara, for today's lunch.'

Tuesday 9 May
We attend a rehearsal run-through of the next Market show, a revival of Fugard's *The Island*, with its original cast, John Kani and Winston Ntshona. I never saw the original production and have never read the play, so the whole thing is a fresh experience for me.

The Island has been rehearsing in one of the Market's first-floor front rooms – you see their huge, domed windows in all the photos of the building. They're used, respectively, as a gallery and as a junk room. In the latter, this morning, Greg, I and a stage manager (they have no director) watch John and Winston pour out their hearts. I can't describe it better than John did the other week:

'Protest theatre? Man, we didn't even know how to spell protest. We were just telling the stories of our lives.'

This morning's run-through has gone straight into my top ten of Best Theatre.

Wednesday 10 May

The last few shows are racing by, but not towards an end; somehow, more a beginning. Everywhere you turn there's much eager chat, either about the TV cameras moving into the theatre today (they're doing a trial run tonight), or about the *Titus* tour to London, Leeds and Spain. Half-way through this evening's show, I was passing the small upstairs dressing room and caught a glimpse of Bruce with a mass of guide books on his table, and Paulus leaning over his shoulder, both their faces lit up by the mirror bulbs, and excitement.

Thursday 11 May

God, another one. In the same week. Another remarkable rehearsal run-through.

At the Civic this time – a revival of *Umabatha*, the Zulu *Macbeth*, by its original director-deviser, Welcome Msomi, whom I know from the RSC (he did the dances and ceremonies for *Tamburlaine*).

This morning, with Greg and his parents, sitting in the empty auditorium of the Civic's main house, watching a cross between a Tech and a dress rehearsal, I'm on the edge of my seat from the word go, when a tiny figure dashes from the back of the vast, open stage, kneels at the front, muttering and shivering, and then sneezes. She's one of the witches and the sneeze is a ritual in Zulu witchcraft.

'OK, hold it,' a miked voice says. 'Can we try that again please.'

So she does it again, and again it's like a cold finger stroking my spine.

Seeing the play done in this context, in a society with a *real* relationship to witchcraft – like Shakespeare's society – makes me realise why ninety-nine per cent of modern British *Macbeths* fail. Once you've witnessed the ferocity and conviction of the Zulu witches, you blush at the memory of assorted British actresses in ragged shawls, prosthetic warts and Celtic accents. I'm also very shaken by the sleep-walking scene. Lady

Macbeth gives a wail which turns into a sort of musical note. From the depth of her being, she sings her pain.

It's the best production of the play I've ever seen.

In the next few weeks, this city is going to be so lucky. Like the real things surrounding it, Jo'burg is going to be a goldmine of theatre. Will audiences come though? To a piece of 'protest theatre' at the Market, or to a local version of *Macbeth* (never mind South African accents, they're doing the whole thing in Zulu)?

Friday 12 May

After two months of bleaching it every fortnight, my beard is starting to fall out. Just when I need it for the SABC film of our production. Every morning, I spend hours in front of the bathroom mirror, trying to tease, squeeze or spray the strands together and close the gaps. My invention knows no bounds and has no shame, like those balding people who take a flap of hair from above one ear and wrap it round their scalps.

Last night was the first of our filmed performances. Much excitement and hilarity backstage. There's a monitor in the corridor and the cast got glued to it, almost missing entrances as they waited to see themselves come on.

I was very disappointed with my own performance. No real emotion. Too self-conscious of the cameras, I suppose. Tears are like sperm. If you think about it too much, it doesn't flow.

But tonight, thank God, I gave the cameras my best performance ever. And the reason makes nonsense of any theories about acting.

As I was exiting from the first scene, I pushed through a curtain and dislodged a piece of the TV sound equipment. A small but weighty metal box fell on my head. I was furious – why does a blow to the head always induce such anger? – and did the rest of the show blazing with pain. Afterwards, Sello said to me, 'Hey, you were good tonight. Did you *know* that you were?'

'Mm,' I answered grumpily. 'And I'm too embarrassed to tell you why.'

48

Saturday 13 May

It's the last night and Hollywood is in. Charlie Chaplin and Walt Disney.

Robert Downey Jr is busy filming here in South Africa. When the news filters backstage, Tony looks a little unnerved. Lord Attenborough persuaded Tony to screen test for his film *Chaplin*. Downey Jr got the part.

Also here, unexpectedly, is an old friend, Jay Dyer, who works for Disney Animated Features in LA. In 1994 I was invited by Disney to develop a treatment of *The Odyssey* for them. They were very generous hosts. Everything was 'on the mouse'!

After my first visit, I remember asking how it was that so many of the animated feature department were gay. 'Well put it this way,' came the reply. 'It takes fairies to make things nice!'

It's also the last night of filming for SABC. We've recorded the last three performances, doing pick-up shots during the day. The SABC lighting guys have blasted the stage with light, which has shot Wesley's sensitive lighting design to pieces, but from my position outside the theatre in the control van, watching the monitors, it looks great.

The SABC director, Raymond Sargeant, has been very attentive to my requirements and alert to my suggestions. We've combed the text for weeks putting together the shooting script. There are six cameras in the auditorium and therefore six monitors to choose from in the control van. Catching every little nuance of the action from an appropriate angle is thrilling (and mind-boggling). It reminds me just how detailed all the performances have become.

It's about the five (i.e. ten minutes before curtain up) and I'm just wandering round to front-of-house to check Ma and Pa have got their tickets, when I'm greeted by an unusual sight. A queue. It stretches right outside the doors of the Market and into the precinct. The Lindops and friends have taken Tony's appeal to heart. The crowd is swelling fast.

Keith Lawrence from the British Council in London, who helped us get this whole project off the ground back in January, has come to see tonight's show too, along with 'Marketeers' like Mike Maxwell, Vanessa Cooke, Bruce Koch and Winston Ntshona.

There's a noisy hum, which gets noisier and more aggressive around the box-office. A fluster of raised voices. I slide through the queue and make my way into the box-office. Dale's daughter, Genevieve, is on duty and is trying to hold back the tide.

One man is shouting at her furiously and now starts on me. 'Where are my tickets? I've booked three tickets and now they can't find them!'

I feel like telling him he should have been here last week, he could have had three rows.

'It's no wonder the Market can't get audiences,' he barks. 'You can't deal with them when they do turn up.'

We have to hold the house because of the huge number of people who've arrived. The audience who are already seated are getting restless. Twenty minutes go by and we realise that the eternal flame, which burns away on the stage in the pre-set, will soon be extinguished. The ASM, Bradley, has to come on and relight it. The audience, desperate for anything to happen, applaud him. Finally the last few anxious ticket holders scuttle to their seats, I dash back to the control van and we begin.

The company really go for it, fuelled by the energy of a full house. Tony rises to the occasion and the 'I am the sea' speech in Act III is riveting. He's never done it better. The emotion of having reached the last show must be coursing through his veins. I'm glad we have a record of the performance.

At the curtain call, the swollen audience bursts into loud applause. They stand and cheer. Suddenly Bradley and Heidi launch a surprise shower of balloons from the flies and Toni Morkel and Oupa Mokoena, on the follow spots, fire streamers at the stage. In a riot of colour, the company are called back and back, time and again.

And then it's all over.

49

Monday 15 May

'The morn is bright and grey.' I remember endless discussions about this line – in Titus's speech at the beginning of the hunt scene. What did Shakespeare mean? How could the morn be both bright and grey?

Today we see it, here at the Londolozi Nature Reserve, on the 5 a.m. game drive. It occurs in those few moments, those fast, distinctively African moments, when the sky suddenly changes from pitch black to the shades of dawn. Poised between monochrome and Technicolor, the world looks . . . bright and grey. Maybe in those missing years, when there are no records of what happened to Shakespeare, maybe he came here?

Londolozi is one of the private reserves flanking the vast Kruger National Park in the Eastern Transvaal. Whereas in the Kruger you have to stay on the roads and try to spot distant animal-shaped blobs through a tangle of bushland, here in the private parks you are taken out, in groups of half a dozen, with your own tracker and ranger (armed with a hefty rifle), in an open jeep. They're amazing vehicles, rather like wild animals themselves, bouncing, twisting and crashing through the bush, or churning their way, whining, through the thick sand of dry river beds, or heaving themselves up the sheer faces of *dongas*, going anywhere and everywhere that the game does, and parking right alongside them.

Whether nose to nose with them here in these parks, or sitting in front of David Attenborough TV programmes back in London, watching wildlife is a joy – no, obsession – which Greg and I share. So we're grabbing these few days before returning to the UK, and the British launch of *Cheap Lives*, to catch our breath and to bring John and Margaret here – to show them Africa, wild Africa, as opposed to Jo'burg's skyscrapers and slums.

The Londolozi daily routine is simple: a dawn and dusk drive, each lasting about three hours, and the rest of the day spent eating, drinking, swimming, sunbathing. Our room is on the edge of camp, with a wooden balcony overlooking the jungle, and raided occasionally by the baboons and vervet monkeys that inhabit the surrounding trees.

Greg's Ma, Margaret (on safari)

Tuesday 16 May

Given that there are a *big five* which visitors most want to see – lion,
leopard, rhino, elephant, buffalo – we've had extremely successful sight-
ings. Three lionesses with their cubs lit in the jeep's spotlight last night,
a leopard prowling its territory at sunrise this morning, a bunch of rhino
having an argument alongside us (the *noise* when two of them clashed!)
and my end of the jeep being half-charged by an elephant with an erec-
tion. I don't think it was anything personal.

This evening, on our last game drive, we were specially blessed. Just as the sun was setting, we came across three or four buffalo, and then seven or eight, and then dozens, and then, as we drove on through some trees, hundreds of them crossing a stretch of savannah, their dark mass slowly covering the yellow grass like a tide. Two young bull elephants were caught in the middle of the herd, annoyed, frightened, defensive, flapping their ears and trumpeting. And further still, on the outskirts of the buffalo herd, we found a rhino mother and calf, fleeing the invasion.

'Three of the big five together,' whispered Greg, his eyes bright 'I think we've done rather well.'

In the rays of the sunset, which seemed to illuminate the savannah from within, making the landscape glow, we sat for a long time among the animals, with nobody speaking. Oh, it was good.

Wednesday 17 May
Fly back to Jo'burg. While John and Margaret transfer to a Cape Town plane (Mom and Randall are meeting them at the other end), we drive back – for the last time – to our house in Greenside, to collect our stuff from the last few months. We didn't want to lug it all to Londolozi.

I've been dreading this.

We pack quickly, load the car, pat Laddie and Grunter, and then seek out Selina. She's in her room, sitting on the floor, terribly upset, weeping – 'Oh Tony, oh Greg, oh Selina will miss you!' – reminding me of Katie in the backyard of our Sea Point house on that day in July 1968 when I left South Africa for the first time.

We give Selina a gift and hug her goodbye. She follows us to the car, and as I climb in, she takes my hand and kisses it . . . we drive away, me crying now . . . we look back as we turn the corner . . . she's outside the gates, a small figure with both arms raised high, like Sello's daughter, waving in silence and slow motion . . . I can't bear this . . . I'm still leaving home, still seeking home . . . I feel as young and vulnerable as I did three decades ago . . . and there's something else today as well – I feel completely bloody bruised.

What the hell happened to my triumphant homecoming?

It was exactly like Titus's. Just one shock after another.

I'm thankful that Greg's at my side. The location of *home* might change, and keep changing, but he's always there.

We drive to the airport and fly back to London.

PART VI *The Tour*

London, Leeds, Almagro, June–August 1995

50

Saturday 24 June
'The whole of South Africa is closing down for the day,' says Mom on
the phone this morning.
    'Really – why?'
    '*Why?*' she echoes in disbelief. 'It's the Final!'
    (Oh, the Rugby World Cup.)
    'Don't tell me you won't be watching!' she says.
    'Certainly not! Even if I could. But actually there's something far more
important happening here today.'
    'And what's that, if a person may ask?'
    'The Gay Pride March.'
    She laughs warmly. Since my mother has never had any problem with
my sexuality, I suppose I should be equally open to the queer part of her
nature; to the fact that this theatre-loving, bridge-playing, spiritualist-
worshipping Sea Point lady is a rugger fan!
    It was Dad's great love and something they shared.
    At the parade, together with Market Theatre trustee, Howard Sacks,
who's in town, Greg and I march under the South African flag. Nearby,
the Stonewall banner is being carried by Chris Smith, Mike Cashman
and Ian McKellen, who drops back to chat. He and I squint at one
another's hair. Mine, in urgent need of re-bleaching, is a sort of silver-
green colour and his is dyed reddish, for the film of *Richard III* which
starts shooting next week. When we were together on the Studio visit to
Jo'burg last year, we shared our frustrations about our dream projects:
for him, a film of his *Richard III*, for me, a film of my first novel, *Middlepost*. In the interim, mine has suffered more setbacks, while his has been
realised. Still, I must take hope from this – dreams *can* come true.
    When Greg and I peel off from the parade, we see that the pubs are
crammed with punters watching TV relays of the Rugby Final in
Jo'burg; people spilling out on to the pavements, the last ones watching
on tiptoes, or with their noses pressed to the windows.
    Back at home, we can't resist switching on the telly. To my surprise,
the match is very exciting and, at the end, when South Africa wins, very

moving: the way the team kneel in a tight circle, as though praying together, before they take the ovation; and shots of Mandela wearing the Springbok colours.

'A gay march in the morning, a rugby match in the afternoon,' says Greg. 'Nobody can say we don't have catholic tastes.'

The Rugby Cup has been a massive event in South Africa, hugely supported and celebrated by the locals. It sets me thinking about the apartheid boycotts again.

During that terrific debate on theatre, which Barry Ronge set in motion, one newspaper headline shouted at me: YOU MADE US PHILISTINES (*Sunday Times*, 30/5/95.) Continuing to address me directly, the writer said, 'South Africans, white and black, no longer give a fig for what is happening to our arts and theatre. And blame for this should be laid squarely at your door.' All this because I supported the cultural boycott, which he calls, 'a crass, naïve, and monumentally stupid concept'.

Well, maybe, maybe not, but if the cultural boycott is to blame for the apathy among Jo'burg's theatre audiences (we've heard that *The Island* is playing to only thirty-five per cent at the Market, and up at the Civic, *Umabatha* is doing so badly it's coming off early), then why didn't the sports boycott have the same effect? Why didn't spectators stay away from the Rugby Cup in droves? Why didn't the people say they don't give a fig for what is happening in sport? Or that the stadium was in too dangerous a part of town? Or that they'd rather stay at home and watch videos of American football? Instead, South Africans just welcomed the whole event in the most joyous way.

Monday 26 June
I spoke too soon. This morning's *Guardian* carries a front-page article about how the Springboks' victory has been soured by a speech by Louis Luyt, SA's rugby president, at the closing banquet. It caused walk-outs by the New Zealanders, French, English and Welsh. Referring to the sports boycott, Meneer Luyt proclaimed the Springboks to be the first *true* world champions: 'There were no true world champions in the 1987 and 1991 World Cups because South Africa was not there. We have proved our point.'

His tone is so familiar.

Tuesday 27 June
This week I'm doing the last batch of publicity for *Cheap Lives*.

The launch has been a tiring but happy time, travelling back and forth across the spring countryside, with plenty of highlights – the reading at South Africa House, the Hay-on-Wye and Birmingham Book Festivals, the Platforms at the RNT and Manchester Royal Exchange – and only a couple of low points: a bookshop signing session where just one person turned up, and a radio show where the interviewer forgot to turn up.

Thursday 29 June
Raymond Sargeant has sent us the final version of the telly *Titus* and we're delighted with it. It's much better than most filmed theatre, because it was done live, with an audience. It's great for us to have a record of the whole show. It's also an opportunity to fulfil what the Minister for Arts, Dr Ngubani, said at the opening, 'I wish all South Africans could see this show.'

Friday 30 June
A beautiful English summer morning. I arrive home to find Greg out and an unusual number of messages on the answer-machine. Three of them – from Howard Sacks and Regina Sebright in Jo'burg, and Diane Borger at the RNT Studio – all say the same thing: 'Just to let you know that Barney Simon has died.'

I sit at the kitchen table, trying to absorb the news.

Barney Simon, co-founder of the Market Theatre . . . Barney is dead.

This evening, not sure what to do with our feelings, Greg and I drive over to the Tricycle Theatre in Kilburn, where *The Suit* is playing – it's the closest we can get to the Market.

Two weeks ago, Barney's production of Can Themba's short story, *The Suit*, arrived in London as part of the LIFT Festival, but without its director–deviser. Sello (who gives a terrific performance as a township Othello, consumed with marital jealousy) told us that when Barney was abroad recently, he felt ill. His brother, a doctor, recommended a check-up. Barney returned to SA, re-rehearsed *The Suit*, then had the check-up. They immediately rushed him into hospital and operated for a heart condition. Barney was not a good patient ('I feel invaded,' he kept telling people. 'My body has been invaded'), but made a good recovery and, although not well enough to travel with *The Suit*, he was thought to be out of danger.

Tonight, we go into the auditorium to watch the last scene.

Sello's character has been out on a piss-up with his mates. Very drunk, he arrives home to find his wife – whom, earlier, he has humiliated publicly – lying in bed. He cuddles up to her, randily. Then discovers she's killed herself. Sobbing, he carries her body round the house. At the same time, his two friends stagger across the front of the stage, talking drunken gibberish, oblivious of the tragedy behind them. The audience, who've been shocked and moved, start giggling. The juxtaposition is a perfect Barney moment.

I watch Sello closely. Barney was his great mentor and champion, changing his fortunes from that of a TV soap star to SA's leading young black theatre actor, John Kani's natural successor. I wonder what Sello must feel as he *acts* grief tonight?

At the curtain call, the cast carry on a candle, then Sello steps forward. In a subdued but controlled voice (I would've said *dignified*, except I know Sello hates the way black actors are always described with this word), he announces, 'The man who has so delicately woven the tapestry of this play . . . he has left us. Barney Simon died early this morning in Johannesburg.'

There's a gasp from the audience. Then Sello asks for a moment of silence. And then the cast break into song, 'Makube Njalo' ('Let it be so').

When we reach the dressing-room, Sello is sitting forward in his chair, still wearing his costume, his face alight with sweat and tears.

'That man will leave a big void,' he says to us. 'A big void. That man . . . Barney Simon.'

Saturday 1 July

The *Evening Standard* has asked me to write an appreciation of Barney. As I try to compose it, I wonder if I'm the right man for the job? I didn't really know him. But then, did anybody? He was a very solitary, very odd, chap, whose work was greatly respected (more overseas than in SA, naturally), and whose personality inspired love and devotion in some, while completely mystifying others. I remember, after meeting him for the first time (he came up to Stratford to see me play Shylock and we had dinner in the Dirty Duck), saying to Greg, 'That man is either a genius or a pseud.'

To be completely honest, I think the truth lay somewhere in between. But it doesn't matter. For whatever reason, he became one of the best and bravest creative artists that SA has produced. His invention of the Market Theatre (with Mannie Manim) in 1976, during apartheid's most violent years, is among the most remarkable things that theatre has done this century; it allowed the voices of protest – or, as John Kani would say, 'the story of our lives' – to echo round the world. And in terms of Barney's own career, as a witty and simple story-teller (like in *Woza Albert!* and *The Suit*), he made miniature masterpieces.

Sunday 2 July

6.30 a.m., Heathrow. The South Africans arrive on two flights, first the Capetonians – Ivan, Oscar and our new actor, Ricky Rudolph (taking over Lesley Fong's roles) – then all the others from Jo'burg. Here we are again. South African actors arriving in London at a time of crisis for the Market. Everyone is in shock over Barney's death. They tell us that Bruce Laing (Barney's lodger and devoted friend) has taken it very badly – he's stayed behind for the funeral today and will fly out this evening.

The other thing uppermost on everyone's tongue is the Rugby World Cup. Duncan's T-shirt says it all: WE WON 15–12. Dale and Gys tell me about their experience of the big day:

Dale: 'We watched it together at my house   '

Gys: 'Almost all of it. But towards the end I got too excited and I went to the nearest bar – I needed to be with lots of people.'

Dale: 'I was pacing around so much, Karen said sit down man, you'll have a heart attack.'

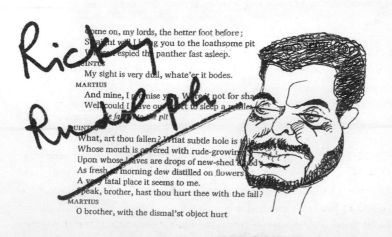

Come on, my lords, the better foot before;
Straight will I bring you to the loathsome pit
Where I espied the panther fast asleep.
QUINTUS
My sight is very dull, whate'er it bodes.
MARTIUS
And mine, I promise you. Were it not for shame,
Well could I leave our sport to sleep a while.
                      He falls into the pit
QUINTUS
What, art thou fallen? What subtle hole is this,
Whose mouth is covered with rude-growing briers,
Upon whose leaves are drops of new-shed blood
As fresh as morning dew distilled on flowers?
A very fatal place it seems to me.
Speak, brother, hast thou hurt thee with the fall?
MARTIUS
O brother, with the dismal'st object hurt

Gys: 'And then we won.'

Dale: 'Then we won.'

Gys: 'And then the streets started cooking!'

Dale: 'Jesus, I've never seen the streets of Jo'burg like that.'

Gys: 'Agh no, I have. That night after the elections. People *jawling* through till dawn, everyone just friends with everyone else, everyone just so fucking happy!'

It's wonderful to see that special Gys de Villiers gleam again – from his bald head and bright gaze – that big-eyed appetite for life, which is somehow boyish and vulpine at the same time. Wonderful to see the whole company; brimming with a kind of wrecked energy, as though the flight was just another all-night party.

Gys

(They all have that particular South African talent, which Dad turned into his catch-phrase – 'I work hard and I play hard' – and it's one they're going to exploit to the limit over the next four weeks.)

Paulus has minimal luggage, but it includes the Chocolate Log sports bag. He's never flown before. 'How was it, Thapelo?' I ask, using his tribal name. As usual, he doesn't reply with words, but describes the experience by licking his lips, jiggling his shoulders, widening his eyes.

Dorothy tells us that Paulus woke her with a phone call at seven o'clock yesterday morning, saying that he was at the meeting place, outside the Market and asking where everyone else was? 'Paulus, we're meeting at seven o'clock *tonight!*' she explained blearily.

When he returned in the evening, the whole of his group, Squint Artists, had come along from Alexandra Township to wave him off. Apparently they'd all been there in the morning as well.

(I'm remembering the loyalty of that group – several of whom are orphans – and how, when our tour was extended by the invitation to Spain, he said he'd have to check with them first, because it meant missing their monthly meeting.)

As Greg and I drive him and Daphney (she's elected to be his minder – a sort of chaperone–translator) to their digs in Kilburn, I ask him about the departure. In his soft, halting way, he says, 'We were up all Saturday night, the Squints . . . a party for my big journey . . . and then, when the time has come for me to go, they give me this . . .' Smiling with pride, he reaches into his jacket and produces a greetings card. It is covered in signatures from all the Squints and a large message in Sotho.

'What does this say?' I ask.

His smile widens. 'It says, "Go, Paulus, go!" '

Afternoon. We make a *braai* for our *Titus* company, and the cast of *The Suit* come along as well. The weather is warm, but grey, and eventually drizzly. We open champagne, and in our small Islington garden the South Africans gather in a circle to hold a wake for Barney. Someone mentions that he had a passion for ice-cream and says, 'That's what he'll be doing now, in heaven, eating strawberry ripple with Joe Slovo.' People propose a variety of toasts ('. . . now raise your glass if Barney ever infuriated you,' chuckles Dale, and everyone's glass shoots up) and tell stories about him. My favourite (told by Dorothy) is of Vanessa Cooke overhearing an actor being rude about Barney, and her flying at him, bringing him down on to the floor and beating him up.

Like Paulus and the Squints – such loyalty, such love.

Monday 3 July

I feel very happy, infused with a romantic sensation of belonging to a
group of travelling players.

Jo'burg, London, Leeds, Spain.

Our long, strange, wonderful journey with this play winds on through
various landscapes, which are sometimes different, sometimes the same,
but always echoing with familiar things. For example, this morning, in
the main rehearsal room of the RNT Studio, here I am again, standing to
attention in a military jeep as the Goth prisoners drag it into Rome, and
we come to a halt, and I give a salute, and then take a deep breath:

> 'Hail Rome, victorious in thy mourning weeds . . .'

A different shiver goes up my spine as I do the opening speech today:

> 'Cometh Andronicus . . .
> To re-salute his country with his tears . . .'

The country which I'm now thinking of as *mine*, and which I'm re-saluting with my 'tears of true joy' – and with this production – is England.

For me, one of the most valuable things to come out of the Jo'burg
experience is the chance to reappraise my career here in England and,
quite frankly, to thank my cotton socks for it! In recent years, I'd become
complacent, jaded even, focusing on the minor irritants (the critics who
don't like my work, the occasional half-full audience), instead of celebrating the privilege of having a career in a country that truly values theatre. Despite the damage inflicted by sixteen years of Tory arts policies,
British theatre is still very much alive and kicking.

Lunch-time. Bruce Laing arrives. Back in Jo'burg, he was more excited
than anyone about coming to London – his first visit. Now, here he is,
looking drawn and subdued, grieving for Barney, his father figure, guru,
friend and landlord.

He tells me about visiting Barney in hospital after the heart surgery.
With tubes in his nose and mouth, Barney could only communicate by
bouncing his eyebrows. (Their joke . . . Barney's nickname for Bruce,
'O.E.O' – One Eyebrow Only.) Soon after that visit, Barney was moved
to the house of some friends – to recuperate – and those friends restricted visitors to a minimum. So Bruce never saw Barney again. His last
image is of Barney with his face full of tubes, yet smiling up at him,
bouncing his eyebrows.

Today, I notice that Bruce has had the middle of his one eyebrow waxed and now has two like everyone else.

He says, 'The funeral yesterday . . . it was incredible. The whole of South African theatre was there.'

'Tell me what happened?'

He frowns, trying to focus on his new surroundings. 'I will . . . another time.'

Even while *Titus* is still in full flow, I have to start thinking about future work. When we got back from SA, a film script was waiting for me with a letter from its author; 'Fancy a gentle summer messing about on the river?' Terry Jones, offering me the part of the villain, Chief Weasel, in his adaptation of *The Wind in the Willows*. (He's also directing, and playing Toad.) Today, I sign up for it.

51

Saturday 8 July

Travel up to Leeds on the two o'clock from King's Cross. By myself.
Tony has to stay behind for fittings for Chief Weasel.

He has had his beard and hair re-dyed for *Titus* by a Miss Tingle at the
London branch of Goldwell. It looked fine on Wednesday night, but on
Thursday he thought it wasn't grey enough and by Friday he decided it
was practically blond. And his fears were compounded this morning
when we woke up to find the front of his hair had turned bright saffron
and the pillows were covered in yellow.

Wondering if this was some weird chemical reaction to stress, I then
realised that he must have accidentally head-butted the star-gazer lilies
on the dining-room table the night before and covered himself in pollen.
It washed out of his fringe sooner than it will wash out of the linen
pillowcases.

The train skims northwards through the flat shires of Beds. and
Northants. Honey-coloured Saxon churches, fields dusky with wheat,
embankments frothing with elderflower and cow parsley, spattered here
and there with rose-bay willow-herb. England stretching into summer.

Skipping through my diary – 'One should always have something sensational to read in the train' – I review the past week's re-rehearsal.

It's been good to be able to bring the company back here after all our
adventures and (quoting Titus) 'to return with precious lading to the bay
from whence at first [we] weighed [our] anchorage'.

The main effort of the week has been to rehearse Martin le Maitre's
replacement, Chris Wells, a rusty rugby player of a man, as Lucius, and
Ricky Rudolph as the Chief Goth.

It's always difficult for actors to take over in a production. I have to
prevent myself and the rest of the company from constantly saying to
Chris, 'Well, Martin used to do it like this . . .' I need to allow Chris to
discover his own way and at the same time preserve the things which we
know can and do work. I have to show him the map and then hurry him
through the maze.

Chris is very well prepared, but there's a lot to take in. One day, during Act III, Scene 1, the great aria of grief, he suddenly grabs his head and says: 'Hold it, hold it . . . What am I thinking here? My sister has been raped and mutilated and has lost her tongue and both her hands. Dad's just had his hand chopped off. What am I thinking?'

Tony suggests, 'It'll be hell at mealtimes?'

Chris Well

Jason Barnes, with the help of Lucy Hemmings, the Studio production manager, and Tracey Wilson, our prop buyer, have assembled all the bits of the production which were too bulky to travel: the mannequin, the junk, even the jeep. It's a Willys, which ironically enough, is the kind of jeep they use in the SADF (South African Defence Force).

Jason is the production manager of the Cottesloe, and next spring he will have been with the National for twenty-five years. With his fierce loyalty, his unquenchable enthusiasm and his rigorous attention to detail, it is no wonder that Richard Eyre describes him as a 'National Treasure'.

We ran the play on Friday afternoon. Because the performances at the Cottesloe have been sold out solidly for weeks, and our answerphone has been jammed with requests for tickets, we sneaked a few friends in to the run. All pros, so they knew what to expect. No costumes, no set etc. Miriam Karlin and Frith Banbury said they felt like Tudor noblemen having the play done specially for them.

'Anybody seen Paulus?'

Paulus was missing.

Somebody said they thought he had gone back to his digs in Kilburn in the lunch-break. Far from being confused by London and the Underground, Paulus loves it. 'It's so easy for a person to go round,' he keeps saying. 'The transport, the transport!' His enthusiasm is understandable. I recall driving past the taxi rank on Bree Street, on our way home from the Market: those Kombis (known as black cabs!) and the queues of black workers stretching right across the vast square. It could take people up to three hours to get to the townships, a journey which by car lasts maybe twenty minutes.

I gave the company a little lecture about looking after Paulus.

We were now half an hour late and couldn't afford to wait any longer. Just as we were about to begin, he came pelting into the room and I bawled him out.

Only later did we discover what had happened. Paulus had nipped back to his digs in the break and was running from Waterloo Station back to the Studio when he was stopped by the police. They presumed he was escaping from the scene of a crime. Why else should a young black boy be running so fast? That very morning the lead story in all the papers had been the contention by the Metropolitan Police Commissioner, Sir Paul Condon, that most muggings are committed by black youths. True or not, the police themselves obviously didn't give Paulus the benefit of the doubt.

Newark, Doncaster, Wakefield, Leeds.

I first worked in Leeds for the Interplay Community Theatre Company; and shared a freezing garret with a friend. This time Tony and I are staying at 42 The Calls.

The Fletland Mill, which now houses this luxury hotel, used to produce flour and horse corn, and dates back to the Industrial Revolution. Our room overlooks the River Aire which rises on the Moors somewhere north of Skipton, meanders down the Airedale Valley, flowing parallel to the Leeds and Liverpool Canal, before losing itself in the Ouse, the Humber Estuary and ultimately the North Sea. Here it is graced by swans. All day, colourful barges putt up and down river with names like *Brighouse Nan, Andromeda II* and *Foxtrot*, and the Kirkstall flyboat ferries schoolchildren and tourists up and down.

Yes, tourists. Leeds has had a face-lift. The sky may still hang over the town like a sodden mattress, but the dark satanic image of a Northern industrial city has gone. The wharves have been scrubbed up, the waterfront now boasts a Heritage Trail and across the Centenary Footbridge,

Tetley's Brewery has opened a Visitors' Centre. I breathe in the warm, malty aroma which drifts over from the brewery and head into the theatre.

The West Yorkshire Playhouse stands on Quarry Hill. The wide Victorian Boulevard of the Headrow, on the other side of the rise, continues its stately march over the roundabout past the Playhouse, and all the way up to an intimidating Fritz Lang edifice commanding the summit. It looks like some New Age temple but turns out to be the Department of Health and Social Security.

I gaze out over the city. How ironic that just as *Titus* took Tony back to South Africa, now it has brought me to the county where I was born. Tony's homecoming was not all he expected. I wonder what mine will be like? Still, I suppose if you are going to dig for your roots, you shouldn't be surprised to find a little soil on them.

Sunday 9 July
Ring Tony to tell him there's a good review for *Cheap Lives* in the *Observer.*

'Aha. How are things?'

God, he can be so irritating. It's a great review. I want to jump up and down; he wants a progress report on the set. But I bet he's jumping up and down inside.

I tell him how things are going. Nadya has managed to achieve the Market stage in miniature, with the sterling help of the National's crew under the supervision of Jason Barnes, Stuart Smith and Mark Jonathan, the RNT head of lighting.

'How was your costume fitting for the Weasel?' I ask.

'I think it's going to be fine,' he says. 'There were about six people here from the wardrobe department, all milling around in the study. So there was no room to try out the tail, so I had to go out and run round the garden for them.'

'In your tail?'

'In my tail.'

I've no idea what the neighbours must make of us. At one moment, Tony's pacing round the lawn practising ventriloquism with a puppet of Hitler (for *Genghis Cohen*); the next, a hoard of noisy South Africans are jamming away on the patio; and now there's a man-sized rodent shimmying up the garden path.

52

Monday 10 July
Tech at West Yorkshire Playhouse. The Market Theatre production of
Jozi Jozi is playing here this week as well, and the management have put
up a display about Barney in the foyer. We're in the Courtyard Theatre,
the smaller of their two auditoria – it was modelled on the Cottesloe, so
it's ideal for our new touring set. The only oddity is the stairways on
either side of the seating. I don't know what they're made of, but they go
'boing, boing, boing' as you walk up or down – we're calling it the Bed-
spring Theatre – and God knows what it'll sound like if audience members arrive late or leave early.

Like all theatres these days, backstage security is hazardous. Locks
everywhere, of the high-tech variety – a digital code which you have to
tap in – so in the second half of the play, when her hands are bound into
stumps, Jenny can't open her dressing-room door.

Because of the rate of exchange, our salary (we're all on the same), £300
a week, turns into a lot of rand – about R1,800 – so the South Africans
are all starting to treat themselves. Last week, Paulus bought himself a
Sony Walkman and is even more difficult to communicate with now, and
Godfrey bought himself a camera. Great excitement today when his first
roll of film was developed, followed by great disappointment when he
discovered that most of the shots were blurred. He nevertheless insisted
on showing every fuzzy snap, cornering each of us, saying mournfully:
'Look at how bad this one is, and oh – look at *this* one!'
    Dan has elected to teach Godfrey how to focus.

Only two things in the production are inferior to their Jo'burg equiva-
lents. The sand, revealed when the paving stones are removed, isn't that
distinctive African red earth (Customs regulations forbade us to bring
the real thing), but from Cornish tin mines; and the pie at the end, in
which Chiron's and Demetrius's heads are baked, isn't a patch on Gramadoelas's. In fact, the one they produced today was *vegetarian*. 'Tamora

is tricked into cannibalising her own children,' I hear Greg explaining tactfully to a West Yorkshire ASM. 'I fear the impact might be lessened if she's munching a handful of chickpeas.'

Tuesday 11 July

First preview and first British performance. The entire Leeds run is sold out. It's wonderful to see an absolutely packed house for the same show that emptied the Market. The auditorium is so full, it looks like people are bulging over the ends of the rows. It's a terrific show, with lots of real emotion, and Act III, Scene 1 is specially good. In the interval, Dumi, whose little band is now perched on the first level, overlooking the auditorium, says, 'If you could see silence, I saw it tonight.' That's a considerable compliment – from a musician. At the end of the show there's huge applause and we're called back for more bows. Afterwards, I discover that Roger Chapman has come up from London, with the RNT's finance wizard, Lorne Cuthbert, and both are very enthusiastic. At last – a palpable sense of excitement about what we're doing. At last – the realisation of our original concept: *What if we could take that Market Theatre energy, that passion and commitment, like in* Woza Albert! *or the Fugard plays, and what if we could put that into Shakespeare?*

Wednesday 12 July

Exhausting day. Working notes from ten to twelve, then a matinée from two to five, then the press night.

Before the latter, Greg assembles the *Titus* cast and crew on stage, and asks the West Yorkshire stage team to join us, as well as the RNT people who've been up here working their socks off. As he thanks them all, I notice that his native Northern accent is creeping back, and can't help smiling. I used to be paranoid about South African vowels popping up in my speech – now I delight in them.

Lifting a little black plastic bag, Greg says, 'I have here some illegal substance, which Tony smuggled out of South Africa, unbeknown to me, I'm pleased to say – since it was in *my* luggage!' Everyone leans forward as he peels open the bag, to reveal a small heap of red Jo'burg earth, which I collected from our set on the last night at the Market.

Greg asks Paulus to sprinkle some on our new set and Daphney to sing something. Without hesitation, her voice soars:

> '*Vumel' abaphansi*
> *Vumel' abaphezulu . . .*'

(A Zulu song to the ancestors, it roughly translates as: 'Agree for them down here/Agree for them up there.') Like all traditional songs, the natural rhythms and repetitive lyric make it easy to join in, and we all do (well, not the Brits), clapping and dancing. I feel moved, happy, proud and frightened again . . .

I didn't think I'd be nervous this time round, but I am. I compensate in my usual way, making myself very available backstage, touring the dressing-rooms and corridors, saying, 'It's going very well,' or, 'That scene sounded terrific.'

Luckily, I'm not forced to lie tonight. The show is extremely good and I'm blessed with real emotion to play with. Standing in the wings, preparing for Act III, Scene 1, I think of Daphney's song, and of ancestors, then whisper, like on the last night in Jo'burg, 'OK Dad, here we go . . .'

At the end of the show, the applause grows to a standing ovation.

Afterwards, in the bar, a woman comes up to me. She's trembling. 'Such violence in the play!' she says. 'Not just what people do to one another, but what's in their minds. I didn't know whether to scream or laugh. And then when *you* laughed . . . !'

(She's referring to one of Shakespeare's most uncharacteristic lines. 'Ha, ha, ha!' which is Titus's response to Marcus's question, 'Now is a time to storm; why art thou still?' I had been playing the laughter as a kind of howl, a noise of pain, but when we were re-rehearsing last week, Greg suggested trying it as *real* laughter, a real fit of graveside giggles, and the moment is more disturbing now. It's one of a whole batch of new discoveries.)

A crowd at the bar. Some of Greg's closest friends (Martin Pople, Amanda Smith, Tony Mulholland) have travelled here to be with him tonight, for *his* homecoming. Jude Kelly, and the ladies from the RNT Studio, Sue H., and Diane B., all seem very pleased with the show, and even more pleased when Dumi opens the piano in the foyer, signalling that it's time for a South African party. Our company is joined by the *Jozi Jozi* lot. 'We're colonising Britain!' yells Sello. He's wearing a red towel round his neck, like a champion athlete (appropriate to the danger and grace with which he performed Aaron this evening). He throws the towel into the air and, bouncing like a kid, whistling and whooping, joins Daphney and Paulus, who are already dancing round the piano. The sing-song takes off like a flight of birds. Traditional songs, songs from shows like *Sophiatown* and *District Six*, and of course 'Nkosi Sikelel'i'. I

"shosholoza
kulezontaba
stimela stimela
sibek' emzazi afrika"

Daphney, Sello, Paulus at W. Yorkshire Playhouse

notice that not all South Africans hold up their fists in the black power salute any more – Dale sings it with his hand on his heart. Sue, Diane and Lucy Hemming sit together, listening, their faces radiant . . . they're back on the Studio visit to the Market . . . where all this began.

Much, much later, walking back to The Calls, I ask Greg, 'So, was it just local critics here tonight?'

'Not at all. All the main ones. From all the main papers.'

'Oo heck,' I say, imitating his rekindled Northern accent.

'It's a compliment – them all travelling up.'

'It is, but . . . *oich*, here we go again.'

53

Thursday 13 July

Discuss the press night over lunch. The Pools Court is very cool and dapper, with the odd discreet vase of agapanthus. The menu is crammed from the *amuse bouche* to the *bavarois* with those glorious words you only find in posh restaurants. They tantalise the brain cells before tickling the palate. I'm seduced by the '*pithivier*' of wild mushrooms.

'But that's vegetarian!' Tony sneers, as if no self-respecting carnivore should be seen dead in that suburb of the menu.

I tell him which critics were in last night: Billington, Coveney, Nightingale, Tinker.

'Did you speak to Billington?' he asks.

'I couldn't make up my mind,' I say. 'Wasn't sure of the etiquette.'

I first met Michael Billington when he was invited up to Stratford in 1987, to explain a review he had written decrying the standard of verse speaking among the younger members of the company. Like Daniel into the lions' den, he came. I asked him if he had ever directed a play. He had, back in Lincoln in the early sixties, before he was lured, or retreated, to the other side of the footlights. So we hatched a plot. He came to direct a delicate Marivaux play called *The Will* for the RSC Fringe and to complete the exercise Terry Hands reviewed it for the *Guardian*.

So last night, for old times' sake, I slipped over to say 'Hello'. During our chat, Michael told me he remembered people being carried out of the Brook production of *Titus*. 'It was the noise,' he said, the loud electronic score which caused this reaction, not the horrors. I told him that backstage during Deborah Warner's *Titus* the actors kept a tally of audience faintings. In Jo'burg they used to vomit. One man, in a projectile eruption worthy of *The Exorcist*, vomited over several rows. I realised, as I scuttled back up the aisle, that I had just told a critic my production made people throw up.

Friday 14 July

Wake up to find Tony reading the papers. Standing there in his dressing-gown, with his silver hair, he looks like some Old Testament prophet.

'What are they like?'

'God,' he mutters.

'What?'

'Phew-ie.'

'WHAT!' I bellow.

'Nothing,' he says. 'Just the review of our dreams. We're "a marvel of modern theatre", according to the *Daily Mail*. Jack Tinker says it's "a triumphant production" and 'cos it's sold out at the National he'd be willing to sell programmes to see it again.'

I feel a sudden rush of affection for Jack Tinker.

'And the rest?'

'Benedict Nightingale in *The Times* has got it spot on. He says it's a crazy piece for a crazy place. That's good isn't it?'

I pick up the *Telegraph*. 'Did you order this?' I ask.

'No, it's compulsory reading in this hotel. All the guests get a copy.'

The review is headlined SO BAD IT ISN'T EVEN SCARY. Sick pit in my stomach. I read it in silence. Tony can tell from my grunts it's bad. 'He says it's misconceived, lackadaisical and sounds ugly in South African accents. But he thinks you are excellent.' I start seething. 'He begins the whole review by saying he thinks the play's "a revolting piece of work", so what the fuck is the point of coming to it at all?' I rage. 'You don't ask a vegetarian what he thinks of your beefsteak tartare!'

Tony takes the paper. 'He also says the play seems "grotesquely at odds with the transformation of South Africa".' He grunts. 'Typically sentimental right-wing point of view. Anyway no one we know reads the *Daily Telegraph*.'

'Oh, only all my parents' friends,' I don't reply.

'What else is out today?' he asks.

'The *Guardian* and the *Yorkshire Post* should be,' I say, busy ogling the *Daily Mail*, revelling in the evident perspicacity and indubitable good taste of their critic.

'Weather's a bit sketchy today,' the taxi driver says, as we set out to Shipley for a morning out.

We stop in Briggate ('Briggit' the driver calls it) so Tony can buy the other papers. When Tony gets back into the taxi, I slide the *Yorkshire Post* from under his arm. He's already half-way through the *Guardian* review.

'Well?' I ask.

'He thinks the production is fascinating and confirms the play's status as a masterwork.'

'Great,' I slaver, grabbing the paper from him. ' "Billington hails Antony Sher in a politically focused *Titus Andronicus*," ' I read aloud, and am about to continue when Tony interrupts: 'He does worry a bit about the stylisation of Lavinia's rape.'

'Oh,' I mumble.

'And thinks the toilet scene falls between two stools. But you know Billington, he can't resist a bad pun.'

'It's good for you though,' I rally. ' "A Pretoria Patton, grizzly and ramrod-backed." '

Tony is thrilled with the Patton reference. George C. Scott's performance was an early source of inspiration.

'What's the *Yorkshire Post* like?' Tony asks.

'It says your performance is mesmerising and calls the production ground breaking and unique. Says it should be writ large in the annals of theatre.'

Tony rubs his finger gently on the back of my hand. 'You must be very pleased,' he says fondly. 'Your homecoming's been a bit of a triumph.'

'Except the *Telegraph*,' I mumble.

I flop the papers to the floor, gaze out of the window and spend the rest of the journey marvelling at the beauty of this county where I was born.

All my mother's family came from Yorkshire. My grandfather was the fastest man in the West Riding in his day; his great-grandfather founded the first Zionist Chapel in Salandine Nook; and my great-great-aunts Melinda and Susan ran a sweet-shop in Lindley. I have a tiny photograph of Melinda and Susan, standing on their whitewashed front step. Melinda, in black bombazine, with her arms braced beneath an ample bosom, peers sternly through gold-rimmed spectacles, while Susan, in her flowery pinnie and rolled sleeves, looks a little flustered, as if she has just been interrupted hammering the toffee or turning out the oven-bottom cake. Neither sister ever married. They were known as the 'unclaimed blessings'.

My family defected across the Pennines to the Red Rose County shortly after my twin sister and I were born, but I can still prove my Yorkshire credentials by properly pronouncing Slaithwaite, where Auntie Mary and Uncle Bob lived, as 'Slawit'. Every summer we would trek back in the Hillman Minx through Oswaldtwistle and Bacup to

Todmorden and Hebden Bridge in the foothills of the Pennines. When the houses got sootier I knew there wasn't far to go. Today, my Yorkshire family sit nattering in my head as we drive to sandblasted Saltaire.

We're going to visit another Titus. Titus Salt. Now there's a no-nonsense, down-to-earth, bollocky sort of Yorkshire name. Titus Salt was a virtuous industrialist who realised his Utopian vision to nurture harmony and fellowship in his workforce and build a model factory. So it was, that in 1853, Salt's Mill arose in the model village of Saltaire.

Today, Salt's Mill is an arts complex, run by another industrious entrepreneur, Jonathan Silver, who has made the place a hub of artistic life in the area and attracted some great Yorkshire names there. He got Tony Harrison to write a play for the Mill. Barrie Rutter rehearses Northern Broadsides here, and David Hockney displays much of his work in the gallery. His current exhibition is devoted to forty-seven paintings of his dachshunds, Little Boogie and Stanley. Looking round it, I begin to wonder if Hockney still has all his chairs at home. But I don't say this to Tony. Hockney is one of his great heroes. One of mine is Alan Bennett. In the canteen, there's an enlarged photograph of them both sitting side by side. They look for all the world like the town and country mouse.

Tony disappears to fax a copy of our reviews to Barry Ronge in South Africa, as a final postscript to the *Star* debate. I sit there quietly, dunking a scone in hot coffee. The accents around me are as familiar as my skin. I feel comfortable and proud to be back working in my home county.

54

Sunday 16 July
Now that I'm reading reviews, it's going the way of all bad habits and
turning into a kind of addiction. I wake early, and lie tensely (*will the
Sundays be as good as the weeklies?*), listening for a tell-tale sound in the
two way cupboard at the door. With access from both the room and the
corridor outside, the cupboard allows papers or food to be delivered
without guest and porter having to meet.

At last – a shuffle of feet, a sliding of panels and that turd-like 'plop,
plop' of newspapers arriving. I collect them and, not wanting to disturb
Greg, crawl across the floor to where a strip of sunlight is spilling under
the long wooden shutters (when open, they hang along the wall, wide
and hinged, like bat wings).

Sprawling naked on the floor, my nose pressed to a sunlit patch of carpet and newsprint, my nervous fingers fumbling towards the arts pages, I
feel more and more like I'm in the grip of some ghastly drug. The
Observer first. The headline above Coveney's review talks of a 'riveting
Titus' – good, good – and yes, his review is terrific for both the show and
me (he remarks that I look like Spike Milligan in the role, which makes a
change from Terre'Blanche or Castro), also Dorothy and Jenny. *Sunday
Times* next, but there's no surprise here. They sent their second-string,
Robert Hewison, and he has stated publicly – at an RSC press confer-
ence – that he can't stand my work. So today, true to form, he dismisses
my performance, while praising the production – 'a worthy tribute to
Barney Simon' – also Dorothy, Oscar and Charlton.

By now my fellow junkie has woken and crawled across the floor to get
his own early morning fix. Slightly better than mine today. He goes
chirpily into the bathroom, to soak in a tub, while I open the shutters,
thinking 'Smarmy sod'. It's a beautiful morning, bright and still, and the
air isn't infused with that weekday smell from the brewery opposite, that
smell of hops: warm and pudgy and not to my taste. To compensate for
my *Sunday Times* review, God lays on a little entertainment. A bunch of
attractive skinheads, who've clearly been clubbing all night (can't tell
whether they're gays or yobbos or both), stagger to the river bank, strip

off completely, swim and sunbathe.

Our group of travelling players assemble at the railway station for the
return to London. Like the naked skinheads, the South Africans have
also been partying all night. Some of the chaps struck lucky with the
ladies of Leeds and look well-fucked, while some others just look, well,
fucked.

To catch up, we buy champagne and orange juice for our table – with
Dorothy and Sello – as the train sets off and trundles in that Sunday-
slow way across England.

What is it about this country in summer? Its beauty never stirs me like
Africa's, but it does make me feel calm and well. What is it? Particularly
these hot summers, when England is less green than usual. All the fields
go yellow and even the sky, pale with heat, is yellow at the edges. It
reminds me of old photos, or of British films of the fifties, in the glow of
early Technicolor. Gentle comedies with Kenneth More, James Robert-
son Justice and bright vintage cars. Those films gave me my first sight-
ings of the land that was to become home, and left me with a strange
affection, a strange nostalgia for places I never knew.

Sello and I start talking. He tells me about the first night of *The Island*,
and how it was a familiar Market Theatre affair, including a frantic, last-
minute campaign to get a full house – because the President was coming.
Sello brought Lerato, his daughter, to see Mandela, and she was pleased,
but unfazed, when he stopped to greet her. Sello explained about Lerato's hearing.

Sello says to me, 'Communicating with her is holy – because you *really*
have to communicate. So her deafness is a kind of gift.'

He does have a fine way of expressing himself, in his strong, throaty
voice ('A classical actor's vibrato', said Janet Suzman when she saw
Titus), but then, of course, he used to be a lay preacher. I ask whether
Lerato misses music?

He answers, 'Well, no, because she sort of hears it, that's the funny
thing. The other day I was watching her play and suddenly she started to
hum to herself. Now where did that come from? I think our feelings
make melodies.'

55

Monday 17 July

'Objectivity is the cardinal function of the critic,' said Shaw. He is also quoted as saying that his own criticism had no other fault 'than the inevitable one of extreme unfairness'. Whether models of objectivity or unfairness, the rest of our reviews go something like this:

Jeffrey Wainwright, the critic in Monday's *Independent*, says the cutting at the end of the play is inspired, the production is 'powerfully voiced' and he likes the stylisation of the rape waltz and the discreet treatment of the play's excesses. He is particularly nice about Dale and Sello, but he doesn't mention Tony's performance – other than to say he looks 'blimpishly pink'.

A critic (M. Coveney)

Time Out praises Tony's 'remarkable' performance, and the 'rich variety' created by our multi-racial cast 'more so than in any such Shakespearean production over here', and places the production on its Critics' Choice list.

And the *Glasgow Herald* glows with superlatives. It claims the production shows 'how stale and lifeless most English productions of Shakespeare have become', and finds ours 'a hundred times more entertaining'. Heart-warming stuff to read.

Of course the production might be riveting to one critic and bore another rigid. One might think it a gripping exposure of inhumanity; another just a tedious piece of Grand Guignol. One finds the production clumsy, another finds it magnificent.

I am glad that we have a multiplicity of very personal perspectives, and that our theatre is not dominated by one tyrannical point of view, as it is in New York. But it can be confusing. Admittedly, as Ken Tynan said, a critic's last responsibility is to the people who read him first. But if a critic's function is not just reactive, but also prescriptive, how are we, the poor patients (many of us vulnerable hypochondriacs) to choose which of these contradictory prescriptions to take?

Critics perpetuate a transient art. They write letters to posterity. It is, after all, by reading critics that we know what some of the great performances of the past were like. I know from Hazlitt that Kean's acting was 'an anarchy of the passions'. I know what Irving was like in *The Bells* or Beerbohm Tree as Falstaff, or Ellen Terry as Portia by reading Shaw. From Agate I know that Gielgud's Hamlet was 'conceived in the key of poetry and executed with beautiful diction'; whereas Mrs Patrick Campbell in *Ghosts* was 'like the Lord Mayor's coach with nothing in it'.

And from Tynan I know that Olivier transformed Titus 'from a five-finger exercise to an unforgettable concerto of grief', and that Vivien Leigh as Lavinia received the news that she was about to be ravished on her husband's corpse 'with little more than the mild annoyance of one who would have preferred foam rubber'.

56

Tuesday 18 July
London. Driving to work on my own (Greg had to be in earlier), I feel a kind of joy, a kind of exhaustion. Tonight's opening is an important landmark in the journey . . . a journey I started twenty-seven years ago, when I left home for the UK, and a journey which these other fifteen South African actors have experienced in the last few months. Who would have thought any of us would be opening at the Royal National Theatre of Great Britain tonight?

The RNT stage-doorkeepers are struggling valiantly to pronounce the names of our company. Over the tannoy, this call: 'Geese de Villiers, please ring the switchboard . . .'
    Wait till they have to summon Sello Maake ka Ncube.

Our set only *just* fits into the Cottesloe. The jeep can barely be hidden from the audience and then hardly has any distance to travel before it reaches centre stage. Greg says, 'It's not so much a triumphal entry any more . . . it's triumphal parking.'

At 6.45 p.m., a repeat of our little ceremony, sprinkling the set with authentic Jo'burg earth, while singing to the ancestors. Mark Jonathan, Jason Barnes and Stuart Smith, who had stood silent and a bit embarrassed in Leeds, now join in with gusto.

So, our third opening night . . . (As Greg says, 'It seems unfair to have so many!')
    The Cottesloe is packed, even the standing-room at the back. Terrific applause at the end – extra bows – and terrific responses from people who are in: my agent Jeremy Conway (who tactfully refrains from any comparisons to his other client, B. Cox), our new chum from the Hay-on-Wye Literary Festival, Sarah Dunant, and the king of first-nighters, the actor Vernon Dobcheff.
    Among theatre circles, the word 'ubiquitous' might eventually be

replaced by 'Dobcheffesque'. Tall and humorous, a walking encyclopaedia of drama, Vernon is often sighted at several openings on the same evening and rumours abound that there's more than one of him. Tonight, he leaves the dressing-room before us, but we overtake him several corridors on, and here he is again, at the stage door when we depart, and yet when we reach Joe Allen's he's already there. '*And*,' he says to me, as if in mid-conversation, 'I want to know why you didn't look in that bag with the heads? After all, you've only got the messenger's word it's your sons!'

Wednesday 19 July
Hot, grey day. Apparently, that fierce heatwave from America is on its way over.

I've got a photo shoot with Lord Snowdon – as part of *Vanity Fair*'s feature on British Theatre. He's photographing me, in Titus costume and make-up, as a sort of military statue, on a plinth, which he's borrowed from Shepperton film studios and positioned at the back of the RNT. Snowdon is charming and giggly. He helps me on to the plinth, admires the congruity of my stained grey-green uniform and the surrounding architecture, adds a squashed Coke tin to the composition and starts clicking away.

An Oriental man, whom I take to be a passing tourist, appears, takes out a camera and, ignoring me completely, starts photographing my photographer. Snowdon's assistants try to block his view, but he's very persistent, shifting round until he's in front of the plinth and he and Snowdon have one another in their viewfinders, as if for a duel. Snowdon gives up and takes him aside. I watch a heated discussion. RNT press officers move in, and now a policeman.

'What's going on?' I ask, as Snowdon pops over to apologise.

'Paparazzi,' he explains with a sigh and a giggle. 'I felt like saying to him, "Bugger off you idiot," but one can't, you know, so I just said, "Are you English?"'

After the show, Greg and I watch our episode of *African Footsteps*, screened on BBC2 earlier tonight. A series of travel programmes, it follows various people (Viv Richards, Paul Boateng and others) through various African countries. When they contacted me, I assumed they wanted me to go to South Africa. But no. Would Greg and I investigate why Morocco attracted gay writers like Bowles, Burroughs, Capote,

Orton, etc? We accepted the offer – it was another chance for us to show ourselves as an out couple. When I grew up, knowing I was gay (from aged four, having first fallen in love at kindergarten), I felt I was a freak. Tonight, when our programme was screened, I'd be content if just one person, frightened by their gayness, saw it and thought, Hey, this is *ordinary*. Particularly since the last time there was any publicity about an Islington gay couple visiting Morocco, it was Orton and Halliwell, which is like an advert for heterosexuality by Fred and Rosemary West.

MOROCCAN FILM...
The Hon. David Herbert (leading
Light of Tangier's Beau Monde)
and young men in the souk.

Thursday 20 July
The heatwave is here. Two very sweaty shows ahead of us today.

I open my dressing-room window wide. All the dressing-rooms here look out into a kind of concrete courtyard. It's ugly really, reminiscent of the Soviet-built tenement blocks I saw during the Studio's visit to Lithuania, but it's also one of the joys of working here. You can peer into all the other dressing-rooms. It's like a cross-section of an anthill. There's Richard (Wilson) preparing for his matinée of *What the Butler Saw*; there's Simon Russell Beale in the middle of the *Volpone* Tech, trying on different wigs; and there's Gambon sunning himself on his window ledge (in his *Volpone* costume and make-up, he looks like a great fleshy clown from a Fellini film or a Russian circus); and there too are the South Africans in their group dressing-room, noisier than their British colleagues. 'How did you get a dressing-room on your own?' Gys yells down to me. 'Who's cock do I have to suck?'

'Oi!' shouts Gambon. 'No swearing! Show some respect! This is the National fucking Theatre!'

Actors appear at the other windows – dressed in costumes from *Volpone*, *Titus* and *What the Butler Saw*. Gambon's courtyard performances are very popular here, as are his water fights.

Evening performance. In the audience, Lord Gowrie, chairman of the Arts Council, and Sir John Hansen, director general of the British Council. Also Harvey Lichtenstein of BAM (Brooklyn Academy of Music) in New York (where the RNT took *Richard III* and *The Madness of George III*), over here to scout for shows.

Greg and I spread the word among the cast and the effect is electric. Bruce whispers to me in the wings, 'It's like the play is being spoken for the first time tonight!'

Tonight's show *is* that good. Maybe also because we've already done it once today. I've noticed that I sometimes act better when I'm tired or even ill. I think this is true of other actors too. We try less hard, the performance just seems to *flow* more.

In the second half, I'm sitting, slumped and sweating, in the scene dock, when Chris Wells walks through. 'I have to keep pinching myself,' he says.

'I know,' I reply. 'I'm whacked as well.'

He frowns at me. 'No, no. Because I'm working *here*!'

I suspect I'll experience similar feelings if Harvey Lichtenstein likes our show and invites us to BAM. I've never played New York (in fact, I've never even visited it), and it's something I'm keen to do.

When I did *Richard III* it was Broadway-bound, until the *New York Times* reviewed it in Stratford and said I wasn't that hot. *Singer* was also headed across the Atlantic, until the *New York Times* reviewed it at the Barbican and said that while I was good, the show was anti-Semitic (whereupon the NY producers dropped it like a hot latke!). *Vanya* was going too, until the *New York Times* reviewed it here at the Cottesloe, and said that while the show was good, I was miscast as Astrov.

Given that Sean Mathias's production of *Vanya* was one of the most successful shows I've been in, in terms of the buzz round town and the hotness of the tickets, it was also, for me, curiously jinxed.

Tonight, as I tour the Cottesloe backstage corridors and stairways, I'm reminded of a particular performance of *Vanya* . . . The sequence of events began just after Astrov's Act II drunk scene. In the scene dock, I bumped into Karl Johnson (playing Waffles). 'Have you heard?' he said. 'Sean has been nominated for an Olivier Award for this.'

'No, I hadn't,' I said. 'How splendid!'

A little later, bumping into Ian McKellen (Vanya), I said excitedly, 'Did you know? – Sean's been nominated for an Olivier.'

'Yes,' said Ian, looking uneasy, then quickly confessed, 'So have I.'

'Oh. That's terrific. Congratulations.'

Later still, I bumped into Janet McTeer (Yelyena), waiting for an entrance just behind the stage, and whispered, 'Sean and Ian have both been nominated for Oliviers.'

'I know,' she whispered back. 'And I have too.'

'Wow, that's . . . that's wonderful. Great stuff.'

Now nearing the end of the performance, I bumped into Lesley Sharp (Sonya) on the stairs. 'Lesley!' I said. 'Sean, Ian *and* Janet have all been nominated for Oliviers. Isn't it just . . . ?'

'And me,' she said. 'Me as well.'

'Goodness. But that's . . . I mean, that's just . . .' Aware that my smile might be looking a bit numb, I said, 'Well done,' and hurried on.

After the show, in the bar, I saw our director. 'Sean!' I said. 'You, Ian, Janet, Lesley, all nominated. How tremendous. Four nominations, that's really . . .'

'Five,' he said.

'Five?' I repeated, my eyebrows raised in a last flicker of hope. 'Why, what's the uhm . . . fifth for?'

'Best revival.'

'Best revival, of course – congrats, mazeltov, what can I say?'

Dazed, I wandered over to where my guests for the evening were waiting. My psychotherapist, Monty Berman, and his wife Myrtle.

'That was terrific,' Monty said. 'The show, you, the rest of the cast, the whole kaboodle, one of the best things we've seen in ages. I'm so glad you managed to get us seats tonight.'

'So am I,' I answered. 'Because I've got bad news for you – you're on duty.'

Friday 21 July

Roger Chapman rings. Harvey Lichtenstein has just left his office. He's inviting *Titus* to New York. Roger sounds as excited as we are. He says he'll help and advise as much as possible, though it'll have to go as a Market Theatre production.

6 p.m. Company meeting. Cheers greet the news of the BAM invitation. *Once again* we've got good news to report. All through *Titus*'s dogged history we've had these occasions, announcing the British–Spanish tour, or the TV version, or the book which Methuen has commissioned. Greg also reads them a letter from today's mail:

> 'Dear Greg and Tony, I saw *Titus* yesterday at the matinée and thought it tremendously effective in the transposition of time and place . . . altogether a production not to be missed, as the audience told you . . . it was exciting, and pulled different worlds together very successfully, and the company is impressive. Chalk one up for proper theatre.'

The group listen politely, nodding in an appreciative but calm way, until Greg reads the signature at the end of the letter – 'Tom Stoppard'.

Greg is looking less happy when I see him next, five minutes before the show starts . . . 'Both Adrian Noble and Terry Hands are in the audience!' he gulps.

Two RSC artistic directors, present and past! 'Thanks a bunch,' I reply. 'Why the hell did you have to tell me?'

'Why should I suffer on my own?'

'Because you don't have to go out there and *do* it!'

*

The performance gets off to a slow start – the heat is incredible – but quickly moves into top gear, and the cheers at the end are the loudest yet.

Patsy Rodenburg is first to my dressing-room afterwards, enthusing about the show. It's as if, by doing Shakespeare in their own accents, the company have achieved something at the heart of her teaching. Finding your own voice.

Adrian also seems genuinely enthusiastic (he did the play at Bristol with Simon Callow), while Terry grins behind his back, as if saying, 'In a moment, I'll tell you what it was *really* like.'

And indeed, once Adrian has left, Terry lights up another cigarette and twinkles in a way which I recognise from the many, and happy, times we've worked together (*Red Noses, Singer, Tamburlaine*). It's an invitation to spar. 'It's probably my fault,' he says without conviction, 'but I was confused by the first half. The trouble is, I think very politically. So I couldn't work out what the parallels were.'

I smile back. 'Yes, one or two other people have made the same mistake. Trying to simplify it too much.'

He laughs. 'And I was very confused by your Terre'Blanche look.'

'Terre'Blanche? It's meant to be Spike Milligan.'

' . . . But then, in the second half, things became clearer. Obviously a township setting,' he says, in that way which can stamp his opinion over yours. 'I enjoyed it much more then.'

'You've never done *Titus*, Terry. Must be one of the few Shakespeares you haven't done. Why's that?'

'Well, I've missed my chance now,' he replies, then turns his smoky smile on to Greg. 'It's a young director's play. Brooky was thirty when he did his, Trevor was thirty-two, Adrian and Deborah were both twenty-eight.'

Before Greg can reply, I say, 'But you could do a mature version, Terry. Seems a shame not to. It's your sort of territory. All that mutilation, rape and cannibalism.'

'Oh no, I get all that at home,' he says, and we surrender, all laughing together.

Saturday 22 July
Two more shows today – our last at the RNT, and in Britain.

Lunch-time. Canteen. *Titus* veterans everywhere. Trevor Peacock (who played Titus in the BBC Shakespeare version) is at one table; at another sits Judi Dench. 'Have you ever given a Tamora or Lavinia?' I ask.

'Lavinia,' she replies, 'on radio.'

It takes a moment for the implications to sink in. 'Lavinia *on radio?*' I say. 'Couldn't have been easy.'

'It was impossible,' she says. 'After I'd lost my tongue and had to do that scene when, y'know, she writes the names of the rapists in the sand with her stumps and a stick, Michael Hordern started laughing so much, they had to put a screen round me.'

11 p.m. Already it's over, our week at the RNT. The brief run typifies something about theatre, something that's both glorious and frustrating. You can't hold on to it. With its brightly lit performers and its shadowy audiences, theatre is a totally unnatural world, and yet it behaves just like the real one. You experience a consuming incident – it burns into you – but only momentarily, and then it exists just as a memory, a story, a photograph. Whether a show runs for one week or a thousand, it's a fleeting thing.

As we're leaving the stage door, Jenny says, 'It's been so different doing the show here in the UK. It felt like people were holding us up in the air. In Jo'burg, people seemed to be standing on us, holding us down.'

Monday 24 July
Roger rings again. The offer from America has grown. Michael Kahn from the Shakespeare (formerly the Folger) Theatre in Washington also flew in to see the show last week and he wants it too.

57

Wednesday 26 July

'I don't believe it. I don't believe it.' Daphney is shaking her head and tutting, like some Zulu version of Victor Meldrew. We're driving from Madrid airport on our way down to Almagro. On the ragged outskirts of the city there is a shanty town of tin shacks.

Daphney is astonished. 'But it's just like a squatter camp in Soweto,' she says. 'I just don't believe it.'

On the journey south everybody makes their own connections.

Driving through one dusty town, Dorothy says the place reminds her of Bloemfontein.

We stop for a pee-break at a wayside café. As we clamber off the air-conditioned coach, the temperature hits you, like a dog breathing in your face, and Chris tugging his shirt-front says: 'This heat . . . it's Namibian.'

And the bleached landscape reminds Tony of the Karoo, the arid desert in South Africa where his father was born and his first novel *Middlepost* is set.

As we drive further south, the table-land seems to expand, the horizons lengthen and the earth becomes drained of colour. In my head imaginary guitars are strumming the florid strains of Rodrigo and de Falla; and I'm looking out for whitewashed windmills. For this is Don Quixote country, the high, dry plain of La Mancha.

Everybody pesters Jennifer, our only Spanish speaker, to translate road signs and advertising hoardings for them. But there's one sign which needs no translation, the huge black bull cut-outs which you see on every other hilltop. They say 'Spain' loud and clear. In fact they advertise a brand of Spanish liquor. Testosterone perhaps.

Three hours later we arrive in Almagro. Our hosts are the British Council and their representative is Ann Bateson. Ann is a Yorkshire lass from North Allerton and she'll be looking after us while we are here. We leave everyone to settle in at the Comfortel Hotel, and walk into town with Ann.

*

In the days of the great order of the Knights of Calatrava, Almagro was a flourishing town, with numerous monasteries, convents and churches. It owed its wealth to the influential Fugger family. From their Golden Counting House in Augsburg, these merchant princes were bankers to the kings and emperors of the Renaissance, furnishing funds to the exchequer of the Holy Roman Empire. The Fuggers settled in Almagro and built themselves grand palacios with magnificent galleried cloisters.

Walking around the narrow streets we keep coming across stately porticoes which attest to the town's former glory: great panelled oak doors with sandstone timpanums bursting with foliage and pomegranites. Even Almagro's modern guttering has a certain baroque flare. All over town, shiny aluminium gargoyles in the shape of pigs or crested lizards spike the gables. Tony thinks they look like township art.

There seems to be a lot of renovation going on in town. One palacio is being turned into a National Theatre Museum (there are three major theatres in this tiny town), while another fine eighteenth-century edifice is destined to house a casino.

We wander into the Plaza Mayor. The life of the town centres around this ancient parade ground. One side is in shade, the other side in the sun. *Sol y Sombre*. It is lined on both sides by long colonnades, with stocky stone columns which seem to belong somewhere else. The balconies are glassed-in and painted saracen green, and above them, endless undulating terracotta roofs.

While I admire the architecture, Tony watches the people. Some fascinating characters have started to emerge, right up his street, very Felliniesque. There's a man with no arms, who wears a big gold watch on one rubbery stump and strolls around with a swagger; an old chap with a tiny loudspeaker in his throat, walking his chihuahuas; a matron in black, delivering great hunks of meat wrapped in cloth to each of the bars.

Under the colonnades there are craft shops selling lace, ceramics and assorted baskets, and plenty of bars where you can grab a *cerveza* (beer) and a *platos Manchego*, a local dish: fried red peppers, or stuffed aubergines, or the delicious hard Manchegan cheese made from sheep's milk.

Ann has a knack for observing life's little absurdities, reminiscent of Victoria Wood. When we stop at Airen's bar, to sample a few of these Almagran delicacies, Ann translates for us. 'Here's a good one,' she says. "*Duelos y Quebrantos*".'

'What does that mean?' Tony asks.

' "Broken cry of pain". That sounds tasty. Oh and here's a cracker,

"*Pinchos Morunos*" – "Moorish pricks"! Or how do you fancy "*Rape a la marinera*"?' she asks.

'Why what is it?' I say.

' "Rape, Sailor-style." '

Back in June, when we came over to do a recce of the theatre, I asked Ann why on earth they have an International Festival of Classical Theatre here in this remote little town. Apparently, some eighteen years ago, the good burghers of Almagro were busy knocking down an old inn in the main square, the Plaza Mayor, when they uncovered the courtyard of a corral theatre dating back to the Golden Age of Spanish drama. It was this discovery which inspired the Festival.

When Tony and I first saw the Corral de Comedias, it took our breath away. While Shakespeare was presenting his plays in the Globe on Bankside, the townsfolk of Almagro were thronging the timbered galleries of this courtyard theatre. And this is no reconstruction. It's the real thing. We stood on the tiny stage examining the devil trap and the ranks of neat little oil lamps around the yard, and wished we were performing *Titus* here. However, we are not. We are gracing the stage of the Teatro Municipal, a quaint nineteenth-century theatre with a cloudy pink auditorium and a tinkling chandelier. The *Titus* set, with its torn camouflage nets, rusted steel decks and red earth, looks rather odd in this refined interior.

The National team, led by Stuart Smith and Fiona Bardsley, with stage technician Len Thomas and the Studio's Lucy Hemmings, have been here for a couple of days, setting up everything. And Mark Jonathan's delegation, Tim Bray and Hugh Llewellyn, have ingeniously recreated the lighting design. They've done a good job under difficult circumstances – like negotiating three-hour siesta breaks in the middle of the day.

At 6 p.m., fresh from their siestas, the company arrive to start the tech.

'Anybody seen Paulus?' Adam shouts up the stairwell backstage. We all laugh.

This cry is becoming a catch-phrase in the company. Paulus hasn't turned up for the call. What can it be this time? Suddenly he comes hurtling through the pass door. He hadn't understood about putting his watch forward by an hour when we arrived in Spain and woke up from his siesta to find the hotel deserted.

Anyway, he's here now and we can start.

58

Thursday 27 July

'I'm in agony!' I call to Roger Chapman as he crosses Almagro's main square, arriving for *Titus*'s fourth and final opening night (for now). Roger looks at me with his familiar startled smile. I explain. 'It's nine o'clock on a beautiful Spanish evening, and I'm sitting in a beautiful Spanish square, and the whole thing feels like the most beautiful holiday, except I'm drinking Diet Coke!'

Weeks ago, when we were told that our Spanish performances would start at 11 p.m. (when it's finally cool enough for people to contemplate sitting in a theatre), the first thing I said to Greg was 'How are we going to keep the company off booze till then? – they're South Africans!' At the moment, I feel like the rest of them look: sitting listlessly in little clumps at the various bars round the square, or taking one more stroll round its shops, staring blankly at the endless displays of lace and pottery. Spain loses some of its sexiness when you're on Diet Coke. And when you're waiting to start work at 11 p.m. And when all around you, the place is thronging with Festival-goers.

We finally go to the theatre at about 10. Backstage is airless and still very hot. I'm sweating just making-up.

As the show starts, we all experience a similar feeling. A kind of panic, but in slow-motion, like a dream. Here we are in the middle of the night, starting a three-hour story, which we're going to tell in English – Shakespearian English at that, and in South African accents – to a group of Spaniards.

Dressed in what looks like beachwear, many of them busily fanning themselves, the audience sit in the pink-and-gilt auditorium of the Teatro Municipal, under its large chandelier, in a sort of eerie silence. Our voices seem to echo round the place because, I suppose, most of the audience aren't really *hearing* the play. No laughs, of course, which is a pity; the humour has been one of the strengths of the production. Tonight it is perhaps Lavinia, with her missing tongue and desperate mimes, whose story the audience follow most clearly.

Yet at the end, we get bravos and a distinctive, rhythmic clapping

which Ann said might happen – it's very complimentary – and we're
called back several times. Suddenly this foreign audience is very familiar,
giving us the same welcome as the people of Leeds and London. I guess
at this moment in history, South Africans are among the most loved
people on earth.

'Ja, it's a blissful time to be in the South African diplomatic service,'
agrees Awie J. Marais, SA's Spanish Ambassador. We're at the reception
after the performance – it's now about 3 a.m. – in the beautiful, clois-
tered courtyard of the sixteenth-century Palacio de los Fucares, a few
streets away from the theatre. Open to the warm night sky, the courtyard
is crammed with people, some of whom have come down specially from
Madrid, like Peter Taylor, the director of the British Council here, and
the SA Ambassador.

Awie J. Marais turns out to know Dorothy from when they were
schoolkids in Durban. He beams at us all. 'You guys have made me so
bloody proud tonight!' Feeling the same way myself, I glance round our
group, then burst out laughing. When we were all marking time before
the performance, strolling round the shops in the Plaza, many of us
bought identical straw hats. Instead of a troupe of travelling players, we
look like a visiting bowls team.

Saturday 29 July
As well as sustaining three theatres during Festival time, this small town
also has several all-night discos, so after each performance, the company
go *jawling* (partying) through the night. They're having a wonderful
holiday to end this phase of *Titus*'s life. Jennifer has taught everyone a
Spanish toast:

> *A la vida*
> *A la muerte*
> *A la danza!*

(To life, to death, to dancing!)
    Greg and I can't keep up at all and tend to stagger back to the hotel
after the show. For us, things have settled into a peculiar, topsy-turvy
routine. We wake at about 11, we don't breakfast, except for coffee, and
then at about 1 we walk into the hot, still town, with Ann and whichever
members of the company are conscious, and we lunch at the El Corregi-
dor restaurant; a long lunch, complete with plentiful vino. This induces

the siesta – back at the hotel – and then, at about 7, it's off into town
again to hit the Diet Coke and start the long evening . . .

Dorothy in Spain

It's been tough playing to small houses again. In the middle of the night.
To non-English-speakers. But it has also been typical of this whole journey – this whole hair-raising, exhilarating journey. Like the play itself,
the journey always seems poised on a tightrope.

Maybe it's just true of all creative art? Training, skill, technique and
even talent isn't enough. For the good stuff. (And, yes, I'm being arrogant and saying that's what I think *Titus* is.) Maybe Art only works well
when there's that bit extra . . . that risk.

A lot of people here in Spain regard bullfighting as an art. I don't
know enough about the subject to judge whether this is true or not. I can
only speak as a spectator, an enthusiastic, un-p.c. spectator, who tries not
to miss the bullfight on any visit to this country. To me, it's a primitive,
and mesmerising, form of theatre.

There's no bullfight in the immediate vicinity of Almagro this weekend, but when the RNT sent Greg and me here in early June, we
stopped over in Madrid and saw a bullfight one afternoon. The star of

the show was a young matador called El Tato and he seemed to defy every rule that the other, older ones followed. The most spectacular example was the way he met the bull.

The animal is at its fastest, and most dangerous, when it first charges into the ring, intoxicated by the sudden freedom, the sunlight, the baying crowd, and not yet weakened by the loss of blood which the matador's team – his *picadores* and *banderillos* – will induce with their spears and pikes, before the boss goes in for the passes, and the kill. So most matadors stand well back when the bull arrives – more like a rocket than a beast – usually on the other side of the ring, where they can observe its size, speed, form, whatever. Not so, young El Tato. His speciality turn was to approach the tunnel through which the animal would appear, to stand directly in front of it and then to kneel down – and to take the first pass as the bull enters.

The first time he did it, the audience went wild with shocked excitement.

When his second turn came, you could feel everyone thinking, He's not going to do *that* again. But he strolled over to the entrance of the tunnel, teased us by just staying there – upright – for a few moments and then, sure enough, knelt down and shook out his cape.

Within the dark tunnel, a gate crashed open, and in the next split second the bull shot into the light and El Tato misjudged something, or the bull swerved, and the two collided. Or rather, it was like watching someone being run over by a truck. The human being stood no chance – *bang!* – and fell sideways like a puppet. The bull ran on for a few yards, before registering that something had happened, then wheeled round, lowered its horns and aimed at the limp, foetal-shaped figure in the dust. There was a flurry of capes as the other matadors and their teams dashed forward to distract the animal, while El Tato was carried out of the ring.

We all sat in silence. A silence without electricity, just flat and dreadful. I expected someone to stop the show and make an announcement, telling us whether the injury was as bad as it looked. But of course one of the players didn't know the show had gone wrong – in fact, probably sensed the opposite – and was still in fighting spirit. So another matador took over and we all watched listlessly as he took the bull through its paces and eventually killed it. We later heard, through Ann, that El Tato had got off lightly and only broken his neck.

I think what struck me most during that incident was that I had witnessed a performer taking a risk and succeeding brilliantly, and then taking another and failing – horribly.

*

Anyway, *Titus* took lots of risks and hasn't broken its neck. It's alive and kicking. Like other Market shows before, it has wowed audiences in the UK and Europe, and is now bound for America.

So what is it about that converted fruit-and-vegetable market in Jo'burg's dangerous downtown, what is it about that underfunded, beaten-up building that fires the imagination of theatre audiences round the world?

I must remember to ask Bruce about Barney's funeral.

59

During the week in Almagro Ann Bateson has taken me to see what else was happening in the Festival. The Comediants company from Catalonia did an adaptation of a thirteenth-century Bestiary in the modern theatre recently opened in the Hospital de San Juan. And the celebrated Compania de Miguel Narros performed a sparkling production of *La Discreta Enamorada* by Lope de Vega in the Cloister of the Dominican Convent. Posters for this production, bearing a large fondled nipple, have been torn down all over town.

In the corral theatre, the Teatro de Mundo company were presenting another Lope de Vega play, *La Boba para los otros y discreta para sí*, which Ann elegantly translated as 'the stupid girl who everybody else thinks is stupid but she doesn't think she is'. In between fighting in the Spanish Armada and serving as an officer for the Inquisition, Lope de Vega wrote one and a half thousand plays, so I suppose he was bound to be stuck for a catchy title now and then.

Sunday 30 July
Tonight is the last performance. The company are all in the theatre, even Paulus. I sit in the plush pink auditorium, trying to translate the Spanish programme (Tamora is Queen of '*los Godos*') and watch the company prepare for the show.

The musicians jam while Gys warms up his saxophone and Fiona mops the stage. Chris Wells likes to run his lines for articulation; Dotty likes to run round the auditorium. Dale gently checks out the stage, Ricky does some quick diaphragm panting, Ivan rolls his neck and shoulders. Dan lies on his back with his knees tucked up, Charlton quietly Tai-chis in a corner with Sello, and Jenny does some tough Afrikaans tongue twisters:

> *'Brie jy swart*
> *Brie jy blou*
> *Brie jy glat*
> *Brie jy grou'*

Oscar has arrived and starts a few arm swings and Tony appears, half made-up, to set his gourd rattle for the end of the show. As Adam checks the sound cues, a gentle chorus of hadedahs fills the air with Africa.

I'm impressed that the company, even now on the last performance of the tour, still make the effort to warm up.

Adam calls the half and the stage is cleared so they can open the house.

'*Mucha Mierde* everyone,' I call out. It's the Spanish equivalent of 'Break a Leg'. It means 'Big Shit'.

I suddenly feel very emotional. Ann seems to understand, and as the company get ready for the show she takes my arm and we go out for some air.

By now Almagro has softened into darkness. The bats flit about in the buttery light. From behind a blind at an upstairs window we hear the clicking of lace bobbins, and from the basement of one municipal building the cicada rattle of castanets as a group of teenagers in sweat pants and track shoes learn the rudiments of flamenco.

'You can tell he's English by the way his trousers hang,' Ann whispers as we pass a group of tourists.

We stop for a drink at Airen's bar and I try to summon some service. The waiter's eye is impossible to catch, unless you are Jennifer. ('Jenni-*fair*' he calls her.) But having listened to Jen ordering a round or two, I think I've caught his name, and I start calling 'Guapo, Guapo!'

'What are you doing?' Ann hisses.

'I'm calling the waiter, Guapo!'

'Yes, but what are you calling him?' She laughs. '*Guapo* means sexy.' Thanks, Jenni*fair*.

After the show, backstage is a blizzard of Gillette foam, as actors shave off their beards. There's much slapping of baby-bottom cheeks and audible sighs of relief. Dan Robbertse pupates from a chrysalis of matted red hair into a strawberry-blond butterfly.

In dressing-room number one, things take a little longer as not only the beard, but the grey-green thatch is removed as well. By the time I've finished helping Tony shave himself back to normal, the theatre is empty and everyone has headed for the Plaza Mayor. As we wander through the dark streets, I try to recollect when last I saw my partner like this. I quite like the skinhead (which he had for *Singer* and then the film of *Genghis*

Cohen) and I don't think I've seen his chin since 1994.

'Hello, *Guapo*,' I say. 'Haven't seen you for a long time.'

The company are gathered at Airen's bar. I introduce my new lover.

60

Monday 31 July

Last night, after the last show, and after the haircut and shave, we had a farewell meal with Ann Bateson and she described Spain like this: 'Every time I come back here and step off the plane, three smells hit me. The black tobacco, the cologne – they even comb the kids' hair with cologne – and the heat. And the way the heat lifts the other two smells. It always makes me blub.'

Today, as flight BA2465 takes off from Madrid, I find that you can actually *see* the heat. The plains of Spain are so burnt, they look white, like ash.

I seek out Bruce, plop myself into the seat next to him and say, 'You promised to tell me about Barney's funeral.'

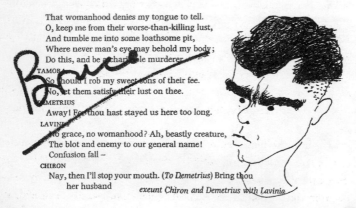

He nods, thinking deeply. I wonder if he wants to talk about it? In Almagro, he was *jawling* hard, getting away from it all. But now he takes a deep breath: 'I woke up that Sunday morning knowing I was leaving for London in the evening. It was an incredibly cold day and there was a heavy mist in Jo'burg.

'Outside the Market, hundreds of people were waiting, actors, directors, writers, all the staff from the theatre, all waiting to go to Westcliffe, the Jewish cemetery. Barney was going to be buried next to his father, mother and sister.

'It was so cold, we decided to open up the Market and let people wait inside. There was a sort of shrine in the foyer, with those Jewish candles that burn for days, and letters and telegrams stuck on the walls, from all round the world, and obituaries from papers in London and New York and everywhere, and faxes from Peter Brook, Ariel Dorfman, Theatre de Complicite, every theatre in the world, yours and Greg's too.

'One of the Market staff, this woman called Angie, with a huge, incredible voice, she started singing . . . y'know, traditional songs, celebrating the spirit of the person. Even white people, who didn't know the words, sang along – *"Hambe Kahle, Barney Simon!"* – dancing and clapping and singing, celebrating Barney's life. He would have loved it. Such a sense of energy and excitement. Such a sense of performance!

'There was a long convoy to the cemetery, hundreds of cars, and there were even more people at the other end, every actor and actress you can name, people had flown up from Cape Town.

'The rabbi – he was the same one who'd done Joe Slovo's funeral – he told us to go into the room with the coffin. So then I saw it for the first time. It was covered in a black flag with the Jewish Star of David. I couldn't believe it. Just a few weeks ago, Barney was walking round the house. He'd just got a video of *A Place in the Sun*. He idolised Montgomery Clift and Elizabeth Taylor. I went and bought cheesecake from Woolworths to watch it with. He'd wanted that video for years.

'An actress called Camilla Waldman was next to me. I said to her, "Please hold my hand." I felt so young. I hadn't had a great relationship with my own parents. For the first time there had been someone – Barney.

'We went into the main room. Athol was meant to begin the speeches, but he was late, which is incredible, he's never late. So John Kani went first. Some people got upset by what he said, but you've got to realise he'd been on the phone for days, taking calls from round the world, and then performing *The Island* in the evenings. And anyway, you get selfish in grief – I understand that. He said, "Barney is not yours, he's ours. We claim him from you. He's not Jewish, he's African!" John meant it as the ultimate compliment, but it upset some people.

'By now Athol had arrived and he got up to speak. He didn't have a yarmulka . . . there was a whole box for us all . . . so he grabbed someone's fez. A gold and black fez. He looked phenomenal. I wish I could remember his whole speech, he really tapped into what everyone was feeling . . . the way he couldn't resolve what had happened. The loss of

such a friend, such a father figure. At one point he sounded like Johnnie
in *Hello and Goodbye* – you know Barney directed him in the original
production – he kept saying, "Daddie is dead, daddie is dead . . ." Then
in the middle of a sentence he couldn't talk any more.

'Finally the rabbi got up to speak. Some of us smiled, because he
immediately reclaimed Barney to the Jewish faith, reclaimed him from
John Kani. Then he talked about how Barney's spirit was separate from
his flesh, and how his energy would live on. I found that comforting.

'Then the first lot of pallbearers lifted the coffin. I'd been chosen as
one. There was also Mannie and Athol. Barney's head must've been
right next to my hand. It all seemed very clumsy, carrying him. The path
was uneven and got steep at one point. Anyway, Barney would've liked
the clumsiness, things not being smooth.

'When we got to the graveside, I was surprised the hole wasn't that
deep. I was next to Rose, Barney's *domestic*. She was sobbing so much,
she had to sit down, sit on the ground. When it came to shovelling soil
on to the coffin, Rose – who's a huge woman – took the spade but could
only manage about a tablespoon of soil. People started to sing 'Nkosi
Sikelel'i', but badly, y'know, the timing was all out. Barney would've
liked that too, and the fact that his coffin was off-centre in the hole, it
was skew.

'And that was it. Back at the building, you have to wash your hands,
wash off the soil. I seemed to be fine, but then, when people kept coming
up to me to console me, then I got really upset. I had to walk away. The
deepest, *deepest* centre of my being, the most vulnerable point, just
opened up and I started wailing . . . it was so painful, worse than any
physical pain. Karen Cutts and Vanessa came to support me.

'We walked past Mannie and Athol. They were just standing there
with these empty expressions on their faces.

'We held a wake at Bob's Bar. Claire Stopford proposed the toast. She
said, "Everyone here has been touched and inspired by Barney. Now it's
time for all of us to grow up. To take his gift."

'When Vanessa drove me to the airport, to join you all in London, she
told me a story about her and Barney. One night they got into a terrible
argument, really vicious, like family, like father and daughter. The argument was about financial things. Then suddenly they stopped and began
crying. They had realised that what they were arguing about was not one
another, but the Market Theatre. Which was their life.'

61

Monday 31 July
Gatwick Airport.

So this is farewell. For now. The next time we all meet up will be to re-rehearse the show for New York. Most people are heading back to South Africa tomorrow. Godfrey is looking forward to getting back to Elsie whom he's been missing, and Dumi is looking forward to having his wife Lulu read him sonnets in the bath-tub.

We all scoop up our luggage from the carousel, piece by piece. There's a bout of hugging. I find myself incapable of saying anything meaningful. Tony is embracing Sello and wiping away tears. This makes Sello smile and say, 'You know? I do like you.'

So we disperse, heading off in ones and twos to run the gauntlet of Customs. It feels suddenly as if someone has snapped a cord that has bound us together for six months, and like beads spilling off a necklace, we scatter in all directions. It'll need a huge effort to thread the whole thing back together.

Tony and I hang back to see everyone through and are just about to steer our trolley towards the green channel, when Daphney appears. 'Anyone seen Paulus?' she says. Not again! Then we see a solitary figure loitering at the end of the baggage hall. It's Paulus. His luggage hasn't come through; the Chocolate Log bag. It contains his entire wardrobe.

'I'm sure it'll turn up, sir,' says the lady at the lost luggage desk. 'They usually do. Can I have your surname?'

Paulus looks bewildered, and so does the lady, as she tries spelling 'Kuoape'. Nevertheless, she seems confident that the bag will appear. 'If you'll give me your number, sir,' she says to Paulus, 'I'll give you a ring when they find it.'

I decide to short-circuit this, give her our number and suggest to Paulus that he goes back to his digs via Islington. 'We can wait for a phone call there and sort out some insurance, if your bag hasn't turned up before you leave tomorrow.'

The Customs hall is empty by the time we go through except for Gys sitting at one table with the entire contents of his suitcase on display, and a Customs officer about to confiscate two suspicious-looking tins. They turn out to be pickled aubergines, an Almagran speciality! If Gys tells them they are 'moorish pricks' the latitude for misunderstanding could be substantial. Paulus and I go on ahead, while Tony stays, in case Gys is charged with possessing illegal aubergines.

Most of the company have dispersed by the time we get through. One or two are left, including Oscar. He'd been so forlorn when his fiancée split up with him. Now he has found somebody new in London and fallen in love. He's wrapped up in his own happy ending, in the arms of Jade, a beautiful girl with almond eyes and jet black hair, who has come to the airport to meet him.

The company tube it back to London. We've got a car laid on, a sleek cream Mercedes. This is not some preferential policy of the National Theatre, it's the film company who are doing *Wind in the Willows*. They need to rush Tony to another fitting for his Chief Weasel teeth this afternoon.

As we glide up the M23, Paulus and I list the contents of his luggage for the claim form. His big regret, if the bag has been swallowed up, is losing his *Titus* T-shirt. 'Was there any money in the bag, Paulus?' I ask.

There wasn't. But he begins to explain to me that he's managed to save almost every scrap of his wages and per diems, and will be taking back to Alexandra Township a figure of nearly £3,000, which is well over R15,000.

By the time we get home there's a message from BA to say the bag hasn't turned up. I realise that I'm more upset than Paulus. He seems to be taking it all in his stride. Perhaps theft is just more routine to him, more a fact of daily life.

With the help of Sue Higginson, we manage to extract an immediate compensation of £50 from BA, plus more later. I suggest to Paulus that we meet up tomorrow to replace the few items of clothing he needs. Then I put him in a taxi home.

I close the door. In the hallway hangs the panorama of London in Shakespeare's day. I've been lucky enough to go all over the world, with Shakespeare as my passport, but since we embarked on that London tour, way back in January, I've never travelled so far.

Tuesday 1 August
Long Acre. Paulus is so excited to be going on a shopping spree, it feels like that Rodeo Drive scene from *Pretty Woman*. He's decided to blow

the £50 on something he really likes.

In one shop, he pulls out a pair of linen trousers with matching vest. That's it. He charms the shopgirls into doing the alterations for him on the spot. But two shops further along he discovers a dream item: a black leather waistcoat, just like the one his hero, Sello, wears. It's £40 in the summer sale. But that's still a lot of money and he's already spent his compensation. He's contemplating dipping into the cash he's saved up.

'What do you think, Paulus?' I ask, stopping myself from saying to him, like Squint Artists did, Go for it, Paulus, go!

62

Tuesday 1 August

London. The first day of the new job. Terry Jones's film of *Wind in the Willows*. I wake early (they're sending a car at 6.30), feeling an inexplicable depression, like jet lag. But that's not far from the truth. Our body clocks were turned upside down by the bizarre schedule in Spain.

Fall asleep in the car, wake at Shepperton Studios, am led to the fitting-rooms and stand before the large mirrors, watching as the designer, Jim Acheson, and his team fit costumes, whiskers, tail and teeth on to a bald, beardless, blank-faced man who was Titus Andronicus a moment ago.

Titus one moment, Chief Weasel the next, heigh-ho, an actor's life . . .

Chief Weasel

Now to one of the smaller sound stages, where we're rehearsing for the week. I did Terry Jones's last film *Erik the Viking*, and it's good to see him again, and to meet Eric Idle, who's playing Ratty. I warm to him immediately. We discuss our teeth.

Eric: 'I've elbowed the bottom set. Couldn't talk.'

Me: 'Know what you mean, but I'm quite liking what it's doing to my speech. Makes me sound a bit like Terry Thomas.'

Eric: 'Hold it, hold it, *I'm* doing Terry Thomas.' (He calls across the room): 'Mister Director, over here please, work demarcation areas to be sorted out.' (Terry Jones waves back, busy with something else. Eric says to me): 'Tell you what, here's a compromise. I'll do Terry Thomas and you do Dustin Hoffman doing Terry Thomas.'

The door of the sound stage is open to the sunlight. Suddenly a shadow falls across it. Badger has arrived. Tall, pallid, thin, Nicol Williamson shakes hands without meeting your eyes. He radiates solemnity while wisecracking in an odd American accent. We all laugh politely at his patter, but he doesn't seem to notice, his gaze skimming our foreheads.

When I get home at about four, I'm pleased to find Paulus still here, after his shopping expedition with Greg. He's like a visitor from another planet, a former life.

He shows his new clothes – which include a black leather waistcoat, similar to Sello's – and then his photos from the last few weeks. Rather like Godfrey in Leeds, but laughing, he warns us, 'Oh my goodness they're bad!' (I wonder if he's always said, 'Oh my goodness'?) The snaps are of red London buses, the coach that took us from Madrid Airport to Almagro, the planes at Gatwick (all this transport, this easy, *safe* transport!) and then views from the plane windows – pieces of England, pieces of Spain – and then some close-ups of himself in his Kilburn digs, grinning as he stretches over the lens to press the button, and then finally, in pride of place, the bust of Mandela on the South Bank, with the inscription, *The Struggle is My Life*.

It's time for him to go – the South Africans all return tonight. Armed with a sheaf of forms about his lost luggage, his Covent Garden shopping bags, and a replacement *Titus* T-shirt (which Greg asked the Studio to send round), he starts to bolt for the taxi, then stops, and we do the African handshake – that little dance of the hands.

Inside the taxi, he twists round and grins and waves, right down to the bottom of the street.

Catching one another wiping away tears, Greg and I break into laughter. 'Oo,' says Greg, playing camp. 'I don't think I could take one more farewell! It's like the end of a Chekhov play.'

I go into the garden for a siesta. The weather this summer is miraculous. Perhaps I'm thinking in spiritual terms because I've just been sent a new Pam Gems play (which she says she's written with me in mind) about the painter Stanley Spencer, and one of his main themes was resurrection. That's how a good English summer strikes you – as a phenomenal return to life, and *light*.

Woza summer!

Spreading out on the lawn, under the apple tree, I'm surrounded by so much fluid green light I could be underwater. Above me, the branches hang like nets, heavy with sun and shade, and above them, like above the surface, I can glimpse the blue of the sky. It's clear but soft. Very English; very different from a Spanish sky, and very, *very* different from an African one.

So what happens now? I spend the next few months doing *Wind in the Willows*, then there's a gap, though my agent Jeremy says there's the possibility of another film, *Indian Summer* (an excellent Martin Sherman screenplay apparently, on an AIDS theme, but upbeat), and then there's *Stanley* at the National, before the American tour of *Titus*.

One thing is clear. All those discussions Greg and I had, at least half seriously, about moving back to SA . . . we've stopped having them now, stopped mentioning the subject. It's simply not practical. I wouldn't be able to earn a living as an actor there, not doing the kind of theatre I like. Also, I think I may have underestimated how attached I am to this place, the house in Islington, and how much London has become *home*.

And so, on this fine English summer afternoon – which could be from a Stanley Spencer painting – I drift off, feeling very land-of-hope-and-glory.

But no doubt I'll feel different again, in a month or two . . .

Postscript

Paulus British Airways never found his luggage, so they awarded him another £150 – about R900. Together with all the money he saved on *Titus*, he bought a house in Alexandra Township, for Squint Artists, some of whom are orphans. Shortly afterwards, he was attacked in a shebeen, and stabbed – seriously – in the neck – several times. He spent two weeks in intensive care, but then gradually mended and went back to the house with Squint Artists. It's thought the attack occurred because he was now identified as a wealthy man.

Awards In Britain, *Titus*'s short visit to West Yorkshire Playhouse won it Best Overall Production and Best Actor at the 1995 Martini TMA Awards, for British Regional Theatre, i.e. all work outside the capital. In London itself, the show was highly commended at the prestigious *Evening Standard* Awards. One of the judges, Michael Coveney (critic of the *Observer*) called Antony Sher 'the outstanding Shakespearian performer of the year' as Titus, and the presenter Ned Sherrin called the production 'the best I've seen of that play'. In South Africa, *Titus* was not nominated in any category for any of their numerous theatre awards.

The Market Theatre Nobody has yet replaced Barney Simon as Artistic Director. But Claire Stopford (who directed *Hysteria*) has been appointed Associate Artistic Director of the Market. The government subsidy, which Dr Ngubani announced on *Titus*'s opening night, has been increased.

American Tour Plans for the American tour of *Titus* turned into a hairraising succession of deadlines – touch-and-go attempts to raise the money, alternating green and red lights – just like the build-up to the original production. And, as before, the outcome was vaguely enigmatic, vaguely improbable and all hinged on one or two individuals. But whereas the 'hoaxer', Deb, had been a curious benefactor, this time luck went the other way. A big American foundation was prepared to put up the necessary money for the tour on two conditions: first, that the Market use the opportunity for a big fund-raising gala (to help secure their finances), and second, that this gala be organised by those members of the Market trustees who had wealthy American friends. Unfortunately the trustees in question declined – for reasons which were never made clear. As a result the revival was cancelled. America never saw the show, the Market lost a huge fund-raising opportunity and alternative employment for the autumn had to be sought by twenty-three South African actors, musicians and stage managers, as well as one British director, and one actor (then playing Stanley Spencer) who wasn't sure what nationality he was. On the night of 29 March 1996, when the tour abruptly fell through, Antony Sher and Gregory Doran sat in their Islington home and consoled themselves, as they often had during the *Titus* experience, by saying, 'Well, at least it'll make a good story in the book.'